"A captivating fantasy thriller rife with magic and intrigue."—*Foreword Reviews* (Starred Review)

"Dabos has managed the rarely seen triad of complex worldbuilding, nuanced character development, and enthralling plot."—*Kirkus Reviews*

"Today, *The Mirror Visitor* stands on the same shelf as Harry Potter."—*Elle*

"Darkly enchanting . . . employs vibrant characters, inventive worldbuilding, and a sophisticated plot that will dazzle readers."—*Publishers Weekly* (Starred Review)

"*A Winter's Promise* is certain to ensnare you in its unique, dizzyingly magical world of treachery, illusion, and intrigue."—Margaret Rogerson, *New York Times* best-selling author of *An Enchantment of Ravens*

"Ophelia is a hero for the ages."
—Adrian Liang, *Ominvoracious: The Amazon Book Review*

"Holds as much appeal for adult fantasy readers as for teens."—*Booklist*

"Today, *The Mirror Visitor* stands on the same shelf as Harry Potter."—*Elle*

Christelle Dabos

THE MIRROR VISITOR
BOOK 1

A WINTER'S PROMISE

*Translated from the French
by Hildegarde Serle*

Europa
editions

Europa Editions
1 Penn Plaza, Suite 6282
New York, N.Y. 10019
www.europaeditions.com
info@europaeditions.com

Copyright © 2013 by Gallimard Jeunesse
First Publication 2018 by Europa Editions
This edition, 2020 by Europa Editions
Fifth printing, 2021

Translation by Hildegarde Serle
Original title: *La Passe-Miroir. Livre 1. Les fiancés de l'hiver*
Translation copyright © 2018 by Europa Editions

Library of Congress Cataloging in Publication Data is available
ISBN 978-1-60945-607-8

Dabos, Christelle
A Winter's Promise

Book design by Emanuele Ragnisco
www.mekkanografici.com

Cover illustration by Laurent Gapaillard
© Gallimard Jeunesse, 2013

Prepress by Grafica Punto Print – Rome

Printed in Italy

Contents

A WINTER'S PROMISE

Fragment

In the beginning, we were as one.

But God felt we couldn't satisfy him like that, so God set about dividing us. God had great fun with us, then God tired of us and forgot us. God could be so cruel in his indifference, he horrified me. God knew how to show his gentle side, too, and I loved him as I've loved no one else.

I think we could have all lived happily, in a way, God, me, and the others, if it weren't for that accursed book. It disgusted me. I knew what bound me to it in the most sickening of ways, but the horror of that particular knowledge came later, much later. I didn't understand straight away, I was too ignorant.

I loved God, yes, but I despised that book, which he'd open at the drop of a hat. As for God, he relished it. When God was happy, he wrote. When God was furious, he wrote. And one day, when God was in a really bad mood, he did something enormously stupid.

God smashed the world to pieces.

The Promise

The Archivist

It's often said of old buildings that they have a soul. On Anima, the ark where objects come to life, old buildings tend mostly to become appallingly bad-tempered.

The Family Archives building, for example, was forever in a foul mood. It spent its days cracking, creaking, dripping, and puffing to express its disgruntlement. It didn't like the drafts that made doors, left ajar, slam in the summer. It didn't like the rains that clogged up its gutter in the autumn. It didn't like the damp that seeped into its walls in winter. It didn't like the weeds that returned to invade its courtyard every spring.

But, above all, the Archives building didn't like visitors who didn't stick to the opening hours.

And that's doubtless why, in the early hours of that September morning, the building was cracking, creaking, dripping, and puffing even more than usual. It sensed someone arriving when it was still far too early to consult the archives. And that particular visitor didn't even stand at the front door, on the steps, like a respectable visitor. No, that visitor entered the Archives building like a thief, straight from the cloakroom.

A nose was sprouting, right in the middle of a mirrored wardrobe.

The nose kept coming. Soon after, a pair of glasses emerged, then the arch of an eyebrow, a forehead, a mouth, a chin, cheeks, eyes, hair, a neck, and ears. Suspended there, above the shoulders, in the center of the mirror, the face looked to the right, then to the left. Next, a bit further down, a bended knee poked through, and in tow came a body that pulled itself right out of the mirrored wardrobe, as if from a bathtub. Once clear of the mirror, the figure amounted to nothing more than a worn-out old coat, a pair of gray-tinted glasses, and a long three-colored scarf.

And under these thick layers, there was Ophelia.

All around Ophelia, the cloakroom was now protesting from its every wardrobe, furious at this intrusion that flouted the Archives' rules. The pieces of furniture creaked at the hinges and stamped their feet; the hangers clanged noisily, one against the other, as though propelled by a poltergeist.

This display of anger didn't intimidate Ophelia in the slightest. She was used to the Archives being temperamental. "Gently does it," she murmured. "Gently does it . . . " Instantly, the furniture calmed down and the hangers fell silent. The Archives building had recognized her.

Ophelia went out of the cloakroom and closed the door. On the panel was written:

BEWARE: COLD ROOMS
TAKE A COAT

With hands in pockets and long scarf trailing, Ophelia passed a succession of labeled filing cabinets: "Register of Births," "Register of Deaths," "Register of Consanguinity Exemptions," and so on. She gently opened the door of the consulting room. Not a soul. The shutters were closed but they let in a few rays of sun that lit up a row of desks in the gloom. The singing of a blackbird from the garden seemed to make this burst of light even more luminous. It was so cold in the Archives, you felt like opening all the windows to usher in the warm air outside.

Ophelia stood still for a moment in the doorway. She watched the threads of sunlight slide slowly across the floorboards as the day broke. She inhaled deeply the scent of old furniture and cold paper. That aroma, in which Ophelia's childhood had been steeped . . . soon she would smell it no longer.

With slow steps she made her way towards the archivist's quarters. All that shielded the private apartment was a curtain. Despite the early hour, a strong smell of coffee was already wafting through. Ophelia coughed into her scarf to make her presence known, but an old operatic aria drowned it out. So she slipped around the curtain. She didn't have to search for the archivist as the room served simultaneously as kitchen, living room, bedroom, and reading room: there he was, sitting on his bed, nose in a periodical.

He was an old man with untamed white hair. He'd wedged a loupe under his eyebrow, making that eye look enormous. He wore gloves and, under his jacket, a badly ironed white shirt.

Ophelia coughed again, but he didn't hear it due to the gramophone. Engrossed in his reading, he sang along to the little aria—somewhat out of tune, in fact. And then there was the humming of the coffeepot, the rumbling of the stove, and all the usual little noises of the Archives building.

Ophelia soaked up the particular atmosphere pervading these quarters: the off-key singing of the old man; the waxing light of day filtering through the curtains; the rustling of care-fully turned pages; the smell of coffee and, underlying it, the naphtha whiff of a gas lamp. In one corner of the room there was a draughtboard on which the pieces moved of their own accord, as though two invisible players were taking each other on. It made Ophelia want, above all, to touch nothing, to leave things just as they were, to turn right back, for fear of spoiling this familiar scene.

And yet she had to steel herself to break the spell. She approached the bed and tapped on the archivist's shoulder. "Lordy!" he exclaimed, jumping out of his skin. "Couldn't you warn people before springing on them like that?"

"I did try to," said Ophelia, apologetically. She picked up the loupe that had rolled onto the carpet and handed it back to him. Then she took off the coat that engulfed her from top to toe, unwound her endless scarf, and placed the lot over the back of a chair. All that remained of her was a slight figure, untidy thick, brown curls, two rectangles for glasses, and an outfit more suited to an elderly lady.

"You've come straight from the cloakroom again, huh?" growled the archivist, wiping his loupe clean with his sleeve. "This obsession with traveling through mirrors at ungodly hours! You know very well my little abode is allergic to sur-prise visits. One of these days you're going to get whacked on the head, and you'll have asked for it!"

His gruff voice made his splendid moustache, which reached his ears, quiver. He got up from his bed with diffi-culty and seized the coffeepot, muttering in a dialect that he was the last to speak on Anima. With all his handling of archives, the old man lived entirely in the past. Even the periodical he was leafing through dated back at least half a century.

"A mug of coffee, dear girl?" The archivist wasn't a very sociable man, but whenever he set eyes on Ophelia, as now, those eyes began to sparkle like cider. He'd always had a soft spot for his great-niece, doubtless because, of all the family, she was the one who most resembled him: just as old-fashioned, just as solitary, just as reserved.

Ophelia nodded. She had too much of a lump in her throat to speak right then, right there.

Her great-uncle poured out a steaming cup for each of them. "I was on the phone with your ma yesterday evening," he chomped into his moustache. "So excited, she was, I couldn't grasp half of her jabbering. But still, I got the gist: you're finally taking the plunge, it seems."

Ophelia confirmed this without saying a word. Her great-uncle promptly knitted his huge brows. "Don't pull that long face, please. Your mother's found you a chap, and that's the end of it."

He handed her cup to her and sat back heavily on his bed, making every spring creak. "Park yourself down. We need a serious chat, godfather to goddaughter."

Ophelia pulled a chair over to the bed. She stared at her great-uncle and his magnificent moustache with a sense of unreality. She felt as though, through him, she were watching a page of her life being torn out, right under her nose.

"I can well imagine why you're eyeballing me like that," he said, "except that this time the answer's *no*. Those sloping shoulders of yours, those gloomy glasses and those sighs of total despair, you can just pack them all away." He was gesturing with thumb and forefinger, both bristled with white hairs. "There's those two cousins you've already rejected! Granted, they were ugly as pepper mills and gross as chamber pots, but it was the whole family you were insulting with each rejection. And what's worse, I made myself your accomplice in sabotaging those betrothals." He sighed into his moustache.

"I know you as if I'd made you. You're more accommodating than a chest of drawers, never raising your voice, never throwing tantrums, but the minute anyone mentions a husband, you send more sparks flying than an anvil. And yet you're the right age for it, whether the chap's your type or not. If you don't settle down, you'll end up banished from the family, and that I'm not having."

Ophelia, her nose in her cup of coffee, decided that it was high time she spoke up. "You've got nothing to worry about, uncle. I didn't come here to ask you to oppose this marriage." At that moment, the needle of the gramophone got stuck in a scratch. The endless echo of the soprano filled the room: "If I . . . If I . . . If I . . . If I . . . If I . . . "

The great-uncle didn't get up to free the needle from its groove. He was too flabbergasted. "What are you babbling to me? You don't want me to intervene?"

"No. The only favor I've come to ask you today is to have access to the archives."

"My archives?"

"Today."

"If I . . . If I . . . If I . . . If I . . . " the record player stuttered on. Fiddling with his moustache, the great-uncle raised a skeptical eyebrow. "You're not expecting me to plead your case to your mother?"

"It wouldn't do any good."

"Nor to bring your feeble father round?"

"I'm going to marry the man that's been chosen for me. It's as simple as that."

The gramophone needle suddenly jumped and then carried on where it had left off, with the soprano proclaiming triumphantly: "If I love you, look out for yourself!"

Ophelia pushed up the glasses on her nose and held her godfather's gaze without blinking. Her eyes were as brown as his were golden. "Splendid!" said the old man, breathing a sigh of relief. "I must admit, I thought you were incapable of uttering those words. He must have really taken your fancy, that fellow. Spill the beans and tell me who he is!"

Ophelia rose from her chair to clear away their cups. She wanted to rinse them but the sink was already full to the brim with dirty plates. Normally, Ophelia didn't like housework, but this morning, she unbuttoned her gloves, rolled up her sleeves, and did the washing-up. "You don't know him," she said at last. Her muttering was drowned by the sound of running water. The great-uncle stopped the gramophone and went closer to the sink. "I couldn't hear you, dear girl." Ophelia turned the tap off for a moment. Her voice was quiet and her diction poor, so she often had to repeat what she'd said.

"You don't know him."

"You're forgetting whom you're talking to!" sniggered the great-uncle, crossing his arms. "My nose may never be out of my archives, but I know the family tree better than anyone. There's not one of your most distant cousins, from the valley to the Great Lakes, that I don't know about."

"You don't know him," insisted Ophelia.

She wiped a plate with her sponge while staring into space.

Touching all these dishes without protective gloves had sent her back in time. She could have described, down to the smallest detail, everything her great-uncle had eaten off these plates since he'd first owned them. Usually, being very professional, Ophelia never handled objects belonging to others without her gloves on, but her great-uncle had taught her to read right here, in this flat. She knew each utensil personally, inside out.

"This man isn't part of the family," she finally announced. "He's from the Pole."

A long silence ensued, broken only by gurgling in the pipes. Ophelia dried her hands with her dress and looked at her godfather over her rectangular glasses. He had suddenly shrunk into himself, as though he had just shouldered another twenty years. Both sides of his moustache had drooped like half-mast flags. "What's this nonsense?" he whispered in a flat voice.

"I know nothing more," Ophelia replied gently, "except that, according to Mom, he's a good match. I don't know his name, I've never seen his face."

The great-uncle went to fetch his snuff tin from under a pillow, stuffed a pinch of tobacco deep into each nostril, and sneezed into a handkerchief. It was his way of clarifying his thoughts. "There must be some mistake . . . "

"That's what I'd like to think, too, dear uncle, but it seems there really isn't."

Ophelia dropped a plate and it broke in two in the sink. She handed the pieces to her great-uncle, he pressed them back together, and, instantly, the plate was as good as new. He placed it on the draining board.

The great-uncle was a remarkable Animist. He could mend absolutely everything with his bare hands and the most unlikely objects yielded to him like puppy dogs.

"There has to be a mistake," he said. "Although I'm an archivist, I've never heard of such an unnatural combination. The less Animists have to do with these particular strangers, the better they feel. Full stop."

"But the marriage will still happen," Ophelia muttered, resuming her washing-up.

"But what the devil's got into your mother and you?" exclaimed the great-uncle, aghast. "Of all the arks, the Pole's the one with the worst reputation. They have powers there that send you out of your mind! They're not even a real family—they're wild packs that tear each other apart. Are you aware of all that's said about them?"

Ophelia broke another plate. Consumed by his outrage, the great-uncle didn't realize the impact his words were having on her. It wouldn't have been obvious in any case: Ophelia had been endowed with a moonlike face on which her feelings rarely surfaced. "No," she simply replied, "I'm not aware of all that's said and I'm not interested. I need serious documentation. So the only thing I'd like, if you don't mind, is access to the archives."

The great-uncle pieced together the second plate and placed it on the draining board. The room's beams started cracking and creaking—the archivist's black mood was spreading to the whole building. "I don't recognize you anymore! You put up a terrible fuss about your cousins, and now that they're shoving a barbarian into your bed, here you are, just resigned to it!"

Ophelia froze, sponge in one hand, cup in the other, and closed her eyes. Plunged into the darkness behind her eyelids, she looked deep within herself. Resigned? To be resigned you have to accept a situation, and to accept a situation you have to understand the whys and wherefores. Ophelia, however, had no clue. Just a few hours earlier, she didn't even know that she was engaged. She felt as though she were heading towards an abyss, as though her life were no longer her own. When she dared to think of the future, it was just the endless unknown. Dumbfounded, incredulous, dizzy— she was all of these, like a patient who's just been diagnosed with an incurable illness. But she wasn't resigned.

"No, I certainly can't conceive of such nonsense," continued her great-uncle. "And then, what would he be coming over here to do, this stranger? All this, what's in it for him? With all due respect, my dear, you're not the most lucrative leaf on our family tree. What I mean is, it's just a museum that you run, not a goldsmith's!"

Ophelia dropped a cup. This clumsiness wasn't about being recalcitrant or temperamental; it was pathological. Objects were forever slipping between her fingers. Her great-uncle was used to it—he mended everything in her wake. "I don't think you've quite understood," stated Ophelia, stiffly. "It's not this man who's coming to live on Anima, it's me who's got to follow him to the Pole."

This time it was the great-uncle who broke the crockery he was busy putting away. He swore in his old dialect.

A clear light was now coming through the flat's window. It cleansed the atmosphere like pure water and cast little glimmers on the bedstead, the stopper of a decanter, and the gramophone's horn. Ophelia couldn't understand what all that sun was doing there. It felt wrong in the middle of that particular conversation. And it made the snow of the Pole feel so distant, so unreal that she no longer really believed in it herself. She took off her glasses, gave them a polish with her apron, and put them back on her nose—as a reflex, as though doing that could help her see things more clearly. The lenses, which had lost any color when removed, soon regained their gray tint. These old spectacles were an extension of Ophelia; the color they took on matched her moods.

"I notice that Mom forgot to tell you the most important thing. It's the Doyennes who betrothed me to this man. For now, they alone are privy to the details of the marriage contract."

"The Doyennes?" gulped the great-uncle. His face, along with all its wrinkles, was contorted. He was finally understanding the scenario in which his great-niece found herself involved. "A diplomatic marriage," he whispered, flatly. "Poor soul . . . " He stuffed two fresh pinches of snuff into his nose and sneezed so hard he had to push his dentures back in place. "My poor child, if the Doyennes have got involved, there's no longer any conceivable way out. But why?" he asked, making his moustache quiver. "Why you? Why over there?"

Ophelia washed her hands under the tap and rebuttoned her gloves. She had broken enough china for today. "It would seem that this man's family made direct contact with the Doyennes to arrange the marriage. I have no idea what made them target me rather than someone else. I'd like to believe it was a misunderstanding, really."

"And your mother?"

"Delighted," muttered Ophelia, bitterly. "She's been promised a good match for me, which is much more than she was hoping for." In the shadow of her hair and her glasses, she set her lips. "It's not in my power to reject this offer. I'll follow my future husband wherever duty and honor oblige me to. But that's as far as things will go," she concluded, pulling at her gloves with determination. "This marriage isn't about to be consummated."

Looking upset, the great-uncle stared at her. "No, dear girl, no, forget that. Look at yourself. You're the height of a stool and the weight of a bolster . . . However he makes you feel, I advise you never to set your will against that of your husband. You'll end up with broken bones."

Ophelia turned the handle of the gramophone to get the deck moving again and clumsily placed the needle on the record's first groove. The little opera aria rang out once again from the horn. With arms behind her back, she looked at him with a vacant expression and said nothing more. This is what Ophelia was like: in situations where any young girl would have cried, moaned, shouted, implored, she usually just observed in silence. Her cousins liked to say that she was a bit simple.

"Listen," muttered the great-uncle while scratching his ill-shaven neck, "let's not overdramatize, either. I doubtless went over the top when telling you about this family earlier on. Who knows? Maybe you'll like your guy?"

Ophelia looked closely at her great-uncle. The strong sunlight seemed to accentuate the features on his face and deepen each wrinkle. With a twinge of sorrow, she suddenly realized that this man, whom she had always thought to be solid as a rock and impervious to the passing of time, was today a tired old man. And she had just, unintentionally, aged him even more. She forced herself to smile. "What I need is some good documentation."

The great-uncle's eyes regained a little of their sparkle. "Put your coat back on, dear girl, we're going down!"

The Rupture

Ophelia's great-uncle dived into the entrance of a stairway barely lit by safety lamps. With hands deep in her coat and nose in her scarf, Ophelia followed him down. The temperature fell from one step to the next. Her eyes were still full of sunlight and she truly felt as if she were plunging into icy black water.

She jumped when the gruff voice of her great-uncle reverberated from wall to wall: "I can't get used to the idea that you're going to leave. The Pole really is the other end of the world!"

He stopped on the stairs to turn to Ophelia. Still not accustomed to the darkness, she bumped right into him. "Say, you're pretty skilled when it comes to mirror-traveling. Couldn't you do those little journeys of yours from the Pole to here, every now and then?"

"I'm unable to do that, uncle. Mirror-traveling only works over small distances; covering the void between two arks is unthinkable."

The great-uncle swore in old dialect and continued down the stairs. Ophelia felt guilty for not being as skilled as he thought. "I'll try to come and see you often," she promised in a small voice.

"When are you off, exactly?"

"December, if I can believe the Doyennes."

The great-uncle swore again. Ophelia was grateful not to understand a word of his dialect.

"And who'll take over from you at the museum?" he grumbled. "No one else can evaluate antiquities like you!"

To that, Ophelia could find no reply. That she would be wrenched from her family was bad enough, but being torn from her museum, the only place where she felt totally herself, that was tantamount to losing her identity. Reading was all that Ophelia was good at. If that were taken from her, all that would remain of her would be a clumsy lump. She didn't know how to keep house, or make conversation, or finish a household chore without doing herself an injury. "Apparently, I'm not as irreplaceable as all that," she muttered into her scarf.

In the first basement, the great-uncle swapped his usual gloves for clean ones. By the light of the electric safety lamps, he slid open his filing cabinets to trawl through the archives that had been deposited, generation after generation, beneath the cold vault of the cellars. He expelled condensation, mid-moustache, with every breath.

"Right, these are the family archives, so don't expect miracles. I know that one or two of our ancestors did set foot in the Great North, but it was a dashed long time ago."

Ophelia wiped away a drop hanging from her nose. It couldn't be more than 40 degrees here. She wondered whether her future husband's house would be even colder than this archives room. "I'd like to see Augustus," she said. This was clearly shorthand—Augustus had died long before Ophelia's birth. "Seeing Augustus" meant looking at his sketches.

Augustus had been the great explorer of the family, a legend in his own right. At school, geography was taught based on his travel journals. He had never written a sentence—he didn't know his alphabet—but his drawings were a mine of information.

Since the great-uncle, deep in his filing cabinets, didn't reply, Ophelia presumed he hadn't heard. She tugged at the scarf that was wrapped round his face and repeated in a louder voice: "I'd like to see Augustus."

"Augustus?" he chomped, without looking at her. "Of no interest. Insignificant. Just old scribbles."

Ophelia raised her eyebrows. Her great-uncle never denigrated his archives. "Oh," she blurted, "really that terrifying?"

With a sigh, the great-uncle emerged from the fully extended drawer in front of him. The loupe he'd wedged under his brow made that eye double the size of the other one. "Bay number four, to your left, bottom shelf. Handle with care, please, and put clean gloves on."

Ophelia moved along the filing cabinets and knelt down at the specified location. There she found all of Augustus's original sketchbooks, classified by ark. She found three at "Al-Anda-loose," seven at "City," and around twenty at "Serenissima." At "Pole" she found only one. Ophelia couldn't afford to be clumsy with such precious archives. She placed the sketchbook on a consulting lectern and, with the utmost care, turned the pages of drawings.

Pale plains, just above the rock, a fjord imprisoned in ice, forests of great firs, houses encased in snow . . . These landscapes were austere, yes, but less daunting than Ophelia had imagined the Pole to be. She even found them quite beautiful, in a way. She wondered where her fiancé lived, in the midst

31

of all this whiteness. Close to this river edged with pebbles? In this fishing port lost in the night? On this plain invaded by tundra? This ark looked so poor, so wild! How could her fiancé be such a good match?

Ophelia fell on a drawing that she didn't understand: it looked like a beehive suspended in the sky. Probably the outline of an idea. She turned a few more pages and saw a hunting portrait. A man was posing proudly in front of a huge pile of pelts. Hands on hips, he had rolled up his sleeves to show off his powerfully muscled arms, which were tattooed up to the elbows. His look was hard, his hair fair.

Ophelia's glasses turned blue when she realized that the pile of pelts behind him was in fact but a single pelt—that of a dead wolf. It was as big as a bear. She turned the page. This time the hunter was standing in the middle of a group. They were posing together in front of a heap of antlers. Elk antlers, no doubt, except that each skull was the size of a man. The hunters all had the same hard look, the same fair hair, the same tattoos on their arms, but not a single weapon between them, as though they had killed the animals with their bare hands.

Ophelia leafed through the sketchbook and found those same hunters posing in front of different carcasses—walruses, mammoths, and bears, all of an unbelievable size. She slowly closed the book and put it back in its place. "Beasts" . . . These animals afflicted with gigantism, she'd already seen them in children's picture books, but they bore no relation to Augustus's sketches. Her little museum hadn't prepared her for that kind of life. What shocked her more than anything was the look in the hunters' eyes. A look that was brutal, arrogant, accustomed to the sight of blood. Ophelia hoped her fiancé wouldn't have that look.

"So?" asked her great-uncle as she returned to him.

"I understand your reluctance a bit more now," she said.

He returned to his research with renewed vigor. "I'm going to find you something else," he muttered. "Those sketches, they must be a hundred and fifty years old. And they don't show everything!"

That was precisely what was worrying Ophelia: what Augustus didn't show. She said nothing, however, merely shrugging her shoulders. Anyone other than her great-uncle would have misread her nonchalance, confusing it with a certain weakness of character. Ophelia seemed so calm, behind her rectangular glasses and half-closed eyelids, that it was almost impossible to imagine that waves of emotion were crashing violently in her chest.

The hunting sketches had scared her. Ophelia wondered whether that was really what she had come to find here, in the archives. A draft blew between her ankles, lightly raising her dress. This breeze came from the entrance to the stairway that led down to the second basement. Ophelia stared for a moment at the passage barred with a chain on which swung a warning sign: "PUBLIC ACCESS PROHIBITED."

There was always a draft lingering in the archive rooms, but Ophelia couldn't resist interpreting this one as an invitation. The second basement was calling for her presence, now.

She tugged on her great-uncle's coat, as he was lost in his reports, perched on his library steps. "Would you allow me to go down?"

"You know very well that I'm not normally authorized to do

that," the great-uncle muttered, with a bristling of his moustache. "It's Artemis's private collection—only archivists have access to it. She honors us with her trust; we must not abuse it."

"I'm not intending to read with bare hands, rest assured," Ophelia promised, showing him her gloves. "And I'm not requesting your permission as your great-niece, I'm requesting it as curator of the family museum."

"Yes, yes, that old chestnut," he sighed. "It's partly my fault. Too much of me has rubbed off on you."

Ophelia unhooked the chain and went down the stairs, but the safety lamps didn't come on. "Light, please," she requested, plunged in darkness. She had to repeat the request several times. The Archives building disapproved of this latest bending of the rules. Finally, and reluctantly, it turned the lamps on; Ophelia had to put up with their flickering light.

Her great-uncle's voice reverberated from wall to wall, down to the second basement: "Only touch with your eyes, yes! I'm as wary of your clumsiness as of the smallpox!"

With her hands deep in her pockets, Ophelia advanced through the rib-vaulted room. She passed beneath a pediment on which the archivists' motto was carved: *Artemis, we are the respectful keepers of your memory*. There were Reliquaries, well protected under their glass cloches, as far as the eye could see.

If Ophelia sometimes seemed like an awkward adolescent, with her long untamed locks, her clumsy movements, and her shyness hiding behind her glasses, she became a different person when in the presence of history. Her cousins all loved pretty tearooms, strolls along the river, trips to the zoo and ballrooms. For Ophelia, the second basement of the Archives was the most fascinating place in the world. That's where, safe and sound under those protective cloches, the shared heritage of the whole family was jealously preserved. Where the documents of the very first generation of the ark resided. Where all the repercussions of year zero had ended up. Where Ophelia got closest to the Rupture.

The Rupture was her professional obsession. She dreamt sometimes that she was running after a skyline that was forever eluding her. Night after night, she went further and further, but it was a world without end, without a crack, round and smooth as an apple; that first world whose objects she collected in her museum: sewing machines, internal combustion engines, cylinder presses, metronomes . . . Ophelia wasn't remotely drawn to boys of her own age, but she could spend hours in the company of a barometer from the old world.

She took stock in front of an ancient parchment under protective glass. It was the founding text of the ark, the one that had linked Artemis and her descendants to Anima. The next Reliquary contained the first draft of their judicial arsenal. On it could already be found the laws that had endowed mothers and matriarchs with a decisive power over the whole community. Under the cloche of a third Reliquary, a manuscript book of statutes continued with the fundamental duties of Artemis toward her descendants: ensuring that everyone got enough to eat, had a roof over their head, received an education, learnt to put their power to good use. Written in capital letters, a clause specified that she must neither abandon her family nor leave her ark. Had Artemis imposed this line of conduct upon herself, so as not to become lax with the passing of the centuries?

Ophelia wandered like this, from Reliquary to Reliquary. The more she delved into the past, the more she felt a great calm descend upon her. She briefly lost sight of the future. She forgot that she was being betrothed against her will; she forgot the look of those hunters; she forgot that she would soon be sent to live far away from all that was dear to her.

Usually, the Reliquaries contained handwritten documents of great value, such as mappings of the new world or the birth certificate of Artemis's first child, the eldest of all the Animists. However, some of them contained the banal artifacts of everyday life: hair scissors that clicked in the air; a crude pair of spectacles that changed hue; a little storybook whose pages turned themselves. They weren't from the same era, but Artemis wanted them to be part of her collection in a symbolic capacity. Symbolic of what? Even she could no longer remember.

Ophelia's steps led her instinctively towards a particular cloche, on which she respectfully laid her hand. Beneath it a register was starting to disintegrate, its ink faded by time. It was a record of the men and women who had rallied to the family spirit to create a new society. It was in fact but an impersonal list of names and numbers, but not insignificant ones: those of the survivors of the Rupture. These people had witnessed the end of the old world.

It was at this moment that Ophelia understood, with a little twinge in her chest, the nature of the call that had drawn her to her great-uncle's archives, deep in the second basement, in front of this old register. It wasn't the simple need to gather information; it was returning to one's roots. Her distant ancestors had witnessed the breaking up of their world. But had they just lain down and died, for all that? No, they had invented a different life for themselves.

Ophelia tucked the locks of hair flopping over her forehead behind her ears, to uncover her face. The glasses on her nose grew clearer, shedding the grayness that had been building up for hours. She was experiencing her very own Rupture. She still felt sick with fear, but she knew now what she still had to do. She had to take up the challenge.

On her shoulders, the scarf started to move. "You're waking up at last?" Ophelia teased it. The scarf rolled sluggishly along her coat, changed position, retightened its loops around her neck, and stopped still. A very old scarf, it spent all its time sleeping.

"We're going back up," Ophelia told it. "I've found what I was looking for."

Just as she was about to turn back, she came across the most dusty, most enigmatic, and most disturbing Reliquary in Artemis's whole collection. She couldn't leave without bidding it farewell. She turned a handle and the two panels of the protective dome slid apart. She laid her gloved palm on the binding of a book, the Book, and was overcome by the same frustration she'd felt the first time she'd made contact with it like this. She couldn't read a trace of any emotion, any thought, any intent. Of any origin whatsoever. And it wasn't just due to her gloves, whose special weave acted as a barrier between her gifts as a reader and the world of objects. No, Ophelia had already touched the Book once with bare hands, like other readers before her, but, quite simply, it refused to reveal itself.

She held it in her arms, stroked its binding, rolled the smooth pages between her fingers. Right through it there were strange arabesques, a script long forgotten. Never in her life had Ophelia handled something even approaching such a phenomenon. Was it just a book, after all? It had the texture neither of vellum nor of rag paper. Awful to admit, but it resembled human skin, drained of its blood. A skin that would benefit from exceptional longevity.

Ophelia then asked herself the ritual questions, those of many generations of archivists and archaeologists. What story was this strange document telling? Why did Artemis want it to feature in her private collection? And what was that message engraved on the base of the Reliquary—*Never, on any account, attempt to destroy this Book*—all about?

Ophelia would carry all these questions away with her to the other side of the world, a place where there were neither archives nor museum nor a duty to remember. None that concerned her, at least.

Her great-uncle's voice resonated right down the stairs and kept reverberating beneath the low vault of the second basement in a ghostly echo: "Come back up! I've dug out a little something for you!"

Ophelia placed her palm on the Book one last time and then closed the dome. She had said her farewells to the past, in due form.

Over to the future now.

The Journal

Saturday June 19th. Rudolf and I have arrived safely. The Pole has turned out to be very different from all I expected it to be. I don't think I have ever felt so dizzy in my life. The ambassadress kindly received us on her estate, where an eternal summer evening reigns. I'm dazzled by so many marvels. The people here are courteous, very considerate, and their powers surpass all understanding.

"May I interrupt you in what you're doing, dear cousin?"

Ophelia jumped, as did her glasses. Immersed in the travel journal of her forebear, Adelaide, she hadn't noticed the arrival of this scrap of a man, bowler hat in hand and smile stretching from one jug-ear to the other. The puny fellow couldn't have been much more than fifteen. With a sweeping flourish of his arm he indicated a group of jovial chaps not far off, all guffawing in front of an old typewriter. "My cousins and I, myself, were wondering whether you might grant us permission to read a few of the curios in your august museum."

Ophelia was unable to stifle a frown. She couldn't, of course, claim to know personally every family member who came through the turnstile at the entrance to the Museum of Primitive History, but she was certain she'd never come across these characters before. From which branch of the family tree did they spring up? The guild of hatters? The caste of tailors? The clan of confectioners? Whichever, there was certainly a strong whiff of the farcical about them. "I'll be right with you," she said, putting her cup of coffee down.

Her suspicions proved justified when she went over to Mr. Bowler Hat's group. Far too much grinning going on.

"And here's the museum's star exhibit!" cooed one of the gang, with a telling look for Ophelia. His irony was, in her opinion, somewhat lacking in subtlety. She knew she wasn't attractive, with her messy plait releasing dark wings over her cheeks; her scarf trailing; her old brocade dress; her mismatched boots; and the incurable clumsiness she was stuck with. She hadn't washed her hair for a week and had dressed in whatever first came to hand, not caring whether it all went together.

This evening, for the first time, Ophelia would meet her fiancé. He had come especially from the Pole to present himself to the family. He would stay a few weeks, then he would take Ophelia away with him to the Great North. With a bit of luck, he would find her so off-putting that he would abandon the idea of their union on the spot.

"Don't touch that," she said, addressing a great lump of a man whose fingers were moving towards a ballistic galvanometer.

"What are you mumbling on about, cousin?" he chortled. "Speak up, I couldn't hear you."

"Don't touch that galvanometer," she said, raising her voice. "I'm going to provide you with some samples specifically for reading."

The great lump shrugged. "Oh, I only wanted to see how this contraption works! Anyhow, I can't read."

Ophelia would have been amazed to hear the opposite. The reading of objects wasn't a widespread power among Animists. It sometimes manifested itself at puberty, in the form of vague intuitions at the tips of the fingers, but it waned in a few months if a tutor didn't swiftly take charge. Ophelia's great-uncle had performed that role with her—after all, their branch worked in the preservation of the family heritage. Going back into the past of objects at the slightest contact? Rare were the Animists who wished to take on such a burden, especially if it wasn't their line of work.

Ophelia glanced at Bowler Hat, who was touching the frock coats of his companions and giggling. He himself could read, but probably not for much longer. He wanted to play with his hands while he still could.

"That's not the problem, cousin," Ophelia remarked calmly, returning to the great lump. "If you wish to handle a piece from the collection, you have to wear gloves like mine."

Since the last family decree on the preservation of the heritage, going anywhere near the archives with bare hands was forbidden without special permission. Coming into contact with an object was to contaminate it with one's own state of mind, adding a new stratum to its history. Too many people had sullied rare items with their emotions and thoughts.

Ophelia went over to her key drawer. She pulled it too far open: the drawer remained in her hand and its contents scattered on the tiled floor in a joyous cacophony. Ophelia heard sniggering behind her back while bending to pick up the keys. Bowler Hat came to her aid with his mocking smile. "We mustn't poke fun at our devoted cousin. She's going to place at my disposal a bit of reading, to educate me!" His

smile turned carnivorous. "I want something tough," he said
to Ophelia. "You wouldn't have a weapon? A war thing, you
know."

Ophelia replaced the drawer and took the key she needed.
The wars of the old world fired up the imagination of the
young, who had only experienced minor family quarrels. All
these greenhorns were after was having fun. Mockery of her
little self didn't bother her, but she wouldn't tolerate anyone
showing so little consideration for her museum, today of all
days. She was determined to remain professional to the end,
however. "Please follow me," she said, key in hand.

"Submit your samples to me!" trilled Bowler Hat, with an
exaggerated bow.

She led them to the rotunda where flying machines of the
first world were displayed—the most popular part of her collection. Ornithopters, amphibious aircraft, mechanical birds,
steam helicopters, quadruplanes, and hydroplanes were suspended on cables like giant dragonflies. The group laughed
even more at the sight of these antiquities, all flapping their
arms like geese. Bowler Hat, who had been chewing gum for
some time, stuck it onto the fuselage of a glider.

Ophelia observed him doing it without batting an eyelid.
That was the limit. He wanted to entertain the crowd? Well,
they'd soon be laughing.

She led them up some mezzanine stairs, then past some
glass shelves. She popped her key into the lock of a display
cabinet, slid back the glass panel, and, with a handkerchief,
picked up a tiny lead ball, which she handed to Bowler Hat.
"An excellent starting point towards a better understanding
of the wars of the old world," she stated flatly. He burst out

laughing as he snatched the ball with his bare hand. "What's this you're offering me? An automaton's dropping?"

His smile gradually faded as, with the tips of his fingers, he went back into the object's past. He became pale and still, as though time had frozen around him. Seeing the look on his face, his beaming companions started poking him in the ribs, but became concerned when he didn't react. "You've given him something horrid!" said one of them in a panicky voice.

"It's an item highly prized by historians," countered Ophelia in a professional tone.

From pallid, Bowler Hat turned gray. "It's not . . . what I . . . was asking for," he struggled to get out.

With her handkerchief, Ophelia retrieved the lead ball and replaced it on its little red cushion. "You wanted a weapon, didn't you? I gave you the projectile from a cartridge that, in its time, punctured the stomach of a soldier. That's what war was about," she concluded, pushing her glasses back up her nose. "Men who killed and men who were killed."

Since Bowler Hat was clutching his stomach and looking queasy, she softened a little. It was a tough lesson, she was aware of that. This boy had come here with his head full of heroic epics, and reading a weapon was like looking his own death in the face. "It will pass," she told him. "I'd advise you to go outside and get some air."

The whole group left, but not before shooting a few dirty looks at her over the shoulder. One of them called her "scarecrow" and another "four-eyed sack of spuds." Ophelia hoped that, later on, her fiancé would think the same of her.

Armed with a spatula, she attacked the chewing gum Bowler Hat had stuck on the glider. "I definitely owed you a small revenge," she whispered, affectionately stroking the side of the aircraft as she would that of an old horse.

"My darling! I've been looking everywhere for you!"

Ophelia turned around. With skirts hitched up and parasol tucked under arm, a splendid young woman was trotting towards her, clicking her white boots on the flagstones. It was Agatha, her elder sister, who was as red-haired, well-dressed, and stunning as her little sister was brown-haired, scruffy, and withdrawn. Day and night.

"But what are you still doing here?"

Ophelia tried to dispose of Bowler Hat's chewing gum, but it was stuck to her gloves. "I'll remind you that I work at the museum until 6 o'clock."

Agatha theatrically squeezed both of Ophelia's hands in her own. She immediately grimaced: she'd just squashed the gum onto her pretty glove. "Not any longer, stupid," she said, annoyed, while flapping her hand. "Mom said you must think only of your preparations. Oh, little sister!" she cried, throwing herself onto Ophelia. "You must be so excited!"

"Er . . . " was all Ophelia managed to get out.

Agatha instantly pulled away to look her up and down. "Holy hot water bottle! Have you looked at yourself in a mirror? You can't possibly, with any decency, show yourself to your betrothed in that state. What will he think of us?"

"That's the least of my worries," Ophelia declared, going over to her counter.

"Well, that's not the case for your kin, you little egoist! We're going to remedy this at once!"

With a sigh, Ophelia got out her old shopping bag and put her belongings into it. If her sister was convinced she had a sacred mission, she'd never let her work in peace. There was nothing she could do but close the museum. While Ophelia took her time gathering her things with a heavy heart, Agatha was stamping her feet with impatience. She perched up on the counter, her white boots swinging under her lace bloomers.

"I've got some gossip for you, and it's juicy! Your mysterious suitor has finally got a name!"

For that, Ophelia lifted her head from her bag. A few hours before they were to be introduced, it was about time! Her future in-laws must have insisted on the utmost discretion. The Doyennes had maintained a deathly silence throughout autumn, divulging not a single piece of information about her fiancé, to an extent that had become ludicrous. Ophelia's mother, furious not to have been taken into their confidence, had been fuming for two months. "Well?" she asked, as Agatha was savoring her little moment.

"Mr. Thorn!"

Ophelia shuddered behind the coils of her scarf. Thorn? She was already allergic to the name. It rang hard on the tongue. Rough. Almost aggressive. A hunter's name.

"I also know that this dear man won't be much older than you, sis. No old codger incapable of fulfilling his conjugal duties for you! And I've kept the best for last," Agatha continued without drawing breath. "You're not going to end up in the middle of nowhere, believe me—the Doyennes have really treated us right. Mr. Thorn has apparently got an aunt who's as beautiful as she's powerful, who ensures that he has an excellent position at the Pole's court. You'll be living the life of a princess!"

Agatha, eyes shining, was triumphant. As for Ophelia, she

was devastated. Thorn, a court gentleman? She would have preferred even a hunter. The more she learnt about her future husband, the more he made her feel like fleeing.

"And what are your sources?"

Agatha adjusted her hat, from which quivering little red curls were escaping. Her cherry mouth puckered into a smug smile. "Rock solid! My brother-in-law Gerard got this information from his great-grandmother, who herself got it from a close cousin who is the actual twin sister of a Doyenne!"

Like a little girl, she clapped her hands and leapt to her booted feet. "You've got yourself a serious ring on your finger, my dear. For a man with such a position and of such a rank to ask for your hand in marriage, it's unhoped for! Come on, get a move on sorting out your mess, we don't have much time before Mr. Thorn's arrival. We've got to make you presentable!"

"Go on ahead," muttered Ophelia, fastening her bag. "There's one last thing I must do."

With a few dainty steps, her sister was off. "I'll save a carriage for us!"

Ophelia stood stock-still behind her counter for a long while. The abrupt silence that had returned to the place once Agatha had left almost hurt her ears. She reopened her forebear's journal at random and scanned the fine, lively handwriting, nearly a century old, with which she was now so familiar.

Tuesday July 16th. I find myself obliged to curb my enthusiasm somewhat. The ambassadress has gone traveling, leaving us in the hands of her countless guests. I feel as though we have been completely forgotten. We spend our days playing cards and walking round the gardens. My brother has adapted to this life of leisure

*better than I have—he is already besotted with a duchess. I will
have to bring him into line since we are here for purely professional
reasons.*

Ophelia was flummoxed. This journal and Agatha's gossip
didn't match up at all with Augustus's sketches. The Pole now
appeared to be a highly refined place. Was Thorn a card player?
He was a court gentleman, he must play cards. That's probably
all he had to do with his days.

Ophelia slipped the little travel journal into a felt cover and
thrust it to the bottom of her bag. Behind the reception counter, she opened the lid of a writing case to get out the inventory register. Several times already, Ophelia had forgotten the
museum keys in a lock, lost important administration documents, and even broken unique exhibits, but if there was one
duty that she had never neglected, it was the keeping of this
register.

Ophelia was an excellent reader, one of the best of her generation. She could decipher the life of machines, layer after layer,
century after century, through the hands that had touched
them, used them, been fond of them, damaged them, patched
them up. This ability had allowed her to enrich the description of each piece in the collection with a hitherto unequalled
level of detail. Where her predecessors confined themselves to
dissecting the past of a former owner, two at a pinch, Ophelia
went back to the birth of an object at the hands of its maker.

This inventory register in some ways told her own story.
Custom dictated that she hand it to her successor in person,
a procedure she would never have imagined carrying out so
early in her life, but no one had yet responded to the request
for applications. So Ophelia slid a note under the binding

addressed to whomever took over at the museum. She replaced the register in the writing case and locked the lid with a turn of the key.

Moving slowly, she then leant with both hands on her counter. She made herself breathe deeply, and accept the unavoidable. This time, it really was over. Tomorrow she wouldn't open her museum, as she did every morning. Tomorrow she would depend forever on a man whose name she would end up sharing.

Mrs. Thorn. Might as well get used to it from now on.

Ophelia grabbed her bag. She looked around her museum for the last time. The sun was coming through the rotunda's glass roof in a cascade of light, wreathing the antiquities in gold and casting their dislocated shadows on the tiled floor. Never had the place seemed as beautiful to her.

Ophelia dropped the keys off at the caretaker's office. She hadn't even passed under the museum's glass canopy, which was swamped by a carpet of dead leaves, when her sister shouted out to her from the door of a carriage: "Get in! We're off to Goldsmiths' Street!"

The cabman snapped his whip, even though there was no horse hitched to his carriage. The wheels took off and the vehicle tore along the river, guided only by the will of its master, from the height of his perch.

Through the back window, Ophelia observed the bustle of the street with a new clarity. This valley, in which she'd been born, seemed to be slipping away from her as fast as the carriage was crossing it. Its half-timbered facades, its market squares, its lovely workshops were all already becoming less familiar to her. The whole town was telling her that this was no longer her home. In the russet glow of this late autumn, people were leading their daily lives. A nanny pushed a pram while blushing at the admiring whistles of workmen up scaffolding. Schoolchildren munched their roast chestnuts on the way home. A messenger rushed along the pavement with a parcel under his arm. All these men, all these women were Ophelia's family, and she didn't know half of them.

The burning breath of a tramcar went past their carriage with a jangling of bells. Once it had vanished, Ophelia gazed at the mountain, criss-crossed by lakes, that overlooked their Valley. The first snows had fallen, up there. The summit had disappeared under a gray shroud—one couldn't even make out Artemis's observatory. Crushed under this cold mass of rocks and clouds, crushed under the dictates of a whole family, Ophelia had never felt so insignificant.

Agatha snapped her fingers under her nose. "Right, trouble, let's get straight to the point: your whole trousseau has to be revised. You need new clothes, shoes, hats, lingerie, lots of lingerie . . . "

"I like my dresses," Ophelia said firmly.

"Oh, be quiet, you dress like our grandmother. Holy curler! Don't tell me you're still wearing this old pair of horrors!" Agatha said, grimacing as she took her sister's gloves in her own. "Mommy's ordered you a load of them from Julian's!"

"They don't make reader's gloves in the Pole, I have to be thrifty."

Agatha was impervious to this sort of reasoning. Smartness and elegance were worth all the money in the world. "Pull yourself together, in Heaven's name! You're going to straighten that back for me, hold that tummy in, show off that top a little, powder that nose, rouge those cheeks, and for pity's sake, change the color of your glasses—that gray is so sinister! As for your hair," sighed Agatha, lifting the brown plait with her fingertips, "if it were up to me, I'd shave it all off and start from scratch, but sadly we no longer have time. Quick, get out, we're there."

Ophelia went around as though leaden-limbed. To every petticoat, every corset, every necklace that was presented to her, she responded with a shake of the head. The dressmaker, whose long Animist fingers shaped fabrics without thread or scissors, shed tears of rage. After two fits of hysterics and about ten shopkeepers, Agatha had only managed to convince her little sister to replace her mismatched boots.

Ophelia was just as recalcitrant at the hairdresser. She wanted to hear nothing of powder, plucking, curling tongs, or the latest style of ribbon.

"I'm certainly patient with you," fumed Agatha, trying her best to lift Ophelia's heavy locks to reveal her neck. "You think I don't know all that you're feeling? I was seventeen when they betrothed me to Charles, and Mommy two years younger when she married Daddy. See what we have become: radiant wives, fulfilled mothers, accomplished women! You've been overprotected by our great-uncle—he did you no favors."

With her vision blurry, Ophelia looked at her face in the mirror of the dressing table before her, while her sister struggled with the knots in her hair. Without her unruly locks and without her glasses, now lying on the comb tray, she felt naked. In the mirror she saw Agatha's auburn head resting its chin on her own head. "Ophelia," she whispered sweetly, "you could be attractive if you just tried a little."

"What's the point? Attractive to whom?"

"But Mr. Thorn, of course, you twit!" said her exasperated sister, giving her a tap on the neck. "Charm is the strongest weapon given to women, you must use it without scruples. A mere trifle is enough, a timely wink, a radiant smile, to have a man at one's feet. Look at Charles, putty in my hands."

Ophelia fixed her eyes on those in her reflection, chocolate-flavored eyes. Without glasses she couldn't see herself clearly, but she could make out the glum oval of her face, the paleness of her cheeks, her white neck throbbing under the collar, the shadow of a characterless nose and those too-thin lips that disliked speaking. She attempted a timid smile, but it looked so false that she dropped it instantly. Was she attractive? How can one tell? From the gaze of a man? Would that be the gaze Thorn would direct at her, this evening?

The idea seemed so grotesque to her that she would have laughed out loud if her situation weren't so pitifully dire. "Have you finished torturing me?" she asked her sister, who was ruth-lessly tugging at her hair.

"Nearly." Agatha turned to the manageress of the salon to request some hairpins. That moment of inattention was all Ophelia needed. She quickly put her glasses back on, grabbed her bag, and dived headlong into the mirror of the dressing table, which was barely wide enough for her. Her head and shoulders emerged through the wall mirror in her room, a few districts away, but she could move no further. On the other side of the mirror, Agatha had grabbed her by the ankles to pull her back to Goldsmiths' Street. Ophelia let go of her bag and used the papered wall for support, struggling with all her might against her sister's grip.

Without warning, she tumbled right into the room, knocking over a stool and the potted plant on it as she did so. Somewhat dazed, she stared blankly at the bare foot sticking out from under her dress; a boot from her new pair had remained with Agatha in Goldsmiths' Street. Her sister couldn't pass through mirrors, so she finally had some respite.

Ophelia picked her bag up from the carpet, limped over to a solid wooden chest at the foot of the bunk beds, and sat down. She pushed her glasses back up her nose and surveyed the little room, which was cluttered with trunks and hatboxes. This particular mess wasn't her usual mess. This room that had witnessed her growing up already smacked of departure.

She carefully got out the journal of her forebear Adelaide and pensively leafed through its pages again.

Sunday July 18th. Still no news from the ambassadress. The women here are charming and I don't think any of my Anima cousins are their equals in grace and beauty, but I sometimes feel uncomfortable. I get the impression that they are forever casting aspersions on my clothes, my manners, and my way of speaking. Or maybe I'm just working myself into a state?

"Why are you home so early?"

Ophelia looked up towards the top bunk. She hadn't noticed the two patent-leather shoes sticking out beyond the mattress; this scrawny pair of legs belonged to Hector, the little brother with whom she shared the room.

She closed the journal. "I'm escaping from Agatha."

"Why?"

"Little female problems. Does Mr. Say-Why want details?"

"Not remotely."

Ophelia half-smiled; she had a soft spot for her brother. The patent shoes disappeared from the top bunk. They were soon replaced by lips smeared with compote, a turned-up nose, a pudding-basin haircut, and two placid eyes. Hector had the same look as Ophelia, but without the glasses: unperturbed in all circumstances. He was holding a slice of bread and apricot jam, which was dripping all over his fingers.

"We said no snacks in this room," Ophelia reminded him.

Hector shrugged his shoulders and pointed with his slice of bread towards the travel journal on her lap. "Why are you still going over that notebook? You know it by heart."

That was Hector. He always asked questions and all his questions began with "why."

"To reassure myself, I suppose," muttered Ophelia.

In fact, Adelaide had become familiar to her over the weeks, almost close. And yet Ophelia felt disappointed each time she ended up on the last page.

Monday August 2nd. I'm so relieved! The ambassadress has returned from her travels. Rudolf has finally signed his contract with one of Lord Farouk's solicitors. I am not allowed to write anything more—it is a professional secret—but we will meet their family spirit tomorrow. If my brother puts on a good show, we will become rich.

The journal finished with these words. Adelaide had felt it necessary neither to enter into details nor to give an account of what had happened next. What contract had she and her brother signed with Farouk, the family spirit? Had they returned rich from the Pole? Most probably not, it would have been common knowledge . . .

"Why don't you read it with your hands?" Hector asked next, grinding his bread and jam between his teeth while also languidly chewing it. "If I could, that's what I'd do, myself."

"I'm not allowed to, as you know."

In truth, Ophelia had been tempted to remove her gloves to uncover the little secrets of her ancestor, but she was too professional to contaminate this document with her own anxiety. Her great-uncle would have been very disappointed if she had succumbed to such an urge.

Beneath her feet, a shrill voice rose through the floor from downstairs: "This guest room, it's a total disaster! It was supposed to be fit for a court gentleman, it needed much more pomp, more decorum! How low is Mr. Thorn's opinion of us going to be? We'll make amends with the meal this evening. Rosaline, dash to the restaurateur's to get news of my fattened chickens—I entrust the directing of operations to you! And you, my poor dear, try to set a bit of an example. It's not every day that one marries one's daughter!"

"Mom," said Hector, placidly.

"Mom," confirmed Ophelia with the same tone.

It certainly didn't make her feel like going downstairs. As she drew the floral curtain at the window, the setting sun gilded her cheeks, nose, and glasses. In the dusk, through a corridor of crimson-turning clouds, the moon already stood out, like a china plate, against the mauve backcloth of the sky.

For a long time, Ophelia contemplated the side of the valley, turned golden by autumn, which loomed over their house, and the carriages going by in the street, and her little sisters playing with a hoop in their courtyard, surrounded by dead leaves. They were singing nursery rhymes, daring each other, pulling each other by the plait, going from laughter to tears and tears to laughter with disconcerting ease. They brought to mind Agatha at that age, with their winning smiles, noisy chatter, and beautiful light-auburn hair, shimmering in the gloaming.

Ophelia was suddenly overcome by a burst of nostalgia. Her eyes widened, her lips thinned, her impassive mask cracked. She would have liked to gambol after her sisters, shamelessly hitch up her skirts and chuck stones into Aunt Rosaline's garden. How long ago those days seemed to her this evening . . .

"Why do you have to go? It's going to be tedious being left alone with all those brats."

Ophelia turned towards Hector. Busy licking his fingers, he hadn't budged from the top bunk, but he had followed her gaze through the window. Despite his phlegmatic demeanor, the tone was accusatory.

"It's not my fault, you know."

"Why didn't you want to marry our cousins, then?"

The question felt like a slap in the face. It's true, Hector was right, she wouldn't be in this situation if she'd married the first comer.

"But regrets are pointless," she muttered.

"Look out!" warned Hector. He wiped his mouth with a swipe of his sleeve and flattened himself on the bed. A sudden draft blew through Ophelia's dresses. With disheveled bun and glistening forehead, their mother had just burst into the room like a whirlwind. Cousin Bertrand followed right behind.

"I'm going to put the little ones in here, as they've given up their room for their sister's fiancé. These trunks are taking up all the space, I just can't handle it! Take this one down to the shed, and be careful, what's in it is fragi—"

Her mother broke off, openmouthed, when she caught sight of Ophelia's silhouette, outlined against the sunset.

"Ancestors alive, I thought you were with Agatha!" She pursed her lips with indignation as she clocked Ophelia's old-lady outfit and dust-collecting scarf. The expected metamorphosis had not taken place. She struck her ample breast with her hand. "You want to finish me off! After all the trouble I go to for you! What are you punishing me for, my girl?"

Ophelia blinked behind her glasses. She'd always had poor taste in clothes—why should she change her getup now?

"Do you even know what time it is?" her mother asked, panicking and slapping her varnished nails over her mouth. "We've to go up to the air terminal in less than an hour! Where's your sister gone? And me in this ghastly state, gadzooks, we'll never make it in time!"

She pulled out a powder compact from inside her bodice, dabbed a pink puff on her nose, rewound her light-auburn bun with an expert hand, and pointed a scarlet nail at Ophelia. "I want you presentable before the next strike of the clock. And that goes for you, too, you disgusting creature!" she scolded in the direction of the top bunk. "You stink of congealed jam, Hector!"

Ophelia's mother bumped into Cousin Bertrand, who had remained standing there, arms dangling. "And that trunk, are you planning on doing it today or tomorrow?"

In a whirlwind of skirt, the storm departed from the room just as it had arrived.

The Bear

As night had fallen, so had heavy rain. It hammered down on the metal latticed roof of the airship hangar, fifty meters above. Hoisted on a neighboring plateau, this base was the most modern in the valley. Designed for receiving long-distance flights in particular, it benefited from steam heating and had its own hydrogen-gas plant. Its vast track-sliding doors were wide open, revealing an interior of wrought iron, brick, and cables, in which many gabardine-clad mechanics were rushing around.

Outside, along the goods quay, a few lamps spat out a light made murky by the damp. A guard, soaked to the bone, was checking the protective tarpaulins on mail crates ready for loading. He grimaced on encountering a forest of umbrellas, right in the middle of the quay. Beneath the umbrellas huddled men in frock coats, women in their finery, and well-combed kids. There they all stood, silent and expressionless, scanning the clouds.

"Well, 'scuse me, my good cousins, might one be of some assistance?" he asked.

Ophelia's mother, whose red umbrella dwarfed all the others, indicated the standing clock around which they had set up camp. Everything about this woman was enormous: her bustled dress, her bullfrog's throat, her beehive bun, and, towering above it all, her feathered hat.

"Well, you could start by telling me if this here's the correct time. It's been a good forty minutes we've been looking out for the Pole airship!"

"Late, as usual," the guard informed her with a cheery smile. "Waiting for a delivery of furs?"

"No, son. We're waiting for a visitor."

The guard squinted at the crow-beaked nose that had just replied to him. It belonged to a lady of extremely advanced years. She was dressed all in black, from the mantilla around her white hair to the taffeta of her stiff-bodiced dress. The elegant silver braiding on her outfit revealed her status of Doyenne, mother among mothers. The guard took off his cap as a sign of respect. "An envoy from the Pole, dear mother? You're sure there hasn't been some misunderstanding about the visitor? I've worked the quays since I were a lad and I've never seen a Northerner drag himself over here for anything but business. Don't mix with just anyone, those people!"

He tipped his cap to salute them and returned to his crates. Ophelia gazed after him gloomily, then returned to contemplating her boots. What was the point of putting on a brand-new pair? They were already covered in mud.

"Lift your chin and try not to get wet," whispered Agatha, with whom she was sharing a lemon-yellow umbrella. "And smile—you look miserable as sin! Mr. Thorn won't be swinging from the chandeliers with a killjoy like you."

Her sister hadn't forgiven her for escaping through the mirror—you could hear it in her voice—but Ophelia was barely listening to her. She was focusing on the sound of the rain, which drowned out the panicky palpitations in her chest.

"Okay, why don't you just let her breathe?" asked Hector, annoyed.

Ophelia shot a grateful look at her brother, but he was already busy jumping into puddles with his little sisters and cousins. They embodied the childhood that she would have liked to have relived one last time this evening. Totally care-free, they had all come along not to see the arrival of the fiancé, but rather that of the airship. It was a rare spectacle for them, one big party.

"It's Agatha who's right," declared the mother under her enormous red umbrella. "My daughter will breathe when she's told to and how she's told to. Isn't that right, my dear?"

The question, for appearances' sake, was just for Ophelia's father, who stammered a vaguely assenting formula. This poor man, balding and graying, prematurely aged, was crushed by his wife's authority. Ophelia couldn't recall ever hearing him say no. She looked for her old godfather among the crowd of uncles, aunts, cousins, and nephews. She spotted him brood-ing, away from the umbrellas, buttoned up to his moustache in his navy-blue mackintosh. She was expecting no miracle from him, but the kindly salutation he directed at her from a distance did her good.

Ophelia's head felt like sludge and her stomach was churn-ing. Her heart thumped deep in her chest. She would have liked this waiting in the rain not to have an ending.

Exclamations all around hit her like dagger blows:

"Over there!"

"That's it."

"About time, too . . . "

Ophelia looked up to the clouds, her stomach in knots. A dark mass, shaped like a whale, was breaking through the mist and stood out against the night sky, while emitting ominous creaking sounds. The whirring of the propellers became deafening. The children squealed with joy. Lace petticoats were blown upwards. Ophelia's and Agatha's lemon-yellow umbrella flew off into the sky. Having arrived above the landing strip, the airship released its cables. The mechanics grabbed hold of them and pulled with all their weight to bring the aerostat down. They clung on, in groups of about ten, to the manual-steering rails, guiding it straight into the great hangar, and then moored it to the ground. A gangway was put in place for disembarkation, and, clutching crates and mailbags, the crew members proceeded down it.

The whole family rushed, like a swarm of flies, to the front of the hangar. Only Ophelia remained behind, dripping under the cold rain, her long brown hair plastered to her cheeks. Water trickled down the surface of her glasses. All she could see in front of her was a formless mass of dresses, jackets, and umbrellas.

Above the hubbub, her mother's booming voice rang out: "Just let him come through, you lot, make way! My dear, my dearest Mr. Thorn, welcome to Anima. So, you came without an escort? Ancestors alive, Ophelia! Where's she disappeared to now, that moon head? Agatha, go find your sister, quick. What awful weather, my poor friend; if you'd arrived an hour earlier, we'd have welcomed you without all this rain. Someone give him an umbrella!"

Ophelia was rooted to the spot. He was there. The man who

was about to devastate her life was there. She wanted neither to see him nor to speak to him.

Agatha grabbed her by the wrist and dragged her through the throng of relatives. Drunk on all the noise and rain, and barely conscious, Ophelia passed from face to face before finally collapsing onto the breast of a polar bear. Dazed, she didn't react when the bear muttered an icy "good evening," from up there, way above her head.

"The introductions are over!" her mother shouted hoarsely in the midst of the polite applause. "To your carriages! No point us catching our death."

Ophelia allowed herself to be shoved into a vehicle. The whip cracked the air, and the carriage moved off with a jolt. A lantern was lit, casting a reddish glow on the passengers. The rain seemed to be battering the windowpanes. Squashed against the door, Ophelia focused on that beating rhythm of the water, long enough to recover her senses and emerge from her torpor. She gradually became aware of the animated conversation going on around her. It was her mother, who talked enough for ten. The bear, was he there, too?

Ophelia pushed up her glasses, still flecked with raindrops. First she saw her mother's huge beehive bun, which flattened her onto the carriage seat, then the Doyenne's crow nose, right in front of her, and finally, on the other side, the bear. He was staring determinedly through the door window, responding from time to time to her mother's jabbering with a laconic nod of the head, but without bothering to exchange a glance with anyone.

Relieved not to be in his line of sight, Ophelia was prepared to take a closer look at her fiancé. Contrary to her initial impression, Thorn wasn't a bear, even if he seemed like one. A voluminous white fur, spiked with fangs and claws, covered his shoulders. In fact, he wasn't that bulky. His arms, crossed on his chest, were tapered like swords. On the other hand, as slender as he was, this man had the stature of a giant. The top of his head was pressed against the ceiling of the carriage, forcing him to bend his neck. He was even more towering than Cousin Bertrand, and that was saying something.

Ancestors alive, thought a shocked Ophelia, that will be my husband, all that?

Thorn had an attractive carpetbag balanced on his knees, a contrast to his animal-skin clothing that lent him a touch of civilization. Ophelia observed him surreptitiously. She daren't stare too hard at him, fearing the he would sense this attention and suddenly turn to her. In two glances, however, she got an impression of his face, and what she had glimpsed made her flesh creep. Pale eyes, sharp nose, light hair, scar across temple, the whole profile was full of disdain. Disdain for her and her whole family.

Taken aback, Ophelia realized that this man was also getting married against his will.

"I have a gift for Mrs. Artemis."

Ophelia shuddered. Her mother suddenly went quiet. Even the Doyenne, who had nodded off, half-opened her eyes. Thorn had uttered this sentence reluctantly, as though speaking to them pained him. His pronunciation of each consonant was hard—it was the accent of the North.

"A gift for Artemis?" stammered her mother, disconcerted. "But of course, sir!" she said, pulling herself together. "It will be a signal honor to introduce you to our family spirit. You doubtless know of her observatory by repute, yes? If it would please you, I propose we go there tomorrow."

"Now."

Thorn's response struck with the snap of the cabman's whip. Her mother turned deathly pale. "The thing is, Mr. Thorn, it wouldn't be acceptable to disturb Artemis this evening. She no longer receives visitors after dark, do you see? And," she added, proudly and with a friendly smile, "we have planned a little meal especially for you . . . "

Ophelia's eyes darted from her mother to her fiancé. A "little meal," that was quite a euphemism. She'd requisitioned Uncle Hubert's barn for her Pantagruelian banquet; organized the slaughter of three pigs; ordered Bengal lights from the hardware store; packaged up several kilos of sugared almonds; and planned a costumed ball to last until dawn. Rosaline, Ophelia's aunt and godmother, was completing the preparations at that very moment.

"It can't wait," declared Thorn. "Anyhow, I'm not hungry."

"I understand, my son," the Doyenne suddenly conceded with a crumpled smile. "You must do things properly."

Ophelia blinked behind her glasses. She, on the other hand, didn't understand. What was this behavior all about? Thorn was proving to be so coarse that he made her seem like a paragon of good manners. With his fist he hit the little rectangle of glass behind him, separating the driver from his carriage. The vehicle screeched to a halt. "Sir?" asked the cabman, nose pressed to the glass.

"To Mrs. Artemis's," ordered Thorn, with that hard accent of his. Through the back window, the cabman looked questioningly at Ophelia's mother. Shock had turned her white as a ghost and caused a slight trembling of her lip. "Drive us to the observatory," she said, finally, her jaw tense.

Gripping the strap on her seat, Ophelia felt the vehicle doing a U-turn to go back up the hill it had just hurtled down. Outside, cries of protestation greeted the maneuver; they came from the carriages carrying the rest of the family.

"What's got into you?" screeched Aunt Mathilda through a door. Ophelia's mother lowered her window. "We're going up to the observatory," she said.

"What d'you mean?" asked an affronted Uncle Hubert. "At this hour? And what about the feast? The celebrations? Our stomachs are rumbling in all directions, over here!"

"Eat without us, feast yourselves, then all go home to bed!" instructed her mother.

She closed her window again to curtail the outcry and signaled to the cabman, whose questioning face was again pressed to the back window, that he could go on. Ophelia bit her scarf to stop herself from smiling. This man from the North had just mortally offended her mother; all things considered, he was exceeding her expectations.

As their carriage set off again under the flabbergasted gaze of the family, Thorn leant against the window, focusing solely on the rain. He no longer seemed willing to continue the conversation with the mother, and even less to start one with the daughter. His eyes, tapered like flashes of metal, didn't alight for a second on the young lady he was supposed to be courting.

With a satisfied gesture, Ophelia pushed away a dripping lock of hair that was plastered to her nose. If Thorn deemed it unnecessary to make any effort to appeal to her, there was some hope he wouldn't expect any such effort in return either.

The way things were going, the engagement would be broken off before midnight.

With lips pursed, her mother no longer bothered to fill any silences; her eyes glinted with rage in the half-light of the carriage. The Doyenne blew out the lantern and, with a sigh, fell back to sleep, shrouded in her great black mantilla. The journey promised to be long.

The carriage took a potholed mountain road that twisted and turned on a pinhead. Queasy from the jolting, Ophelia focused on the landscape. At first she was on the bad side of the carriage and saw only jagged rock on which the first snows had appeared. A turning later, and her view plummeted into the void. The rain had stopped, swept away by a west wind. This had blown a scattering of stars between the clouds, but down below, at the bottom of the Valley, the sky was still glowing red in the dusk. Forests of sweet chestnut and larch had given way to fir trees, whose resinous scent swept over the cab.

Thanks to the darkness, Ophelia could look less guardedly at the bent-in-three figure of Thorn. The night had cast a bluish glow on his closed eyelids; Ophelia noticed another scar that cut through his eyebrow and glowed white against his cheek. So this man actually was a hunter, in the end? He was certainly a bit thin, but she had recognized in him the same hard look that Augustus's subjects had. Rocked by the jolting of the carriage, she would have thought him asleep if it hadn't been for the annoyed furrow in his brow and the nervous drumming of his fingers on his case. She turned away when Thorn's eyelids suddenly let through a gray glint.

The cabman had pulled up. "The observatory," he announced.

The Observatory

Only twice in her life had Ophelia got the chance to meet the spirit of her family. She couldn't recall the first, the occasion being her baptism. At the time, she was but a mewling shawl that had sprinkled the Doyenne with tears and urine.

The second time, on the other hand, had left a vivid impression on her. At fifteen, she had won the reading competition organized by the Society of Sciences, all thanks to a shirt button. It had led her back more than three centuries and revealed the escapades of its owner in the smallest detail. Artemis herself had given her the top prize: her first reader's gloves. The very same gloves, now threadbare, that, this evening, she was nibbling at the seams as she got out of the carriage.

An icy wind made her coat flap. Ophelia remained still, her breath taken away by the amazing vault of the white dome, whose long telescope was poking the night in the eye. Artemis's observatory was not only a center of research in astronomy, meteorology, and rock mechanics, it was also an architectural marvel. Set in a mountain rock-face enclosure, the palace incorporated a dozen buildings specifically to house the great instruments, from meridian circle to equatorial telescope, astrograph to magnetic pavilion. The pediment of the main building, stamped with a black-and-gold sundial, looked down from its lofty heights over the Valley, where the town's night-time lights twinkled.

This sight was even more impressive than Ophelia had remembered. She offered her arm to the Doyenne, who was struggling to alight from the carriage. This was more a man's duty, but Thorn had commandeered the carriage seats to open up his case. With eyes set deep under stern brows, he did what suited him, not remotely concerned about these women whose guest of honor he was.

On the terrace of the observatory, a frantic scientist was running in pursuit of his top hat as it rolled between two rows of columns. "Excuse me, learned father," shouted out Ophelia's mother, holding down her fine feathered hat with one hand. "Do you work here?"

"Absolutely." The man had abandoned his top hat to turn his wide forehead, which was being whipped by his quiff, towards her. "A splendid wind, isn't it!" he enthused. "Absolutely splendid! It cleared the sky for us within half an hour."

Suddenly, he frowned. Enlarged by his lorgnette, his suspicious eye bounced from the three women to the carriage, parked outside the main entrance, in which Thorn's huge shadow was busy unpacking the case. "What is it? What do you want?"

"An audience, my son," the Doyenne chipped in. She was leaning with all her weight on Ophelia's arm.

"Impossible. Absolutely impossible. Come back tomorrow." The scientist held up his cane to the night sky, pointing at the clouds that were dissolving in the wind like spiderwebs. "First clear night sky for a week. Artemis is up to her eyes in work, absolutely up to her eyes."

"It won't take long." Thorn had blurted this assurance while extricating himself from the carriage, a casket under his arm.

The scientist pushed away the quiff flapping over his eyes, to no avail. "Were it only to take a fraction of a second, I repeat, it's absolutely impossible. We're right in the middle of an inventory. Fourth edition of the catalog, *Astronomiae instauratae mechanica*. It's absolutely a priority."

"Six!" marveled Ophelia to herself. She'd never heard "absolutely" repeated so many times in one go.

Thorn scaled the entrance steps in two long strides and stood to his full height in front of the scientist, who instantly took a step back. The wind was making the light hair of this great scarecrow stand on end and tugging on the laces of his fur, revealing the grip of a pistol at his belt. Thorn's arm stretched out. This sudden movement made the scientist jump, but it was a simple fob watch that Thorn had just brandished under his nose.

"Ten minutes, not a second more. Where can I find Mrs. Artemis?"

The old man indicated the main dome with his cane; there was a slot cut into it, like a moneybox. "At her telescope."

Thorn clicked his heels across the marble without a backward glance, without a word of thanks. Red-faced with humiliation under her bulky feathered hat, Ophelia's mother lost none of her fury. So she took it out on Ophelia when she skidded on a patch of ice, nearly pulling the Doyenne down with her. "And you, are you never going to grow out of your clumsiness? You cover me in shame!"

Ophelia felt around on the flagstones for her glasses. Once she'd put them back on, she saw her mother's voluminous dress in triple. The lenses had cracked.

"And that man who doesn't wait for us," grumbled her mother, gathering up her skirts. "Mr. Thorn, slow down!"

With his little casket under his arm, Thorn ignored her, entering into the hall of the observatory. He continued at marching pace, opening all the doors he came across without ever knocking. With his stature, he towered over the troupe of scientists dancing up and down the corridors while commenting loudly on their constellation charts.

Ophelia went with the flow, nose behind scarf. All she could see of Thorn were pieces of a fragmented silhouette. He stood so tall in his shaggy fur that, from the back, he could be mistaken for a polar bear. She was thoroughly relishing the situation. This man's attitude was so offensive, it seemed almost too good to be true. As Thorn started going up a spiral staircase, Ophelia offered the Doyenne her arm again to help her up the stairs.

"May I ask you a question?" she whispered to her.

"You may, dear girl," said the Doyenne, smiling.

A scientist sweeping down the stairs like a whirlwind knocked into them without apologizing. He was tearing his hair out and screaming like one possessed that he'd never got his calculations wrong and he wasn't about to start this evening.

"How many insults must our family endure before thinking of reconsidering the betrothal?" asked Ophelia.

Her question cast a chill. The Doyenne withdrew her hand from Ophelia's proffered arm. She repositioned her black mantilla on her head so that all that remained visible was her beak of a nose and a deeply wrinkled smile. "What are you complaining about, dear girl? This young boy seems totally charming to me."

Perplexed, Ophelia looked at the black and shriveled figure of the Doyenne, who was heaving herself laboriously from one step to the next. So did she not care, either?

Thorn's gloomy voice reverberated around the rotunda he'd just entered: "Madam, your brother has sent me to you."

Ophelia didn't want to miss the audience with Artemis. She hurried to get through the metal door on which still swung this sign: DO NOT DISTURB: OBSERVATION IN PROGRESS.

She blinked behind her broken glasses as she entered into the darkness. She heard what sounded like a fluttering of wings in front of her; it was her mother, increasingly enraged, who'd taken out her fan to refresh her thoughts. As for Thorn, she only made out his fur spiked with claws once the wall lamps gradually came on.

"My brother? Which one?" This hoarse whisper, sounding more like the scraping of a millstone than a woman's voice, had rebounded across the whole metal framework of the room. Ophelia searched for its source. She scanned the gangways that spiraled up around the dome, then looked down again, along the copper cylinder whose focal range was almost six times her height. She found Artemis bending over the lens of the telescope.

She saw her splintered into three pieces. She must take care of her glasses as soon as possible.

The spirit of the family slowly tore herself away from the spectacle of the stars, unbending each of her limbs, each of her joints, until she stood taller than Thorn himself, much taller.

71

Artemis studied at length this stranger who had disturbed her contemplation of the galaxy, and who didn't even blink under the intensity of her scrutiny.

A few years had passed since she was fifteen, but Ophelia felt as disturbed by Artemis's appearance as she had that day she'd handed her the top prize. It wasn't that she was ugly; in fact, there was something formidable about her beauty. Her auburn hair escaped at her neck in a loose coil and rippled over the marble flagstones, around her bare ankles, like a river of molten lava. The graceful curve of her figure put even the ark's most beautiful young girls in the shade. Her skin—flesh so white and supple that, from afar, it seemed liquid—flowed over the perfect structure of her face. By an irony of fate, Artemis didn't value the supernatural radiance that Nature had bestowed upon her and that was the envy of so many coquettes. Thus she only had men's clothes tailor-made to fit her great height. That night, she was wearing a red velvet frock coat with simple knee breeches, leaving her calves bare.

It wasn't her mannish ways, either, that made Ophelia feel uncomfortable—a trifling annoyance when compared with such splendor. No, it was something else. Artemis was beautiful, but it was a cold beauty, indifferent, almost inhuman.

The slit of her eyes, between which one could glimpse two yellow irises, expressed nothing while she studied Thorn at length. Not anger, not boredom, not curiosity. Just a waiting.

At the end of a silence that seemed to last an eternity, she broke into a smile that was devoid of all emotion, neither kind nor unkind. A smile that had but the shape of a smile.

"You have the accent and manners of the North. You are of Farouk's lineage." Artemis leant backwards in one long, graceful movement; the marble surged up from the flagging like a fountain to furnish her with a seat. Of all the Animists who populated the ark, no one was capable of such a feat, not even the line of blacksmiths, who could twist metal with just a press of the thumb.

"And what does he want from me, my dear brother?" she asked in her rasping voice.

The Doyenne moved a step forward, lifted her black dress to curtsey to her and replied: "The marriage, beautiful Artemis, do you recall?"

Artemis's yellow eyes swiveled towards the old woman in black, then towards the feathered hat of the mother, who was fanning herself feverishly, before landing straight on Ophelia. She shuddered, her damp hair clinging to her cheeks like seaweed. Artemis, of whom she could only see a blurred and fragmented image, was her great-great-great-great-great-great-great-grandmother. And there were doubtless still one or two greats missing.

Evidently, her relation didn't recognize her. The family spirit never recognized anyone. For a long time now she had given up trying to memorize the faces of all her descendants, faces that were too ephemeral for this ageless goddess. Ophelia sometimes wondered whether Artemis had once been close to her children. She wasn't a very maternal creature, she never left her observatory to join her offspring, and she had long since delegated all her responsibilities to the Doyennes.

It wasn't entirely Artemis's fault, however, if she had so little memory. Nothing stuck firmly in her mind, events flowed over her without lingering. This predisposition to forget was probably to compensate for her immortality, a safety valve to avoid sinking into madness or despair. Artemis knew nothing of her past; she lived in an eternal present. No one knew what her life had been like before founding her own dynasty on Anima, several centuries back. For the family, she was there, she had always been there, she would always be there.

And this was how it went for each ark and each family spirit.

With a nervous gesture, Ophelia pushed her broken glasses back up her nose. Sometimes she still asked herself this question: what really were the family spirits and where did they come from? That the blood of a phenomenon such as Artemis should run in her own veins seemed barely credible to her, and yet run it did, spreading its Animism to the whole line without ever running dry.

"Yes, I do remember," Artemis finally admitted. "So what do you call yourself, my daughter?"

"Ophelia."

There was a disdainful snort. Ophelia looked at Thorn. He had his back to her, as rigid as a large stuffed bear. Although she couldn't see the expression on his face, she didn't doubt that this snort came from him. Her reedy little voice had clearly not pleased him.

"Ophelia," said Artemis, "I offer you my congratulations for your marriage and I thank you for this alliance that will reinforce the cordial relations between my brother and me."

It was a fitting formula, devoid of enthusiasm, spoken only for the sake of protocol. Thorn moved towards Artemis and offered her the lacquered-wood casket. Approaching so close to this sublime creature, who could turn the heads of a whole procession of old scientists, left him cold as marble.

"On behalf of Lord Farouk."

Ophelia consulted her mother with a flash of her glasses. Would she also be expected to offer a tribute to the spirit of her in-laws' family, the day of her arrival in the Pole? Judging by her mother's shocked lipstick grimace, she realized that she was asking herself the same question.

Artemis accepted the offering with a nonchalant gesture. Her face, impassive up to now, tensed slightly as soon as she had discovered, through the surface of her skin, the contents of the casket. "Why?" she asked, looking through half-closed eyelids.

"I don't know what this casket contains," Thorn informed her, bowing very stiffly. "Indeed, I have no other message to pass on to you."

The family spirit stroked the lacquered wood, pensively, turned her yellow eyes back to Ophelia, seemed about to say something to her, then casually shrugged a shoulder. "You may leave, all of you. I have work to do."

Thorn hadn't waited for a blessing to turn on his heels, watch in hand, and go back down the stairs with his energetic step. The three women hastily took their leave of Artemis and hurried after him, fearing that he would be rude enough to set off in the carriage without them.

"Ancestors alive, I refuse to give up my daughter to this lout!"

Ophelia's mother had exploded in the midst of animated whispering, right in the center of a planetarium in which a crowd of scientists were all talking about the imminent passage of the comet. Thorn didn't hear her. His ill-bred bearskin had already left the dark room in which the globes' mechanisms were humming like clockwork cogs.

Ophelia's heart leapt in her chest, racing with hope, but the Doyenne shattered all her illusions with a mere smile. "An agreement has been reached between two families, dear girl. No one, apart from Farouk and Artemis, can go back on that without sparking off a diplomatic incident."

Her mother's large bun had collapsed under her fine hat, and her pointed nose was visibly turning purple, despite the layers of makeup. "Yes, but all the same, my magnificent meal!"

Ophelia scowled behind her scarf while gazing up at the ballet of the stars under the vault of the planetarium. Between the behavior of her fiancé, of her mother, and of the Doyenne, she couldn't decide which was most infuriating. "If, by chance, you should ask me for my opinion . . . " she muttered.

"No one is asking you for it," cut in the Doyenne, with her little smile.

In other circumstances, Ophelia wouldn't have insisted. She valued her tranquility too much to debate, argue, stick up for herself, but this evening, it was the rest of her life that was at stake. "I'm giving it to you anyway," she said. "Mr. Thorn feels no more like chaining himself to me than I do to him. I think you must have made a mistake at some stage."

The Doyenne came to a halt. Her body, all twisted with arthritis, slowly straightened up, getting taller and taller, as she turned towards Ophelia. Beneath the web of wrinkles, the kindly smile had disappeared. The dull blue iris, on the verge of blindness, locked on to her glasses with such coldness that Ophelia was staggered. Her mother herself shrank upon witnessing this metamorphosis. It was no longer a shriveled old woman who stood before them, amid this whirlwind of overexcited scientists. It was the incarnation of the supreme authority on Anima. The worthy representative of the matriarchal Council. The mother among mothers.

76

"There is no mistake whatsoever," the Doyenne said, icily. "Mr. Thorn put forward an official request to marry an Animist. Among all the marriageable young girls, you are the one that we chose."

"It would appear that Mr. Thorn doesn't approve of your choice," Ophelia commented, calmly.

"He will have to put up with it. The families have spoken."

"Why me?" insisted Ophelia, not caring about the horrified expression on her mother's face. "Are you punishing me?"

That was her firm belief. She had turned down too many proposals, too many arrangements. She stuck out among all her cousins, who were already housewives, and that false note was disliked. The Doyennes were using this marriage as an example to others.

With her pale eyes, the old woman looked deep into Ophelia's glasses, beyond the broken lenses. When not bent double, she was taller than Ophelia. "We have granted you a final chance. Be an honor to our family, child. If you fail at this task, if you make this marriage fail, I swear to you that you will never again set foot on Anima."

The Kitchen

Ophelia ran fast as the wind. She crossed rivers, cut through forests, flew over towns, passed through mountains, but the horizon remained out of reach. Sometimes she sped across the surface of a vast ocean, and the watery landscape went on forever, but she always ended up reaching land. This wasn't Anima. This wasn't even an ark. This world was all of a piece. It was whole, with no break, round like a ball. The old world of before the Rupture.

Suddenly, Ophelia spotted a vertical arrow piercing the horizon like a flash of lightning. She didn't think she'd ever seen it before, this arrow. Curious, she ran towards it, faster than the wind. The closer she got to it, the less the arrow looked like an arrow. On second thought, it was more a kind of tower. Or statue.

No, it was a man.

Ophelia wanted to slow down, change direction, turn back, but an irresistible force pulled her, against her will, towards this man. The old world had disappeared. There was no longer a horizon, just Ophelia rushing, despite herself, towards this thin, huge man, who stubbornly kept his back turned to her.

Ophelia opened her eyes wide, head on pillow, hair fanning

around her like some wild vegetation. She blew her nose. It sounded like a blocked trumpet. Breathing through her mouth, she gazed at the slatted base of Hector's bed, just above hers. She wondered whether her little brother was still asleep, up there, or had already climbed down the wooden ladder. She hadn't the slightest idea what time it might be.

Propping herself up on an elbow, she peered myopically around the room, where bedding had been improvised on the carpet, now a tangle of sheets and bolsters. Her little sisters were all up. A cold wind whistled around the window frame, making the curtains billow. The sun was already up, the children must have left for school.

Ophelia noticed that the family's old cat had curled up in the gap between her feet, at the end of the bed. She dived back under her patchwork quilt and blew her nose once more. She felt as though she had cotton wool in her throat, ears, and eyes. She was used to it—she caught colds from the slightest draft. She groped around for her glasses on the bedside table. The cracked lenses were already starting to heal up, but they'd still need several more hours to get the all clear. Ophelia placed them on her nose. An object repaired itself quicker if it felt useful, it was all a question of psychology.

She stretched her arms under the covers, in no hurry to leave her bed. Ophelia had struggled to get to sleep once they'd got back home. She knew she wasn't the only one. From the moment he'd shut himself in it, with a snort by way of "good night," Thorn hadn't stopped pacing up and down the room above, making the floor creak, back and forth. Ophelia had tired before him, finally sinking into sleep.

With head deep in pillow, she tried hard to untangle the

emotions tightening her chest. The Doyenne's chilling words echoed in her head: "If you fail at this task, if you make this marriage fail, I swear to you that you will never again set foot on Anima."

Banishment was worse than death. Ophelia's entire world was on this ark; if she were cast out, she'd never have any family to turn to, ever again. She'd have to marry this bear, she had no choice.

A marriage of convenience always served a purpose, particularly if it reinforced diplomatic relations between two arks. It could be supplying new blood to avoid the degeneration linked to too much consanguinity. It could be a strategic alliance to benefit business and commerce. It could also, though that remained rare, be a marriage of love arising from a holiday romance.

However much Ophelia examined the question, its most important aspect continued to elude her: this man, who seemed disgusted by everything on Anima, what benefit did he really hope to reap from this marriage?

She nosedived back into her checked handkerchief and blew with all her might. She felt relieved. Thorn was a barely civilized madman, who towered two heads above her, and whose long, tense hands had surely handled weapons. But at least he didn't like her. And he'd like her no better by the end of summer, when the traditional period between betrothal and wedding was over.

Ophelia blew her nose one last time, then pushed back the covers. A furious meowing rumbled under the patchwork quilt when she pushed it; she'd forgotten about the cat. In the wall mirror she contemplated, not without a certain satisfaction,

her dazed face, her skew-whiff glasses, her red nose and her
messy hair. Thorn would never want to put her in his bed.
She had sensed his disapproval, she was not the woman he
was looking for. Their respective families could force them to
marry, but together they would ensure that it remained a union
in appearance only.

Ophelia wrapped an old dressing gown around her nightdress. If it were only up to her, she'd stay toasty in bed until
midday, but her mother had imposed a crazy timetable for
the days to come, before the great departure. Picnic in the
family park. Tea with the grandmothers, Sidonia and Antoi-
nette. Walk along the river. Drinks at Uncle Benjamin's with
his new wife. Evening at the theatre followed by dinner and
dancing. Ophelia had indigestion just thinking about it all. She
would have preferred a less frantic pace to bid farewell properly
to her native ark.

The wood creaked under her feet as she came down the
stairs. The house seemed too quiet to her. But she soon realized that everyone had gathered in the kitchen; she could hear
muffled conversation through the small glass door. Silence fell
as soon as she opened it.

All eyes were focused on Ophelia. The scrutinizing eyes of
her mother, stationed close to the gas stove. The apologetic
eyes of her father, half-slumped on the table. The disapproving
eyes of Aunt Rosaline, her long nose wedged in her cup of tea.
The pensive eyes of her great-uncle, over the top of the newspaper he was leafing through, his back to the window.

All told, it was only Thorn, on his stool, busy filling a pipe,
who wasn't remotely interested in her. His silver-blond hair
wildly thrown back, his ill-shaven chin, his thinness, his flimsy

tunic and the dagger stuck down his boot all spoke more of a vagabond than a court gentleman. He seemed out of place in the middle of the kitchen's hot copper pans and aroma of jam.

"Morning," croaked Ophelia.

An uncomfortable silence followed her to the table. She'd known more cheery mornings. She pushed her broken glasses up with a finger, purely mechanically, and poured herself a full mug of hot chocolate. The plashing of the milk on the china, the protesting of the tiles as she pulled in her chair, the scraping of her butter knife on the bread, the whistling from her blocked nostrils . . . She felt as though each sound that emanated from her, even the tiniest one, assumed gigantic proportions.

She jumped when her mother's voice rang out once again: "Mr. Thorn, you've still not swallowed a thing since your arrival among us. Won't you allow yourself to be tempted by a mug of coffee and some buttered bread?"

The tone had changed. It was neither warm nor sharp. Polite, the bare minimum. Her mother must have spent the night thinking about what the Doyenne had said and calming herself down. Ophelia looked questioningly at her, but her mother turned away, pretending to check on her oven.

Something wasn't right; there was a whiff of conspiracy in the air.

Ophelia looked to her great-uncle, but he was fuming behind his moustache. So she turned to the balding, dithering head of her father, sitting opposite her at the table, and stared as hard as she could at him. As she was expecting, he gave in. "Daughter, something . . . slightly unexpected has cropped up."

He had measured his "slightly unexpected" between thumb

and index finger. Ophelia's heart pounded in her ears and, for one crazy second, she thought the engagement was off. Her father cast an eye over his shoulder in Thorn's direction, as though hoping for a denial. From his stool, the man offered them only a penknife-hewn profile, obdurate brow, teeth gnawing at the horn of his pipe. His long legs twitched with impatience. If, stripped of his fur, he no longer looked as much like a bear, Ophelia now saw in him the stance of a peregrine falcon, alert and restless, about to take flight.

She turned back to her father when he gently patted her hand. "I know your mother had an amazing schedule for the week . . . "

He was interrupted by the furious coughing of his wife, as she leant over her gas stove, but he continued with a sigh: "Mr. Thorn was explaining earlier to us that duties await him back home. Duties of the utmost importance, d'you see? In short, he can't waste time on great receptions, on various amusements and . . . "

Exasperated, Thorn cut him short by snapping the cover of his fob watch. "We're leaving today on the airship at four o'clock sharp."

The blood drained from Ophelia's cheeks. Today. Four o'clock sharp. Her brother and her sisters wouldn't be back from school. She wouldn't say goodbye to them. She would never see them grow up.

"Go home then, sir, as duty calls. I'm not stopping you." Her lips had moved of their own accord. It was but a barely audible whisper, partly due to her cold, but it had the effect of a thunderbolt in the kitchen. Her father's face fell, her mother looked daggers at her, Aunt Rosaline spluttered into her tea, and her great-uncle took cover behind a fit of sneezing. Ophelia looked at none of them. Her attention was focused on Thorn, who, for the first time since they'd met, was studying her closely, straight on, from top to bottom. His lanky legs had jerked him straight up off his stool, like a spring being released. She was seeing him in triple, thanks to her broken lenses. Three towering figures, six eyes as sharp as razors, and thirty clenched fingers. It all added up to a lot for just one guy, even such a massive one . . .

Ophelia expected an explosion. The response was but a deep murmur: "Is this a refusal?"

"Of course not," chided her mother, thrusting out her enormous bust. "She hasn't a word to say on the matter, Mr. Thorn, she will accompany you wherever you please."

"And me, my word, am I allowed to have it?"

This question, issued in a shrill voice, came from Rosaline, who was glaring venomously at the bottom of her empty teacup.

Rosaline was Ophelia's aunt, but more importantly, she was her godmother, and as such had been designated her chaperone. A widow and childless, her status made her the natural choice to accompany her goddaughter in the Pole until her marriage. She was a mature woman, with horse's teeth, thin as a bag of bones, nervy as a cutlet. She wore her hair in a bun, like Ophelia's mother, but hers resembled a pincushion.

"No more than I'm allowed to have mine," grumbled the great-uncle into his moustache while scrunching up his newspaper. "In any case, no one in this family asks me my opinion anymore!"

Ophelia's mother put her fists on her enormous hips. "Oh, you two, this is neither the time nor the place!"

"It's just that, everything's going a bit faster than we at first envisaged," her father broke in, addressing the engaged couple. "The kid's intimidated, she'll get over it."

Neither Ophelia nor Thorn paid them the slightest attention. They were sizing each other up, she seated in front of her hot chocolate, he from the summit of his absurd height. Ophelia didn't want to give way to the metallic eyes of this man, but upon reflection, she didn't think it smart to provoke him. In her situation, the most sensible thing was still to shut up. In any case, she had no choice.

Head down, she spread butter on another slice of bread for herself. When Thorn sat back on his stool, shrouded in a cloud of smoke, everyone breathed a sigh of relief.

"Get your things ready immediately," he said, simply. For him, the incident was over. Not for Ophelia. Behind her hair, she vowed to make his life as difficult as he was making hers.

Thorn's eyes, gray and cold as the cutting edge of a blade, flashed at her once again. "Ophelia," he added, without smiling.

Coming from this sullen mouth, and hardened by the Northern accent, her name seemed to slice the tongue. Sickened, Ophelia folded her napkin and left the table. She slipped quietly upstairs and shut herself in her room. With her back against the door, she didn't move, didn't blink, didn't cry, but inside she was screaming. The furniture in the room, sensitive to the rage of its owner, began to tremble, as though nervous jitters were running through it.

Ophelia was rocked by a spectacular sneeze. The spell was instantly broken, the furniture once again perfectly still. Without even passing a comb through her hair, Ophelia pulled on her dreariest dress, a corseted antiquity, gray and austere. She sat on the bed and while pushing her bare feet into her boots, her scarf slithered, slid, and wound itself, like a snake, up to her neck.

There was a knock on the door.

"C'min," mumbled Ophelia, her nose blocked. Her great-uncle poked his moustache round the half-opened door. "May I, dear girl?"

She nodded from behind her handkerchief. The uncle's large shoes cut a path through the confusion of sheets, eiderdowns, and pillows cluttering the carpet. He signaled at a chair to come closer, which it did on the double, and flopped onto it. "My poor child," he sighed, "that chap, he's certainly the last husband I wished for you."

"I know."

"You're going to have to be brave. The Doyennes have spoken."

"The Doyennes have spoken," repeated Ophelia. (But they won't have the last word, she thought to herself, even though she hadn't the slightest idea what she was hoping by thinking that.)

Much to Ophelia's surprise, her great-uncle started laughing. He pointed at the wall mirror. "Do you remember your first passage? We ended up thinking you'd be stuck like that forever, one leg kicking out here, the rest of you writhing in my sister's mirror! You put us through the longest night of our lives. You weren't yet thirteen."

"I'm still suffering a few aftereffects," sighed Ophelia, looking at her hands, which, through her broken glasses, appeared splintered.

Suddenly, her great-uncle returned to looking seriously at

her. "Precisely. And yet that still didn't stop you from trying again and getting stuck again, until you finally got the hang of it. Mirror-travelers are rare in the family, dear girl, and do you know why?"

Ophelia looked up behind her glasses. She'd never broached the subject with her godfather. And yet everything she knew, she'd learnt from him. "Because it's a rather particular form of reading?" she suggested.

Her great-uncle snorted into his moustache and widened his golden eyes under the wings of his eyebrows. "Nothing to do with it! To read an object requires forgetting oneself a little, to leave room for the past of someone else. Traveling through mirrors, that requires facing up to oneself. One has to have guts, y'know, to look oneself straight in the peepers, see oneself as one really is, plunge into one's own reflection. Those who close their eyes, those who lie to themselves, those who see themselves as better than they are, they could never do it. So, believe me, it's no run-of-the-mill thing."

Ophelia was struck by this unexpected outpouring. She'd always traveled through mirrors in an intuitive way, she didn't see herself as particularly brave. Her great-uncle then pointed at the old three-colored scarf, scruffy with age, resting lazily across her shoulders.

"Isn't that your first golem?"

"Yes."

"The very one that almost deprived us forever of your company."

Ophelia concurred, after a time. She sometimes forgot that this scarf, which she always dragged around after her, had once tried to strangle her.

"And despite that, you never . . . stopped . . . wearing . . . it," pronounced the great-uncle, punctuating each word with a slap of his thigh.

"I sense you're trying to tell me something," Ophelia said, gently. "Trouble is, I don't quite understand what."

Her great-uncle grunted gruffly. "You don't cut much of a figure like that, dear girl. You hide behind your hair, behind your glasses, behind your muttering. Of your mother's whole brood, you're the one who's never shed a tear, never howled, and yet I swear, you were definitely the one who got into the most scrapes."

"You're exaggerating, dear uncle."

"Since you were born, you've never stopped hurting yourself, making mistakes, falling flat on your face, pinching your fingers, getting lost . . . " he went on, gesticulating wildly. "You can imagine how worried sick we were—for ages we thought that, one day, one of your endless disasters would be the death of you! 'Calamity Jane,' that's what we called you. Now listen carefully to me, dear girl . . . "

The great-uncle kneeled, with some pain, at the foot of the bed on which Ophelia had remained slumped, her feet deep in her unlaced boots. He seized her elbows and shook her, as though better to imprint each syllable on her memory. "You have the strongest character in the family, my child. Forget what I said to you last time. Here, before you, I predict that your husband's will is going to shatter against yours."

The Medal

The cigar-shaped shadow of the airship scudded across fields and rivers like a solitary cloud. Through the curved window, Ophelia scanned the landscape, hoping to see, in the distance, for one last time, the watchtower from which her family were waving scarves. Her head was still spinning. Barely minutes after takeoff, when the airship was negotiating a turn, she'd had to leave the starboard promenade in a panic to find the lavatories. By the time she was back, all she could see of the Valley was a distant stretch of shadow at the foot of the mountain.

She couldn't have imagined a more disastrous leave-taking.

"A girl of the mountains who's airsick! Your mother's right, you never miss a chance to make a spectacle of yourself . . . "

Ophelia tore her eyes from the viewing window to look around the Map Room, so called due to the planispheres on the wall depicting the fragmented geography of all the arks. At the other end of the room, the bottle-green dress Aunt Rosaline was wearing stood out against the honey-colored plush of the carpets and armchairs. She was studying the cartographic images with a stern eye. It took Ophelia a while to realize that it wasn't the arks she was scrutinizing like this, but the quality

of the printing. An occupational defect: Aunt Rosaline special-
ized in the restoration of paper.

She came back to Ophelia with wary, mincing steps, sat in
the neighboring chair, and nibbled with her horsey teeth at the
biscuits they'd been served. Feeling nauseous, Ophelia looked
away. The two women were alone in the room. Apart from
them, Thorn, and the crew, there were no other passengers on
board the airship.

"Did you notice Mr. Thorn's expression when you started to
redistribute your meal all over the airship?"

"I was rather preoccupied right then, dear aunt."

Ophelia peered at her godmother over the rectangles of
her glasses. She was as narrow, dried-up, and jaundiced as
her mother was plump, moist, and rubicund. Ophelia didn't
know this aunt, who would be her chaperone for the coming
months, very well, and it felt strange to find herself alone with
her. Normally, they saw little of each other and hardly spoke.
The widow had always lived solely for her old papers, just as
Ophelia had always lived solely for her museum. Which hadn't
left them much chance to get close.

"He nearly died of shame," declared Aunt Rosaline in a
harsh voice. "And that, young lady, is a spectacle I never, ever
want to witness again. The honor of the family rests on your
shoulders."

Outside, the airship's shadow was merging into the water of
the Great Lakes, which shimmered like mercury. In the Map
Room, the late-afternoon light was fading. The honey-colored
plush of the furnishings appeared less golden, more beige. All
around, the airship's framework was creaking, its propellers
droning. Ophelia absorbed, once and for all, these sounds, this

gentle rolling beneath her feet, and felt better. It was just something to get used to.

She pulled a spotty handkerchief out from her sleeve and sneezed once, twice, three times. Her eyes were watering behind her glasses. The nausea had gone, but not the cold. "Poor man," she said, amused, "if he fears ridicule, he's not marrying the right person."

Aunt Rosaline's skin turned pale yellow. She threw a panicked look over to the small room, trembling at the thought of seeing the bearskin in one of the armchairs. "Ancestors alive, don't say such things!" she whispered.

"He worries you?" asked Ophelia, amazed. She herself had feared Thorn, yes, but that was before meeting him. Since the stranger had got a face, she was no longer scared of him.

"He sends shivers down my spine," shuddered her aunt, neatening her tiny bun. "Have you seen his scars? I suspect he tends towards violence when in a bad mood. I'd advise you to keep a low profile after this morning's little scene. And then try to make a good impression on him—we're going to be with him, me for the next eight months, you for the rest of your life."

When Ophelia's gaze wandered out of the large observation window, what she saw took her breath away. The flaming autumnal forests, gilded by the sun and battered by the wind, had just been replaced by a sheer wall of rock that disappeared into a sea of fog. The airship moved on, and Anima, hanging in the sky, appeared entirely surrounded by a ring of clouds. The further they moved away, the more it looked like a sod of earth and grass that an invisible spade had dug from a garden. So that was it, then, an ark seen from a distance? That little clod lost in the middle of the sky? Who would imagine that lakes, meadows, towns, woods, fields, mountains, and valleys stretched across this ridiculous chunk of world?

With her hand pressed to the glass, Ophelia imprinted this vision on her mind as the ark disappeared, blotted out by the curtain of clouds. She had no idea when she would return there.

"You should have brought a spare pair with you. We look like paupers!"

Ophelia turned back to her aunt, who was looking at her with disapproval. It took her a moment to realize that she was talking about her glasses. "They've almost healed up," Ophelia reassured her. "By tomorrow, nothing will show." She took them off to puff mist on the lenses. Apart from a little crack in one corner of her vision, she didn't really have a problem and no longer saw everything in triple.

Outdoors, there was now just endless sky, in which the first stars were starting to twinkle. When the light came on in the room, the windows became mirrors and it was no longer possible to see anything. Ophelia needed to fix her eyes on something. She went over to the wall of maps. They were veritable works of art, created by illustrious geographers. The twenty-one major arks and the one hundred and eighty-six minor arks were all depicted with the most scrupulous attention to detail.

Ophelia could go back in time as easily as others cross a room, but she didn't know much about cartography. It took her a while to find Anima, and even longer to find the Pole. She compared the one with the other, and was amazed by their difference in size: the Pole was nearly three times as big as Anima.

With its interior sea, its springs, and its lakes, it called to mind a large tank full of water.

But nothing fascinated her as much as the central planisphere, which offered a general view of the Core of the World, and the fixed ring of arks surrounding it. The Core of the World was the biggest fragment of the original Earth; it was but a mass of volcanoes, forever struck by lightning, permanently uninhabitable. It was shrouded in the sea of Clouds, a compact mass of vapor the sun never penetrated, but, for clarity's sake, the map omitted that. It did, on the other hand, trace the wind corridors that allowed airships to travel with ease from one ark to another.

Ophelia closed her eyes and tried to imagine this map in three dimensions, as one might see it from the Moon. Fragments of stone suspended above a great, an immense and eternal storm . . . Come to think of it, this new world was a true miracle.

Bells rang out in the Map Room. "Supper," guessed Aunt Rosaline with a sigh. "Do you think you'll be able to sit at table without totally embarrassing us?"

"You mean without vomiting? Depends what's on the menu."

When Ophelia and her godmother pushed open the door of the dining room, they thought for a moment they'd made a mistake. The buffets weren't set up and a shadowy half-light lurked between the paneled walls.

A friendly voice stopped them just as they were about to turn tail: "This way, ladies!" A man—white uniform, red epaulettes, double cuff links—came towards them. "Captain Bartholomew, at your service!" he proclaimed pompously. He broke into a wide smile, in which a few gold teeth glittered, and flicked dust off his stripes. "In fact, I'm just second in command, but let's not quibble. I hope you'll forgive us, but we've started on the hors d'oeuvres. Come and join us, ladies, a touch of femininity will be most welcome!"

The first mate showed them to the back of the room. Between a long openwork screen and the lovely picture windows, a small table was catching the final glow of the sunset on the starboard promenade. Ophelia spotted immediately the tall, thin figure that she didn't want to see there. Thorn had his back to them. All she saw of him was an endless spine under his traveling tunic; pale, shaggy hair; and elbows moving to the rhythm of knife and fork, with not a thought of stopping for them.

"But, for goodness sake, what are you doing?" asked a shocked Bartholomew.

Ophelia hadn't even sat down on the chair beside her aunt before he was grabbing her by the waist, making her dance a couple of steps, and sitting her straight beside the last person she wanted to be near. "At the table, one must always alternate men and women."

With nose down towards plate, Ophelia felt completely swamped by Thorn's shadow, higher by two heads as he sat bolt upright in his chair. She buttered her radishes without much appetite. Opposite her, a small man saluted her with a friendly inclination of the head, his smile stretching between salt-and-pepper side whiskers. Within seconds, only the clicking of cutlery filled the silence around the table. Crudités were munched, wine drunk, butter passed from hand to hand. Ophelia tipped over the saltcellar she was handing to her aunt.

The first mate, on whom the silence was clearly weighing, spun like a weather vane towards Ophelia. "How are you feeling, my dear child? Has that nasty sickness gone away?"

Ophelia wiped her mouth with a flick of the napkin. Why was this man talking to her as though she were ten years old? "Yes, thank you."

"I beg your pardon?" he guffawed. "You have a tiny little voice, miss."

"Yes, thank you," articulated Ophelia, stretching her vocal cords.

"Don't hesitate to let our onboard doctor know about any discomfort. He's a master in his field."

The man with the salt-and-pepper side whiskers, opposite her, displayed a polite modesty. It must be him, the doctor.

Another silence fell around the table, which Bartholomew broke by drumming his restless fingers on his cutlery. Ophelia blew her nose to conceal her annoyance. The first mate's twinkling eyes kept dragging themselves from her up to Thorn, and from Thorn back down to her. How bored he must be to seek entertainment from them.

"Well, I must say, you're not very chatty!" he said, chuckling. "Yet, if I understand correctly, you're traveling together, no? Two ladies from Anima and a man from the Pole . . . quite rare, a combination like that!"

Ophelia risked stealing a glance at Thorn's long, thin hands as he sliced his radishes in silence. So, the crew knew nothing of what had prompted their meeting? She decided to adopt his attitude. She just gave a weak but polite smile, without clearing up the misunderstanding.

Her aunt didn't see it like that at all. "These young people are going to be married, sir!" she cried, outraged. "So you weren't aware of that?"

To the right of Ophelia, Thorn's hands clenched around his cutlery. From where she sat, she could see a vein bulging on his wrist. At the head of the table, Bartholomew's gold teeth gleamed.

"I'm terribly sorry, madam, but, indeed, I wasn't aware of that. Come now, Mr. Thorn, you should have told me that this charming child was to be yours! How does it make me look, now?"

Like someone who is relishing the situation, replied Ophelia, to herself.

Bartholomew's glee didn't last long, however. His smile faded as soon as he saw Thorn's countenance. Aunt Rosaline went pale when she, in turn, noticed it. Ophelia, on the other hand, couldn't see it. She would have had to lean over and unscrew her head from her shoulders to see right up there. In any case, she had no trouble guessing what was going on above her. Eyes as sharp as razors and a hard line instead of a mouth. Thorn didn't like to make a spectacle of himself—at least they had that in common.

The doctor must have noticed the awkwardness since he hastened to change the subject. "I'm very intrigued by your family's little talents," he said, addressing Aunt Rosaline. "Your control over the most banal objects is quite simply fascinating! Please forgive my indiscretion, but might I ask you what your specialty is, madam?"

Aunt Rosaline dabbed her mouth with her napkin. "Paper. I smooth out, I restore, I mend." She grabbed the wine menu, unceremoniously tore it, and then, with a mere slide of the finger, resealed the edges.

"That's most interesting," commented the doctor, twisting the little points of his moustache while a waiter served the soup.

"I should say so," the aunt said, puffing herself up. "I've saved archives of immense historic value from decay. Genealogists, restorers, curators, our branch of the family is at the service of Artemis's legacy."

"Is that the case for you, too?" asked Bartholomew, turning his sparkling smile towards Ophelia.

She didn't get the chance to correct him by saying: "It *was* the case, sir." Her aunt took it upon herself to answer for her, between two spoonfuls of soup: "My niece is an excellent reader."

"A reader?" repeated the perplexed first mate and doctor in unison.

"I ran a museum," explained Ophelia, succinctly. With her eyes, she beseeched her aunt to let it drop. She didn't want to talk about what belonged to her former life, especially not in the vicinity of Thorn's long fingers tightening around the soup spoon. The image of her family waving farewell with scarves from the watchtower haunted her. She wanted to finish her vegetable velouté and go to bed.

Unfortunately, Aunt Rosaline was cut from the same cloth as her mother. They weren't sisters for nothing. She was keen to impress Thorn. "No, no, no, it's much more than that, don't be so modest! Gentlemen, my niece can empathize with objects, go back into their past, and draw up highly reliable evaluations."

"Sounds like fun!" enthused Bartholomew. "Would you agree to give us a little demonstration, dear child?" He pulled on a chain attached to his fine uniform. Ophelia thought at first that it was a fob watch, but she was wrong. "This gold medal is my lucky charm. The man who gave it to me informed me that it had belonged to an emperor of the old world. I'd so love to know more!"

"I can't." Ophelia retrieved a long brown hair from her soup. She could gather as many curls as possible at her nape, using hairpins, ties, and slides, but they still managed to escape.

Bartholomew was put out. "You can't?"

"Deontology prevents me, sir. It's not the past of the object that I retrace, it's that of the owners. I would be violating your private life."

"It's the ethical code of readers," confirmed Aunt Rosaline, revealing her horse's teeth. "A private reading is only permitted with the consent of the owner."

Ophelia turned her glasses towards her godmother, but she was determined that, at all costs, her niece should distinguish herself in the eyes of her betrothed. Indeed, the gnarled hands slowly rested the cutlery on the tablecloth and moved no more. Thorn was paying attention. Or then, he was no longer hungry.

"In that case, I grant you that permission!" Bartholomew declared, very predictably. "I want to get to know my emperor!" He handed her his old gold medal, which matched his stripes and his teeth. Ophelia first examined it through her glasses. One thing was certain, this charm didn't date back to the old world. In a hurry to get it over with, she unbuttoned her gloves. As soon as she closed her fingers around the medal, lightning flashes shot out between her half-open eyelids. Ophelia let herself be immersed, without yet interpreting the stream of sensations flooding into her, from the most recent to the oldest. A reading always proceeded in an anticlockwise direction.

Promises in the air, whispered to a pretty girl in the street. It's so boring up there, facing the infinite alone. The little wife and the kids are waiting for him at home. They're far away, they almost don't exist. Journey follows journey without leaving any trace. As do women. The boredom is stronger than the remorse. Suddenly, there's a white flash from a black cape. It's a knife. It's for Ophelia, this knife, a husband is taking revenge. The blade hits the medal, in the pocket of the uniform, and is thus deflected from its mortal trajectory. Ophelia is still bored. A hand of three kings, surrounded by bursts of anger, is worth a lovely medal to him. Ophelia feels herself getting younger. The teacher summons him to the rostrum with a kind smile. He gives him a present. It shines, it's pretty.

"Well?" asked the first mate, amused.

Ophelia put her gloves back on and returned his lucky charm to him. "You were duped," she murmured. "It's a medal of merit. A simple prize for a child."

The gold teeth disappeared with Bartholomew's smile. "Excuse me? You can't have read carefully, miss."

"It's a medallion for a child," insisted Ophelia. "It isn't real gold and it isn't even half a century old. That man you beat at cards, he lied to you."

Aunt Rosaline coughed nervously; this was not the feat she'd hoped for from her niece. The doctor suddenly developed a passionate interest in the inside of his plate. Thorn's hand wound up his fob watch with obvious boredom.

Since the first mate seemed crushed by this revelation,

Ophelia took pity on him. "It's no less excellent a lucky charm. That medal still saved you from that jealous husband."

"Ophelia!" said Rosaline, choking. The rest of the meal continued in silence. When they rose from the table, Thorn was first to leave the room, without even mumbling a polite word.

The following day, Ophelia explored the gondola of the airship, from one end to the other. With nose buried in scarf, she strolled around the port and starboard promenades; took tea in the sitting room; discreetly visited, with Bartholomew's permission, the command bridge, the navigation cabin, and the radio room. Mostly, she killed time by looking at the view. Sometimes it was just an intensely blue sky as far as the eye could see, in which very few clouds popped up. Sometimes it was a damp fog that spluttered all over the windows. Sometimes it was the steeples of a town, when they were flying over an ark.

Ophelia got used to the tables with no cloths, the cabins with no passengers, the armchairs with no occupants. No one ever came on board. Stops were rare: the airship never touched the ground. But the journey wasn't shorter for that, as they made various detours to jettison postal packages and mailbags onto the arks.

If Ophelia allowed her scarf to trail all over the place, Thorn never poked the tip of his snout out of his cabin. She saw him neither at breakfast nor at dinner, nor at tea, nor at supper. And that's how it remained for several days.

When the corridors started to feel chilly and the portholes to deck themselves in frosty lace, Aunt Rosaline declared that it was high time for her niece to have a real conversation with her fiancé. "If you don't break the ice now, later it will be too late," she warned her one evening, arms deep in a muff as they walked together on the bridge.

The picture windows were ablaze in the sunset. Outdoors, it was doubtless terribly cold. Fragments of the old world, too small to become arks, were coated in frost and sparkled like a river of diamonds in the middle of the sky.

"What's it to you, whether Thorn and I like each other or not?" asked Ophelia, sighing and huddling inside her coat. "We're getting married, isn't that all that matters?"

"Good grief! In my time, I was a more romantic marriage-able girl than you."

"You're my chaperone," Ophelia reminded her. "Your role is to watch that nothing indecent happens to me, not to push me into the arms of that man."

"Indecent, indecent . . . there's not too much risk on that score," muttered Aunt Rosaline. "I hardly got the impression that you ignited uncontrollable desire in Mr. Thorn. In fact, I don't think I've ever seen a man going to such lengths not to cross a woman's path."

Ophelia couldn't stifle a sideward smile, which, luckily, her aunt didn't see.

"You're going to offer him a herbal tea," her aunt sudden-ly decreed with a determined look. "A lime-blossom tea. It soothes the nerves, lime blossom."

"My dear aunt, it's this man who insisted on marrying me, and not the other way round. I'm hardly going to go after him."

"I'm not asking you to make advances to him, I just want a bearable atmosphere for us in the days to come. You're going to just grin and bear it, and be friendly to him!"

Ophelia watched her shadow lengthening, widening and disappearing at her feet as the russet disc of the sun faded into the mist on the other side of the windows. Her darkened glasses adapted to the changing levels of light, gradually becoming paler. They were completely healed now. "I'll think about it, aunt."

Rosaline held her by the chin to force her to look at her. Like most of the women in the family, her aunt was taller than her. With her fur hat and too-long teeth, she no longer looked like a horse, but like a marmot. "You must try your hardest, do you hear me?"

Night had fallen behind the promenade windows. Ophelia was cold without and within, despite the scarf that was tightening its grip around her shoulders. Deep down, she knew that her aunt wasn't wrong. They still knew nothing about the life that awaited them in the Pole.

She would have to put aside the grievances she harbored against Thorn, long enough for a little talk.

The Warning

The shy knocks on the metal door got lost somewhere along the gangway. Darkness surrounded Ophelia and her little steaming tray. It wasn't total darkness: the safety lights allowed one to distinguish the striped wallpaper, the numbers on the cabin doors, the vases of flowers on the consoles.

Ophelia waited a few heartbeats, listened for a sound from the other side of the door, but only the background humming of the propellers cadenced the silence. She awkwardly gripped the tray with one glove and knocked again twice. No one opened to her.

She had every right to come back later. Tray in hand, Ophelia carefully swiveled round. Immediately, she had to step backwards. Her back hit the door she'd just been turning from; the cup slopped a little of its herbal tea.

Standing at full altitude, Thorn looked piercingly down at her. Far from softening his angular features, the safety lights deepened the scars and also magnified his fur's spiky shadow on the corridor walls.

Ophelia decided he was definitely much too tall for her.

"What do you want?" He had asked his question in a flat

voice, devoid of warmth, his Northern accent harshly stressing each consonant.

Ophelia held her tray out to him. "My aunt insists that I serve you a herbal tea." Her godmother would have disapproved of this candor, but Ophelia was a bad liar. Stiff as a stalagmite and with arms dangling, Thorn made not a move to take the cup she was handing to him. It made one wonder whether, deep down, he wasn't more stupid than scornful.

"It's a lime-blossom tea," she said. "Apparently, it sooth—"

"Do you always speak so quietly?" he interrupted her, abruptly. "One can barely understand you."

Ophelia maintained a silence, and then spoke even more quietly: "Always."

Thorn frowned while seeming to search, in vain, for something worthy of interest in this slip of a woman, behind her heavy brown locks, behind her rectangular glasses, behind her old muffler. Ophelia became aware, after an endless face-to-face, that he wanted to access his cabin. She, along with her tray of herbal tea, stepped aside.

Thorn had to bend his extendable form until he could fit under his door's lintel. Ophelia remained on the threshold, encumbered by her tray. Thorn's cabin, like all those in the airship, was very cramped. An upholstered bench that turned into a bed, a luggage rack, a narrow passage for moving around, a work surface at the back of the room with a writing case on it, and that was it. Ophelia found moving around her suite hard enough, but it was almost miraculous that Thorn could get into his without banging himself, left, right, and center.

He pulled the cord of a ceiling bulb, threw his bear fur across the bench, and leant with both hands on the work surface. On it there were notebooks and pads covered in scrawls. Once he was leaning, back bent in two, over this bizarre paperwork, Thorn didn't budge. Ophelia wondered whether he was thinking or reading. He seemed quite simply to have forgotten her, out in the corridor, but at least he hadn't shut door behind him.

It wasn't in Ophelia's nature to bother a man with questions, so she waited with all the patience in the world outside the cabin, frozen to the bone, creating clouds of condensation with every breath. She studied carefully the tense muscles at the nape; the bony wrists sticking out from the sleeves; the jutting shoulder blades under the tunic; the long, restless legs. This man was totally on edge, as though uncomfortable in this too-tall, too-thin body that was electrified by a constant tension.

"Still there?" he grunted, not bothering to turn round. Ophelia realized that he wouldn't touch the herbal tea, so, to lighten her load, drank it herself. The hot liquid did her good.

"Am I distracting you?" she murmured, sipping at the cup.

"You won't survive."

Ophelia's heart skipped a beat. She had to spit her tea back into the cup. It was either that, or it going down the wrong way. Thorn obstinately kept his back turned to her. She would have given anything to see him from the front and check he wasn't making fun of her. "What is it that you reckon I won't survive?" she asked.

"The Pole. The court. Our engagement. You should go back to your mother's apron strings while you still can."

Disconcerted, Ophelia couldn't take in these barely concealed threats. "Are you renouncing me?"

Thorn's shoulders tensed up. He half-turned his lanky scare-crow body and looked at her, uncaringly. Ophelia wondered whether the twist of his mouth was more smile or grimace. "Renouncing?" he rasped. "You have a very saccharine vision of our customs."

"I'm not following you," whispered Ophelia.

"This marriage is as loathsome to me as it is to you, be in no doubt, but I have committed to your family in the name of my own family. I'm not in a position to go back on my pledge without paying the price, and it's a high one."

Ophelia took the time to take these words in. "I'm not in a position to either, sir, if that's what you're hoping from me. For me to reject this marriage for no admissible reason would be to dishonor my family. I would be summarily banished."

Thorn knitted his brows—one being sliced in two by his scar—even more. Ophelia's response wasn't the one he would have liked to hear. "Your customs are more flexible than ours," he countered with a condescending look. "I've sniffed around the nest you grew up in. Nothing to compare with the world that awaits you."

Ophelia tightened her grip around the cup. This man had turned to tactics of intimidation and she didn't like it. He didn't want her—she understood that perfectly and didn't hold it against him. But for him to expect the woman he'd asked in marriage to take all responsibility for a split, that was pretty cowardly. "You're deliberately painting a bleak picture of the situation," she accused him in a whisper. "What benefit can our families hope to reap from our union if I'm considered not up to it? You're affording me an importance I don't have . . . "

She let an angel pass before finishing, and watching for

Thorn's reaction: " . . . or you're keeping something important from me."

The metallic eyes became more piercing. This time, Thorn
didn't look at her over his shoulder, from above and afar. On
the contrary, he looked at her very closely while rubbing his
ill-shaven jaw. He made a face when he noticed that Ophelia's
scarf, which hung down to the ground, was flicking back and
forth like the tail of an annoyed cat.

"The more I see of you, the more my first impression is
reinforced," he grumbled. "Too sickly, too slow, too pampered . . . You're not cut out for the place I'm taking you to. If
you follow me there, you won't last through winter. Just you
wait and see."

Ophelia held the look he was boring into her. A look of
iron. A look of defiance. Her great-uncle's words resounded in
her memory and she heard herself replying to him: "You don't
know me, sir."

She placed the cup of herbal tea back on its tray and, slowly,
calmly, she closed the door between them.

Several more days went by without Ophelia coming across
Thorn again, whether in the dining room or at the turn of
a gangway. Their exchange had left her perplexed. In order
not to worry her aunt unnecessarily, she had lied to her:
Thorn was too busy to receive her, they'd not said a word
to each other. While her godmother was already cooking
up new romantic strategies, Ophelia nibbled at the seams of
her gloves. On what kind of chessboard had the Doyennes
placed her? The dangers evoked by Thorn, were they real,
or was he just trying to terrify her in the hope that she'd go

back home? Was her position at court really as assured as her family believed it to be?

Plagued by her aunt, Ophelia needed to be alone. She shut herself inside the airship's lavatories, took off her glasses, pressed her forehead to the freezing porthole, and stayed like that for a long time, her breath leaving an increasingly dense veil of condensation on the glass. She could see nothing outside, due to the snow encrusting the porthole, but she knew it was night-time. The sun, driven away by the Polar winter, hadn't shown itself for three days.

Suddenly, the electric bulb flickered feverishly and the floor started swaying under Ophelia's feet. She left the lavatories. All around her, the airship was screeching, groaning, and creaking while gearing up for mooring, right in the middle of a snowstorm.

"I don't believe it, you're not yet ready?" exclaimed Aunt Rosaline as she burst into the corridor, muffled under several layers of fur. "Go quickly to gather up your things, and if you don't want to freeze before leaving the gangway, cover yourself up well!"

Ophelia threw on two coats, a thick hat, mittens over her gloves, and wound her endless scarf around several times. In the end, she couldn't lower her arms, so restricted was she by all the layers of clothes.

When she joined the rest of the crew in the airship's airlock, her trunks were being offloaded outside. A wind as cutting as glass swept through the door and was already turning the floor white with snow. The temperature in this room was so low that Ophelia had tears in her eyes.

Impassive under his bearskin cloak, yet battered by the

wind, Thorn set off without hesitation into the storm. When Ophelia, in turn, descended the gangway, she felt as though she were gulping lungfuls of ice. The snowy crust covering her glasses made her blind and the gangway ropes were slippery under her mittens. Each step was challenging; it felt as though, deep in her boots, her toes had instantly turned to ice. Somewhere behind her, smothered by the north wind, her aunt's voice was shouting at her to watch where she put her feet. That was all Ophelia needed. She immediately skidded but somehow, with one leg dangling in the void, stopped herself from falling thanks to the security cordon. She didn't know the distance remaining between the gangway and the ground, and she didn't want to know.

"Come down slowly," a member of the crew advised her while gripping her elbow. "There!" Ophelia reached solid ground more dead than alive. The wind was buffeting her coats, her dresses, her hair, and her hat was sent flying into the distance. Impeded by her mittens, she tried to knock off the snow that had accumulated on her glasses, but she became stuck to the lenses, fast as a lead seal. Ophelia was obliged to take them off her nose to see where she was. Wherever she directed her blurred vision, all she glimpsed were patches of night and snow. She had lost Thorn and her aunt.

"Your hand!" a man screamed to her. Disorientated, she randomly stretched out her arm and was immediately dragged on to a sleigh that she hadn't seen. "Hold on tight!"

She clung onto a handle as her whole body, frozen stiff, was shaken by all the jolting. Above her, a whip was being cracked, again and again, producing more and more speed from the team of dogs. Through the crack between her eyelids, Ophelia thought she could see intertwined streaks of light within the darkness. Street lamps. The sleighs were cutting right through a town, sending white flurries across pavements and doors. To Ophelia, this race across the ice felt never-ending, but finally the pace slowed, leaving her intoxicated with wind and speed on her pile of furs.

The dogs were crossing a massive drawbridge.

The Gamekeeper

"Over 'ere!" shouted a man swinging a lantern.

Shivering and with hair flying in the wind, Ophelia stumbled out of the sleigh to find herself ankle-deep in powdery snow. It poured over the top of her boots like cream. She had only a confused idea of where they now were. A narrow courtyard, wedged by ramparts. It had stopped snowing, but the wind was lacerating.

"Good journey, m'lord?" asked the man with the lantern as he walked towards them. "Didn't think you'd be away that long, we was starting to worry. Well, here's a strange delivery!" He swung his lantern in front of Ophelia's stunned face. All she could see of him through her glasses was a blurred glow. His accent was much stronger than Thorn's; she could barely understand him.

"Holy smoke, she's a skinny 'un! Not too steady on the pegs, that one. Hope she ain't going to croak on us. Could at least have given you a filly with more fat on her . . . "

Ophelia was dumbfounded. As the man stretched his hand towards her with the clear intention of fingering her, he got a whack on the head. It was Aunt Rosaline's umbrella. "Keep your paws well away from my niece, and mind your language, you uncouth individual!" she protested from under her fur hat. "And you, Mr. Thorn, you might say something!"

But Thorn had abstained from saying anything at all. He was already far away, his huge bearskin silhouetted against the lit rectangle of a doorway. Delirious, Ophelia plunged her feet into the footprints he'd left in his wake, tracking him up to the threshold of the house.

Warmth. Light. Carpet.

The contrast with the tempest outside was almost violent. Half-blind, Ophelia crossed a long hall and dragged herself instinctively over to a stove, which set her cheeks ablaze. She was starting to understand why Thorn thought she wouldn't survive the winter. This coldness bore no comparison to that of her mountain. Ophelia was struggling to breathe; her nose, throat, lungs were burning her from within.

She jumped when a woman's voice, even louder than her mother's, burst out behind her: "Nice breeze, no? Give us yer fur, my good lord, soaked through it is. Business good? And company for madam, you've brought some at last? It's just that time mustn't 'alf drag for her, up there!"

The woman seemingly hadn't noticed the shivering little creature curled up by the stove. As for Ophelia, she found her hard to understand due to her accent, also very strong. Company for madam? As Thorn, true to form, didn't answer, the woman moved away as discreetly as her clogs permitted. "I'm off to help me husband."

Ophelia slowly looked at her surroundings. As the snow melted from her glasses, strange shapes became clearer around her. Animal trophies, with mouths agape and eyes staring, jutted out from the walls along a vast hunting gallery. These were Beasts, judging by their monstrous size. The antlers of an elk, in pride of place above the entrance, had the dimensions of a tree.

At the end of the room, Thorn's shadow stood before a huge fireplace. He'd placed his carpetbag at his feet, ready to grab it at the first opportunity.

Ophelia gave up her little brazier for this fireplace, which she decided was more appealing. Her boots, which were soaked through, squelched with every step. Her dress had also sucked up the snow and felt as though weighed down with lead. Ophelia lifted it a little, and noticed that what she had thought was carpet was in fact an immense gray fur. The sight sent shivers down her spine. What animal could be so gigantic alive that it could cover such a vast surface once skinned?

Thorn had plunged his cast-iron stare into the open fire; he ignored Ophelia when she approached. His arms, saber-like, were crossed on his chest, and his long, restless legs shuddered with contained impatience, as though unable to stay still. With a quick snap of the lid, he consulted his fob watch. Click, click.

Holding her hands out to the flames, Ophelia wondered what her aunt was up to. She shouldn't have left her alone with the lantern man outside. When she listened, she thought she could hear protestations about their luggage. She waited until her teeth had stopped chattering to speak to Thorn. "I must admit that I can't really understand these people . . . "

Ophelia thought, from his stubborn silence, that Thorn wouldn't respond to her, but he finally unclenched his jaws: "In the presence of others, and as long as it pleases me, you will be two lady's companions that I've brought over from abroad to entertain my aunt. If you want to make it easier for me, watch your language, in particular that of your chaperone. And don't stand alongside me," he added with an exasperated sigh. "It will arouse suspicion."

Ophelia moved back a couple of steps, tearing herself reluctantly from the warmth of the fireplace. Thorn was certainly going to a lot of trouble to keep their marriage quiet; it was becoming worrying. She was, moreover, troubled by the unusual relationship linking him to this couple. They called him "lord," and their apparent familiarity towards him concealed a certain deference. In Anima, everyone was the cousin of someone, and no one bothered to stand on ceremony. Here, there was already a kind of inviolable hierarchy that Ophelia couldn't quite fathom.

"Is this where you live?" she asked in a barely audible whisper, from her withdrawn position.

"No," Thorn condescended to reply, but only after a silence. "It's the gamekeeper's lodge."

That reassured Ophelia. She didn't like the deathly stench of the Beast trophies, barely masked by the smell of the open fire. "Are we spending the night here?"

While Thorn had hitherto stubbornly shown only his roughhewn profile, her question made him turn a falcon stare towards her. Astonishment had instantly relaxed the hard features of his face. "The night? What time do you think it is then?"

"Clearly much earlier than I thought it was," Ophelia muttered to herself.

The oppressive darkness of the sky had confused her internal clock. She was tired and she was cold, but she said nothing about it to Thorn. She didn't want to show any weakness in front of this man who already judged her to be too delicate.

Suddenly, a thunderbolt hit the hall. "Vandals!" boomed the voice of Aunt Rosaline. "Clumsy oafs! Boors!"

Ophelia noticed Thorn tensing up. Crimson with rage under her fur hat, the aunt made a grand entrance into the trophy gallery, with the gamekeeper's wife following hot on her heels. This time Ophelia had a chance to see what the woman looked like: she was a creature as pink and chubby as a baby, with a golden plait wrapped around her forehead like a crown.

"Who'd just turn up at the home of decent folk with a contraption like that?" the latter protested. "Think we're a duchess, do we!"

Rosaline spotted Ophelia in front of the hearth. Brandishing her umbrella like a sword, she immediately sought her support: "They've wrecked my beautiful, my magnificent sewing machine!" she exclaimed with outrage. "And how am I going to hem our dresses? How am I going to mend any tears? I specialize in paper, I do, not material!"

"Like everyone else does, say," retorted the woman with disdain. "With a needle and thread, my dear!"

Ophelia wanted to question Thorn with her eyes to know what attitude to adopt, but, seemingly uninterested in these fishwife quarrels, he had resolutely turned back to the fireplace. She could guess, however, from his stiffness, that he disapproved of Aunt Rosaline's indiscretion.

"It's intolerable," the latter said, choking. "Do you at least know to whom you—"

Ophelia placed a hand on her arm to make her pause for thought. "Calm yourself, dear aunt, it's not the end of the world."

The gamekeeper's wife rolled her pale eyes from aunt to niece. She cast a telling look at her soggy hair, pallid complexion, and ridiculous getup, which was dripping like a mop. "Expected something more exotic, I did. Hope Lady Berenilde's got the patience!"

"Go and get your husband," Thorn said, abruptly. "He must harness his dogs. We still have to cross the woods; I don't want to waste any more time."

Aunt Rosaline parted her long, equine teeth to ask who Lady Berenilde was, but with one look, Ophelia stopped her.

"You wouldn't prefer to go there by airship, m'lord?" asked the gamekeeper's wife, amazed.

Ophelia would have liked a "yes," the airship appealing more than the frozen woods, but an annoyed Thorn replied: "There's no connecting service before Thursday. I've no time to lose."

"Right, m'lord," said the woman, bowing.

Clutching her umbrella, Aunt Rosaline was outraged. "And us, Mr. Thorn, no one asks our opinion? I would prefer to sleep at a hotel while waiting for this snow to melt a little."

Thorn grabbed his bag without looking at Ophelia or her godmother. "It won't melt," was all he said.

They went out through a large covered terrace, not far from a rustling forest. Ophelia, breath seized by the cold, could see the landscape here more clearly than when coming down from the airship. The polar night wasn't as black and impenetrable as she had imagined it to be. Indented by the tops of the firs, all swollen with snow, the sky was an almost phosphorescent indigo, turning a delicate blue just above the ramparts that separated the neighboring town from the forest. The sun was hiding, yes, but it wasn't far away. It was waiting there, almost visible, just above the horizon.

Hiding behind her scarf, her nose in a handkerchief, Ophelia got a shock when she saw the sleighs that were being harnessed up for them. With their coats ruffled by the wind, the wolfhounds were as big as horses. It was one thing to see Beasts in Augustus's sketchbook, quite another to encounter them for real, all fur and fangs. Aunt Rosaline almost fainted at the sight of them.

Boots planted firmly in the snow, his face inscrutable, Thorn was pulling on sleigh-driving gloves. He had exchanged his white bearskin for a gray fur cloak, less bulky and less heavy, which clung to his wiry body. He was listening without paying much attention to the verbal report of the gamekeeper, who was complaining about poachers.

Once more, Ophelia wondered who Thorn was to these people. Did the forest belong to him, then, to be entitled to this official account?

"And our trunks?" Aunt Rosaline asked, interrupting them, between two chatterings of her teeth. "You're not loading them onto the sleighs?"

"They'll slow us down, lady," said the gamekeeper while chewing a quid of tobacco. "Worry not, we'll get 'em delivered pronto to Lady Berenilde's."

Aunt Rosaline couldn't understand him at first, due to his accent and his quid. She had to make him repeat his sentence three times. "Women cannot travel without the bare essentials!" she declared with outrage. "And Mr. Thorn, he gets to keep his little case, doesn't he?"

"That's not the same thing at all," hissed the gamekeeper, very shocked.

Thorn clicked his tongue with annoyance. "Where is she?" he asked, conspicuously ignoring Rosaline. With a wave of his hand, the gamekeeper indicated a vague area beyond the trees. "She's 'anging about near the lake, m'lord."

"Who are you talking about?" Aunt Rosaline asked, impatiently.

With head wrapped in scarf, Ophelia didn't understand either. She hadn't a clue. The cold made her head ache and prevented her from thinking straight. She was still drowning in cotton wool when the sleighs set off again into the night, the drafts inflating her petticoats. Huddled at the back of the sleigh and thrown around like a rag doll by the jolting, she was using her mittens to stop her hair from whipping her nose. In front of her, Thorn was driving their sleigh, his huge shadow, straining forward, embracing the wind like an arrow. The muffled bells of the other sleigh, carrying the gamekeeper and Aunt Rosaline, followed them discreetly in the dark. All around, the bare branches of the trees were clawing the landscape, cutting into the snow, and spitting out, here and there, scraps of sky. Shaken in all directions, fighting the viscous drowsiness that was dogging her, Ophelia felt as though this race had no end.

All of a sudden, the swarming shadows of the woods were shattered and a night that was vast, crystal-clear, dazzling, unfolded its starry mantle as far as the eye could see. Ophelia's eyes widened behind her glasses. She sat up in the sleigh and, as the icy breath of the north wind swept through her hair, what she saw stunned her.

Hanging there, in the middle of the night sky, its towers steeped in the Milky Way, a marvelous citadel floated above the forest, with nothing attaching it to the rest of the world. It was a totally crazy spectacle, an enormous beehive disowned

by the earth, a tortuous interlacing of keeps, bridges, crenella-
tions, stairs, flying buttresses, and chimneys. Jealously guarded by a frozen ring of moats, their long streams solidified in
the void, the snowy city soared above and plunged below this
line. Spangled with lit windows and street lamps, it reflected
its thousand-and-one lights onto the mirror of a lake. As for its
highest tower, it speared the very crescent of the moon.

"Inaccessible," reckoned Ophelia, elated by the sight. So it
was this floating city that Augustus had drawn in his sketchbook?

At the front of the sleigh, Thorn swung a look over his
shoulder. Through the pale strands of hair whipping his face,
his eyes were brighter than usual. "Hold on!"

Perplexed, Ophelia gripped the first thing to hand. An indraft,
powerful as a torrent, took her breath away, while the enormous dogs and the sleigh itself caught that current and soared
away from the snow. Her godmother's hysterical scream almost
reached the stars. Ophelia, on the other hand, was incapable
of making the slightest sound. She could feel her heart beating
wildly. The higher they got in the sky, the more they gained
speed and the heavier the weight at the pit of her stomach. They
traced a sweeping loop that seemed as unending as her aunt's
screaming. Showering sparks, the runners landed hard on the
moat's ice. Ophelia was suddenly bounced from the floor of the
sleigh; she almost went overboard. Finally, the dogs curbed their
speed and the sleigh came to a halt before a colossal portcullis.

"The Citaceleste," announced Thorn, laconically, as he got
down.

He didn't look back once to check that his fiancée was still
actually there.

The Citaceleste

Ophelia twisted her neck, unable to tear her eyes from the monumental city towering up to the stars.

Perched on top of a high rampart wall, a road wound its way around the middle of the fortress and snaked up in a spiral to the summit. The Citaceleste was far more strange than beautiful. Turrets in a variety of shapes—some bulbous, some slender or else crooked—spewed out smoke from their every chimney. Arcaded stairways awkwardly straddled the void, and certainly didn't inspire confidence. Windows—stained-glass or casement, in a palette of clashing colors—spangled the night sky.

"I thought I was going to die . . . " said a voice behind Ophelia.

"Ware, lady. With them shoes, that's a proper skating rink." Supported by the gamekeeper, and close to collapse, Aunt Rosaline tried to keep her balance on the moat's surface. In the lantern light, her complexion appeared even more jaundiced than usual.

Ophelia was next to place a wary foot out of her sleigh and she tested the grip of her shoes on the ice. She promptly fell flat on her back. As for Thorn's ridged boots, they gripped the thick frosty layer perfectly as he unharnessed his dogs to combine them with those of the gamekeeper.

"All done, m'lord?" inquired the last, winding the tethers round his wrists.

"Yes."

With a flick of the reins, the sleigh took off without a sound, caught an air current, and, along with its lantern, disappeared into the night like a shooting star. Slumped on the ice, Ophelia followed it with her eyes, sure that it took with it all hope of turning back. She couldn't fathom how it was physically possible for a sleigh harnessed to some dogs to fly like that.

Thorn's large, stiff body was bent over behind his empty sleigh and he apparently expected Ophelia to do likewise. She skidded over to him as best she could. He indicated a stake that he'd just planted in the snow. "Press your foot against it. At my signal, push as hard as you can."

She agreed to try, but wasn't convinced: she could barely feel her toes against the stake. As soon as Thorn gave her the signal, she leant with all her weight against the sleigh. The vehicle, which had moved so easily behind the great wolf-hounds, seemed to have got stuck in the ice since the dogs had been released. Ophelia was relieved to see the runners responding to their pushing. "Again," demanded Thorn, his tone flat, while he planted more stakes.

"Will anyone actually explain to me what this whole pala-ver is in aid of?" asked an outraged Aunt Rosaline, observing their activity. "Why is no one coming to meet us, as is customary? Why are we being treated with so little consideration? And why do I get the impression that your family hasn't been informed of our arrival?"

She was gesticulating in her brown fur coat while struggling to find her balance. The look that Thorn shot at her transfixed her on the spot. His eyes stood out like two flashes of a blade in the bluish dark of the night. "Because," he hissed between his teeth. "A little discretion, madam, would it really kill you?"

He turned his sullen face back down to Ophelia and indicated to her to push. By repeating their maneuver over and over again, they reached a massive barn whose huge doors, loosely fastened with chains, were creaking in the wind. Thorn lifted up his fur cloak, revealing a bag slung across his body, and pulled out a bunch of keys. The padlocks sprang open, the chains slid apart. Rows of sleighs similar to theirs were lined up in the dark. An access ramp had been installed inside and Thorn parked their vehicle in the barn without needing help from Ophelia. He retrieved his case and signaled to them to follow him to the back of the barn.

"You're not letting us in through the front door," commented Aunt Rosaline.

Thorn glared down at the two women, one after the other. "From now on," he said in a voice full of thunder, "you will follow me without questioning, without dithering, without dragging your feet, without a sound."

Aunt Rosaline pursed her lips. Ophelia kept her true thoughts to herself since, in any case, Thorn didn't seek consent. They were sneaking into the citadel like outlaws, but he had his reasons. Whether they were good or bad was another matter.

Thorn slid back a heavy wooden door. Barely had they entered a dark room with a pungent animal smell when there was movement in the shadows. Kennels. Behind the bars of every pen, large paws scratched, enormous snouts snorted, huge muzzles whined. The dogs were so big, Ophelia would have thought she were in a stable. Thorn whistled between his teeth to calm them down. He ducked into a cast-iron goods lift, waited while the women got in, pulled across the safety shutter, and turned a crank. With a metallic clatter, the lift gained height, clambering from floor to floor. Clouds of ice crystals rose up around them as the temperature increased.

The warmth entering Ophelia's veins soon became a trial, burning her cheeks and misting up her glasses. Her godmother stifled a squeal when the goods lift screeched to a halt. Thorn pulled back the lift's concertina shutter, and swung his long neck from one side of the landing to the other.

"Turn right. Hurry up."

This floor strangely resembled a seedy alley, with half-loose cobblestones, badly maintained pavements, walls covered in old bill posters, and a thick fog. Wafting in the air was a vague aroma of baking and spices that made Ophelia's stomach rumble.

Clutching his case, Thorn led them through deserted districts, using hidden paths and dilapidated stairs. Twice he shoved them into the shadow of a passageway, prompted by the passing of a carriage or a distant burst of laughter. Then he dragged Ophelia by the wrist to speed her up. Each of his long strides required two of her own.

By the light of the street lamps, she observed Thorn's clenched jaw, his very pale eyes, and, right up there, his determined brow. Once again she wondered quite how legitimate her place at court really was, for him to be acting in this way. His long, tense fingers released her arm once they had made it to the backyard of a pitifully decrepit house. A cat nosing around the dustbins bolted at the sight of them. After a final wary glance, Thorn pushed the two women behind a door, which he immediately closed behind him and double-locked.

Aunt Rosaline gasped with astonishment and Ophelia's eyes widened behind her glasses: resplendent at the close of day, a country park flaunted its autumn foliage all around them. No more night. No more snow. No more Citaceleste. By some unbelievable conjuring trick, they had popped up somewhere else entirely. Ophelia turned on her heels: the door they'd just come through was just standing there, absurdly, in the middle of the lawn.

Since Thorn seemed to be breathing easier, they thought his prohibitions were now lifted. "This is extraordinary," stammered Aunt Rosaline, her long, pinched face opening up in admiration. "Where are we?"

Case in hand, Thorn had immediately set off again, between the rows of elm and poplar. "On my aunt's estate. Kindly keep your other questions for later and don't delay us any further," he added, cuttingly, as Rosaline was about to continue where she'd left off.

They followed Thorn along the well-maintained avenue, which was bordered by two-tiered streams. The aunt unfastened her fur coat, relishing the warm breeze. "Extraordinary," she repeated with a smile that displayed her long teeth. "Quite simply extraordinary . . . "

Less effusive, Ophelia blew her nose. Her hair and clothes wouldn't stop weeping melted snow and she was leaving scattered puddles in her wake.

She looked at the grass of the lawn at her feet, then at the sparkling streams, then at the leaves trembling in the breeze, then at the sky turning pink in the dusk. She couldn't dismiss a slight uneasiness—the sun wasn't in its place here; the lawn was far too green; the russet trees shed not a leaf. And neither the singing of birds nor the buzzing of insects could be heard.

Ophelia remembered the travel journal of her forebear, Adelaide: *The lady ambassador kindly received us on her estate, where an eternal summer evening reigns. I'm dazzled by so many marvels. The people here are courteous, very considerate, and their powers surpass all understanding.*

"Don't take your coat off, aunt," Ophelia said quietly. "I think this park is fake."

"Fake?" repeated Rosaline, baffled.

Thorn half-turned. Ophelia caught but a brief glimpse of his scarred and unshaven profile, but the look he'd thrown at her had betrayed a flicker of surprise.

A grand residence was outlined in filigree behind a lace of branches. It appeared to them in its entirety, standing out clearly against the red backcloth of the sunset, where the avenue left the rustic wood for pretty symmetrical gardens. It was a manor house draped in ivy, topped with slate, and adorned with weather vanes.

On the stone perron, with its concave steps, stood an elderly lady. With her hands linked on her black apron and a shawl around her shoulders, she seemed to have been looking out for them forever. She eyed them hungrily as soon as they were climbing the steps, her wrinkles spreading around a radiant smile. "Thorn, my little boy, what a joy to see you again!"

Despite her tiredness, despite her cold, despite her doubts, Ophelia couldn't hide her amusement. In her eyes, Thorn was everything but "little." She frowned, however, when he rebuffed the overtures of the old woman with no consideration. "Thorn, Thorn, so you're not going to kiss your grandmother?" lamented the woman.

"Stop that," he hissed.

He rushed into the hall of the manor, leaving the three of them on the threshold. "What a heartless man!" said a shocked Rosaline, who seemed to have forgotten any policy of rapprochement. But the grandmother had already found herself another victim. Her fingers were squeezing Ophelia's cheeks as though to ascertain how fresh she was, almost knocking off her glasses. "So here's the new blood coming to save the Dragons," she said with a dreamy smile.

"I beg your pardon?" stammered Ophelia. She hadn't understood a single word of this formula of welcome.

"You've got a good face," said the old woman with amusement. "Very innocent."

Ophelia thought to herself that, more than anything, she must look dazed. The grandmother's wrinkled hands were covered in strange tattoos. The same tattoos as on the arms of the hunters in Augustus's sketches. "Forgive me, madam, I'm getting water on you," said Ophelia as she pulled back her dripping hair.

"By our illustrious forefathers, you're shivering, my poor child! Come in, come right in, ladies. Supper will soon be served."

The Dragon

Deep in the steaming water, Ophelia was coming back to life.

Normally, she didn't really like using someone else's bath—reading these small private places could be embarrassing—but she was taking full advantage of this one. Her toes, which the cold had turned numb as stone, had just returned to a reassuring color under the water. Drowsy in the hot steam, Ophelia let her eyes wander sleepily along the long enameled edge of the bath, to the pewter kettle, to the fleur-de-lys borders of the tapestry, and to the fine porcelain vases on the console. Every element of the decor was a veritable work of art.

"I'm both reassured and concerned, my dear!"

Ophelia turned her misted-up glasses towards the canvas screen on which Aunt Rosaline's shadow was gesticulating, like at some children's theatre. She was pinning up her little bun, putting on her pearls, powdering her nose.

"Reassured," continued the aunt's shadow, "because this ark isn't as inhospitable as I feared it would be. Never have I seen such a well-kept house, and, although her accent does offend my ears somewhat, that venerable grandmother is a sweetie!"

Rosaline came around the screen to lean over Ophelia's bath. Her blond hair, neat as a new pin, smelt strongly of eau de toilette. She had squeezed her narrow body into a lovely dark-green dress. The grandmother had given it to her as a present to make up for the damage to her sewing machine at the gamekeeper's.

"But I'm concerned because the man you're about to marry is a lout," she whispered.

Ophelia slid her heavy, dripping locks off her shoulders and stared at her knees, emerging from the foam like two pink bubbles. For a moment, she wondered whether she shouldn't tell her godmother about Thorn's warnings.

"Get out of there," said Aunt Rosaline, snapping her fingers. "You're turning as wrinkled as a prune."

When Ophelia dragged herself out of the hot bathwater, the air felt like a cold slap to her whole body. Her first reflex was to put on her reader's gloves. Then she gladly wrapped herself in the white bath sheet her godmother held out to her and rubbed herself down in front of the fire. Thorn's grandmother had put several dresses at her disposal. Spread out on the large canopied four-poster bed, like languishing women, they rivaled each other in elegance and style. Paying no attention to Rosaline's protestations, she chose the plainest among them: a pearl-gray outfit, belted at the waist and buttoned to the chin. She perched her glasses on her nose and darkened the lenses. When she saw herself in this getup, with her hair plaited at the nape, in the mirror she missed her usual scruffiness. She held out her arm to her scarf, which was still cold, and it coiled its three-colored loops into their familiar position around her neck, its fringe sweeping the carpet.

"My poor niece, you're irredeemably lacking in taste," said an irritated Rosaline.

There was a knock on their door. A young girl in white apron and white bonnet bowed respectfully. "The meal is served, if these ladies would care to follow me."

Ophelia looked at this pretty face sprinkled with freckles. She tried, in vain, to guess how she was related to Thorn. If she was a sister, she looked nothing like him. "Thank you, miss," she replied, returning her formal reverence. The young girl looked so taken aback that Ophelia thought she must have made a faux pas. Should she have called her "cousin" rather than "miss," to be polite?

"I think she's a servant," her aunt whispered in her ear as they were descending the velvet-lined stairway. "I'd already heard of them, but it's the first time in my life I've seen one with my own eyes." Ophelia knew nothing about them. She'd read some scissors that had belonged to a maid, while at the museum, but she thought such occupations had disappeared with the old world.

The young girl showed them into a huge dining room. It felt gloomier than the corridors, with its brown paneling, its high coffered ceiling, its chiaroscuro paintings, and its cased windows, through which one could just make out, between two lead lattices, the park by night. The candelabras barely dispelled this darkness along the large table, casting delicate golden glimmers on the silverware.

In the midst of all these shadows, a luminous creature sat enthroned at the head of the table, deep in a carved armchair. "My sweet child," she said in a sensual voice, to greet Ophelia. "Come closer now, so that I can admire you."

Ophelia awkwardly offered her hand to the delicate fingers extended towards her. The woman to whom they belonged was breathtakingly beautiful. Her supple, voluptuous body made her dress, of blue taffeta banded with cream ribbon, rustle with its every movement. The milky skin of her neck flowed up from the bodice, and was haloed with a blond cloud. An ethereal smile hovered on her sweet face, which was ageless, and once one's eyes had alighted on it, it was impossible to tear them away. Ophelia did have to tear hers away, however, to look at the satin arm the woman had held out to her. The under-sleeve of embroidered tulle, being sheer, allowed a glimpse of intertwined tattoos, the very ones that the grandmother had on her arms, and that the hunters in Augustus's sketches had on theirs.

"I'm afraid to be too ordinary to be 'admired,'" Ophelia muttered, impulsively.

The woman's smile broadened, creating a dimple in her creamy skin. "You're certainly not lacking in candor. Which is a novelty for us, isn't that so, Mother?"

The Northern accent, whose inflections were so hard coming from Thorn's mouth, rolled sensually on this woman's tongue, endowing her with even more charm. Two chairs further along, the grandmother concurred with a kind smile. "That's what I was telling you, my dear. This young person is of an ingenuous simplicity!"

"I'm forgetting all my duties," apologized the beautiful woman. "I've not even introduced myself to you! Berenilde, Thorn's aunt. I love him like a son and I'm sure that, very soon, I'll love you like my own daughter. So you may address me as you would a mother. Take a seat, my dear child, and you, too, Madam Rosaline."

It was when Ophelia sat down in front of her soup plate that she became aware of Thorn's presence, on the opposite side of the table. He blended so well into the surrounding gloom that she hadn't noticed him.

He was only just recognizable. His mane, short and light, was no longer sprouting, weedlike, in all directions. He had shaved off the beard, which had crept up to his cheeks, in such a way that all that remained was an anchor-shaped goatee. The coarse traveling fur had been exchanged for a slim, high-collared, midnight-blue jacket, from which emerged the full sleeves of an impeccably white shirt. These clothes made his long, thin body seem even stiffer, but like this Thorn did look more like a gentleman than a wild animal. The chain of his fob watch and his cuff links caught the candlelight.

His face, long and chiseled, wasn't any friendlier, for all that. He kept his eyelids resolutely lowered onto his pumpkin soup. He seemed to be silently counting every journey between spoon and lips.

"I've not heard much out of you, Thorn!" commented the beautiful Berenilde, glass of wine in hand. "There I was, hoping that a touch of femininity in your life would make you more talkative."

When he raised his eyes, it wasn't his aunt that he blatantly stared at, but Ophelia. A defiant gleam still shone from the leaden sky of his pupils. His two scars, one at the temple, the other across the eyebrow, almost jarred on his newly symmetrical face, well shaved, hair well combed. Slowly he turned to Berenilde. "I killed a man."

He had thrown this out casually, like small talk, between two gulps of soup. Ophelia's glasses went pale. Beside her, Aunt Rosaline choked, nearly passing out. Berenilde calmly put her glass of wine down on the lace tablecloth. "Where? When?"

Ophelia would, herself, have asked, "Who? Why?"

"At the airship terminal, before embarking for Anima," replied Thorn in a steady voice. "A disgraced man whom a malicious individual had set on my tail. I hastened my journey somewhat as a result."

"You did well."

Ophelia stiffened on her chair. Really, that was it? "You're a murderer, perfect, pass me the salt . . ."

Berenilde noticed her stiffness. With a graceful flourish, she placed her tattooed hand on Ophelia's glove. "You must find us terrifying," she whispered. "I notice that my dear nephew, true to form, hasn't bothered to put you in the picture."

"Put us in the picture of what?" Aunt Rosaline asked, sounding offended. "There's never been any question of my goddaughter marrying a criminal!"

Berenilde turned the limpid pools of her eyes towards her. "This has little to do with crime, madam. We have to defend ourselves against our rivals. I fear that many nobles at the court look extremely unfavorably on this alliance between our two families. What makes some stronger weakens the position of others," she told her gently, with a smile. "The tiniest change in the balance of power precipitates intrigues and backstairs murders."

Ophelia was shocked. So that's what it was, the court? In her ignorance, she had imagined kings and queens who spent their days philosophizing and playing cards.

As for Aunt Rosaline, she also seemed to be thunderstruck. "Ancestors alive! You mean to say that those are common practices? They calmly assassinate one another, and that's it?"

"It's a trifle more complicated than that," Berenilde replied, patiently.

Men wearing black tailcoats and stiff, white shirtfronts discreetly entered the dining room. Wordlessly, they took away the soup tureens, served some fish, and disappeared in three blinks of an eye. No one at the table thought there was any point introducing them to Ophelia. So all these people who lived here weren't part of the family? Is that, then, what servants were? Anonymous drafts?

"You see," continued Berenilde, resting her chin on linked hands, "our way of life is somewhat different to yours on Anima. There are the families who are favored by our spirit Farouk, those who no longer are, and those who never were."

"Families plural?" queried Ophelia in a murmur.

"Yes, my child. Our family tree is more tortuous than yours. Since the creation of the ark, it has divided into several branches, all totally distinct from each other, branches that never mix with each other without misgivings . . . or without killing each other."

"Totally charming," commented Aunt Rosaline, with two napkin wipes of the mouth.

Ophelia tackled her salmon apprehensively. She was incapable of eating fish without getting a bone stuck in her throat. She glanced surreptitiously at Thorn, feeling uncomfortable with him just in front of her, but he was paying more attention to his plate than to all those at the table put together. He was chewing his fish sullenly, as though swallowing food revolted him. Not surprising he was so thin . . . His legs were so long that, despite the width of the table, Ophelia had to tuck her boots under her chair to avoid kicking his feet.

She pushed her glasses back up her nose, and observed, this time discreetly, the shriveled figure of the grandmother, seated beside him, who was eating her salmon with gusto. What was it again that she had said when welcoming them? "So here's the new blood coming to save the Dragons."

"The Dragons," Ophelia suddenly whispered, "is that the name of your family?"

Berenilde raised her finely plucked eyebrows and looked at Thorn with amazement. "You explained nothing to them? So what did you spend your time doing during the journey?"

She shook her pretty little blonde curls, half-annoyed and half-amused, and gave Ophelia a twinkling wink. "Yes, my dear child, it's the name of our family. Three clans, including ours, currently hold sway at court. As you now know, we all don't like each other very much. The clan of the Dragons is powerful and feared, but small in number. Not too many of them for you to meet, my dear!"

A shiver ran down Ophelia's spine, from nape to lower back. Suddenly she'd had an ominous premonition as to the role she would be made to play within this clan. Bring new blood? A broodmare, that's what they were planning to turn her into. She looked at Thorn straight on, his hard and unpleasant face, his large angular body, his disdainful eyes that avoided hers, his curt manner. Just thinking about getting close to this man made Ophelia drop her fork on to the carpet. She was about to bend down to retrieve it, but an old man in tails instantly materialized from the shadows to give her another one.

"Forgive me, madam," Aunt Rosaline interrupted once again, "but are you now insinuating that my niece's marriage could put her life in danger, due to the idiotic whim of some courtier?"

Berenilde dissected her salmon without losing her composure. "My poor friend, I fear that the attempt to intimidate Thorn is but one link in a long chain."

Ophelia coughed into her napkin. Sure enough, she'd almost swallowed a fish bone.

"Ridiculous!" exclaimed Rosaline, while shooting her a meaningful look. "This child wouldn't hurt a fly! What could anyone fear of her?"

Thorn raised his eyes to the ceiling, exasperated. Ophelia, meanwhile, was gathering the fish bones on the edge of her plate. Despite seeming distracted, she was listening, observing, thinking.

"Madam Rosaline," said Berenilde in a silken voice, "you must understand that an alliance forged with a foreign ark is seen as a seizure of power at the Citaceleste. How can I explain this without shocking you too much?" she murmured, screwing up her large, limpid eyes. "The women of your family are known for their wonderful fecundity."

"Our fecundity . . . " repeated Aunt Rosaline, caught off guard.

Ophelia again pushed up her glasses, which slipped down her nose as soon as she put her head down to eat.

There we were, it had been said.

She studied Thorn's expression, opposite her. Even if he was studiously avoiding catching her eye, she could read on his face the same disgust that she felt, which certainly reassured her. Slowly, she emptied her glass of water, to clear her throat. Should she announce now, right in the middle of this family meal, that she had no intention of sharing this man's bed? It would doubtless not give the best of impressions.

And anyhow, there was something else . . . Ophelia wasn't sure precisely what, but Berenilde's eyelashes had quivered, as though she'd had to force herself to look them in the eye while revealing her motives. A hesitation? Something unspoken? It was hard to determine, but Ophelia stood by her opinion: there was something else.

"In the meantime, we know nothing about your situation," Aunt Rosaline finally stammered, sounding more embarrassed. "Madam Berenilde, I will have to consult the family on this. This development could call into question the engagement."

Berenilde's smile softened. "Maybe you're not aware, Madam Rosaline, but that's not how your Doyennes see it. They accepted our offer fully aware of the facts. I'm awfully sorry if they didn't inform you of all that, but we were obliged to proceed with the utmost discretion, to ensure your protection. The fewer the people who know about this marriage, the better we'll feel. You are at liberty, needless to say, to write to your family if you doubt my word. Thorn will take care of your letter."

Beneath her tight bun, Ophelia's godmother had gone very white. She was gripping her cutlery so hard that her fingers were shaking. When she planted her fork in her plate, she didn't seem to notice that a caramel custard tart had replaced the salmon on it. "I refuse for my niece to be assassinated because of your little intrigues!"

Her outburst had scaled the high notes, on the edge of hysteria. Ophelia was so moved by it that she forgot her own agitation. At this precise moment, she realized how alone and abandoned she would have felt without this grouchy old aunt by her side. She lied to her as best she could: "Don't fret. If the Doyennes gave their consent, it's because they believe the danger to me can't be that great."

"A man is dead, you simpleton!"

Ophelia had run out of arguments. She didn't much like the views being served up to them, either, but losing her cool wouldn't change her situation in the slightest. She stared hard into Thorn's eyes, now just two narrow slits, silently willing him to break his silence. "I have many enemies at court," he said, brusquely. "Your niece isn't the center of the world."

Berenilde looked at him for a moment, somewhat surprised by what he'd just said. "It's true that your position was already tricky from the start, irrespective of any nuptial considerations," she admitted.

"Of course! If this great blockhead strangles anything that moves, I can quite imagine that friendship doesn't come pouring through his door," Rosaline added.

"More caramel, anyone?" the grandmother hastened to suggest, seizing the sauce boat.

No one replied to her. Under the flickering light of the candles, a flash had escaped between Berenilde's eyelids and Thorn's jaws had tightened. Ophelia bit her lip. She understood that if her aunt didn't hold her tongue very soon, someone would see to it that she shut up, one way or another.

"Please forgive this outburst, sir," she then murmured, bowing her head to Thorn. "Traveling fatigue has made us a little sensitive."

Aunt Rosaline was about to protest, but Ophelia pressed her foot under the table while keeping her attention riveted on Thorn. "You apologize, godmother, and I do, too. I now realize that all the precautions you took earlier, sir, were just for our safety, and for that I am grateful to you."

Thorn stared at her cagily, arching his brow, spoon in midair. He took Ophelia's thanks for what they were, a mere façade of politeness.

She put down her napkin and invited a dumbfounded Rosaline to leave the table. "I think we need a good rest, my aunt and I."

From deep in her chair, Berenilde directed an appreciative smile at Ophelia. "It's always wise to sleep on things," she said, philosophically.

The Bedroom

Ophelia peered into the darkness, hair disheveled, eyelids still half-shut with sleep. Something had woken her up, but she didn't know what. Sitting up in bed, she gazed at the blurred contours of the room. Beyond the brocade drapes of the four-poster, she could just about make out the latticed window. Night was fading through the misted panes; it would soon be dawn.

Ophelia had struggled to get to sleep. She'd shared her bedroom with her brother and sisters all her life, so it felt strange to spend the night alone in a house she didn't know. That conversation at supper hadn't helped, either.

She listened carefully to the silence that was punctuated by the clock on the mantelpiece. What on earth could have woken her up? Suddenly, small knocks could be heard on the door. So she hadn't been dreaming.

As soon as Ophelia pushed off her eiderdown, the cold took her breath away. She slipped a cardigan over her nightdress, tripped against a footrest on the carpet, and turned the doorknob. An abrupt voice instantly boomed down at her: "It's not for want of warning you."

A huge black coat, lugubrious as death itself, could only just be made out in the gloom of the corridor. Without glasses,

Ophelia guessed it was Thorn more than saw it was him. He certainly had his own peculiar way to start a conversation.

Still half-asleep, she shivered in the icy draft coming through the door, just long enough to collect her thoughts. "I can no longer pull out," she ended up muttering.

"It is, indeed, too late. From now on, we'll have to compromise, one with the other."

Ophelia rubbed her eyes, as though that could help lift the veil of her shortsightedness, but of Thorn she could still only see a huge black coat. It didn't really matter. His tone had made it quite clear how little this prospect appealed to him, which Ophelia found very reassuring. She thought she could make out a bag hanging from his arm. "Are we leaving already?"

"I'm leaving," the coat corrected her. "You, you're staying here with my aunt. My absence has already been too prolonged; I have to get back to my activities."

Ophelia suddenly realized that she still didn't know what work her fiancé did. Because she'd always seen him as a hunter, she'd forgotten to ask him the question. "And what do your activities consist of?"

"I work at a finance office," he replied, impatiently. "But I haven't come to see you to make small talk; I'm in a hurry."

Ophelia half-opened her eyelids. She just couldn't imagine Thorn as a bureaucrat. "I'm listening to you."

Thorn pushed the door so roughly towards Ophelia that he crushed her toes. He turned the bolt three times to show her how it worked. He really took her for a half-wit. "From today onwards, you must double-lock yourself in every night, is that totally clear? You must eat nothing other than what is served

144

to you at the table, and, for pity's sake, make sure your wittering chaperone tones down her remarks. It's not very smart to offend Lady Berenilde under her own roof."

Although it wasn't polite, Ophelia couldn't stifle a yawn. "Is that advice or a threat?"

There was a leaden silence from the huge black coat. Finally, he said: "My aunt is your best ally. Never leave her protection, go nowhere without her permission, trust no one else."

"'No one else'—doesn't that include you?"

Thorn sniffed and shut the door in her face. He clearly didn't have a sense of humor.

Ophelia went in search of her glasses, somewhere between the pillows, and then posted herself at the window. She rubbed a pane with her sleeve to clear the condensation. Outside, dawn was painting the sky mauve and adding its first touches of pink to the clouds. The majestic autumnal trees were bathed in mist. It was still too early for the leaves to have shed their grayness, but before long, when the sun had taken over the horizon, there would be a blaze of red and gold across the park.

The more Ophelia contemplated this magical landscape, the more convinced she became. This decor was a trompe l'oeil: a very convincing facsimile of nature, but a facsimile all the same.

She looked down. Between two beds of violets, Thorn, in his huge coat, was already heading off along the avenue, bag in hand. That fellow had managed to quell her desire to sleep.

With teeth chattering, Ophelia turned her attention to the dead cinders in the fireplace. She felt as though she were in a tomb. She took off her night gloves, which stopped her from reading randomly in her sleep, and tipped a ewer over the pretty china washbowl of the dressing table.

"And now?" she asked herself, splashing her cheeks with cold water. She didn't feel in the mood to stay put. Thorn's warnings had intrigued her much more than scared her. Here was a man going to great lengths to protect a woman that he didn't like . . .

And then there was that little something, that indefinable hesitation that Berenilde had betrayed at supper. Maybe it was just a small thing, but it was playing on her mind.

Ophelia gazed at her reddened nose and her eyelashes beaded with water in the mirror of the dressing table. Were they going to keep a close watch on her? The mirrors, she suddenly decided. If I want to maintain freedom of movement, I must locate all the mirrors around here.

She found a velvet dressing gown in the wardrobe, but no slippers for her feet. She winced as she slid into her boots, stiffened by the sodden journey. Ophelia sneaked out of the room. She proceeded along the main corridor of that floor. The two guests occupied the best bedrooms, on either side of Berenilde's private apartments, and in addition there were six small, unoccupied bedrooms, which Ophelia visited one by one. She discovered a linen room and two bathrooms, and then went downstairs. On the ground floor, men in frock coats and women in aprons were already busy, despite the earliness of the hour. They were polishing the banisters, dusting the vases, lighting fires in the hearths, and filling the place with the combined aroma of polish, wood, and coffee.

They greeted Ophelia amiably when she went around the small reception rooms, the dining room, the billiard room, and the music room, but their politeness became uneasy when she also invited herself into the kitchen, the laundry, and the office.

Ophelia made sure that she captured her reflection in every mirror, every cheval glass, every medallion. Mirror-traveling wasn't that different an experience to reading, whatever her great-uncle might think, but it was certainly more enigmatic. A mirror retains a memory of any image imprinted on its surface. By a little-known procedure, some readers could thus create a passage between two mirrors in which they had already captured their reflection, but it didn't work on windows, or on tarnished surfaces, or across great distances.

On Anima, Ophelia had once attempted, without much conviction, to pass through a corridor mirror to get to her childhood bedroom. Instead of turning into a liquid consistency, the mirror had remained solid beneath her fingers, as hard and cold as the most ordinary of mirrors. The destination was much too far; Ophelia knew it, but was still disappointed.

Going back up the service stairs, Ophelia came across a wing of the manor that had been neglected. The furniture in the corridors and antechambers had been draped in white sheets, like sleeping ghosts. The dust made her sneeze. Was this area reserved for other members of the clan when they visited Berenilde?

Ophelia opened a double door at the end of a gallery. The musty atmosphere of the long hall hadn't prepared her for what awaited on the other side. Hangings of brocaded damask, a large carved bed, ceiling decorated with frescoes—never had Ophelia seen such a sumptuous bedroom. Here, a cozy warmth prevailed that made absolutely no sense: there was no fire burning in the hearth and the adjoining gallery was freezing cold.

Her surprise only increased when she noticed rocking horses and an army of lead soldiers on the carpet.

A child's room.

Curiosity propelled Ophelia towards the framed photographs on the walls. A sepia-tinted couple with a baby reappeared in each one.

"You're an early riser."

Ophelia turned around to see Berenilde smiling at her between the two half-opened doors. She was already freshly attired in a loose-fitting satin dress, her hair gracefully coiled above the nape. In her arms she held some embroidery hoops.

"I was looking for you, my dear girl. Where on earth did you lose your way?"

"Who are these people, madam? Members of your family?"

Berenilde's parted lips revealed a glimpse of pearly teeth. She approached Ophelia to look at the photographs with her. Now they were standing side by side, the difference in height between them was notable. She may not have been as tall as her nephew, but Berenilde was a head taller than Ophelia. "Certainly not!" she replied with her delightful accent, laughing heartily. "Those are the former owners of the manor. They've been dead for years."

Ophelia found it a bit strange that Berenilde would have inherited their estate if they weren't part of the family. She looked again at the severe portraits. A shadow deepened their eyes, from lid to brow. Makeup? The photographs weren't sharp enough for her to be sure. "And the baby?" she asked.

Berenilde's smile became more reserved, almost sad. "As long as this child lives, this room will also live. I could cover it in dustsheets, remove the furniture, brick up the windows, but it would always remain looking exactly as you see it now. It's certainly better this way."

Another trompe l'oeil? Ophelia found it a strange idea, but not that strange. After all, the Animists certainly left their mark on their homes. She wanted to ask what this power was that generated such illusions, and what had become of the baby in the photographs, but Berenilde stopped her short by suggesting that she sit with her in the armchairs. A pink lamp bathed them in a pool of light.

"Do you like to embroider, Ophelia?"

"I'm too clumsy for it, madam."

Berenilde placed a hoop on her knees, and her delicate hands, adorned with tattoos, serenely guided the needle. She was as smooth as her nephew was angular. "Yesterday, you defined yourself as 'ordinary,' today as 'clumsy,'" she trilled mellifluously. "And that tiny voice that swallows every word you say! I'm going to end up thinking you don't want me to like you, my dear child. Either you are too modest, or you are false."

Despite its cozy comfort and elegant tapestries, Ophelia felt ill at ease in this room. It felt as though she were violating a sanctuary in which all the toys looked accusingly at her, from the clockwork monkeys to the dislocated puppets. There was nothing more sinister than a child's bedroom with no child. "No, madam, I really am very clumsy. An accident with a mirror when I was twelve."

Berenilde's needle remained suspended in midair. "An accident with a mirror? I confess that I don't quite understand."

"I remained stuck in two places at the same time, for several hours," muttered Ophelia. "Since that day, my body no longer obeys me as readily. I endured some physiotherapy, but the doctor predicted that I'd be left with some aftereffects. Some discrepancies."

A smile spread across Berenilde's lovely face. "You're amusing! You please me."

With her muddy boots and messy hair, Ophelia felt like nothing but a little peasant beside this dazzling society lady. In an impulse full of affection, Berenilde left her embroidery hoop balanced on her knees and seized Ophelia's gloved hands in her own.

"I can imagine that you're feeling a little nervous, my dear girl. All this is so new to you! Don't hesitate to confide your concerns to me, just as you would to your mother."

Ophelia refrained from telling her that her mother was probably the last person in the world to whom she would confide her concerns. And more than pouring out her feelings, it was concrete answers that she needed.

Almost instantly, Berenilde released her hands, apologizing. "I'm so sorry, I sometimes forget that you're a reader."

Ophelia took a while to understand what was making her uncomfortable. "I can't read anything with my gloves on, madam. And even if I took them off, you could hold my hand without fear. I don't read living beings, just objects."

"I'll know better in future."

"Your nephew informed me that he works in a finance office. So who is his employer?"

Berenilde's eyes, as sparkling and exquisite as precious stones, widened. She let out a crystalline laugh that filled the whole room.

"Did I say something stupid, madam?" asked an astonished Ophelia.

"Oh, no, it's Thorn who's to blame," said Berenilde, still laughing. "I recognize his style there, as economical with his words as with his good manners!" Lifting a flounce on her dress, she wiped the corner of her eyelids and became more serious again. "You should know that he doesn't just work 'in a finance office,' as you say. He's Lord Farouk's Treasurer, the principal financial administrator of the Citaceleste and all the provinces of the Pole."

Since Ophelia's glasses were turning blue, Berenilde gently confirmed: "Yes, my dear, your future husband is the chief treasurer of the realm."

It took Ophelia some time to digest this revelation. This shaggy, rude hulk of a man as a top-ranking official—it defied the imagination. Why had they gone and betrothed a simple girl like her to such an individual? It was as if it weren't actually Ophelia being punished, but Thorn.

"I can't really envisage my position within your clan," she admitted. "Leaving aside children, what are you expecting of me?"

"What on earth do you mean?" exclaimed Berenilde.

Ophelia took refuge behind her impassive, ingenuous mask, but inside she was surprised by this reaction. Her question wasn't that incongruous, surely? "I ran a museum on Anima," she explained, quietly. "Are they hoping I'll resume that work here, or something similar? I don't want to sponge off you, not make my own contribution."

What Ophelia was mainly trying to negotiate was her autonomy. A pensive Berenilde turned her lovely limpid eyes towards some picture books in a case. "A museum? Yes, I can imagine that that might be an amusing occupation. Life for women up here can be boring—we're not entrusted with important duties, as is the way where you're from. We'll discuss it further once your position at court is sufficiently established. You're going to have to be patient, my sweet child."

If there was one thing Ophelia wasn't impatient for, it was, indeed, joining this nobility. All she really knew about it was what her forebear's journal had told her—*We spend our days playing cards and walking round the gardens*—and that didn't appeal to her. "And how does one establish it, this position at court?" she asked, rather concerned. "Will I have to attend social events and pay homage to your family spirit?"

Berenilde returned to her embroidery. A shadow had crossed the clear pool of her eyes. The needle piercing the hoop's taut canvas was less lively. For some reason, which escaped Ophelia, she had upset her.

"You won't see Lord Farouk other than at a distance, my dear. As for social events, yes, but not right now. We'll wait until your marriage at the end of the summer. Your Doyennes requested that the traditional year of betrothal be strictly adhered to, so we could get to know you better. And," added Berenilde, with a slight frown, "it will allow us time to prepare you for the court."

Feeling uncomfortable due to the surfeit of cushions, Ophelia shifted to the edge of the armchair and contemplated the muddy toes of her boots, poking out from under her nightdress. Her doubts were justified: Berenilde wasn't revealing to her what she was really thinking. She raised her head and let her attention wander through the window. The first glimmers of daylight were piercing the mist with golden arrows and casting shadows at the foot of the trees.

"This park, this bedroom . . . " Ophelia whispered, "so they're just visual effects?"

Berenilde lifted the needle, calm as a mountain lake. "Yes, my dear girl, but they're not my doing. The Dragons don't know how to conjure up illusions; that's more a specialty of our rival clan."

A rival clan from whom Berenilde had still inherited an estate, noted Ophelia to herself. Maybe she wasn't on such bad terms with them? "And your power, madam, what is it?"

"What an indiscreet question!" Berenilde gently chided, without looking up from her embroidery hoop. "Does one ask a lady her age? It seems to me that it's more the role of your fiancé to inform you about all that."

Since Ophelia was looking disconcerted, she let out a sympathetic little sigh and said: "Thorn really is incorrigible! I guess he leaves you in a fog, never bothering to satisfy your curiosity."

"Neither of us is very talkative," commented Ophelia, choosing her words carefully. "I fear, however, with all due respect, that your nephew doesn't hold me very close to his heart."

Berenilde grabbed a cigarette case from a pocket in her dress. Moments later, she was blowing a tongue of blue smoke between her parted lips. "Thorn's heart . . . " she murmured, rolling the "r"s. "A myth? A desert island? A desiccated lump of flesh? If it's any consolation to you, my dear child, I've never seen him enamored of anyone whatsoever."

Ophelia recalled the unusual eloquence with which he had spoken of his aunt to her. "He holds you in very high esteem."

"Yes," said Berenilde, cheering up and tapping her cigarette case on the edge of a sweet tin. "I love him like a mother, and I believe that he, in turn, feels a sincere affection for me, which touches me even more as that doesn't come naturally to him. For a long time I despaired of his ever knowing any woman, and I know he's annoyed that I rather forced his hand. Your glasses often change color!" she suddenly said, amused. "It's entertaining!"

"The sun's rising, madam, and they adjust to the light." Ophelia looked at Berenilde through the grim gray that had appeared on her lenses, and decided to give her a more honest explanation. "As they do to my mood. The truth is, I was wondering whether Thorn wouldn't have hoped for a woman more like you. I fear I'm the polar opposite of such a desire."

"You're afraid, or you're actually relieved?" With her long cigarette pinched between two fingers, Berenilde studied the expression on her guest's face as though indulging in a particularly amusing game. "Relax, Ophelia, I'm setting no trap for you. Do you really imagine that your feelings are unfamiliar to me? You're forcibly promised to a man you don't know and who turns out to be as warm as an iceberg!" She stubbed out her cigarette on the bottom of the sweet tin while shaking her little curls into a blond waltz. "But I disagree with you, my child. Thorn is a man of duty and I think he just got stuck on the idea of never marrying. Right now you're jostling him out of his little routine, that's all."

"And why didn't he want to? Honoring one's family by starting one's own, isn't that what everyone normally aspires to?" Ophelia used a finger to push her glasses back up her nose, while chuckling inside. It was actually her saying that!

"He was unable to do so," Berenilde gently corrected her.

"Not wishing to offend you, but why else would I have looked so far afield for a wife for him?"

"Does madam desire to be served anything here?" It was an old gentleman that had just interrupted them from the door of the room, amazed to have found them in this part of the manor. Berenilde casually threw her embroidery hoop onto the cushion of a chair. "Some tea and orange biscuits! Have them served in the little sitting room, we're not staying here. What were we saying, my dear child?" she asked, turning her big turquoise eyes back to Ophelia.

"That Thorn couldn't get married. I must admit, I can't quite understand what could stop a man from taking a wife, if that's his wish."

A ray of sunlight decided to enter the room and planted a golden kiss on Berenilde's delicate neck. The little curls clustered at her nape gleamed.

"Because he's a bastard."

Ophelia blinked several times, dazzled by the light emerging beyond the windowpanes. Thorn had been born to an adulteress?

"His late father, my brother, had the weakness of character to frequent a woman from another clan," Berenilde explained to her, "and, as ill luck would have it, the family of this slut has, since then, fallen into disgrace."

The perfect oval of her face had contorted at the word "slut." This is more than disdain, Ophelia thought, this is pure hatred. Berenilde held out her lovely tattooed hand for her to help her up.

"It was touch and go whether Thorn would be banished from the court along with his harlot of a mother," she continued in a more composed voice. "With my dearest brother having had the brilliant idea of dying before he'd officially recognized him, I had to use all my influence to save his son from disaster. I succeeded rather well, as you can see for yourself."

Berenilde shut the double door with a resounding bang. Her pinched smile softened. Her demeanor turned from bitter to sweet. "You keep examining the tattoos that my mother and I bear on our hands. Be warned, my little Ophelia, that they are the mark of the Dragons. That is a recognition to which Thorn can never lay claim. There isn't a female in our clan who would accept to marry a bastard whose parent was disgraced."

Ophelia pondered on these words. On Anima, a relation who brought the honor of the family seriously into disrepute could be banished, but between that and condemning a whole clan . . . Thorn was right, the customs here weren't gentle.

The sonorous chime of a grandfather clock rang out in the distance. Berenilde, deep in her own thoughts, suddenly seemed to return to reality. "The croquet game at Countess Ingrid's! I was about to forget all about it."

She leant her long body, supple and smooth, over Ophelia to stroke her cheek. "I won't invite you to join us, you must still be tired from your journey. So, take tea in the sitting room, rest in your bedroom, and use my lackeys as you please!"

Ophelia watched Berenilde set off with a swish of her dress, along the gallery with the ghostly sheets. She wondered what on earth a lackey could be.

The Getaway

Mother, Father.

The goose quill remained long suspended over the paper once it had scrawled these two little words. Ophelia simply didn't know how to continue. She'd never had a talent, whether speaking or writing, for expressing what affected her closely, for defining precisely what she felt.

Ophelia looked deep into the flames in the hearth. She'd settled herself on the fur rug of the little sitting room with, in lieu of a writing case, a tapestry footrest. Nearby, her scarf had coiled up lazily on the floor, like a three-colored snake.

She returned to her letter, first removing the strand of hair that had fallen onto the paper. It seemed even more of a challenge with her parents. Her mother had an overpowering personality that allowed room for nothing but herself; she spoke, she demanded, she gesticulated, she didn't listen. As for her father, he was but the feeble echo of his wife, always reluctantly agreeing with her without looking up from his shoes.

What Ophelia's mother would like to read in this letter was an expression of profound gratitude, and the first bits of court gossip, which she could then repeat to her heart's content. Ophelia wasn't, however, about to write either. She was hardly going to thank her family for having sent her to the other side of the world, onto such a diabolical ark . . . As for gossip, she had none to tell, and that was the very least of her worries.

So she made a start on her letter with the usual questions: *How are you all? Have you found someone to replace me at the museum? Is great-uncle getting away at all from his archives? Are my little sisters working hard at school? Who's Hector sharing the room with now?*

While writing that last sentence, Ophelia suddenly felt peculiar. She adored her brother, and the thought of him growing up far away from her, of her becoming a stranger to him, made her blood run cold. She decided that that was enough with the questions.

She moistened her quill in the ink pot and had a brainwave. Should she tell them a little about her fiancé and how she was getting on with him? She hadn't the faintest idea of the person he really was. An ill-bred lout? An important official? An evil murderer? A man of duty? A bastard disgraced from birth? There were too many facets for just one man and she didn't know to which, in the end, she would soon be married.

We arrived yesterday, the journey went smoothly, she slowly wrote instead. In that she wasn't lying, but she wasn't mentioning the most important things: Thorn's warning on the airship; their solitary confinement in Berenilde's manor house; the strife between clans.

And then there was the door at the far end of the park, through which they had arrived the previous day. Ophelia had returned to it and found it locked. When she had asked a servant for the key, he had replied that they weren't allowed to give it to her. Despite the bowing and scraping of the staff and the exquisite manners of Lady Berenilde, she felt like a prisoner . . . and she wasn't sure she could write that.

"Done!" proclaimed Aunt Rosaline.

Ophelia turned around. Sitting at a little writing desk, bolt upright on her chair, her godmother placed her quill back on its bronze stand and folded the three pages she'd just blackened with ink. "You've finished already?" asked Ophelia, amazed.

"I certainly have—I had all night and all day to think about what to write. The Doyennes are going to hear all about what's being plotted here, trust me."

By leaving her quill hovering over her letter, Ophelia let a star-shaped inkblot fall right in the middle of a sentence. She pressed a blotter on it and got up. Pensively, she looked at the delicate mantel clock that marked the seconds with a crisp tick-tock. Soon 9:00 P.M., and still no news from either Thorn or Berenilde. Through the window, blackened by the night, one could no longer see the park; due to the light from lamps and hearth, the little sitting room was reflected in it, as though in a mirror.

"I fear your letter will never leave the Pole," she muttered.

"Why do you say such a thing?" asked Rosaline, appalled.

Ophelia held a finger to her mouth to get her to speak less loudly. She went up to the writing desk and turned her aunt's envelope over in her hands. "You heard Lady Berenilde," she whispered. "It's to Mr. Thorn that we have to hand our letters. I'm not so naive as to think he won't check that the contents don't scupper their plans."

Aunt Rosaline rose abruptly from her chair and looked sharply down at Ophelia, somewhat surprised. The lamplight made her complexion even yellower than normal. "So we're totally alone, is that what you're telling me?"

Ophelia nodded. Yes, she was entirely convinced of that. No one would come to find them, the Doyennes wouldn't go back on their decision. They had to extricate themselves, however tricky that might be.

"And that doesn't terrify you?" Aunt Rosaline continued, her eyes half-closed like those of an old cat.

Ophelia puffed some mist on to her glasses and polished them on her sleeve. "A little," she admitted. "Particularly what we're not being told."

Aunt Rosaline's lips tightened; even so, her horse teeth stuck out. She considered her envelope for a moment, tore it in two, and sat back down at her writing desk.

"Very well," she sighed, picking up her quill again. "I'm going to try to be more subtle, even though such ruses are not my forte."

When Ophelia also returned to her footrest, her aunt added, drily: "I always thought that you were like your father, without personality or willpower. I realize now that I really didn't know you, dear girl."

Ophelia contemplated the inkblot on her letter for a long time. She couldn't say why, but these words had instantly warmed her. *I'm glad that Aunt Rosaline is here*, she wrote to her parents.

"Night's fallen," commented her godmother, looking disapprovingly at the window. "And our hosts still haven't returned! I hope they're not going to forget about us altogether. The grandmother's charming, but she's still a bit senile."

"They have to submit to the rhythm of the court," said Ophelia

with a shrug. She didn't dare mention the croquet game that Berenilde had gone off to. Her aunt would have been outraged that
children's games were chosen over them.

"The court!" whispered Rosaline, scratching the paper with
her quill. "A very fine word to define a grotesque stage set
where dagger blows are dispensed in the wings. Given the
choice, I think we're better off here, well away from those
maniacs."

Ophelia frowned while stroking her scarf. On this, she didn't
share her aunt's feelings. The thought of being deprived of her
freedom of movement horrified her. First they put her in a cage
to protect her, then one day that cage would turn into a prison.
A woman confined at home with the sole purpose of producing children for her husband, that's what they'd turn her into
if she didn't take control of her future, as of now.

"Are you in need of anything, my dears?"

Ophelia and Rosaline looked up from their correspondence.
Thorn's grandmother had opened the double door so discreetly that they hadn't heard her enter. She really did remind one
of a tortoise, with her bumpy back, wrinkly neck, slow movements, and that wizened smile cutting right across her face.
"No, thank you, madam," replied Aunt Rosaline, enunciating
each word loudly. "You're most kind."

Ophelia and her aunt had noticed that if they sometimes
found the Northern accent hard to understand, the reverse was
also true. The grandmother sometimes seemed a bit lost when
they spoke too fast.

"I've just had my daughter on the telephone," the old woman
announced. "She asks that you forgive her, but she has been held
up. She'll be home tomorrow, mid-morning." The grandmother

was shaking her head ruefully. "I'm not very keen on this social whirl that she feels she has to join. It's not reasonable . . . "

Ophelia noticed some anxiety in the sound of her voice. Was Berenilde also taking risks by appearing at court? "And your grandson?" she inquired. "When will he be back?" In truth, she was in no hurry to see him again, and the old woman's reply totally reassured her:

"My poor child, he's such a serious boy! He's always busy, watch in hand, never standing still. He barely takes the time to feed himself! I fear you will only ever see him in short bursts."

"We'll have some letters to give him," said Aunt Rosaline. "We'll need to give our family the address at which they can contact us in return."

The grandmother was nodding her head to such an extent that Ophelia wondered whether she wouldn't end up tucking it in between her shoulders, like a tortoise into its shell.

It was past noon the following day when Berenilde returned to the manor and collapsed onto her chaise longue, pleading for coffee. "The shackles of the court, my little Ophelia!" she exclaimed when the latter came to greet her. "You don't know how lucky you are. Would you pass that to me, please?"

Ophelia spotted the pretty little mirror on the console that she was pointing at and passed it to her, having first almost dropped it on the floor. Berenilde propped herself up on her cushions and anxiously examined the small line, barely visible, that had imprinted itself on her powdered forehead. "If I don't want to totally ruin my looks, I'm going to have to take a rest."

A servant poured her the cup of coffee she had pleaded for, but she pushed it away with a look of disgust, and then directed a weary smile at Ophelia and Aunt Rosaline. "I'm terribly sorry, most terribly sorry," she said, rolling her "r"s sensually. "I didn't think I'd be away so long. You didn't languish too much, I hope?"

The question was purely rhetorical. Berenilde dismissed them both and shut herself away in her room, which made Aunt Rosaline choke with indignation.

The days that followed were much the same. Ophelia barely saw her fiancé; caught Berenilde fleetingly between absences; exchanged a few polite words with the grandmother when their paths crossed in a corridor; and spent most of her time with her aunt. Her existence soon slipped into a dreary routine consisting of solitary walks in the gardens; meals eaten without a word being uttered; long evenings reading in the sitting room; and a few other attempts to keep boredom at bay. The only noteworthy event was the delivery, one afternoon, of the trunks, which somewhat reassured Aunt Rosaline. For her part, Ophelia ensured that she had a resigned expression on her face at all times, so as not to arouse suspicions when she disappeared for too long at the back of the park.

One evening, she retired early to her room. When the chime sounded four times, she stared wide-eyed at the canopy above her bed. Ophelia decided that the time had come for her to stretch her legs. She buttoned up one of her old, outmoded dresses and threw on a black cloak, whose roomy hood swallowed her head right up to her glasses. She didn't have the heart to wake up her scarf, dozing at the bottom of the bed, curled in a ball. Ophelia dived, body and soul, into the mirror in her room, sprang out from the mirror in the hall, and, taking every precaution, pulled back the latches on the front door.

Outside, a fake starry night hung over the park. Ophelia

walked on the lawn, merging her shadow with those of the trees, crossed a stone bridge, and leapt over the streams. She arrived at the little wooden door that separated Berenilde's estate from the rest of the world.

Ophelia knelt down and placed her hand flat on the surface of the door. She'd made the most of all her strolls in the park in preparation for this moment, whispering friendly words to the lock, breathing some life into it, bringing it out of its shell, day after day. Everything now depended on her performance. For the door to consider her as its owner, she had to behave as such. "Open up," she whispered in a firm tone.

A click. Ophelia seized the handle. The door, which stood in the middle of the grass with nothing in front or behind it, half-opened on to a flight of stairs. Wrapped in her cape, Ophelia closed the door after her, proceeded into the small, badly paved courtyard, and had one final look back. It was hard to believe that this decrepit building concealed a manor house and its estate.

Ophelia plunged into the foul-smelling fog of the alleyways, which the light of the street lamps only just penetrated. A smile came to her lips. For the first time in what seemed to her an eternity, she was free to go wherever she fancied. It wasn't an escape, she just wanted to discover for herself the world in which she was about to live. After all, it wasn't emblazoned on her forehead that she was Thorn's fiancée, so why should she worry?

She disappeared into the half-light of the deserted streets. It was noticeably colder and damper here than in the manor's park, but she was happy to breathe in "real" air. Noticing the area's boarded-up doors and bricked-up windows, Ophelia wondered whether each of these buildings concealed castles and gardens. At the turning of an alley, she was stopped by a strange noise. Behind a streetlight, a panel of white glass was vibrating between two walls. That was a window; a real window. Ophelia opened it. A flurry of snow went straight into her mouth and nose, blowing her hood backwards. She turned away, had a good cough, held her breath, and used the support of both hands to lean out of the window. With half her body above the void, Ophelia recognized the anarchy of the wonky turrets, soaring arcades, and ramshackle ramparts that rose from the surface of the Citaceleste. Far below, the frozen water of the moats glittered. And even farther down, beyond reach, a forest of white fir trees shivered in the wind. The cold was almost unbearable; Ophelia pushed shut the heavy pane of glass, shook her cape, and returned to her exploring.

She hid just in time in the shadows of a dead end as a metallic clicking approached from the far end of the pavement. It was an old man who was splendidly adorned, with rings on each finger and pearls threaded into his beard. A silver cane rang out his every step. A king, Ophelia would have thought. His eyes were strangely shadowed, just like those of the people in the photos in the child's bedroom.

The old man was getting closer. He passed the dead end in which Ophelia was lurking without noticing her presence. He was humming, his eyes like half-moons. They weren't shadows on his face, but tattoos; they covered his eyelids right up to his brows. At that precise moment, a firework dazzled Ophelia. The ditty the old man had been mumbling exploded into carnival music. A crowd of cheery masks gathered around her, blew confetti into her hair, and vanished as suddenly as they

1

2

had appeared, while the man and his cane went off along the pavement.

Disconcerted, Ophelia shook her hair for confetti, found none, and watched the old man disappearing into the distance. A weaver of illusions. Did he belong to the Dragons' rival clan? Ophelia decided it would be safer to turn back. Since she had no sense of direction, she could no longer find the road back to Berenilde's manor. These stinking alleys, clogged in fog, all looked the same.

She went down some stairs that she didn't recall having gone up, dithered between two avenues, went under an arch that stank of sewage. As she passed some advertising posters, she slowed down.

HAUTE COUTURE:
BARON MELCHIOR'S GOLDEN FINGERS
WILL TACKLE ANYTHING!
ASTHMA? RHUMATISM? NERVES?
EVER CONSIDERED A THERMAL CURE?
THE EROTIC DELIGHTS OF MADAME CUNEGONDE
LUMINOUS MIME SHOWS—OLD ERIC'S OPTICAL THEATER

There was anything and everything . . . Ophelia frowned when she came across a poster that was more incongruous than the rest:

SANDGLASSES FROM HILDEGARDE'S WORKSHOP
FOR A WELL-DESERVED REST

She tore off the bill to study it closely. Then found herself nose to nose with her own face. The advertisements were stuck on to a reflective surface. Ophelia forgot the sandglasses and advanced along the corridor of advertisements. The posters became fewer, but her reflection, on the contrary, kept multiplying.

It was the entrance to a hall of mirrors. Too good to be true: a mirror was all she needed to get back to her room. Ophelia gently strolled among the other Ophelias, hooded in their cloaks, their eyes a little wild behind their glasses. Lured by the fun of the labyrinth, she followed the maze of mirrors and soon noticed that the appearance of the ground had changed. The paving had given way to a fine polished parquet, the color of a cello.

A burst of laughter froze Ophelia to the spot, and, before she had time to react, the triple reflection of a couple surrounded her. She did what she was best in the world at doing: she didn't speak, didn't panic, didn't make the slightest movement that might attract attention. The man and woman, fabulously dressed, brushed past without noticing her. They both wore masks on their faces.

"And your husband, my dear cousin?" teased the gentleman, smothering the gloved arms with kisses.

"My husband? Squandering our fortune at bridge, naturally!"

"Let's be sure, in that case, to bring him a bit of luck . . . " With these words, the man carried his companion off into the distance. Ophelia remained still for a moment, still incredulous that she'd so easily gone unnoticed. A few steps further on, and the hall of mirrors led to additional, increasingly complex halls. Soon, other reflections mingled with her own, drowning her in a crowd of veiled women, uniformed officers, feathered hats, bewigged gentlemen, porcelain masks, glasses of champagne, wild dancing. As the cheerful music broke into a waltz, Ophelia realized that she was circulating in the middle of a costumed ball.

So that was why she hadn't been noticed under her black cloak. She might just as well have been invisible.

Ophelia blackened her glasses as a precaution, and then even made so bold as to snatch a glass of something bubbly as it flew past on a servant's tray, to quench her thirst. She walked along the mirrors, ready to melt into her reflection at any moment, and observed the ball with great curiosity. She listened to the various conversations, all ears, but was soon disenchanted. They were all exchanging sweet nothings, trying to be witty, having fun seducing each other. They tackled no really serious subjects, and some had too strong an accent for Ophelia to grasp what they were saying.

In truth, this outside world of which she'd been deprived all that time didn't seem as threatening as it had been depicted to her. Much as she loved calm and valued her tranquility, seeing new faces, albeit masked, was doing her good. Each gulp of champagne made her tongue tingle. She realized, from her enjoyment at being among these strangers, how much the manor's oppressive atmosphere had weighed on her.

"Mr. Ambassador!" called out a woman just beside her. She was wearing a magnificent farthingale dress and a mother-of-pearl-and-gold lorgnette. Leaning against a pillar, Ophelia couldn't take her eyes off the man coming towards them. Could he be a descendant of that ambassadress that her forebear Adelaide had mentioned so often in her travel journal? Tatty frock coat, fingerless gloves full of holes, flattened opera hat: his costume was a blatant contrast to the festive, brash colors of the party. He wore no mask, his face exposed. Ophelia, usually little susceptible to masculine charm, had at least to recognize that this one wasn't lacking in it. That honest face—harmonious, youngish, totally beardless, too pale, maybe—seemed open to the sky, so light were his eyes.

The ambassador bowed politely to the woman who had shouted out to him. "Lady Olga," he greeted her, raising his hat. When he straightened up, he shot a sidelong glance that went straight through Ophelia's dark glasses, deep within her hood. The glass of champagne almost fell from her hands. She didn't blink, didn't draw back, didn't turn away. She must do nothing to betray the fact that she was an intruder.

The ambassador's eyes skated casually over her and returned to Lady Olga, who was playfully rapping him on the shoulder with her fan. "Not enjoying my little party? You're staying alone in your corner, like a lost soul!"

"I'm bored," he stated, frankly.

Ophelia was astonished at his candor. Lady Olga let out a laugh that sounded a bit forced. "Of course, it doesn't come up to the receptions at Clairdelune. All this is a bit too 'tame' for you, I presume?"

She half-lowered her lorgnette, so her eyes were revealed. She was looking at the ambassador adoringly. "Be my partner," she suggested, cooingly. "You'll no longer be bored."

Ophelia froze. This woman had the same tattoos on her eyelids as the old man she'd come across earlier. She considered the crowd of dancers around her. Did all those masks hide that distinctive marking?

"I thank you, Lady Olga, but I can't stay," declined the ambassador with an enigmatic smile.

"Oh!" she exclaimed, greatly intrigued. "Are you expected elsewhere?"

"In a way."

"There are far too many women in your life!" she scolded him, laughing.

The ambassador's smile broadened. A beauty spot between his eyebrows gave him a strange expression. "And there'll be yet another this evening."

Ophelia didn't find his face that honest, after all. She told herself that it was high time she got back to bed. She put her glass of champagne down on a sideboard, made her way through the dancing and the streamers, and dived back into the halls of mirrors, ready to plunge into the first mirror she came to. A firm grip around her arm made her swivel round on her heels. Disorientated among all the Ophelias spinning around her, she ended up squinting at the smile the handsome ambassador was directing at her.

"And there I was, telling myself that it was impossible for me not to recognize a woman's face," he said, calm as anything. "To whom do I have the honor, little young lady?"

170

The Garden

Ophelia lowered her chin and stammered the first thing that came into her head:

"A servant, sir. I'm new, I . . . I've just come on duty."

The man's smile instantly vanished and his eyebrows shot up beneath the top hat. He clasped her around the shoulders and dragged her forcibly through the halls of mirrors. Ophelia was stunned. At the back of her mind, a thought that wasn't hers was commanding her not to utter another word. As much as she hit out with arms and legs, she had no choice but to plunge back into the fetid fog of the town. There would be many cobbles and many alleys before the ambassador slowed his pace.

He pulled back Ophelia's hood and, with a disconcerting familiarity, pensively stroked her thick brown curls. He then lifted her chin to study her at leisure in the light of a street lamp. Ophelia stared back at him. The light falling on the ambassador's face turned his skin white as ivory and his hair pale as a moonbeam. This just made the blue of his exceptionally light eyes stand out more. And it wasn't a beauty spot between his eyebrows, it was a tattoo.

This man was beautiful, yes, but it was a rather terrifying

beauty. Despite the crown of his hat flipping open like a tin, he certainly didn't make Ophelia want to laugh in his face.

"That little accent, that ludicrous outfit, those provincial manners," he listed with increasing glee, "you're Thorn's fiancée! I knew he was pulling the wool over our eyes, that rogue! And what's hiding behind these black goggles?" The ambassador gently slid Ophelia's glasses down until their eyes met. She had no idea what her expression was at that moment, but the man instantly softened. "Don't be anxious, I've never hurt a woman in my life. And you're so small! It prompts an irresistible desire to protect you."

He had said that while patting her on the head, as an adult would a lost child. Ophelia wondered whether, in fact, he wasn't openly making fun of her.

"You're a reckless little young lady!" he chided in an unctuous voice. "Strutting about like that, nose in the air, bang in the middle of Mirage territory. Are you already tired of life?"

These words shocked Ophelia. So Thorn's and Berenilde's warnings hadn't been exaggerated. "Mirage"—was that the name of those people with the tattooed eyelids? A fitting term for illusionists. But then, she really couldn't understand: why had these people handed over an estate to Berenilde if they so hated the Dragons and anything to do with them?

"Has the cat got your tongue?" the ambassador teased her. "Do I terrify you?"

Ophelia indicated no with her head, but uttered not a word. All she was thinking about was how she could give him the slip.

"Thorn would kill me if he knew you were with me," he gloated. "How ironic; I'm really loving this! My dear young lady, you're going to join me for a little stroll."

Ophelia would have definitely turned the offer down, but the arm he wrapped around hers was overpowering. Her great-uncle was right. In the hands of a man, she really didn't carry much weight.

The ambassador led her into even fouler-smelling areas, if that were possible. The bottom of her dress was getting soaked in puddles so black that they couldn't be water.

"You arrived here recently, isn't that so?" the ambassador asked while eyeing her hungrily and with intense curiosity. "I daresay Anima's towns are much prettier. You'll soon discover that over here, all the filth is hidden under a triple layer of varnish."

He suddenly went quiet as they turned off a pavement. Once again, a thought came to Ophelia that wasn't her own: she must put her hood back up. Unnerved, she raised her glasses towards the ambassador, and he responded with a wink. So it wasn't a figment of her imagination—this man could superimpose his thoughts onto hers. She didn't like the thought of that.

The ambassador led her through warehouses packed to the ceiling with crates and canvas sacks. Many laborers were hard at work in them, despite it being so late at night. They respectfully touched the peaks of their caps as the ambassador went by, but paid no attention whatsoever to the hooded little woman accompanying him. The lighting, coming from lamps hanging at the end of long, iron chains, emphasized their blank, tired expressions. It was seeing these worn-out men that really allowed Ophelia to take the measure of this world in which she found herself. There were those who danced at the ball, enclosed in their bubbles of illusion, and those who kept the whole machine going. "And me?" she wondered. "Where will I fit into all that?"

"We're there," trilled the ambassador. "Just in time!" He indicated a grandfather clock to Ophelia showing it was already almost six in the morning. She found it strange to encounter such a lovely grandfather clock in the middle of warehouses, but then realized that they were now in what looked like a little waiting room, with an elegant green carpet, comfortable armchairs, and paintings on the wall. In front of her, two wrought-iron gates stood before empty cages.

There had been no transition from the previous setting; it was mind-boggling. The ambassador burst out laughing when he noticed Ophelia's expression—behind her dark glasses, her eyes were popping out of her head.

"Precisely what I was telling you, varnish over filth! There are illusions lurking almost everywhere around here. It doesn't always make much sense, but you'll soon get used to it." He sighed wearily. "Masking poverty! Saving appearances—that, in some ways, is the designated role of the Mirages."

Ophelia wondered whether it was just to be provocative that he himself wore the clothes of a tramp.

Shortly after the clock struck six, there was a humming sound and a lift cage arrived behind one of the gates. A liftboy opened to them. It was the first time Ophelia had entered such a luxurious lift. The sides were of padded velvet and a record player provided background music.

But still not a mirror in sight.

"Have you stopped recently at the summer garden?" asked the ambassador.

"No, sir," the liftboy replied. "It's out of fashion; the smoking rooms are more popular."

"Perfect. Take us to it and ensure that we're not disturbed." He handed a small object to the liftboy, who beamed back at him.

"Yes, sir."

Ophelia felt as though she had completely lost control of the situation. As the liftboy operated a lever and the lift went gently up, she was considering how she could escape from the man now imposing himself on her. The journey past the different levels of the Citaceleste felt interminable to her. She counted the levels to herself: "Eighteen . . . nineteen . . . twenty . . . twenty-one . . . " It was never-ending and each landing further distanced her from the manor house.

"The summer garden!" the liftboy suddenly announced, jamming the lift's brake on. The door opened onto dazzling sunshine. The ambassador closed the wrought-iron gate behind him and the lift continued upwards to the higher floors. Ophelia shielded her eyes with both hands: despite her glasses' dark lenses, she felt overwhelmed by the colors. A field of poppies spread as far as the eye could see, like a red carpet billowing under a sky of brilliant blue. The cicadas' chittering filled the air. The heat was stifling.

Ophelia turned around. The two lift shafts were still there, set into a wall that, absurdly, was planted in the middle of the poppies.

"Here, we can talk at our leisure," declared the ambassador, whirling his opera hat around.

"I have nothing to say to you," Ophelia warned him.

The ambassador's smile stretched like elastic. His eyes

looked even bluer than the sky above his head. "Well, there you astound me, little young lady! I've just saved you from almost certain death. You should rather start by thanking me, don't you think?"

Thanking him for what? For having put her out of reach of a mirror? Bothered by the heat, Ophelia threw off her hood and unbuttoned her cloak, but the ambassador rapped her on the knuckles as he would have done to a child. "Don't take anything off, you'll catch cold! The sun here is as illusory as that lovely cloudless sky, those pretty poppies, and the chittering of the cicadas."

He extended his tatty cape over Ophelia to give her some shade, and calmly started walking, hat pointing skywards. "So tell me, Thorn's fiancée, what's your name?"

"I think there's been a misunderstanding," she whispered, timidly. "You think I'm someone else."

He shook his head. "Oh no, I don't think so. I'm the ambassador, and as such, I can recognize a stranger just from their pronunciation. You're an Artemis girl. And those," he said, delicately taking her wrist, "I'd wager that they're reader's gloves."

He'd said that without the slightest accent, to Ophelia's ears. She had to admit that she was impressed—this man was very well informed.

"You reek of your little province," he jeered at her. "You have neither the manners of an aristocrat nor those of a servant. I must say, it's charmingly exotic." Not releasing Ophelia's wrist, he kissed her hand, a mischievous smile playing on his lips. "My name is Archibald. Will you, Thorn's fiancée, finally tell me yours?"

Ophelia retrieved her hand and trailed her fingers on

the poppies. A few red petals fell at her touch. The illusion really was perfect, even more successful than Berenilde's park. "Denise. And for your information, I'm already married to a man from my family. I'm only passing through here. As I said, you're mistaking me for someone else."

Archibald's smile flickered. Suddenly inspired, Ophelia had concocted this charming lie. Since she could no longer deny that she was an Animist, she might as well pretend that she was a relation. The main thing was to prevent this man, at all costs, from establishing any personal link between her and Thorn. She already felt that she had done something irredeemably stupid, so now she mustn't make the situation worse.

In silence, under his canopied cape, Archibald studied Ophelia's impassive face, as though he wanted to see beyond her dark glasses. Could he hear thoughts? Just in case, Ophelia recited a childhood nursery rhyme to herself, over and over again.

"So it's 'Mrs.?'" asked Archibald, looking thoughtful. "And how are you related to Thorn's fiancée?"

"She's a close cousin. I wanted to know about where she'll be living."

Archibald finally let out a deep sigh. "I'll admit to you that I'm a little disappointed. It would have been frightfully amusing to have Thorn's betrothed at my disposal."

"And why's that?" she asked, frowning.

"Well, to deflower her, of course."

Ophelia fluttered her eyelashes foolishly. It was the most unexpected declaration she'd ever received. "You intended to force yourself on my cousin in the tall grasses of this garden?"

Archibald shook his head looking exasperated, almost

offended. "Do you take me for a boorish brute? Killing a man means nothing to me, but never would I raise a hand against a woman. I would have seduced her, by Jove!"

Ophelia was so staggered by the cheek of this ambassador, she couldn't even get angry. His frankness was disconcerting. Her foot caught on something in the middle of the poppies; she would have fallen flat on her face in the grass if Archibald hadn't caught her. "Watch out for the cobbles! One can't see them, but one trips up on them."

"And what if my cousin had turned you down?" insisted Ophelia. "What would you have done then?"

He shrugged his shoulders. "I'm not too sure; such a thing has never happened to me."

"You definitely don't suffer from self-doubt."

Archibald broke into a fierce smile. "Do you have the slightest notion of the man she's destined to marry? Believe me, she would have been very susceptible to my advances. Let's sit down here a moment," he suggested, without allowing her time to reply. "I'm dying of thirst!"

Grabbing Ophelia by the waist, he lifted her off the ground and placed her on the edge of a well, as easily as if she weighed nothing. He tugged on the pulley chain to draw up some water.

"Is it real?" asked an astonished Ophelia.

"The well is. Feel how freezing the water is!" He had tipped a few burningly cold drops onto Ophelia's wrist, where it was unprotected by her glove. She couldn't understand how an actual well could have been dug between two floors of the Citaceleste. Could illusions distort space as they pleased?

With the sun on her face and heady with the aroma of the warm grass, Ophelia waited for the ambassador to slake his thirst. At least she was lucky, in this sorry misadventure, to have fallen on a chatterbox. Water was cascading down his beardless chin. The harsh daylight emphasized the perfect smoothness of his skin. He was younger than he'd appeared to her in the light of the street lamps.

Ophelia studied him with curiosity. Archibald was handsome—that was undeniable—but he didn't quicken her pulse. No man had ever quickened her pulse. She'd once read a romantic novel lent by her sister. All those amorous outpourings had done nothing for her and the book had bored her to death. Was this abnormal? Would her body and heart be forever deaf to that call?

Archibald wiped his mouth with a handkerchief as full of holes as his hat, jacket, and fingerless gloves. "None of that explains to me what a little Animist was doing at that time of night, without an escort, in the middle of a Mirage party!"

"I got lost." Ophelia was a bad liar, so she preferred to stick as close to the truth as possible.

"You can say that again!" he exclaimed gleefully as he sat beside her on the edge of the well. "And where should I be escorting you to, proper gentleman that I am?"

Ophelia's only response was to stare at the tips of her boots beneath her dress, stained by the puddles. "May I ask you why, sir, you were planning to seduce my cousin before her marriage?"

Archibald raised his fine profile to the light. "Stealing the virginity of a courtier's wife, that's a game that's always succeeded in dispelling my boredom. But Thorn's fiancée, my little Denise, you can't imagine what a thrill that would be! Everyone hates the Treasurer, and the Treasurer hates everyone.

I pity his little protégée if she were to fall into other arms than mine. I know of those who would settle their score with Thorn without scruples."

The wink he flashed at her sent shivers down her spine. Ophelia nibbled the seam of her glove. Some people bite their nails when they're nervous; with Ophelia, it was her gloves. "You're not cut out for the place I'm taking you to." Thorn's words in the airship suddenly made total sense.

Archibald gave a little flick to his hat to make it tilt to one side. "He knows us well, the bastard," he chuckled. "That dear Berenilde spread the rumor that his fiancée would only travel here for the marriage itself. But since you're here," he added with an angelic look, "I deduce that your cousin is, in reality, not that far away. Would you agree to introduce me to her?"

Ophelia thought of the workers in the warehouses a few floors down, of the hollow look in their eyes, of their weary shoulders, of the crates that they would load and unload until they dropped dead. With a few blinks she lightened her glasses until they were transparent, so that she could look Archibald straight in the eye. "Really, sir, have you nothing more useful to do? Your life must be pretty empty!"

Archibald seemed totally flummoxed. Usually so talkative, he now opened and closed his mouth without finding a reply.

"A game, you said?" Ophelia continued, sternly. "Because dishonoring a young girl and risking a diplomatic incident, that amuses you, Mr. Ambassador? You are unworthy of the responsibilities incumbent upon your office."

Archibald was so dumbfounded that Ophelia thought his smile would be wiped from his lips for good. He stared wide-eyed at her as though seeing her differently. "It's a long time

180

since a woman has spoken to me so sincerely," he finally declared, looking perplexed. "I'm not sure whether it shocks me or charms me."

"Sincerity, you're not short of it yourself," murmured Ophelia while staring at a solitary poppy sprouting between two cobblestones. "My cousin will be warned of your intentions. I'll reinforce my recommendation that she not leave Anima before it's time for the marriage, exactly as was planned."

It wasn't her most inspired lie, but that was an art in which she didn't particularly excel.

"So you, little Denise, what are you doing so far from home?" asked Archibald in a honeyed voice.

"I told you, I'm on a reconnaissance trip." At least Ophelia didn't have to push the playacting too far—she could hardly have been more sincere. She could look Archibald in the eye without blinking. "That tattoo on your forehead, is that the mark of your clan?"

"Indeed it is," he said.

"Does it signify that you can enter into the minds of others and become their master?" she continued, anxiously.

Archibald burst out laughing. "Thankfully not! Life would be frightfully dull if I could read women's hearts like an open book. Let's say instead that it's I who can make myself transparent to you. This tattoo," he added, pounding his forehead, "is the guarantee of that very transparency that our society is so cruelly lacking. *We* always say what we think and we prefer to be silent than to lie."

Ophelia believed him. She'd seen it for herself.

"We are not as venomous as the Mirages, or as aggressive as the Dragons," Archibald continued, hitting his stride. "My entire family works in the diplomatic world. We act as a buffer between two destructive forces."

At these words, they both fell quiet in thought, the cicadas' chirring filling the silence between them.

"I really must get back now," said Ophelia, softly.

Archibald seemed to hesitate, then slapped his opera hat, which flattened and then popped up like a spring. He got down from the well and offered Ophelia a gallant hand, along with his loveliest smile. "It's a shame you're not Thorn's fiancée."

"Why's that?" she asked, anxiously.

"I would have adored to have you as a neighbor!" He underlined this statement with a tap on Ophelia's head, as though he really saw her more as a child than a woman. They cut across fields and were soon back at the lifts. Archibald checked his fob watch. "We'll have to wait, a lift should soon be on its way down. Would you like me to escort you after that?"

"I would prefer not, sir," she replied, declining as politely as she could.

Archibald took off his hat and, with his finger, fiddled with its crown, which flipped open like a tin. "As you please, but take great care of yourself, little Denise. The Citaceleste is not the best place for a young woman alone, whether married or not."

Ophelia crouched down and picked a poppy. She twirled the downy stalk, which seemed so real, between her fingers. "To be honest, I didn't think I'd meet anyone at such an hour," she murmured. "I just wanted to walk a little."

"Ah, but we're not in your lovely mountains, where day and night mean something! Up here, any time's a good time for dancing, maligning, and plotting. As soon as one gets involved in the social whirl, one loses all control of time!"

Ophelia pulled the flower from its stalk and folded down each petal until it looked like a little doll in a red dress. Agatha had taught her this trick when they were both young. "And do you enjoy that life?"

Archibald now also crouched and took the poppy-doll out of her hands with an amused curiosity. "No, but I know no other life. Little Denise, may I give you some advice? Advice that you can then pass on to your cousin from me."

Ophelia looked at him with astonishment.

"She must never, but never, go near our Lord Farouk. He's as capricious as he is unpredictable—she'll be ruined." He had said this with such solemnity that Ophelia started seriously to wonder who this family spirit was to prompt such mistrust in his own descendants.

"Tell me instead, sir, to whom my cousin might turn without fearing for her life and virtue."

Archibald nodded his head approvingly, his eyes like sparkling water. "Fantastic! You've finally grasped how our world works."

A metallic creaking told them the lift was approaching. Archibald pulled Ophelia's hood back over her head, opened the folding gate, and pushed her gently into the lift's padded interior. This time it was an old lift operator, so lined, so shaky, and so hunched that he must have been a hundred. Ophelia thought it shameful to make a man of that age work.

"Take this lady down to the warehouses," instructed Archibald.

"You're staying here?" asked Ophelia, surprised.

The ambassador bowed and raised his gaping opera hat in farewell. "Me, I must return to loftier heights. I'll take another lift. Goodbye, little Denise, and take care of yourself . . . Oh, a final warning!" He tapped the tattoo between his eyebrows, with a big, mocking smile. "Also tell your cousin not to spout everything and anything to those who bear this mark. It could backfire on her one day."

The lift's gate closed, leaving Ophelia deep in thought.

The Sister

As the lift slowly descended, floor after floor, Ophelia leant against its velvet wall. The ambassador's parting words were still ringing in her ears. What had he meant by saying that? She was no longer so sure to have taken him in with all her lies.

Whether it was the effect of that glass of champagne, the lack of sleep, or all those illusions, Ophelia didn't know, but her head was spinning. Suddenly shivering, she rubbed her arms. The contrast with the summery warmth of the garden was stark. Unless that was where the illusion stopped: while she'd thought she was hot, her body had caught cold. She noticed the record player, which was churning out a little violin tune. "How on earth," she thought, "do these people manage to live, day in, day out, in this irritating atmosphere?" In comparison, her mother's hysterics seemed restful.

In the meantime, if Ophelia didn't get back soon and her room was found empty, her aunt would die of worry. From inside her hood she observed the old lift operator, with his red livery and enormous white side-whiskers sticking out from his elastic-strapped hat. He was gripping his lever as a skipper does his tiller.

"Sir?"

The man took a while to understand that this murmur was addressed to him. He turned two eyes sunk deep in their sockets towards Ophelia. From his dumbfounded look, she realized that no one had ever called him "sir" before.

"Yes, miss?"

"How does one get to Lady Berenilde's from the warehouses, please?"

"It's not just next door—miss should take a stagecoach," the old attendant suggested. "Miss will find one near the big covered market, on the other side of the warehouses."

"Thank you."

He checked his floor counter, on which the numbers were diminishing, and then turned his pale eyes back to Ophelia. "Miss is a stranger, isn't that so? You can hear it by the sound. It's so rare to come across any around here!"

She just nodded timidly in agreement. She was definitely going to have to change that accent and her manners if she wanted to melt into the background.

When the lift arrived at a landing, silhouettes could be seen through the mesh of the gate. The old man jammed on the brake and opened to them. Ophelia pressed herself against the padded wall. A couple with three children entered the lift, asking for "the tearoom." They were all so impressive in their fur outfits that Ophelia felt like a mouse among bears.

The boys, who were rowdy, jostled her without even noticing her. They were as alike as three peas in a pod, with their shaven heads and wildcat smiles. Squashed at the back of the lift, Ophelia wondered whether these little savages went to school. She was hoping the parents would restore a little calm among them, but she soon realized that they had other concerns.

"Try to distinguish yourself, just for a change!" the wife said, bitterly, to the husband. "The doors of Clairdelune will be forever closed to us if you're incapable of coming up with a single witticism. Think of our boys a little and their entrée into society."

With hands deep in a muff, she wore a dress of honey-hued mink that would have made her look stunning if her face hadn't been distorted by spite. Her twitching lips; her pale hair pulled tight under her fur hat; her nose sticking up like a thorn; the line etched between her eyebrows—each feature of her face spoke of constant displeasure, a dissatisfaction rooted deep inside her. So much tension emanated from her body that Ophelia got a headache just looking at her.

The husband scowled. His huge blond beard blended in so well with the fur of his coat that the one seemed an integral part of the other. "And yet I don't believe that it was I who split the ears of the countess. With your tantrums, my dear, you're not doing our social life any favors."

That man had a mountain torrent instead of a voice. Even without shouting, he was deafening.

"She had insulted me! And I have to defend my own honor, since you're too cowardly to do so."

Ophelia kept a low profile in her corner of the lift. She allowed herself to be jostled by the quarreling children and abandoned any thought of complaining.

"But . . . we're going down!" the woman suddenly shouted, outraged. "We asked for the tearoom, you senile old man!"

"If madam and sir would forgive me," said the lift operator, bowing respectfully, "first I have to drop miss off at the warehouses."

The wife, the husband and the three children turned towards the little shadow desperately trying to disappear into its cloak, as though they were finally noticing its presence. Ophelia hardly dared to meet their razor-blade eyes, so high above her. While the man was the tallest and most imposing of them all, with his long blond beard, it was of his wife that she was particularly wary. She wasn't sure how, but this woman gave her a terrible headache.

"And why should you take precedence over us?" the latter spat out with disdain.

Ophelia was afraid that her accent would betray her yet again; she just shook her hood to make them understand that she wasn't that bothered about this *precedence*. Unfortunately, her approach didn't seem to meet with the woman's approval.

"Just look at that," she hissed, appalled. "It would appear that this young person deems me unworthy of a reply."

"Freya, calm down," the husband sighed into his beard. "You're far too touchy, making a scene over nothing. Let's make a detour to the warehouses and say no more about it!"

"It's because of weaklings like you that our clan is destined to decline," she snapped, spitefully. "We cannot let a single insult slip by unchecked if we are to be respected." Then, turning to Ophelia, she added: "Come on, show us your face. Is it because you're Mirage that you hide your eyes like a coward?"

Spurred by their mother's agitation, the children were laughing and stamping their feet. Ophelia just couldn't understand what she'd done to land herself in the soup again. The old attendant, seeing that the situation was turning nasty, decided it was time to intervene: "Miss is a stranger, she won't have really understood madam."

Freya's fury was snuffed out like a flame. "A stranger?"

Her pale, narrow eyes scrutinized Ophelia's glasses, deep in the shadow of her hood, intently. For her part, Ophelia noticed the woman's hands, which she had revealed by relinquishing her muff. They were covered in tattoos identical to those of Berenilde. These people belonged to the Dragon clan. They were her future in-laws.

"Are you what I think you are?" asked Freya in a muted voice. Ophelia nodded yes. She had understood clearly that, in her current situation, it was better to be who she was than to pass for a member of a rival clan. "And might one know what you're up to here?" The surprise had made Freya's face smoother. She looked ten years younger.

"I got lost," whispered Ophelia.

"Take us down to the warehouses," said Freya, capitulating, to the great relief of the lift operator and her husband.

When the lift reached its destination, Freya allowed Ophelia to leave first, following close on her heels. "Haldor, go on ahead with the children," she said, closing the gate.

"Er . . . are you sure, my dear?"

"I'll find you in the tearoom once I've accompanied this girl to her destination, safe and sound. It wouldn't do for her to encounter the wrong sort of people."

Ophelia glanced at the grandfather clock in the waiting room. It was too late now to sneak back into her room. Everyone at the manor must be awake by now.

As they were going through the warehouses, Freya lifted

her mink dress to avoid the puddles. "I presume it's Berenilde you're staying with? We'll take a carriage."

They cut across the covered market, already teeming with people. The smell of fish made Ophelia feel nauseous; right now, it was strong coffee, not fish, that she was dreaming of. Freya hailed a carriage, and settled on one seat. Ophelia sat down opposite her. As the carriage set off, an uncomfortable silence fell heavily between them—the tall, haughty blonde and the small, awkward brunette.

"Thank you, madam," murmured Ophelia.

Freya smiled, but there was no light in her eyes. "Are you enjoying the Pole?"

"It's all a bit new to me," Ophelia replied, choosing her words carefully. She'd realized what a touchy character Freya was, so best to avoid offending her.

"And my brother? Is he to your taste?"

Freya was Thorn's sister? True, they had the same eyes, full of thunder. Ophelia looked out of the window in the carriage door, now vibrating in the strong wind. The carriage had just burst out into the open, the real open. It rattled along a narrow and precipitous cliff road, jolted up to the top of a rampart, and came back down the side of the Citaceleste. Daring to glance down below, Ophelia saw the night paling in the distance, beyond the conifer forest, where the snow was undulating. It was the sun, the real one, the treacherous one, that was pretending to rise but would turn tail before even reaching the horizon, abandoning the Pole, as it did every day, to its winter. After a turning, the carriage plunged back into the bowels of the Citaceleste.

"We don't yet know each other very well," Ophelia finally replied.

"You will never know Thorn!" jeered Freya. "Are you aware that you've been promised to a bastard, an opportunist, and a schemer? It's public knowledge that he hates women. Trust me, as soon as he's got you pregnant, you'll seem no more important to him than an old trinket. You'll be the laughing-stock at court."

Frozen to the bone, Ophelia rubbed her gloves together. Thorn wasn't a saint—that she'd seen for herself—but malicious gossip had always annoyed her more than anything else. She suspected this unsubtle woman of serving her own personal interest in wanting to put her off the marriage. And she was starting to give her a headache again. It was strange to describe: it was like a hostile tingling all around her. "Without wishing to offend you, madam, I'd rather make up my own mind."

On the seat opposite, Freya, hands in muff, didn't move a muscle, and yet an almighty slap flung Ophelia against the window. Completely dazed, she stared wide-eyed in disbelief at the blurred figure before her—her glasses had fallen off her nose with the force of the slap.

"That," Freya said, icily, "is a kindness compared with what that man will have in store for you in private."

With the cuff of her sleeve, Ophelia wiped the blood trickling from her nose down to her chin. So was that the Dragons' power? The ability to hurt at a distance? She felt around on the floor for her glasses and returned them to their perch. "It's not as if I'm being given the choice, madam."

The invisible power hit her other cheek with full force. Ophelia heard the vertebrae in her neck protesting in unison. In front of her, Freya's face was distorted by a smile of disgust.

"Marry that bastard, dear girl, and I will personally see to it that your life is hell."

Ophelia wasn't sure she could survive a third slap from Freya. Luckily for her, the carriage was just pulling up. Through the mist on the window, Ophelia didn't recognize the colonnaded facade it had stopped outside.

Freya opened the door for her. "Think about it with a calm head," she said, curtly.

With the snap of a whip and the clatter of hooves on cobbles, the carriage disappeared into the fog.

Rubbing her sore cheeks, Ophelia contemplated the frontispiece, all marble and columns, that stood before her, hemmed in by two rows of houses. Why had Freya dropped her off here? She warily climbed the stairs leading to a splendid gilded door. A plaque at the entrance read:

MADAM BERENILDE'S MANOR

On the day they'd arrived, Thorn had taken them in through the back door. Ophelia should have known that the manor house would have a proper entrance. She had to sit down for a moment on a step. Her legs could no longer carry her. And she needed to collect her thoughts.

"Everyone hates the Treasurer," Archibald had said. Ophelia had just got the measure of how true that was. That hatred was already being turned on her without her being afforded the smallest chance to exist in her own right. She was Thorn's fiancée, full stop. That was already too much in the eyes of others.

Ophelia pulled a handkerchief from her sleeve and snorted

away the remaining blood in her nose. Then she removed the pins from her hair in order to cover her bruised cheeks with a thick curtain. She'd wanted to see the world that awaited her? Well, she certainly had. It had been a painful lesson, but that would be the reality of her life. Best not to wear blinkers.

Ophelia got up, dusted down her dress, went to the door, and tugged the bellpull three times. A metallic clinking rang out from the other side, the sign that someone was using the little spy hole to identify the visitor. The butler's voice called out, "Madam! Madam!" in the distance, and after a long silence, Berenilde herself came to open to her.

"Come in. We were taking tea while waiting for you."

That was it. No accusation, no reprimand. Berenilde's expression was soft as velvet, but behind her golden curls and flowing silk dressing-gown, there was a rigidity. She was much angrier than she seemed. Ophelia understood that that's what being a society lady was: covering one's true feelings with a sweet smile. Ophelia went inside and entered a stylish little room in which the stained-glass windows threw warm colors onto three harps and a harpsichord. Taken aback, she recognized the music room. Berenilde closed the door of what Ophelia had always thought was a large sheet-music cupboard. Were there other passages between the manor and the outside world?

Before Ophelia could utter a word, Berenilde cupped her face in her lovely tattooed hands. Her big, liquid eyes narrowed in the shadow of her eyelashes as she examined the bruises on Ophelia's cheeks. Holding her gaze, knowing that, sooner or later, she'd have to explain herself, Ophelia let her carry on without daring to tell her that she was hurting her; her neck was but a tangle of knots. She hadn't seen herself in a mirror, but Berenilde's intense stare spoke volumes.

"Who?" was all she asked.

"Freya."

"Let's go to the sitting room," said Berenilde without blinking. "You're going to have to speak to Thorn."

Ophelia put her hands through her hair to draw it back over the bruises. "He's here?"

"We called the Treasury as soon as we noticed your disappearance. It was your scarf that sounded the alarm."

"My scarf?" stammered Ophelia.

"That thing woke us up in the middle of the night by knocking over all the vases in your room."

The scarf must have been panic-stricken when she didn't return; Ophelia felt stupid for not thinking of that. She would have liked a rest before confronting Thorn, but she had to accept the consequences of her actions. So she followed Berenilde without making a fuss. As soon as she entered the sitting room, Aunt Rosaline swooped down on her. She looked like a ghost, with her pale yellow skin, dressing gown, and nightcap.

"But what sort of madness entered your head? Going out like that, in the middle of the night, without me to chaperone you! You made me go insane with worry! You . . . you've got as much sense as an occasional table!"

Each reproach triggered shooting pains at the back of Ophelia's neck. Her aunt must have realized that she wasn't feeling herself since she forced her to sit on a chair and thrust a cup of tea into her hands. "What are those marks on your cheeks? Did you have an unpleasant encounter? Did someone assault you?"

Berenilde gently took Aunt Rosaline by the shoulders to

calm her down. "Not by a man, if that's what's worrying you," she reassured her. "Ophelia met her in-laws. The Dragons sometimes have rather cold manners."

"Rather cold manners?" repeated the aunt, staggered. "Are you making fun of me? Look at her face!"

"If you wouldn't mind, Madam Rosaline, it's to my nephew that your niece owes some explanations. Let's go into the ante-chamber for a while."

As the two women retired into the neighboring room, leaving the door ajar, Ophelia listlessly moved the spoon around in her lemon tea. Thorn's silhouette was outlined against the sitting-room window like a great motionless shadow. Absorbed in surveying the park, he hadn't so much as looked at her since she'd come in. He was wearing a black uniform with golden epaulettes that made him seem even stiffer than usual. His work clothes, no doubt.

Outside, the autumn colors were unusually subdued. Weighing down on the treetops was a covering of dark clouds from which flashes of lightning flickered. There was a storm brewing.

As Thorn turned from the window and slowly moved towards her, Ophelia had a singularly heightened perception of certain things: the bright flashes of lightning on the carpet, the warm cup between her gloves, the febrile hum of the house. However, Thorn's silence in the background was far more disquieting. She looked straight ahead of her. Her stiff neck prevented her from raising her eyes to meet his, located too high up. She found it annoying not to be able to see the expression on his face. Would he slap her just as Freya had?

"I don't make a habit of regretting," Ophelia preempted him.

She'd prepared herself for a reprimand, a scene, a slap in the face from Thorn, anything but this disturbingly calm voice:

"I'm not entirely sure which of my warnings was lost on you."

"Your warnings, they were just words to me. I needed to see your world with my own eyes."

Ophelia had got up from her chair to try to speak to him face-to-face, but it was impossible with this cricked neck before such a tall man. Right now she had a clear view of Thorn's fob watch, its chain hanging from his uniform.

"With whose collusion did you get out?"

"That of your back door. I tamed it."

Thorn's forbidding voice, hardened by his accent, had prompted Ophelia to answer honestly; she didn't want to drag the servants into her wrongdoing. In front of her, the thin hand seized the fob watch and opened its cover with a flick of the thumb.

"Who assaulted you and for what reason?"

His tone was as impersonal as that of an investigating police officer. These questions weren't a sign of concern; Thorn merely wanted to ascertain to what extent Ophelia had compromised them. She decided not to mention her meeting with the ambassador. It was doubtless a mistake, but she would have found revealing the content of their conversation to him very embarrassing. "Only your sister, Freya, whose path I crossed by chance. She doesn't seem to approve of our marriage."

"Half-sister," Thorn corrected. "She hates me. I'm amazed you survived that encounter."

"I hope you're not too disappointed."

Thorn's thumb snapped the cover of his watch shut. "You've

just made a public spectacle of yourself. All we can hope is that Freya holds her tongue and doesn't target us with any unpleasant repercussions. In the meantime, I would advise you to keep a low profile forthwith."

Ophelia pushed her glasses back up her nose. From the way Thorn had been carrying out his questioning, she'd thought him very detached. She'd been wrong: this incident had deeply angered him. "It's your fault," she murmured. "You're not preparing me adequately for this world by keeping me in ignorance."

She saw Thorn's fingers tighten around his watch. Berenilde's return to the room distracted his attention. "Well?" she asked, gently.

"We're going to have to change our strategy," Thorn announced, crossing his arms behind his back.

Berenilde shook her little blond curls as she gave a small smile of derision. She was neither dressed nor made-up, and yet she was more beautiful than ever. "To whom could your sister tell what she saw? She's fallen out with the whole of the Citaceleste."

"Let's say someone else knows and the rumor spreads. If it's known that my fiancée is here, we won't be left in peace." Thorn turned to Ophelia. Though she couldn't meet his eyes, she could almost feel the steely look on her skin. "And it's mainly this foolish girl that we've got to watch out for."

"What do you suggest, then?"

"We must redouble our vigilance and knock a bit of sense into her. You and me both, in turn."

Berenilde's smile became twisted. "If we're not seen very often, up there, it will arouse curiosity, don't you think?"

"Not if there's a good reason for it," retorted Thorn. "I fear, dear aunt, that you may suffer a few complications. As for me, what could be more normal than that I should make myself available to you?"

Berenilde instinctively placed her hand on her stomach. Suddenly, Ophelia put into words all that had continually struck her since her arrival here. Those loose clothes, those bouts of tiredness, that languor . . .

The widow Berenilde was expecting a baby. "It's *he* who should be looking after me," she whispered in a flat voice. "I don't want to be away from the court. He truly loves me, you understand?"

Thorn looked contemptuous. Evidently, these emotional outbursts exasperated him. "Farouk has stopped being interested in you, as you well know."

Ophelia was flabbergasted. The spirit of the family? This woman was pregnant by her own ancestor?

Berenilde had turned whiter than the silk of her dressing gown. She had to force herself to recompose, feature by feature, a serene face. "Fine," she acquiesced. "You're right, dear boy, as always."

Above her smile, the look she gave Ophelia was poisonous.

The Claws

From that day onwards, Ophelia's existence became more restricted than ever. Going on solitary walks or into any rooms in the manor with large mirrors was forbidden to her. The cheval mirror in her room was removed. Until they felt able to withdraw from the demands of the court without arousing suspicion, Thorn and Berenilde had placed her under constant surveillance. Ophelia slept with a lady's maid beside her bed; couldn't walk a step without a servant following close behind; and could hear the grandmother's wheezy cough even behind the door of the lavatory. And it didn't help that, since Freya's two slaps, she'd had her neck stuck in a brace.

Ophelia put up with all these constraints, regardless. Thorn had advised her to keep a low profile and her instinct whispered that he was right, at least for now. What she dreaded most was still to come: the return of master and mistress to the manor. She sensed that that was when her real punishment for breaking the rules would begin. "Knock a bit of sense into her," Thorn had said. What had he meant by that?

One afternoon in January, Berenilde feigned a malaise while watching a fashionable play. Before she'd even returned home, all the Citaceleste's newspapers were already spreading alarmist rumors. *Favorite's Pregnancy Ordeal* was the headline in one of them. *Miscarriage Again for the Widow!* another cynically proclaimed.

"Do put aside all that nonsense, my sweet child," advised Berenilde when she found Ophelia engrossed in a newspaper, in the boudoir. She stretched out voluptuously on an oval ottoman and requested a chamomile tea. "In fact, bring me the book on the table, over there. Thanks to you, I'll have plenty of time to read from now on!"

Berenilde had highlighted these words with a serene smile that sent shivers down Ophelia's spine. The atmosphere suddenly darkened. Outside, the weather vanes on the roofs went crazy as a storm-whipped wind was rising. In the boudoir, a drop of water fell silently on a window, and, just seconds later, a dense curtain of rain was pounding the gardens. Stiff in her neck brace, Ophelia positioned herself at a window. It felt strange to her to see so much rain falling without it making the slightest noise or any puddles on the ground. This illusion really did leave a lot to be desired.

"What gloomy weather, by Jove!" sighed Berenilde, turning the pages of her book. "I can barely see to read." She settled more comfortably on her ottoman and delicately massaged her eyelids.

"Does madam require that we light the lamps?" asked a servant who was stoking the fire in the stove.

"No, don't waste the gas. Well, I suppose I'm not a young thing anymore! I envy you your age, my dear girl."

"Doesn't stop me from having to wear glasses," muttered Ophelia.

"Might you lend me your sight?" asked Berenilde, holding

the book out to her. "You're an eminent reader, after all!" Her tone had become more sensual, as though she were indulging in some strange game of seduction with Ophelia.

"I am not that sort of reader, madam."

"Well, you are now!"

Ophelia took a seat and tucked her hair behind her ears. Unable to bend her neck, she had to hold the book up. She glanced at the cover: *The Morals of the Tower*, by the Marquis Adalbert. The Tower? Shouldn't it have been "the Court?"

"It's some maxims and portraits by a moralist who's very famous up there," Berenilde explained. "Every person of noble birth has to have read it at least once!"

"This 'tower,' what is it? A metaphor?"

"Not in the slightest, my dear girl; Lord Farouk's tower is very real. It overlooks the Citaceleste—you can't have missed it. It's up there that the great and good of this world come to visit our Lord; that the ministers hold meetings; that the most famous artistes give their performances; that the best illusions are created! Anyhow, what about that reading?"

Ophelia opened the book and randomly read a "maxim," on the conflicts between passion and duty.

"Forgive me, but I can't understand you very well," Berenilde interrupted. "Could you speak louder and with a less strong accent?"

Right then, Ophelia knew exactly what form her punishment would take. A familiar tingling was turning into a terrible headache, exactly as had occurred with Thorn's sister. From the cushions of her ottoman, with a smile on her lips, Berenilde was using her invisible power to thrash her.

Ophelia raised her voice, but the pain between her temples

increased and Berenilde interrupted her again: "Like that, it's never going to work! How can I derive any pleasure from listening to you if you're forever muttering into your hair?"

"You're wasting your time," Rosaline intervened. "Ophelia's elocution has always been a disaster."

Seated in an armchair, the aunt was examining, with a magnifying glass, the pages of an old encyclopedia she'd plucked from a bookcase. She wasn't reading; she was just focusing on the quality of the paper. From time to time, she slid her finger over an imperfection, a tear or a damp patch; the paper was as good as new once she'd done so. Aunt Rosaline was so bored at the manor that she was repairing any books she fell upon. With a twinge of sorrow, Ophelia had even caught her repairing the wallpaper in the laundry. Basically, her aunt was like her: she couldn't bear idleness.

"I think it would be good for your niece to learn how to express herself in society," declared Berenilde. "Come along, dear girl, make an effort and push a little on those vocal cords!"

Ophelia tried to continue reading, but her vision was blurring. She felt as though spikes were piercing her skull. Reclining on her ottoman, Berenilde was observing her from the corner of her eye, with that silken smile that never left her. She knew that she was responsible for Ophelia's suffering, and she knew that Ophelia knew it, too.

She wants to see me crack, Ophelia deduced, tightening her grip on the book, she wants me to beg her out loud to stop.

She did no such thing. Aunt Rosaline, focused on her encyclopedia, was unaware of the punishment that was being silently inflicted. If Ophelia weakened, if she revealed her pain, her aunt could do something stupid and be punished herself.

"Louder!" ordered Berenilde.

Ophelia was now seeing double. She was completely losing the thread of what she was reading.

"If you muddle the sense of the words, you're going to reduce this gem of spirituality into potato peelings," lamented Berenilde. "And that dreadful accent, do make an effort!"

Ophelia closed the book. "Forgive me, madam. I think it would be preferable to light the lamp so you can continue reading yourself."

Berenilde's smile spread even further. Ophelia thought how like a rose this woman was. Beneath the velvet, cruel thorns were hiding. "That, my dear girl, is not the problem. One day, when you are married to my nephew and your position will be more established, you will have to make your entrance at court. There's no place up there for the feebleminded."

"My niece is not feebleminded," Aunt Rosaline declared, sharply.

Ophelia, on the verge of nausea, was only half-listening to them. The dull ache that had expanded inside her head had now turned into shooting pains down the back of her neck.

A servant appeared in the doorway at just the right time and lowered a silver salver to Berenilde. On it lay a little envelope.

"That dear Columbine is coming," announced Berenilde, once she'd unsealed the flap. "This is but the start of the visiting—my malaise didn't go unnoticed and a miscarriage would delight more than one of them!" Berenilde rose languidly from her divan and restored a little volume to her golden curls. "Madam Rosaline, my little Ophelia, I'm going to get myself ready. My convalescence must be believable, I need the appropriate makeup. A servant will shortly take you back to your rooms; you will not leave them as long as I'm receiving visitors."

Ophelia breathed a sigh of relief. The diversion had brought an end to her ordeal. She could see clearly again and the headache had gone. She really could have thought that she'd imagined what she'd just lived through if it weren't for the nausea still affecting her stomach.

Berenilde turned her luminous smile on her and stroked her cheek with a disconcerting tenderness. Ophelia felt a shiver running along her neck, just under her brace. "Do me a favor, my sweet girl. Put your free time to good use by working on your diction."

"Holy curler, she doesn't mince her words!" exclaimed Aunt Rosaline once Berenilde had left the boudoir. "That woman is harder than she at first seems. Is it carrying the child of a family spirit that's gone to her head like this?"

Ophelia thought it best to keep her true thoughts to herself. Her godmother closed the encyclopedia, put down her magnifying glass, and took some hairpins out of a pocket in her dress. "But she's not entirely wrong," she continued, lifting up Ophelia's brown curls. "You're destined to become a society lady, so you must take care of your appearance."

Ophelia let Rosaline create a chignon. She was definitely pulling too hard on her hair, but this simple ritual, a touch maternal, gradually soothed her.

"I'm not hurting you too much?"

"No, no," Ophelia lied, in a small voice.

"With this braced neck, it's not easy, doing your hair!"

"I'll soon be able to take it off." Ophelia felt a lump rising in her throat while her aunt cursed the knots in her hair. She knew it was very selfish, but she found the thought that one day this woman would leave unbearable. Curt and harsh she might be, but she was the only person preventing her from freezing up inside since their arrival. "Aunt?"

"Mmmm?" murmured Rosaline, a hairpin stuck between her horsey teeth.

"Home . . . you're not missing it too much?"

Aunt Rosaline gave her an astonished look and stuck the final pin into her chignon. Taking Ophelia by surprise, she held her in her arms and rubbed her back. "And it's you who's asking me that?"

It lasted but the length of a breath. Aunt Rosaline stepped back, regained her stern look, and scolded Ophelia: "You're not giving in now, for goodness sake! Buck up! Just show these toffs what you're made of!"

Ophelia felt her heart beating harder under her ribs. She didn't really know the cause, but a smile rose to her lips. "Will do."

The rain fell all day, as it did the following day, and for the rest of the week. Berenilde was forever receiving visitors at the manor, confining Ophelia and Aunt Rosaline to their apartments. Their meals were brought up, but no one thought of giving them something to read or to occupy them. The hours seemed endless to Ophelia; she wondered how many more days this procession of aristocrats would go on for.

When they all ate supper together, late in the evening, Ophelia had to endure Berenilde's barbs. Charming and gracious for the first half of the meal, she reserved her poisoned arrows for dessert. "How clumsy that girl is!" she'd lament when Ophelia spilt sponge pudding on the tablecloth. "You're so deadly dull!" she'd sigh as soon as a silence lengthened. "When are you finally going to burn that monstrosity?" she'd hiss, pointing her finger at Ophelia's scarf. She'd make her repeat every sentence she uttered, mock her accent, criticize her manners, humiliate her with exceptional skill. And if she thought Ophelia wasn't making enough effort to improve herself, she'd inflict atrocious headaches on her until the end of the meal.

This little ritual somehow comforted Ophelia in its predictability. These weren't the foibles of a pregnant woman; this was Berenilde's true face.

From one day to the next, all visits to the manor ceased. Ophelia, who could at last stretch her legs around the property, understood why when she came across a daily newspaper: *Mr. Thorn announced yesterday that his Treasury would remain closed indefinitely. Complainants, review your schedules accordingly! His secretary informed us that he will withdraw "for as long as required" to be beside his aunt, favorite among favorites, whose health is said to be declining. Might Mr. Thorn be a more caring nephew than he seems? Or maybe this hardened accountant wants to ensure that Berenilde's testamentary provisions remain favorable to him? We'll leave it to our readers to come to their own opinion on the subject.*

Ophelia frowned. Thorn really wasn't a popular man . . . With just the news of his return to the manor, the place had emptied.

When she was released from her brace, she automatically massaged her neck. If it meant that soon she'd be able to see something other than the walls of her room, day in, day out, she wasn't about to complain. While she'd been shut away, she'd not slept well.

As soon as Berenilde learnt that her nephew would soon

be arriving, she became ruthless with the servants. The whole place had to be aired, the bedding changed, every carpet beaten, all chimneys swept, the furniture dusted. She proved to be so persnickety, so intransigent over insignificant details, that a young maid ended up bursting into tears. Ophelia found Berenilde's behavior incomprehensible: she was making more of an effort to welcome her nephew than she had for distinguished guests. It wasn't as if he never came to see her, was it?

The following day, early in the morning, Thorn crossed the entrance to the manor. His arms were loaded with such a stack of files that one wondered how this tall, thin man could still keep his balance.

"It's raining at yours," he said by way of a greeting.

"You've brought all that work here?" Berenilde gently chided him as she came down the stairs, one hand on her stomach. "I thought you were supposed to watch over me!"

"Watch over you, yes. Sit idly by, no." Thorn had replied to her in a monotone without even glancing at her. He was looking higher up, to the top of the stairs, where Ophelia was busy tying the laces of her boot. When she noticed that Thorn, laden with files, was staring impassively at her, she politely nodded at him. All she could hope was that this man wouldn't have the same treatment in store for her as Berenilde's.

That morning, they breakfasted together. Seeing Thorn at this table again didn't please Aunt Rosaline, so she thought it best to maintain a dignified silence. Ophelia, however, was secretly in seventh heaven. For the first time in an eternity, Berenilde had forgotten she existed. She was all over her nephew, winking charmingly at him, teasing him about his thinness, showing interest in his work, thanking him for rescuing her from boredom. She didn't seem to notice that Thorn was both replying and eating reluctantly, as though forcing himself not to be rude.

Seeing Berenilde so animated, her cheeks flushed with contentment, almost amused Ophelia. She was starting to think that this woman had a visceral need to be someone's mother.

The atmosphere changed abruptly when Thorn opened his mouth: "Are you unwell?" He was addressing not his aunt, but his fiancée. At this moment, it would have been hard to decide who, out of Berenilde, Aunt Rosaline, and Ophelia, was the most flabbergasted.

"No, no," Ophelia finally stammered while staring at her fried egg. She knew she'd got thinner, but did she look so sick that Thorn himself was shocked?

"Unlikely, that girl's pampered!" sighed Berenilde. "It's rather I, in fact, who am exhausting myself instilling a little education into her. Your fiancée is as taciturn as she is stubborn."

Thorn threw a suspicious glance towards the dining room windows. The rain was pouring endlessly down, casting an impenetrable veil over the landscape. "Why is it raining?"

It was the strangest question Ophelia had ever heard.

"It's nothing," Berenilde assured him with a winning smile. "My nerves are just a little on edge."

Ophelia now saw the rain, beating soundlessly against the windows, through different eyes. Did the weather here reflect the moods of the lady of the manor?

Thorn pulled off his napkin and rose from the table. "In that case, you can give your nerves a rest, aunt. I'm taking over."

Ophelia was immediately requested to go with her godmother to the library. This didn't particularly thrill them: after the lavatories, it was the chilliest room in the place. Thorn had already methodically arranged his files on a desk, at the back of the room. He opened one window wide and, without a word to the ladies, folded his endless legs behind his desk and threw himself into studying a schedule of repayments.

"What about us?" demanded Aunt Rosaline.

"You pick a book," muttered Thorn. "It seems to me that there's no shortage here."

"Couldn't we at least go outdoors a little? We haven't set foot outside for an eternity!"

"You pick a book," Thorn repeated with that hard accent of his.

Exasperated, Aunt Rosaline furiously grabbed a dictionary, sat as far away from Thorn as possible, at the other end of the room, and started to examine the state of the paper, page after page.

No less disappointed, Ophelia leant on her elbows at the window and breathed in the odorless air of the garden. The rain, which was bucketing down, disappeared the moment it splashed on her glasses, as though the illusion had reached its limits. It was really strange to get water that didn't wet on one's face. Ophelia stretched out her hand; she could almost touch the rosebushes in front of her. She would have preferred a real garden with real plants and a real sky, but she still had a burning desire to climb out of this window. Hadn't her punishment lasted long enough?

She watched Thorn from the corner of her glasses. Too cramped behind the little desk, his shoulders hunched, forehead low, sharp nose buried in a file, he seemed indifferent to everything other than his reading. Ophelia might just as well have not been there. Between Berenilde, who had a real fixation on her, and this man, who seemed barely conscious of her existence, it was definitely going to be hard for her to find her place within this family.

Ophelia took a book, sat on a chair, and got stuck on the first line. There were only scholarly tomes in this library, and she understood not a single word. Staring into space, she stroked her old scarf, rolled into a ball on her knees, and let time wash slowly over her. What, in the end, do these people want from me, she asked herself, deep in thought. They make me only too aware that I'm not up to their expectations, so why go to such lengths to burden themselves with me?

"Are you interested in algebra?"

Ophelia turned towards Thorn, looking amazed, and then massaged her painful neck. Sudden movements weren't recommended, but she'd allowed herself to be taken by surprise. With his elbows on the desk, Thorn was looking sharply at her; she wondered for how long those metallic eyes had been dissecting her in that way. "Algebra?" she repeated.

Thorn indicated with his chin the handbook she was holding. "Oh, that? I picked it randomly."

She drew her feet under her chair, turned the page, and pretended to concentrate on reading. Berenilde had mocked her enough over *The Morals of the Tower*; she hoped Thorn wasn't going to torment her with mathematics. A treasurer like him must be unbeatable in that subject.

"What's going on between my aunt and you?"

This time, Ophelia considered Thorn with utmost seriousness. So she wasn't imagining it—this man really was trying to engage in conversation. She glanced hesitatingly at her godmother; Aunt Rosaline had dozed off, dictionary on knees.

Ophelia gathered up her scarf, put the algebra handbook back on its shelf, and went over to Thorn's desk. She looked at him straight on, he seated, she standing, but found it pretty annoying that she was still the smallest of the two of them. This man truly was the embodiment of austerity, with that over-angular face; that excessively combed pale hair; those eyes tapered like razor blades; those eyebrows forever frowning; those thin hands he held crossed; and that sullen mouth that never smiled. Not exactly the kind of person who instantly made one feel like confiding in them.

"What's going on is that your aunt hasn't forgiven me for my getaway," declared Ophelia.

Thorn let out a derisive snort. "That's putting it mildly. This downpour is symptomatic. The last time the weather deteriorated to this extent, the matter was resolved with a duel to the death between my aunt and a courtesan. I'd rather avoid seeing you going to such extremes."

Ophelia's glasses blanched. A duel to the death? Such practices were beyond her comprehension. "I have no intention of fighting with your aunt," she reassured him. "Maybe she's missing the court?"

"Farouk, more likely."

Ophelia didn't know what shocked her the most: Berenilde carrying the child of her own family spirit, or the disdain that she'd discerned in Thorn's voice. This Farouk certainly inspired the most contradictory feelings in his descendants. She stroked her scarf ruminatively, as she would an old cat. And this man, seated at the desk before her? What should she think of him, after all?

"Why do the people here hate you?"

211

There was a flash of surprise in Thorn's piercing eyes. He was doubtless not prepared for such a direct question. He remained silent for a long time, frowning hard enough to split his forehead, before unclenching his teeth. "Because I respect only numbers."

Ophelia wasn't entirely sure she understood, but supposed she'd better accept this explanation for now. She found it surreal enough that Thorn had made the effort to answer her. She had the impression, maybe a misleading one, that he was no longer as hostile towards her as he had been. That didn't necessarily make him amiable—he was just as morose—but the atmosphere was less tense. Was that due to their last conversation? Had Thorn taken into consideration what she'd told him?

"You should reconcile with my aunt," he resumed, narrowing his eyes. "She's the only trustworthy person, be sure not to make an enemy of her."

Ophelia allowed herself a moment to think, which Thorn took advantage of to bury his nose back in his papers. "Tell me about your family's power," she decided to ask.

Thorn looked up from a report, his eyebrows raised. "I suppose by that you mean my father's family," he grumbled.

As no one ever mentioned it, Ophelia tended sometimes to forget that Thorn was the illegitimate offspring of *two* families. She feared for a second that she'd made a faux pas. "Yes . . . well . . . if you possess this power yourself, it goes without saying."

"Not in its strongest form, but I do possess it. I can't give you a demonstration without hurting you. Why that question?"

Ophelia felt a vague uneasiness. There was a sudden tension in Thorn's voice. "I wasn't prepared for what your sister made

212

me suffer." She thought it best to remain silent about Berenilde's headaches, but Thorn caught her unawares:

"Does my aunt use her claws on you?" With fingers linked against chin, he was watching Ophelia carefully, expectantly. It was probably an optical illusion, but the scar across his eyebrow made his eyes particularly piercing.

Embarrassed, Ophelia couldn't answer this loaded question. If she said, "Yes," with whom would he really be angry, in the end? With his aunt, for giving a rough time to his fiancée? Or with his fiancée, for betraying his aunt? Maybe he wouldn't be angry at all, and this was mere curiosity on his part. "Tell me about these claws," she asked, evasively.

A draft caught her ankles. Ophelia sneezed hard enough to make every bone in her neck ache. After a good blow into her handkerchief, she deemed it more polite to add: "Please."

Leaning on his fists, Thorn extricated his extendable body from behind the desk. He rolled his shirtsleeves up to the elbow. His thin arms were riddled with scars, similar to those he had on his face. Ophelia tried not to stare at them too much, for fear of seeming rude, but she was puzzled. How could a treasurer who held such an important position be this battered?

"As you can see," said Thorn in a gloomy voice, "I don't bear the distinctive mark of the clan. However, I'm the exception that confirms the rule: all nobles have one. Always systematically locate the tattoo on every person you encounter. It's the location that counts, not the symbol."

Ophelia wasn't particularly expressive, yet she struggled to hide her astonishment. Thorn had initiated the conversation, and now here he was answering questions! Curiously, it didn't ring true. This effort seemed to come at a price for Thorn, as though he were forcing himself not to dive back into his files. It wasn't for pleasure that he was being talkative, so why?

"The Dragons bear the mark of the clan on their hands and arms," he continued, meanwhile, undaunted. "Avoid crossing their paths and never respond to their provocations, however humiliating they may be. Trust only my aunt."

That was easily said . . . Ophelia looked at the window that Thorn had closed. The fake rain was beating against it now, unnervingly silent, never leaving the slightest trace of water behind. "Torturing remotely," she whispered, "is that another kind of illusion?"

"It's much more brutal than an illusion, but you've grasped the principle," Thorn muttered while checking his fob watch. "The claws act as an invisible extension of our nervous system, they're not really tangible."

Ophelia never liked speaking to someone without seeing their face. She wanted to look up at Thorn, but she could go no higher than the buttons on his mandarin collar. She still had some stiffness in her neck and this man was outrageously tall. "Your sister's brutality felt very tangible to me," she said.

"Because her nervous system directly attacked yours. If your brain is convinced that your body is suffering, then your body will adapt so that's effectively the case."

Thorn had said that as though it were the most basic of blatant facts. He might be less curt, but he'd lost none of his condescension. "And when one is attacked by a Dragon," murmured Ophelia, "up to what point can the body play the game of the brain?"

"Pains, fractures, hemorrhages, mutilations," Thorn

enumerated, dispassionately. "It all depends on the talent of the person attacking you."

After this, Ophelia no longer dared to look at his scars at all. Was it his people that had done that to him? How could he speak of *talent*? She nibbled at the seams of her glove. Generally, she didn't allow herself to do so in front of anyone, but now, she really felt the need. Augustus's sketches came back to her like a slap. Those hunters with their hard, arrogant look, capable of killing Beasts without using weapons, they would be her new family. Ophelia simply couldn't comprehend how she'd be able to survive among them. "Now I'm fully grasping the significance of your words in the airship," she admitted.

"You're afraid? That's not like you."

Ophelia looked up at Thorn in surprise, but her neck protested and she had to lower her head again. The brief glimpse she'd caught of him, however, left her thoughtful. Those razor-blade eyes watched her from on high and from a distance, but it wasn't really condescension. Rather, a remote curiosity, as though this little fiancée was turning out to be less uninteresting than expected. Ophelia couldn't stop herself from feeling annoyed. "How can you claim to know what's like me or isn't? You've never made the effort to try to get to know me."

To that, Thorn didn't respond. The silence that had suddenly fallen between them seemed eternal. Ophelia was starting to feel awkward, stuck here in front of this man, who was rigid as a monolith, arms dangling, too tall for her to see the expression on his face.

A resounding bang, from the other side of the library, saved her from her predicament. Aunt Rosaline's dictionary had slid off her knees and slammed onto the parquet. The chaperone awoke with a start, casting a dazed look around her. She soon spotted Thorn and Ophelia beside the window. "What on earth is going on here?" she protested. "Kindly step back, sir, you are too close to my niece! You can do whatever you please, once you are united by the sacred bonds of marriage."

The Ear

"Sit down. Stand up. Sit down . . . No, not like that. We've practiced this movement a hundred times, dear girl, is it that hard for you to remember it?"

Berenilde herself sat down on one of the sitting room's bergères, doing so with the natural grace that enhanced every movement she made, then stood up again with the same elegance.

"Like so. You can't just plonk yourself down like a sack of potatoes, you need to be as harmonious as a piece of music. Sit down. Stand up. Sit down. Stand up. Sit down. No, no, no!"

Too late—Ophelia had fallen off the side of her chair. All that sitting down, again and again, had made her dizzy. "Would you mind, madam, if we left it at that?" she asked, picking herself up. "We've been repeating this exercise too much for me to do it properly."

Berenilde raised her perfectly plucked eyebrows and fluttered her fan, smiling knowingly. "I've observed a fine talent in you, my child. You're very good at concealing your insolence behind those little submissive looks of yours."

"And yet I don't consider myself to be either insolent or submissive," Ophelia calmly responded.

"Berenilde, let that poor child breathe! You can see perfectly well that she's ready to drop."

Ophelia smiled gratefully at the grandmother, busy knitting by the fire. The old lady was as slow and silent as a tortoise, but when she did intervene in a conversation, it was often to take Ophelia's defense.

And indeed, Ophelia was shattered. Berenilde had got her out of bed at four in the morning, on a whim, claiming that she urgently needed to work on her deportment. She'd got her to walk forwards with a book balanced on her head; made her go up and down the manor's stairs until satisfied with her bearing; and, for more than hour, had focused obsessively on how she sat on a chair.

Since she'd stopped receiving visitors, Berenilde was devoting her days to reeducating Ophelia: how she behaved at the table, selected her dresses, served tea, paid compliments, pronounced her sentences . . . She was drowning Ophelia in so much advice that she couldn't retain the half of it.

"Alright, Mother," sighed Berenilde. "I'm sure I'm even more worn out than the dear girl. Drilling good manners into her is hardly restful!"

Ophelia reflected that Berenilde was tiring herself pointlessly, that she'd never be an affectionate, graceful, and witty fiancée, and that there were far more important things she should have instructed her on. Of course, she said not a word of this. Criticizing Berenilde wouldn't help in patching things up with her. Instead, Ophelia saved her questions for Thorn, whenever he deigned to lift his nose out of his files or put the telephone down—in other words, rarely. The tone he used to address her was a bit forced, but he never dismissed her. Each day,

Ophelia learnt more about the ancestry of the Dragons, their customs, their extreme touchiness, the gestures to avoid in front of them, and the words never to utter in their presence.

The only subject that was never broached, either by Ophelia or by Thorn, was their marriage.

"Would you pass me the cigarettes, dear girl? You'll find them on the mantelpiece." Berenilde had settled herself deep in an armchair, close to the storm-darkened window. With her hands laid on a stomach not yet rounded, she looked like a blissful expectant mother. It was a deceptive image, as Ophelia knew. Berenilde was carrying the child of a lord no longer interested in her. Concealed behind the exquisite porcelain face was a heart in turmoil and a mortally wounded pride.

With a friendly pat of the hand, Berenilde indicated the seat beside hers to Ophelia as she brought her the cigarettes. "I realize that I've been a little strict lately, so do come and rest beside me."

Ophelia would have preferred to have a mug of coffee in the kitchen, but she could do nothing but comply with this woman's caprices. She'd barely sat down before Berenilde proffered her cigarette case. "Take one."

"No, really," Ophelia declined.

"Take one, I tell you! Smoking rooms are unavoidably convivial places, you must ready yourself for them right now."

Unconvinced, Ophelia reluctantly took a cigarette. If Aunt Rosaline saw her, she'd certainly be very cross. The one and only time she'd smoked tobacco was at the age of eleven. She'd had just a puff of her father's pipe and then been sick all day.

"Always remember this," said Berenilde, tilting her cigarette holder towards the flame of a lighter. "If a man is near you,

219

it's he who must light your cigarette. Inhale the smoke slowly and exhale it discreetly up into the air, like so. Never blow it into someone's face—it'll end up in a duel. Try it a little, just to see?"

Ophelia coughed and spluttered, her eyes watering. Her cigarette escaped from her fingers and she just managed to pick it up before her scarf caught fire. She decided that that would be her final attempt.

Berenilde burst into tinkling laughter. "Is there not one single thing that you can do properly?"

Her laughter died on her lips. Ophelia, still coughing a little, followed her eyes to beyond the sitting room's open doors. Standing mid-corridor, letters in hand, Thorn was silently observing the scene. "Come and join us," Berenilde suggested in an unctuous voice. "We're having a bit of fun, for once!"

Ophelia wasn't having that much fun; her lungs were aching from too much coughing. Thorn remained true to form: rigid from head to toe, sinister as an undertaker's assistant. "I've work to do," he muttered, moving off. His lugubrious footsteps faded as they reached the end of the corridor.

Berenilde stubbed out her cigarette in the ashtray on a low table. Her manner betrayed her displeasure. Even her smile had lost its silkiness. "I don't recognize that boy anymore."

Ophelia was trying to pacify her scarf, as it unwound itself from her neck like an escaping snake. The incident with the cigarette had panicked it. "Where I'm concerned, I find him not that different from usual."

Berenilde's limpid eyes wandered through the window and into the storm-swollen clouds louring down on the park.

"What do you feel for him?" she murmured. "I like to think that I can read the emotions in any face, but yours remains a mystery to me."

"Nothing in particular," replied Ophelia, shrugging her shoulders. "I know the man too little to have the slightest opinion on the subject."

"Nonsense!" With a flick of her wrist, Berenilde used her fan as though she were wilting inside. "Nonsense," she repeated, more calmly. "One can love at first sight. Indeed, one never loves someone more than when one knows the least about them."

Bitter words, indeed, but Ophelia wasn't sentimental enough to feel concerned. "I'm no more enamored of your nephew than he is of me."

Berenilde considered her thoughtfully. The little blond curls, which danced like flames with every movement of her head, were stilled. Caught in the unrelenting beam of her stare, Ophelia suddenly felt as a ewe must, thrown at the paws of a lioness. Her headache returned with renewed vigor. Try as she might to convince herself that this pain wasn't real, that it was Berenilde's mind interfering with hers, it still hurt. What was this woman actually punishing her for, after all?

"Do what you will with your heart, my girl. I only expect you to fulfill your duties and not to disappoint us."

She's not punishing me, Ophelia realized, fists clenched against her dress, she wants to control me. It's my independence of mind that concerns her.

At that moment, the sound of a bell echoed through the manor. A visitor announcing their arrival. Whoever it was, Ophelia silently thanked them for such a timely visit. Berenilde seized a little bell from the low table and shook it. There were similar ones on every piece of furniture in the manor, so a servant could be summoned from any room.

A maid instantly appeared and curtseyed. "Madam?"

"Where is Madam Rosaline?"

"In the reading room, madam. She was most interested in madam's stamp collection."

Cheered by this, Ophelia reflected that as long as there was paper in this house, in whatever form, Aunt Rosaline would find something to keep her hands busy.

"Make sure she stays there while I'm receiving," instructed Berenilde.

"Yes, madam."

"And accompany this child back to her quarters," she added, flicking her hand in Ophelia's direction.

"Very good, madam."

Like a little girl who hadn't been good, Ophelia was double-locked into her bedroom. It was the same ritual every time someone visited the property. Patience was the best tactic— when Berenilde received visitors, it could go on for hours.

Ophelia was teasing her scarf, as it writhed gleefully on the carpet, when the giggling of some maids made her prick up her ears:

"It's Mr. Archibald!"

"Did you see him, with your very own eyes?"

"I even took his hat and his gloves!"

"Oh! Why do such things never happen to me?"

Ophelia pressed her ear to the door, but the hurried footsteps were already moving away. Could it possibly be the Archibald from the summer garden? She wound her hair around her fingers. Supposing it was him, what would happen if he mentioned his meeting with an Animist, right in the middle of a Mirage party? Berenilde would tear me to shreds with those claws, Ophelia concluded. And if I survive, Thorn will never answer any of my questions ever again. In what kind of soup have I landed myself now?

She paced up and down her room. Not knowing what was brewing behind her back, right at this very moment, made her extremely tense. She'd already found the atmosphere stifling since her getaway; she didn't want her relationship with her in-laws to deteriorate completely.

Unable to stand it any longer, she hammered on her bedroom door until someone came to open it.

"Yes, miss?"

Ophelia breathed a sigh of relief. It was Pistache, her lady's maid. This adolescent was the only member of the staff who dared to be a little familiar when the mistress wasn't around. "It's a little chilly in my room," said Ophelia with an apologetic smile. "Might it be possible to light a fire?"

"For sure!" Pistache came in, relocked the door, and then removed the grate from the fireplace.

"I understand Madam Berenilde is receiving an important visitor?" Ophelia whispered in a low voice. Pistache placed some logs in the hearth and threw her a twinkly look over her shoulder. "Oh yes!" she whispered back, excitedly. "Mr. Ambassador's 'ere! And it's an almighty surprise for ma'am." With a coquettish gesture, she re-pinned her lace bonnet to improve its appearance. "Oh my, miss! Don't never go near 'im, or 'e'll soon 'ave you in 'is bed! An' I'm told even ma'am couldn't resist 'im!"

The pronounced accent of the adolescent, fresh out of her native province, prevented Ophelia from understanding all she said, but she'd grasped the essential. It was indeed the Archibald she knew. She kneeled close to Pistache, in front of the fire that was taking hold with a heady smell of resin. "Say, mightn't I observe the meeting between Madam Berenilde and this ambassador? Very discreetly, of course." Pistache made a face. She likewise couldn't always understand Ophelia's accent. When Ophelia repeated herself more slowly, Pistache went so pale that her freckles stood out like a firework trail. "Can't! If ma'am finds out I let you out without permission, I'm a goner! I'm awful sorry, miss," sighed Pistache, "I bet you's dead lonely 'ere, an' all. An' you treat me with respect, you's polite and listen kindly to me, but you 'ave to understand . . . Can't, end of!"

Ophelia put herself in her position. Berenilde didn't play games when it came to the loyalty of her servants. If just one among them betrayed her, they would all surely be hanged. "All I need is a mirror," she ventured. The maid shook her plaits, looking apologetic. "Can't! Ma'am said you couldn't—"

"Big mirrors, yes. Not pocket mirrors. I couldn't get out of this room with a pocket mirror, could I now?" Pistache stood up and dusted down her white apron. "True. I'll fetch you one right away!"

A few moments later, Pistache returned with a hand mirror, a veritable work of art in embossed silver and surrounded with pearls. Ophelia took it carefully and sat on her bed. It wasn't the most practical object, but it would do. "Where, as far as you know, is Madam Berenilde receiving the ambassador right now?"

Pistache thrust her fists deep into the pockets of her apron, a casual stance she would never have assumed in front of her mistress. "A quality guest, always in the red sittin' room!"

Ophelia visualized the red sitting room, named after its splendid exotic tapestries. There were two mirrors in there, one above the fireplace, the other at the back of a silver cabinet. The second would be the ideal hiding place.

"Pardon me askin', but what you gonna do with that mirror?" asked Pistache, really intrigued. Ophelia smiled at her, put a finger to her lips, and took her glasses off. "It stays between us, doesn't it? I trust you."

Before a stunned Pistache, Ophelia placed the mirror against her ear until it had been entirely engulfed. The ear reemerged inside the silver cabinet in the red sitting room, at the other end of the manor. Ophelia immediately recognized Archibald's jocular voice, somewhat muted by the cabinet's pane of glass:

" . . . tesque Madam Seraphine, who likes to surround herself with Adonises. Her little gathering was exquisitely decadent, but lacked your special touch! You were missed." Archibald went quiet. A tinkling of crystal. His glass must be being filled. "Just as you're missed at court," he soon added, suavely. Then Berenilde's voice could be recognized, but she spoke too softly for Ophelia to hear what she was saying, even when blocking her other ear.

In front of her stood Pistache, astounded. "Don't tell me, miss, you can 'ear the chat down there!"

Holding the mirror like a telephone receiver, Ophelia indicated to her not to make a sound: Archibald was replying. "I know that, and that's precisely the reason for my coming here today. The newspapers depicted you in such alarming terms, we thought you were on your deathbed! Our Lord Farouk, although not the sort to worry about anything other than his own pleasure, is showing signs of concern about you."

Silence. Berenilde must be replying to him.

"I know those rags always exaggerate," Archibald's voice continued, "especially when they're a conduit for jealousy. However, I must speak candidly to you. You're no longer a very young woman, and childbirth, at your age, can prove hazardous. You're in a vulnerable position, Berenilde. Your property, comfortable as it is, is far from a fortress, and a servant is easily corrupted. Without mentioning all the poisons currently circulating on the market!"

This time, when Berenilde responded, Ophelia picked up "thank you, but" and "nephew."

"Thorn can't be at your side day and night," Archibald gently chided her. "And I'm not saying that solely in your interest. The Treasury needs to reopen its doors. Too many cases are dragging on in the courts; the provincial militia has gone to seed; couriers are circulating without consent; controls are becoming scarce; and everyone is swindling everyone. Only yesterday, the Council of Ministers was denouncing these failures."

Perhaps it was due to irritation, but Berenilde's voice became much clearer inside the silver cabinet: "Well, delegate! My nephew can't keep the Citaceleste functioning single-handedly."

"We've already discussed the matter, Berenilde."

"What are you after, ambassador? If I didn't know you, I would say that you're trying to isolate me . . . or to push me to get rid of my child."

Archibald's burst of laughter was so loud, it gave Ophelia a start. "Berenilde! What sort of odious character do you take me for? And there was I thinking that we understood each other well, you and I. And what's this 'ambassador' all about? Haven't I always been Archibald, and only Archibald, to you?"

A brief silence fell on the red sitting room, and then Archibald continued in a more serious tone:

"It is, of course, out of the question that you cut short your pregnancy. What I would suggest, in fact, is that you come and stay at my place and allow Thorn to return to his Treasury. I consider it a personal duty to care for you and the child you're carrying."

Ophelia's eyes widened behind her glasses. Berenilde at Archibald's. Thorn at the Treasury. So would she and Aunt Rosaline remain alone at the manor?

"I'm afraid I will have to decline your proposal," said Berenilde.

"And I'm afraid I will have to impose it on you. It's an order from Lord Farouk."

In the renewed silence that followed, Ophelia didn't find it hard to imagine how Berenilde must be feeling.

"You have caught me unawares. Would you permit me to summon my nephew?"

"I was going to request that you do so, my dear!"

Once again, Berenilde's footsteps faded, making her words inaudible, but Ophelia had caught the familiar sound of a bell. Berenilde was issuing her orders. Archibald barely had time to utter a few niceties before Thorn made his entrance to the red sitting room.

"Mr. Ambassador."

Purely from the sound of these words, spoken in that chilling tone, Ophelia could visualize those eyes that cut like a knife. Thorn hated Archibald—she could tell instinctively.

"Our indispensible Treasurer!" proclaimed Archibald in a tone dripping with irony. "I haven't yet had the chance to congratulate you on your engagement! We're longing to meet the lucky girl."

He must have stood up since Ophelia was hearing him from a slightly different angle. Her hand had tightened around the mirror. One misplaced word from this man's mouth and she'd never have any peace again.

"My fiancée is perfectly fine where she is for the moment," retorted Thorn in a leaden voice.

"I daresay she is," Archibald murmured, glibly.

That was all. He added nothing more, made no reference to their meeting. Ophelia could barely believe it.

"Let's get to the point," he continued, cheerfully. "Mr. Treasurer, you are summoned to return to your duties forthwith. The Citaceleste has been thrown to the four winds!"

"That is out of the question," declared Thorn.

"It's an order," retorted Archibald.

"I don't need any orders from you. I intend to remain by my aunt's side until the birth of her child."

"It's not an order from me, but from Lord Farouk. I will personally assure, at his request, your aunt's safety."

Ophelia's ear was filled with an endless silence. She'd been so engrossed in what she was hearing that she'd completely forgotten about Pistache, standing in front of her and burning with curiosity. "What they saying, miss? What they saying?"

"I presume that there is no conceivable way out of this," Thorn's voice finally articulated with extreme stiffness.

"None, indeed. Make your arrangements as of today. Berenilde, you will come to Clairdelune this evening. A ball will be organized in your honor! Madam, sir, I bid you good day."

Mime

Ophelia remained still and silent for a long while, her ear hovering in the silver cabinet. Accepting the fact that there was no one left in the red sitting room, she placed the mirror on her bed. It was so heavy that her wrist was aching.

"So, miss?" asked Pistache with a mischievous grin. "What d'you 'ear?"

"There are going to be some changes," muttered Ophelia.

"Changes? What changes?"

"I don't know yet." Ophelia felt a sense of foreboding. Thorn and Berenilde would never risk leaving her alone at the manor, they didn't trust her enough for that. What fate did they have in store for her?

"Miss! Miss! Come and see!"

Pistache was jumping for joy at the window, her plaits dancing on her shoulders. Ophelia blinked behind her glasses, dazzled. A radiant sun was piercing the clouds with its golden arrows. The sky became so blue, the park's colors so blazing, that it hurt the eyes after so much grayness. Ophelia concluded that at least Berenilde wasn't angry with her.

Someone knocked on the door. Quickly, Ophelia hid the hand mirror under her pillow, then indicated to Pistache that she could open the door. It was Thorn. He marched straight in, pushed Pistache into the corridor, and closed the door. He found Ophelia sitting in an armchair, book in hand and scarf on knees. She wasn't a good enough actress to feign surprise, so she just scaled the interminable figure standing before her with her eyes.

"The weather's changed," she remarked.

Thorn positioned himself at the window, rigid as an easel, hands linked behind his back. The daylight made his face in profile seem paler and more angular than it already was. "We have just received an unpleasant visit," he finally said, reluctantly. "In fact, the situation could hardly be worse."

Ophelia was surprised suddenly to see Thorn in blue, but then realized it was her glasses that had turned that shade. Blue was the color of apprehension. "Explain yourself."

"You're leaving this evening." He was expressing himself both abruptly and haltingly. Ophelia had at first thought he was looking out of the window, but not at all. His gray eye glowered under the scarred brow. Anger was strangling him, and it was radiating beyond him, piercing Ophelia's forehead with a thousand pinpricks. It was clearly an odd family trait, this transferring of one's nerves on to other people's brains.

"Going where?" she whispered.

"Into the nest of a vulture by the name of Archibald. He's our ambassador and Farouk's right-hand man. You will be there with my aunt until her pregnancy reaches full term."

Seated in her armchair, Ophelia felt as though the cushions, the stuffing, and the springs were all collapsing beneath her. If Archibald saw her, he would denounce her in front of everyone. "But why?" she stammered. "Wasn't I supposed to be kept in solitary confinement?"

With an exasperated flourish, Thorn drew the curtains across the window, as though all that light were attacking him. "We can't do otherwise. You and your chaperone will pass yourselves off as members of our household staff."

Ophelia stared at the fire crackling in the hearth. Even if she made herself up as a servant, Archibald would recognize her and expose her imposture. He had immediately spotted her right in the middle of a costumed ball—this was a man with fiendish powers of observation.

"I don't want to," she declared, closing her book. "We're not pawns that you can just manipulate as you please, sir. I desire to remain at the manor with my aunt."

In return, Thorn looked down at her with stupefaction. Ophelia thought for a second that he was going to lose his temper and stick his claws into her, but he merely snorted noisily with impatience. "I won't commit the error of taking your refusal lightly. It's better to convince you than to compel you, would I be right?"

Caught off guard, Ophelia raised her eyebrows. Thorn grabbed a chair and sat down not far from her armchair, his joints doing their best to bend outsized legs. He leant his elbows on his knees, rested his chin on his fists, and drilled his metallic eyes deep into Ophelia's glasses. "I'm not very talkative," he said, finally. "I've always considered speaking a waste of time, but, as I hope you will have noticed, I do try to counter my nature."

Ophelia drummed her fingers nervously on the cover of her book. What was Thorn driving at?

"And you're not a chatterbox, either," he went on, in his excessively hard accent. "If that was a relief to me at first, I'll confess that your silences are now more wont to bother me. I'm not pretending to think you're happy, but, basically, I haven't the slightest notion of your opinion of me."

Thorn was silent, as though expecting a response, but Ophelia was incapable of uttering a word. She had been ready for anything except this statement. What she thought of him? Since when had he cared about that? He didn't even trust her.

Deep in thought, Thorn's eyed wandered down to the scarf rolled up in a ball in the lap of the young girl. "You were right, the other day. I haven't taken enough time either to get to know you or to allow you to get to know me in return. It's not something I do often, making concessions, but . . . I admit I should have had a different attitude towards you."

He stopped short when he looked up at Ophelia. With hideous embarrassment, she realized that her nose was bleeding. "It must be the heat from the fireplace," she stammered while pulling a handkerchief from her sleeve.

Ophelia tilted her head into the handkerchief, while Thorn waited, priestlike, on his chair. Only she could get herself into such a ridiculous position in circumstances that couldn't have been worse.

"It doesn't matter," muttered Thorn with a glance at his watch. "In any case, I'm no good at things like this and time is ticking." He breathed in deeply, then continued in a more formal tone: "Here are the facts. Archibald is having my aunt to stay at his home at Clairdelune so that I can turn my attention to my backlog. That's the official version, at any rate, as I fear this pest is cooking up something else."

"Wouldn't it be wisest for me to stay here, then?" insisted Ophelia, nose in handkerchief.

"No. Even in a wolf's lair, you'll be infinitely safer with my aunt than alone in the manor. Freya knows you're here and, believe me, she doesn't wish you only the best. All the servants on this estate wouldn't be sufficient to protect you from her."

Ophelia had to admit that she hadn't thought of that. If the choice was between Freya and Archibald, she would actually prefer Archibald. "Is that what my existence is going to be reduced to forever?" she muttered, bitterly. "Clinging to your aunt's skirts?"

Thorn wound his watch and stared at its face for a long while. Ophelia counted a good many tick-tocks during this silence. "I'm not a man who is available enough to watch properly over you." He pulled a little silver notebook from a pocket and scribbled something down in pencil. "Here's the address of the Treasury. Memorize it well. If you find yourself in difficulty, if you need help, come and see me without attracting any attention."

Ophelia stared at the little piece of paper. It was all very nice, but it didn't solve her problem. "This Archibald, he's never going to suspect my identity, if I spend the coming months in his home?"

Thorn's eyes narrowed to two thin slits. "He must never suspect. Don't trust his inane smiles, he's a dangerous man. If he discovers who you are, he will make it his duty to dishonor you for the simple pleasure of humiliating me. So be very sure to control your Animism."

Ophelia pushed her mass of hair to the back of her shoulders. Not giving herself away was going to be a serious challenge.

"It's not just in front of Archibald that you must take extreme precautions," Thorn continued, emphasizing each syllable, "but in front of his whole family. Those people are all connected to each other. What one sees, they all see. What one hears, they all hear. What one knows, they all know. They're known as 'the Web'—you can spot them by the mark they bear on their forehead."

Archibald's parting words came back to Ophelia like an electric shock: "Tell your cousin not to spout everything and anything to those who bear this mark. It could backfire on her one day." So that night, Archibald's whole family had witnessed their encounter? Did they all now know her face?

Ophelia felt cornered. She couldn't lie any longer to Thorn and Berenilde, she had to tell them what had happened. "Listen . . . ," she whispered, quietly.

Thorn interpreted her awkwardness quite differently. "You must think I'm throwing you into the lions' den with total indifference," he said in a more serious voice. "I don't show it to you very well, but your fate is of real concern to me. If the slightest offense is committed against you behind my back, it will be paid for at the highest price."

With a metallic click, Thorn snapped shut the cover of his watch. He departed as suddenly as he had arrived, leaving Ophelia alone with her bad conscience. She banged a few times on the door of her room, asking to see Berenilde, repeating that it was very important, but nothing could be done for her. "Madam is very, very, very busy," Pistache explained through the half-open door. "Be patient, miss, I'll open to you soon. I 'ave to leave you!" she exclaimed, as the sound of a bell ringing could be heard in the distance.

Ophelia's hopes were falsely raised two hours later when there was the sound of a key turning in the lock. It was Aunt Rosaline, whom they had forgotten in the reading room and who had just been made to come up.

"It's intolerable!" she screamed, purple with rage. "These people are forever locking us up as if we were thieves! And then, what on earth's going on, for a start? There are trunks all over the place downstairs! Is the manor being emptied?"

Ophelia told her what Thorn had just said to her, but that put Aunt Rosaline into an even worse mood. "What do you mean? That boor was alone with you here, with no one to chaperone you? He didn't give you too rough a time, at least? And what's this business about going and pretending to be servants elsewhere? Who is he, this Archimedes?"

Ophelia considered for a moment confiding a bit more, but soon realized that Aunt Rosaline wasn't the right person in whom to do it. She already had a real job explaining to her what Thorn and Berenilde expected of them.

After a long conversation and much repetition, Ophelia sat back in her armchair, while Aunt Rosaline walked around and around the room. They spent a good part of the day listening to the general commotion shaking up the manor. Trunks were being packed, dresses taken out, skirts ironed, as Berenilde, whose loud, clear voice echoed through the corridors, issued her orders.

Outside, daylight was fading. Ophelia drew up her legs and rested her chin on her knees. However much she thought about it, she was cross with herself for not having immediately told Thorn the truth. Whatever she did, right now, it was much too late. Let's recap, she reasoned with herself. The Dragons want to get rid of me because I'm marrying their bastard. The Mirages want me dead because I'm marrying a Dragon. Archibald wants me in his bed because it amuses him; and, through him, I've lied to the whole Web. My only allies are Berenilde and Thorn, but I've managed to turn one against me, and it won't be long before I've done the same with the other.

Ophelia buried her head in her dress. This world was much too complicated for her; a longing for her old life wrenched her stomach. She got a start when the door to her room was finally opened. "Madam desires to converse with miss," the butler announced. "If miss would care to follow me."

Ophelia did follow him into the large sitting room, where the carpet was strewn with hatboxes. "My dear girl, I've been longing to speak to you!" Berenilde was radiant as a star. Powdered from top to toe, she was strutting around in a corset and white petticoat with no concern for modesty. She exuded a strong smell of curling iron.

"As I have you, madam," said Ophelia, who'd suddenly had an idea.

"No, not 'madam!' Into the bin with 'madam's! Call me by my first name, call me 'aunt,' even call me 'mommy,' if you like! And now, give me your honest opinion." Berenilde twirled gracefully to show off her perfect, shapely figure from the side. "Do you find me plump?"

"Plump?" stammered Ophelia, taken aback. "Well, no. But . . . "

Berenilde clasped her theatrically in her arms, covering her clothes in powder. "I regret my childish attitude towards you, dear girl. I held a grudge against you, like a true adolescent. But that's all forgotten now!"

Berenilde's cheeks were flushed with pleasure and her eyes were sparkling. A woman in love, quite simply. Farouk had shown concern for her, she was triumphant. "Thorn explained to you what's happening to us, I believe. I think Archibald's offer is the best opportunity we could be given." She sat in front of her dressing table, on which three mirrors reflected her beautiful face from different angles. She squeezed the bulb on a bottle of perfume to spray her bodice. Ophelia sneezed.

"You see," Berenilde continued, looking more serious, "I feel the life we were leading wasn't viable. It's perilous for courtiers to cut themselves off from everyone else, and, to be perfectly frank, I believe it won't do my nephew any harm to be a little deprived of you." With a hint of irony at the corner of her lips, and also faintly flustered, she smiled at the reflection of Ophelia, who was standing behind her, arms dangling. "That boy has softened since he took you from your family. I find him excessively understanding with you, which isn't like him. And I, who flattered myself in front of you that I alone reigned over his heart, I confess to you that I did feel a touch jealous!"

Ophelia was barely listening to her as she was concentrating too much on the words she now had to utter: Madam, I have already met Mr. Archibald.

"Madam, I—"

"The past is the past!" Berenilde interrupted her. "What matters is what is to come. I will at last be able to initiate you into the scheming subtleties of the court."

"Wait, madam, I—"

"Because you, my dear Ophelia, you are going to be part of my retinue," she added, before shouting: "Mother!"

Berenilde snapped her fingers, imperiously. The grandmother

advanced slowly, her tortoise smile splitting her face in two. She presented Ophelia with a little case smelling strongly of mothballs. A black dress, rather odd-looking, was folded inside.

"Get undressed," ordered Berenilde, lighting herself a cigarette.

"Listen . . . " insisted Ophelia, "I have already—"

"Help her, Mother. The child's far too prissy."

With a gentle touch, the grandmother unfastened Ophelia's dress until it fell around her feet. Shivering, with arms crossed over her chest, she was left wearing nothing but a cotton slip. If Thorn came into the sitting room now, she'd give a fine impression.

"Put this on, dear girl," said the grandmother. She handed over the black dress from the little case. Feeling increasingly uneasy, Ophelia noticed, as she unfolded the heavy velvet embellished with silver braid, that this was not a woman's garment.

"A valet's livery?"

"A vest and hose are on their way. Slip it on, just to see."

Ophelia passed her head through the narrow collar of the uniform, which hung down to her thighs. Berenilde blew out a cloud of smoke through her satisfied smile. "From tonight onwards, you're called Mime."

Startled, Ophelia discovered a reflection in Berenilde's triple mirror that she didn't recognize. A little man with black hair, almond-shaped eyes and bland features was reflecting her own surprise back at her. "What's that?" she stammered. The little man had moved his lips at the same rhythm she'd moved hers.

"An effective disguise," replied Berenilde. "The only drawback is your voice . . . and your accent. But what does that matter if you're mute?"

Ophelia saw the eyes of the young man widen. She put her hand up to her glasses to check they were still there, as she could no longer see them. Her reflection seemed to be touching the air.

"You'll also have to avoid those kinds of mannerisms," mocked Berenilde. "So, what do you think? I doubt you'll interest anyone whatsoever looking like that!"

Ophelia agreed in silence. Her problem had just found a solution.

At Clairdelune

The Key

The Antechamber was the envy of all of Citaceleste. It was decorated like a boudoir and a variety of teas were served. It was called the Antechamber because it was the only means of access to Clairdelune, Archibald's estate. The only people who could ride in it were the ambassador's guests, who were distinguished by their lineage and their eccentricity. Doubtless owing to its weight, it was also the slowest lift: it took half an hour to complete its journey.

Feeling stiff in her uniform, Ophelia crossed her legs, uncrossed them, crossed them again, and rubbed one ankle against the other. It was the first time in her life she'd worn men's clothing, so she wasn't sure how to carry herself, and those stockings were horribly scratchy against her calves.

Seated in a comfortable armchair with cup of tea in hand, Berenilde cast a disapproving look at her. "I do hope you're not going to wriggle around like that at the ambassador's. You will stand up straight, heels together, chin up, and eyes down. And, most importantly, do nothing that I haven't specifically asked you to do."

She put her teacup down on a pedestal table and beckoned Ophelia over. Delicately, she took her gloved hands into her own. Ophelia instantly stiffened at this contact. Berenilde had seemed in a good mood since Archibald's surprise visit, but this lioness's mood swings were unpredictable. "My sweet girl, never forget that only the livery bears the illusion. You have the face and upper body of a man, but your hands and legs are those of a woman. Avoid anything that could draw attention to them."

Women's hands . . . Ophelia looked at her reader's gloves, as black as her livery, and clenched her fingers several times to break in the new fabric. She'd relinquished her usual old pair for one of those her mother had given her. She didn't want to wear anything that might trigger Archibald's memory.

"This disguise is as humiliating as it is indecent!" railed Aunt Rosaline. "Turning my niece into your valet! If my sister found out about this, all the hairpins on her head would stand on end."

"Our luck will change," Berenilde assured her with a confident smile. "A little patience, Madam Rosaline."

"A little patience," repeated Thorn's grandmother with an inane smile. "A little patience."

Too elderly to be apart from her daughter, the old lady had joined Berenilde's retinue. Ophelia had always seen her dressed very simply; it was quite something to see her decked out in her large feathered hat and blue damask dress. Her long tortoise neck had almost entirely disappeared behind the rows of pearls.

"Patience—it strikes me that we've hardly been lacking in that up to now," observed Aunt Rosaline, coldly.

Berenilde glanced slyly at the Antechamber's clock. "We'll be there in fifteen minutes, dear friend. I would advise you to use them to perfect your 'yes, madam's, and to serve us some more of that delicious spiced tea."

"Yes, madam," said Aunt Rosaline with a highly exaggerated Northern accent.

Berenilde arched her brows with satisfaction. She was wearing a light-colored dress with a ruff, and a wig of breathtaking height that resembled an iced wedding cake. She was as radiant as Aunt Rosalind was austere in her severe outfit of a lady's companion. Her tiny bun pulled the skin of her forehead so tight, she no longer had the slightest expression line.

"You are proud, Madam Rosaline," sighed Berenilde as she sipped her spiced tea. "It's a quality that I like in a woman, but it is out of place in a lady's companion. Soon I'll be speaking to you haughtily, and you must simply reply with, 'Yes, madam', or, 'Very well, madam.' There'll no longer be any 'I' or 'you' between us, we'll not be part of the same world anymore. Do you feel capable of enduring that?"

Putting the teapot down abruptly, Aunt Rosaline straightened up, mustering all her dignity. "If it were for the sake of my niece, I would even feel capable of scouring your chamber pot."

Ophelia stifled the smile that rose to her lips. Her aunt had her own very particular way of putting people back in their place.

"From you two, I expect the utmost discretion and unconditional obedience," declared Berenilde. "Whatever I do and whatever I say, whether to one or the other, I won't tolerate any sideways looks. Most importantly, never reveal your Animism in front of a witness. At the first error, the measures that I will find myself obliged to take will be exemplary, in the interests of all four of us."

After this warning, Berenilde bit into a macaroon with voluptuous relish.

Ophelia checked the lift's clock. Still ten more minutes before Clairdelune. Maybe it was the relief of leaving her gilded prison, but she felt no apprehension. She even felt curiously impatient. All the idleness, the waiting, the vacuity that comprised her existence at the manor, it would all have ended up crushing her, bit by bit, until she was reduced to a pile of ashes on her wedding day. This evening, she was finally getting moving again. This evening she would see unknown faces, discover a new place, learn more about the workings of this world. This evening she'd no longer be the fiancée of the Treasurer, but a simple valet, anonymous among the anonymous. This livery was the best vantage point she could have dreamt of, and she was determined to make the most of it. She would look without being seen, listen while remaining mute.

Thorn could think what he liked, Ophelia was totally convinced that there couldn't be only hypocrites, corrupt individuals, and murderers on this ark. There had to be people worthy of trust. It was up to her to know how to spot them. The manor has changed me, she thought, twiddling her fingers in their new gloves. On Anima, Ophelia had only been interested in her museum. Now, by force of circumstance, she had become more curious about other people. She felt the need to find a support network, some honest people who wouldn't betray her over some clan rivalry. She refused to be entirely dependent on Thorn and Berenilde. Ophelia wanted to form her own opinions, make her own choices, and be self-sufficient.

When there were only three minutes left on the lift clock, a concern arose to spoil her fine resolutions. "Madam," Ophelia whispered, leaning closer to Berenilde, "do you think there will be Mirages at Mr. Archibald's ball?"

Busy powdering her nose, Berenilde looked at her in amazement, and then dissolved into tinkling laughter. "But of course! Mirages are inescapable characters, they're present at every reception! You'll come across them continually at Clairdelune, my dear."

Ophelia was taken aback by such nonchalance. "But the livery I'm wearing, it's a Mirage creation, isn't it?"

"Don't worry, no one will recognize it. You're the most insignificant of servants, with no personality or distinctive sign. There will be hundreds of valets looking just like you, so no one will notice any difference between you and them."

Ophelia lifted her head and looked at Mime's reflection in the mirrored ceiling. A wan face, nondescript nose, expressionless eyes, neatly combed hair . . . Berenilde must surely be right. "But you, madam," Ophelia insisted, "are you not worried about openly rubbing shoulders with Mirages? They're your sworn enemies, after all."

"Why would I be worried? Clairdelune is a diplomatic sanctuary. There's conspiring, maligning, threatening there, but certainly no killing. Even judicial duels are forbidden there."

Judicial duels? Ophelia would never have imagined finding those two words in the same sentence. "But what if we bump into Freya and her husband?" she continued. "Your family knows I've been placed under your protection; won't they guess that I'm hiding within your retinue?"

Lifting the folds of her dress, Berenilde stood up, gracefully. "You'll never bump into my niece at Clairdelune. She is forbidden access, due to her vicious ways. So rest easy, my child, we're just arriving at our destination."

The lift was, indeed, slowing down. Ophelia exchanged a look with Rosaline. At this moment they were still aunt and niece, godmother and goddaughter, but soon their relationship would become purely formal, as it had to be between a lady's companion and a mute valet. Ophelia had no idea when she would get the chance to speak freely again with her, so her final words went to this woman who was sacrificing comfort and pride for her: "Thank you."

Aunt Rosaline briefly clasped her hand in her own. The gilded gates of the Antechamber opened onto the estate of Clairdelune. At least, that's what Ophelia had been expecting. She was perplexed to discover instead a large waiting hall. It was a stunning place, with checkered tiles, gigantic crystal chandeliers, and gold statues bearing baskets of fruit.

Following Berenilde's directions, Ophelia undertook to push the luggage trolley out of the lift. It was loaded with such heavy trunks, she felt as though she were moving a brick house. She stopped herself from marveling at the hall's painted ceilings. All manner of landscape came spectacularly to life: the wind whistling through the trees, here; some waves threatening to spill over onto the walls, there. Ophelia also had to refrain from staring at the bewigged nobles, as she tried to avoid them with her trolley. They all wore outrageous make up, spoke in shrill voices, and adopted affected poses. They expressed themselves in such a precious way, with such convoluted turns of phrase, Ophelia could barely understand them, and it wasn't a question of accent. And they all bore, from eyelid to eyebrow, the mark of the Mirages.

As soon as the nobles spotted the beautiful Berenilde, they greeted her in the most eccentric and ceremonious of ways, to which she responded with a distracted flutter of her eyelashes. Ophelia really would have thought, to see them, that there was no rivalry between them. Berenilde took a seat beside her mother on a velvet bench. There were similar ones across the entire waiting hall, on which many ladies sat impatiently fanning themselves.

Ophelia parked the luggage trolley behind Berenilde's bench and remained standing, heels together. She didn't understand what exactly they were waiting for here. It was already well into the evening, and Archibald would end up finding the tardiness of his guest insulting.

On a neighboring bench, an old lady in pink was giving a quick brush to what Ophelia presumed to be a long-haired greyhound. It was the height of a bear, had a ridiculous blue ribbon tied around its neck, and sounded like a steam train as soon as it showed its tongue. She hadn't expected to see a Beast in a place such as this.

Suddenly, silence fell upon the hall. All the nobles turned as a man, who was as round as a barrel, went by. He walked with small, hurried steps, with a huge smile on his lips. Judging by his uniform, which was black with gold braiding, Ophelia concluded that he was a head butler—Berenilde had made her learn the servant hierarchy by heart—but he so lacked the bearing of one that she had her doubts: he was swaying on his legs and his wig was skew-whiff.

"My dear Gustave!" a Mirage called out to him in an ingratiating voice. "My wife and I have been waiting here for two days. I daresay it's merely a little oversight on your part?"

He had said this while discreetly slipping a small object into the butler's pocket; Ophelia couldn't tell what as they were too far away. The butler patted his uniform pocket, looking flattered. "There's no oversight, sir. Sir and madam are on the waiting list."

"But we've already waited for two days," the Mirage insisted, in a sharper tone.

"And others for even longer, sir."

Watched by the rattled Mirage, the butler moved on, with his hurried, mincing steps, offering a beaming smile to all the nobles presenting themselves to him. One put forward his youngest daughter, commending her wit and beauty. Another vaunted the exceptional quality of his illusions. Even the old lady in pink made her giant greyhound sit up and beg to impress the butler, but he cut through the crowd without halting for anyone. He stopped only once he had reached Berenilde's bench, and there he bowed so low he almost lost his badly attached wig.

"Ladies, Mr. Ambassador awaits you."

Berenilde and her mother rose without a word and followed the butler. Ophelia struggled to wheel her trolley through the mass of indignant nobles. Gustave the butler led them to the far end of the hall, and through a door guarded by policemen who looked far from easy-going.

They instantly found themselves on the path of a rose garden. Ophelia looked up to discover, between the arches of white roses, a vast starry night. Clairdelune deserved its name. The warm air was so balmy, the flowers' perfume so heady that she knew for sure they had just entered into an illusion. A very old illusion, at that. She recalled Adelaide's journal: *The lady ambassador kindly received us on her estate, where an eternal summer evening reigns.* So, while Archibald had inherited the estate of his forebear, Ophelia was walking in the footsteps of her own. It felt a little as though history were repeating itself. The butler's high-pitched voice brought her back down to earth.

"It's an honor to escort madam!" he clucked, addressing Berenilde. "Might I be so bold as to confess to madam that I share without reserve the esteem in which Mr. Ambassador holds her?"

Aunt Rosaline raised her eyes skywards at this. Due to the piles of trunks on her trolley, Ophelia couldn't really see what was going on in front of her. A turning in the rose garden path afforded her a closer look at this bizarre butler. With his beaming fat face and purplish drunkard's nose, he reminded her more of a circus performer than a servant. "I'm not unaware of that, my devoted Gustave," whispered Berenilde. "I am indebted to you for more than one favor. And I'll be indebted for another when you've sketched out a current picture of Clairdelune for me." As the Mirage before her had done, Berenilde discreetly slipped a small object to the butler. Baffled, Ophelia saw that it was a sandglass. So here, favors were exchanged for simple sandglasses?

Gustave's tongue instantly loosened. "There's quite a crowd here, and not small fry, either. After all the rumors that circulated about madam's indisposition, madam's rivals made a very conspicuous reappearance at the court. Some vile gossips even suggested that it was a symptom of some disgrace, but hang me if I lent a willing ear to that!"

"My female rivals don't concern me as much as my male rivals," Berenilde said, lightly.

"I won't conceal from madam that the Knight features on today's menu. He rushed here as soon as he heard that madam was to be the guest at Clairdelune. The Knight has privileged access right across the court, and even when it would better for him not to show up, he always does whatever he likes. I do hope his presence won't be an irritant to madam?"

There was a long silence, disturbed only by the wheels of the trolley on the rose garden's paving stones. Ophelia's arms were aching, but she was dying to know more. So who was this Knight who seemed to make Berenilde uncomfortable? A rejected lover?

"Will some members of my family also be present?" Berenilde merely asked.

The butler coughed with feigned embarrassment, but it seemed more like stifled laughter. "With all due respect, madam, the Mr. and Mrs. Dragons are not greatly appreciated by Mr. Ambassador. They cause such mayhem whenever they're here!"

"Archibald is doing me a big favor," Berenilde concurred, lightheartedly. "Save me from my friends, I'm busy with my enemies. At least the Mirages have the good sense not to tear each other apart."

"Madam needn't worry about a thing. My master has reserved his very own apartments for her, and madam will be perfectly safe there. Now, if these ladies would kindly excuse me, I'm going to announce their arrival to him!"

"Do that, dear Gustave. Tell Archibald that we're here."

The butler went off with his hasty little steps. Ophelia nearly lost her balance trying to watch him go: a wheel of her trolley had got stuck in a rut in the paving. As she wrestled to free it,

254

she got a glimpse of how far she still had to go. The rose garden's arched path extended into a vast avenue punctuated by large, wide urns. Archibald's castle, all white stone and blue tiles, stood right at the end; to Ophelia, it seemed almost as unreachable as the fake moon in the sky.

"We're going to take a shortcut," announced Berenilde, offering her arm to her mother.

They went along a large bed of violets, which struck Ophelia as more of a detour. She was starting to get cramps in her hands. Berenilde set off across a bridge, which, spanning a little canal, led to more gardens, and then, without warning, turned on her heels with an elegant swirl of her dress. Ophelia had to brake with both feet not to bang into her with the trolley.

"Now, listen carefully to me," Berenilde whispered. "The butler who's just been conversing with me is the most treacherous and venal man at Clairdelune. He'll seek to corrupt you, one day or another, as soon as some friend of mine, whether Mirage or Dragon, offers him a good price in exchange for my life or that of my child. You will pretend to accept his offer and inform me as soon as you can. Is that clear?"

"What do you mean?" spluttered Aunt Rosaline. "I thought people didn't kill each other here! That it was a diplomatic sanctuary!"

Berenilde directed a venomous smile at her, to remind her that, apart from "yes, madam"s, she wanted to hear nothing from her mouth. "People don't kill each other," she replied, nonetheless, "but unexplained accidents can occur. They can easily be avoided, as long as one remains vigilant."

Berenilde had spoken that last word with a meaningful look towards the figure of Mime, stuck behind the luggage trolley.

Behind the illusion's neutral face, Ophelia was dismayed. In her mind, servants were people who were fundamentally different to nobles, pure souls such as Pistache. The knowledge that she'd have to be wary of them, too, perturbed her.

As Berenilde helped her mother down the slope of the bridge, Ophelia mindlessly pushed her trolley behind them. It took her a while to realize that the landscape on the other side wasn't as expected. Instead of violets, they were now going through a grove of weeping willows. A little waltz melody floated in the air. Ophelia looked up and, above the undulating foliage, saw Archibald's castle, its white turrets soaring into the night sky. The little bridge had conveyed them from one end of the estate to the other! However much Ophelia thought about it, she couldn't understand how illusions could play around with the laws of space in this way.

In the castle's gardens, couples dressed in their finest were dancing by lamplight. The closer Berenilde and her retinue got, the denser the crowd became, a sea of wigs and silk. In the sky, the fake moon was as brilliant as a nacreous sun, and the fake stars evoked a real firework display. As for Archibald's home, it was worthy of a fairy-tale castle, with its towers topped with pointed roofs and its myriad stained-glass windows. In comparison, Berenilde's manor seemed like a country house.

Ophelia didn't remain under the spell of what lay before her for long. The dancers broke off waltzing as Berenilde, calm as a lake, advanced among them. They all had friendly smiles and sympathetic words for the favorite, but their eyes were colder than ice. The women, in particular, whispered behind the cover of their fans while indicating Berenilde's stomach with their eyes. They exuded such hostility, it brought a lump to Ophelia's throat.

"Berenilde, or the art of making oneself desired!" jeered a voice above the music and the laughter.

Ophelia seized up behind her trolley: it was Archibald, opera hat full of holes in one hand, old cane in the other, who was coming to meet them at a sprightly pace. A bevy of ravishing young girls trailed in his wake.

Upon the arrival of the master of the castle, all servants in the gardens bowed. Ophelia mirrored them. Letting go of her trolley, she bent over stiffly and stared at the tips of her shoes for as long as they did. When she finally straightened up, she didn't allow herself to be swayed by Archibald's open smile or big, sky-blue eyes as he kissed Berenilde's hand. She rather held it against him that he'd concealed his family's particular power from her. Coming from a man who claimed to be incapable of lying, she considered this omission a minor betrayal.

"Desiring for a woman to be punctual is not really knowing her," Berenilde responded, teasingly. "Just ask your sisters!" She clasped each young girl to her bosom, as though they were all her own children. "Patience! Melody! Grace! Clarimond! Gaiety! Relish! And here's my little Dulcie," she concluded, hugging the youngest of the seven. "I missed you so much!"

From the safety of Mime's half-closed eyelids, Ophelia's eyes glided from one sister to the next. They were all so young, so blond, so delicate in their white dresses that it might have been a trick of mirrors. The adolescents responded to Berenilde's embraces with an affection that was certainly more sincere than her own. There was true admiration in their beautiful, clear eyes.

The seven sisters all bore the mark of the Web on their foreheads. If Ophelia were to believe Thorn, each one of them had already seen her face through the eyes of their brother. Would they casually mention her in front of Berenilde? If that had to happen, Ophelia congratulated herself for not having given her real name that night.

"You came with a little retinue, so I see," remarked Archibald. He gallantly kissed the grandmother's hand, as she blushed with pleasure, and then directed an obviously amused smile at Aunt Rosaline. So starchy and frosty was she in her black dress that she stuck out in the midst of the colorful ball. If only for that, Archibald seemed to find her fascinating.

"My lady's companion," Berenilde casually introduced her. "I chose her less for the pleasure of her conversation than for her talents as a midwife."

Aunt Rosaline's lips thinned, but she was determined not to react, confining herself to a polite nod of the head. When Archibald approached the luggage trolley, Ophelia forced herself not to recoil. As though on purpose, her stockings made her calves itch again, irrepressibly. She thought the ambassador was going to extend his inspection to Mime, but he merely patted the trunks. "We're going to install your belongings in my apartments. Consider yourself at home there!"

The butler Gustave came forward and opened a casket. From it Archibald took out a fine silver chain from which hung an exquisite little key, set with precious stones. Berenilde turned gracefully around so he could slip the chain around her neck. This strange ceremony was applauded half-heartedly by the crowd.

"How about we dance a little?" Archibald suggested with a wink. "This ball is being held in your honor, after all!"

"I mustn't overdo it," Berenilde reminded him, laying a protective hand on her stomach.

"Just one or two waltzes. And you have my permission to tread on my toes!"

Ophelia observed their little game with a certain fascination. Behind the facade of their lighthearted, almost childish, exchanges, the two of them silently seemed to be saying something else entirely. Archibald wasn't the attentive escort he attempted to appear; Berenilde knew it and Archibald knew that Berenilde knew it. That being the case, what was the one really expecting from the other? Were they blindly obeying Farouk's orders, or were they trying to make the most of the situation?

Ophelia was wondering this certainly as much as they both were as they walked off, arm in arm. Her heartbeat slowly returned to normal. Archibald hadn't even glanced at her! Much as Ophelia knew she was unrecognizable, it was a great relief to have passed this first test with flying colors.

Fox

Ophelia's second test as a valet had just begun. What was she supposed to do with the trunks? Berenilde had gone off to dance without giving her the slightest instruction. The grandmother and Aunt Rosaline had got lost in the crowd. So Ophelia found herself alone beneath the stars, between two weeping willows, lumbered with her luggage trolley. Archibald had spoken of settling Berenilde into his personal apartments, but all the same, Ophelia wasn't just going to go into the castle as if it were her home. And where exactly were they, these apartments? The drawback of being mute is that one can't ask a single question.

She cast a few hesitant glances at the servants serving refreshments in the gardens, hoping that they would understand her predicament, but they all turned away from her with a look of indifference.

"Hey! You!" A valet wearing exactly the same uniform as Ophelia was coming towards her on the double. He was built like a kitchen dresser and had hair so red, it seemed to have caught fire on his head. Ophelia found him very striking.

"So, dawdling are we? Soon as the masters' backs are turned, think we can just stand and gape?" When he raised a hand as big as a carpet beater, Ophelia thought he was going to hit her with full force. Instead, he patted her good-naturedly on the back. "We're going to get on, in that case. My name's Fox and I'm the king of the skivers. So, never been here before? Looked so lost on your own, I felt sorry for you. Follow me, sonny!"

The valet grabbed hold of the luggage trolley and pushed it in front of him as if it were a baby's perambulator. "In fact, my real name is Foster," he continued with gusto, "but everyone calls me Fox. I'm in the service of the master's grandmother, and you, jammy little so-and-so, you're Madam Berenilde's flunky. I'd sell my innards to get near such a woman!"

He kissed the tips of his fingers with ardor, and, smiling greedily, curled his lips back to reveal bright-white canines. As she went along the path with him, Ophelia studied him closely, totally captivated. This Fox made her think of a blazing fire in the hearth. He must have been close to forty, but he had the energy of a really young man.

He looked down at Ophelia in surprise, with eyes the green of emeralds. "Not very chatty, are we! Is it the effect I have on you, or are you always so shy?"

With her thumb, Ophelia drew a cross over her lips, looking helpless. "A mute?" smirked Fox. "Smart, that Berenilde—she knows to surround herself with discreet types! Not deaf as well, I hope. D'you get what I'm on about?"

Ophelia nodded. He had an accent you could cut with a knife, but still not as thick as Pistache's.

Fox maneuvered the luggage trolley onto a small paved path, bordered by two rows of perfectly manicured hedges, in order to skirt around the castle and gardens. They went through a stone porch that opened onto a vast courtyard. There were no lamps here, but the illuminated ground-floor windows became golden rectangles in the night. They were all steamed up, as though it were infernally hot inside. Stovepipes spewed billowing smoke the length of the wall. "The kitchens," explained Fox. "Lesson No. 1, my lad: never set foot in the Clairdelune kitchens. What they're cooking up in there, it's not for little fellows like you."

Ophelia took him at his word. As they went past the misted up windows, screams and insults reached them, along with a smell of grilled fish. She risked a quick peek through a pane the steam had missed, and saw a staggering ballet of silver tureens, bread baskets, tiered cakes, and swordfish stretching across vast platters.

"Over here!" Fox called to her. He was pushing the luggage trolley down the passage of a tradesman's entrance, a bit further on. When Ophelia caught up with him, she found herself in an ancient lobby, freezing cold and poorly lit. No doubt about it, she was in the servants' quarters. Steam was escaping from the kitchen through a double door to the right, filling the lobby with a spice-infused haze. Waiters were forever pushing the doors back and forth, carrying out steaming platters or bringing back trolleys loaded with dishes for washing.

"I'll wait for you here with the trolley," said Fox. "You have to go and register with Papier-Mâché to get your key." With his thumb he indicated a glass door to the left, with a sign saying "Steward" above it. Ophelia hesitated. What key could she possibly need? Berenilde had put her in charge of the trunks, so the thought of leaving them with this stranger didn't feel right.

"Come on, hurry up and get your key," Fox urged.

Ophelia knocked on the door and went in. At first she didn't see the man seated behind the writing desk, quill in hand. His dark suit, grayish complexion, and total stillness made him almost invisible against the wood-paneled wall. "You are?" the steward asked, stiffly. His skin was more wrinkled than that of an old man. Papier-Mâché? The nickname suited him down to the ground. "You are?" he insisted. Ophelia rummaged in her pockets, searching for the letter of recommendation that Berenilde had written specially for Mime. She handed it to the steward, who put on a monocle and skimmed through it with a glum expression. Without ceremony, he pulled a register out of his desk, dipped his quill in the inkwell, scrawled a few words, and handed it to Ophelia.

"Sign." Under a long list of names, dates and signatures, he pointed to a new one: *Mime, service of Lady Berenilde.* Ophelia improvised a clumsy signature.

The steward got up, walked round his desk, and went over to some labeled drawers: Head Waiters; Chefs; Kitchen Boys; Housekeepers; Lady's Maids; Nannies; Linen Maids; Grooms; Chauffeur-Mechanics; Gardeners; Farmhands. He opened the drawer labeled "Valets" and randomly picked a small key, which he passed to Ophelia. On its tag she saw a stamp of what she supposed was the Clairdelune coat of arms. On the other side, a simple address: 6, Baths Road.

"Your room," said the steward. "You are required to leave it as you find it; to have no women visitors in it; and especially not to eat in it—we've just rid that corner of rats. Keep this key on you at all times: it's proof of your temporary status at Clairdelune. We carry out regular identity checks to maintain the security of the master's guests. You have to show this key each time; if you don't, you'll be thrown into the dungeons.

Welcome to Clairdelune," he concluded, in the same monotonous voice.

Ophelia left the steward's office, somewhat baffled. To her
relief, Fox was still waiting for her with the luggage trolley. She
felt less reassured, however, once she realized that he was busy
rowing with a female cook glistening with sweat.

"Slob!"

"Sauce-splitter!"

"Bloated old fox!"

"It's all muscle! I'll give you a taste whenever you fancy,
you pest."

Ophelia put a hand on Fox's arm to calm him down. She
had no desire to see her only guide fighting with a woman.

"Go on then, flex them muscles," jibed the cook. "It's only
your little pets you'll impress." She pushed open the double
door with a theatrical flourish, and disappeared into the steam
of the saucepans.

Ophelia felt embarrassed to have witnessed this exchange,
but Fox stunned her by bursting into laughter. "Don't look so
glum, kid. She's an old friend! We always needle each other a
bit."

Ophelia suddenly understood why this man evoked a strange
sense of familiarity. He reminded her of her great-uncle, only
younger. She really mustn't make such associations. If the head
butler at Clairdelune was corrupt, why should this valet be any
more trustworthy?

"Got your key?" asked Fox.

Feeling awkward, Ophelia shyly nodded.

"Perfect. We'll do our delivery, then I'll talk to you."

Fox pushed the trolley into a spacious wrought-iron goods

lift and pulled a lever. He only jammed the brake on when the lift reached the castle's top floor. They went through a service room reserved for the maids, then along a lengthy corridor with around a dozen doors. On each one there was a golden label: Dulcie; Joy; Relish; Melody; Clarimond; Grace; Patience.

"Here," whispered Fox, indicating the label Clothilde, "are my mistress's apartments—the master's grandmother. She's having a siesta, so not a sound. Don't fancy starting my service too early."

Ophelia frowned. It would soon be midnight, strange time for a siesta. Archibald had warned her that day and night meant nothing at the Pole's court. She noticed a very grand lift, right in the middle of the corridor; it must be reserved for the family. Further along, she saw a door whose label had been covered with a black scarf. Having followed her gaze, Fox leant towards her ear. "The conjugal bedroom of the late master and mistress, parents of the young master. They died years ago, but it's never been erased."

Erase a room? Much as Ophelia questioned Fox with her eyes, he didn't explain. He rolled the trolley up to a door at the end of the corridor, on which were engraved letters spelling Archibald. Ophelia followed him into an antechamber that alone was twice the size of Berenilde's sitting room at the manor. A huge pink-marble fireplace, windows up to the ceiling, full-length portraits, bookcases on every wall, two crystal chandeliers, furniture fashioned like works of art . . . This family certainly had delusions of grandeur. A gramophone, which someone must be continually winding up, was churning out some whining opera.

With a bit of a shock, Ophelia caught sight of her own

reflection in a large wall mirror. A moon face perched on a body as flat as a board. Even with a man's features, she didn't cut much of a dash. Black hair, white face, black livery, white hose: she looked like an old photograph.

"Mr. Ambassador's room," announced Fox, indicating a closed door. "For your service, it'll always be through here." He opened a sky-blue door, at the other end of the antechamber, which led to an exquisite lady's boudoir. It was a large, light room, without excessive decoration. Heating vents, freestanding bath, wall-mounted telephone—all the modern conveniences were there to assure Berenilde's comfort. Archibald hadn't duped his guest: her accommodation was fit for a queen.

Ophelia was, however, shocked not to see a single window. "Originally, it was just a walk-in wardrobe," explained Fox, seizing a trunk, "but the master had it specially extended for this occasion."

Ophelia made a mental note: at Clairdelune, rooms were erased, and new ones created to order. She helped Fox to unload the trolley: trunks full of dresses, cases of shoes, caskets of jewelry . . . "Well, you're not the handiest of fellows!" Fox sniggered when Ophelia knocked over a pile of boxes for the second time.

They piled up all the luggage in the room, beside the folding screen. Ophelia hadn't yet grasped all the subtleties of domestic service, but she did know that, as a valet, she wasn't allowed to touch her mistress's clothes. It would be the maids' job to put them away in the cupboards.

"Give me a closer look at your key," Fox asked when they had finished. "We're going to regulate your mistress's timepiece to match yours."

Ophelia was getting used to not understanding a thing; she didn't balk at giving him her key.

"Baths Road," he said, reading the tag. "Poor kid—Papier-Mâché has shoved you right next to the latrines! Everyone does anything not to end up over there."

Fox went over to the fine mantelpiece clock, and Ophelia followed. She noticed that it displayed words instead of times: "zigzag"; "barely rises"; "ricochet"; "wide-angle" . . . Fox moved the long hand round to "baths." A second smaller dial comprised a series of numbers; he set the hand at six. "Done! Now, seeing as I'm a nice chap, I'm going to show you your room."

Ophelia was starting to suspect that this big redhead wasn't helping her merely out of the goodness of his heart. He expected something in return; you could tell by the way he smiled. She had nothing to give him—how could she make him understand that?

They went back along the corridor, and back down in the goods lift, this time to the castle's basement. First, Fox stopped off at the laundry and gave Ophelia a set of sheets for her room; he took the opportunity to pick up a clean shirt and stockings. Next, they went through a communal washhouse, storerooms, a strong room, and a vast servants' hall. Ophelia felt totally lost when they ventured into the sleeping quarters. There was an endless sequence of numbers right along the winding corridors, all of which had the names of roads. Doors opened and shut on servants, some exhausted after their service, others just emerging from sleep, as though it were at once morning and evening. They all seemed highly irritable, getting annoyed over a slammed door, an aloof greeting, or a funny look. The sound of bells ringing came from all directions.

Dazed by the surrounding hubbub and laden with her sheets, Ophelia was struggling to hear Fox as he walked with long strides ahead of her. "The sleeping quarters are divided into sections," he explained. "Cooks with cooks, gardeners with gardeners, maids with maids, valets with valets. Speed up, boy!" he exclaimed abruptly while checking his pocket watch. "Festivities will soon be starting up there, and my mistress wouldn't want to miss them for anything in the world."

As he closed the cover with a quick flick of the thumb, Ophelia suddenly had a vision of Thorn again, fob watch in his hand, too big for his chair. That was but a few hours ago, and already it seemed like days to her. Why was she suddenly thinking about it?

Ophelia was jolted from her thoughts by the vicious look a woman threw at her, as she turned a corner in the corridor. A half-look, in fact: a black monocle eclipsed her left eye. She was examining Ophelia from top to bottom, without a word, without a smile, and with such intensity that it was embarrassing.

Fox bowed low before her. "Greetings, my lovely! Where've you been sticking those little hands now?"

Ophelia was wondering the same thing. The woman was covered, from head to toe, in soot. She wore a mechanic's uniform, and her curls, dark as night and cropped very short, escaped as fierce spikes on her cheeks.

"I've come from the main stove, which has gone and done it again," she replied, glumly. "And who's that?"

She had indicated Ophelia with a hard look from an electric-blue eye. This small woman wasn't much older than her, but she exuded surprising charisma.

"Madam Berenilde's valet," Fox said, chuckling. "I don't even know his name—he's not very chatty!"

"He looks interesting."

"Come on, don't mock! It's the first time the boy's been here and I'm showing him the ropes."

"Free of charge, of course?" the woman asked, sarcastically.

"Sonny," said Fox, turning to Ophelia, "this charming brunette is Gail, our mechanic. Heating, plumbing, all the piping, she does it."

"I'm not *your* mechanic," grumbled Gail, "I'm in Mother Hildegarde's service."

"And since Mother Hildegarde is the architect of Clairdelune," he smoothly went on, "it comes to the same thing."

The mechanic ignored the handkerchief Fox was offering her. She just continued casually on her way, bumping, as she passed, into Ophelia, whose pile of sheets fell to the floor.

Fox put his handkerchief away, looking peeved. "You took her fancy, it seems. Hands off, hey! Been after her for years, that one."

While gathering up her sheets, Ophelia would have liked to reassure him. The last thing she had on her mind was whispering sweet nothings to a pretty mechanic.

"Baths Road!" Fox finally announced, a few corridors later. They had arrived at a gangway where the bricks were rotting with damp and the air was putrid. Ophelia put her key into the lock of door No. 6. Fox lit the gas lamp and shut the door behind them. When Ophelia saw the private space allotted to her for the months to come, her mouth went dry. Dirty walls, a rickety bed, an old copper basin, an appalling smell . . . It was squalid.

270

"Leave it in the state you find it," the steward had said. He'd certainly had a laugh at Mime's expense.

"That, my boy," said Fox, pointing to a board above the bed, "is your new nightmare." On the board, a set of small bells was linked to multiple labels: ballroom; billiard room; tearoom; smoking room; library . . . Fox showed her the "bedroom" bell. "You're now tied to the personal clock of your mistress. You'll sleep and wake at the same rhythm as her. And at Clairdelune, sonny, that can end up being at any time. The master's never short of inspiration when it comes to entertaining the crowd; it comes to him at all hours of the night."

Fox grabbed a stool, plonked his large, dresser-like body on it, and indicated to Ophelia to sit opposite him. "Now, we talk."

Ophelia and her pile of sheets settled on the bed; the back legs instantly collapsed under the weight.

"Well, you jammy so-and-so, you've fallen on a real gem. I've been slaving away at Clairdelune for twenty-three years now, so you could say that, when it comes to experience, I'm not short of it. And I'm a nice chap, me, not one of the countless perverts swarming around here. When I saw you coming, with your eyes like saucers, I instantly said to myself: 'My dear Foster, that boy there's going to be eaten alive by the first comer, you must give him a nudge in the right direction.'"

Ophelia blinked to encourage him to continue. Making the stool squeak, Fox leant towards her, so close that, for a moment, she feared he'd knock her glasses. And Mime didn't wear glasses.

"So here's what I'm proposing to you. I teach you all you need to know in this place, and in exchange I only ask of you a trifling compensation." He unbuttoned his livery and, from an inside pocket, pulled out a small, red sandglass. "Know what this is?" Ophelia shook her head. "Thought you wouldn't. These things are only made in these parts. In short, the nobles here thank us with these gratuities. These sandglasses, you'll only ever see them in four colors: green ones, red ones, blue ones, and yellow ones. Ah, the yellow ones!" Fox rolled his eyes in ecstasy and then pressed his sandglass into her hand. "Have an eyeful of that."

Ophelia felt the weight of the object. It was no bigger than her thumb, but was as heavy as if the sand had been replaced with lead balls. It had a little copper label: "seaside resort."

"There's a whole load of destinations," Fox explained, since she was frowning. "Shopping streets, women's quarters, gaming rooms, to name but a few! What you need is the luck of the draw, 'cause you never really know where you'll end up. Once, I pulled the pin on one pretentiously labeled 'breath of fresh air,' and found myself in a rotten chalet surrounded by mountains."

Ophelia rubbed her nose; she wasn't sure she quite understood. She turned the sandglass upside down, but, to her great surprise, the sand didn't flow. Fox burst out laughing at her stunned face, and showed her a little metal ring she hadn't noticed. "You can turn this sandglass in any direction you like, it won't work so long as the pin is intact. Don't touch it, now, I don't want you disappearing with my holiday! Just look at this."

He pointed to a golden seal set in the wood:

FAMILY MANUFACTURER
H^{DE} & Co

"It's Mother Hildegarde who makes 'em," Fox explained. "Any knickknack without this stamp isn't worth my toenails. Don't let yourself be fobbed off with rubbish, son; forgery's more rife here than anywhere else."

Abruptly, he took the sandglass from her and put it back in his pocket. "Some friendly advice: if you don't want to get fleeced, use the strong room; or pull your sandglasses' pins without delay. Once, an old mate had accumulated 12 years' salary in what he thought was the perfect hiding place. The day the whole lot was stolen from him, he hanged himself."

Fox got up, pushed the basin under a tap, and filled it with water. "I'm soon back on duty, mind if I freshen up a bit here?"

Ophelia tried to look disapproving to discourage him, but he stripped off in front of her without a modicum of modesty. He soon had nothing on him but a chain around his neck holding his personal key. It really wasn't easy having someone else's face on one's body; Ophelia would have to learn how to work her expressions.

"These sandglasses," continued Fox from the basin, "are our holidays. Don't know how long you've been serving Berenilde, but I imagine it's no picnic. Well here, with these ladies' and gents' way of life, it'll be even worse! It got so crazy for the flunkies that some were getting really angry behind their masters' backs. That's when Mother Hildegarde got the idea of the sandglasses. Lend me a towel, will you?"

Ophelia held a bath towel out to him while avoiding looking at him. She felt extremely uncomfortable. This man was having a wash right under her nose and seemed in no hurry to put his clothes back on.

"As I'm a decent chap, I'll be happy with your first ten

sandglasses, whatever the color," Fox then declared. "What you earn after that will be all yours."

He rose from the basin, wrapped himself in the towel, and rubbed himself down. His red side-whiskers looked wild when he leant over to Ophelia, hand outstretched to shake on it. She shook her head vehemently. She'd understood nothing of this sandglass business, and refused to seal a deal without knowing every clause.

"What, sir's turning his nose up? You realize, buddy, that others will guzzle up your salary without even asking you? Fox, he's just offering to keep you in the know, without malice, and to protect you with his fists if need be. It's worth at least three times what I'm asking you for!"

Offended, he turned his back on her, slipped his clean shirt on, and buttoned his valet's livery on top of it. When he turned once more to face Ophelia, his anger had given way to a wide smile.

"That's good, sonny—mustn't let people take advantage of you. So let's say you only pass me your green sandglasses, how's that?"

Ophelia remained arms dangling before the hand that Fox again held out to her. His smile widened even more. "You're not as naïve as you look, kid. Swear I'm not trying to bamboozle you. Greens are worth the least. D'you want me to explain the whole thing in a few words?"

Ophelia accepted. But she'd have felt more at ease if he'd put some trousers on.

Fox fastened his cuff links with the air of a schoolmaster. "Four colors, hence four values. The greens, the most common, give you the right to a day off in the Citaceleste: big covered market, opium den, fairground stalls, sauna . . . As I said, hope you strike it lucky."

To Ophelia's great relief, he at last buttoned up his trousers and tied his stockings. "The reds, they're an even bigger thrill. A day's leave! Not to be confused with the greens, right? With the reds, you've official permission to go out into the real great outdoors, the world beyond. You choose your destination, you pull out the pin, and you can enjoy it until all the sand's run through. Those I keep for fine weather!"

Fox leant towards a shard of mirror nailed to the wall. He slicked back his red mane and stroked his strong, perfectly beardless jaw with satisfaction. "With the blues, you're getting the pick of the bunch," he went on with a fond sigh. "You'll need to be ambitious to pick 'em up, but it's worth the effort. Those sandglasses drop you into a real waking dream. Twice in my life I've had a taste of it, and I've got goose bumps just talking about it."

He put his arm around Ophelia's shoulders. She was glad she'd rolled her hair up above her nape. If Fox had felt hair where Mime didn't have any, there would have been trouble. "Try to imagine the brightest colors, the most intoxicating perfumes, the most passionate caresses," he murmured to her. "And you'll still be way off what this illusion can do for you. A supreme pleasure, so intense that it's hardly bearable and, once it's vanished, leaves you bereft."

The twelve strikes of midnight rang out in the distance. Fox released Ophelia and hastily checked his appearance. "In short, a dirty trick. They always ensure you get one taste of it. After that, you're under their heel, asking for more, in the totally crazy hope of one day landing the top prize, a one-way ticket to paradise: the yellow sandglass. Get the picture now, sonny?"

What Ophelia certainly got was that these sandglasses were a real flytrap.

"Right, so what have you decided?" Fox pressed her while shaking his watch. "Ten green sandglasses and I'll teach you all you need to know to fit in at Clairdelune. Deal?"

Ophelia raised her chin and looked him straight in the eye. She knew nothing about this world, she needed a guide. Maybe this man would betray her trust, maybe he'd give her bad advice, but how would she know if she didn't give him a chance? She couldn't forge ahead without ever taking the slightest risk.

This time, she willingly accepted Fox's handshake. He crushed her fingers with a cordial smile. "Fine! I'm going to teach you a thing or two, good and proper, and you won't regret it. With that, I must leave you. Midnight's struck. Madam Clothilde requires my services!"

The Child

As soon as Fox had gone, Ophelia felt as if he'd taken with him what little warmth the room had possessed. Narrow, gray, freezing cold, this place had something of the prison cell about it. Ophelia put her hand to her neck, out of habit, but the dear old scarf was no longer there. Berenilde had forced her to leave it in a trunk at the manor. Just the thought of months without seeing that dust-collector writhing around gave Ophelia a pang of anguish.

She wedged something under the wobbly bed and finally lay on it with a sigh. She hadn't slept since Berenilde had roused her that morning at four o'clock, to teach her how to sit in a chair.

While she was familiarizing herself with the cobwebs on the ceiling, Ophelia thought again about the sandglass business. Objects that transport you to all sorts of destinations, just for a few hours . . . She'd imagined that the servants received wages for their services. True, she didn't know much about money—she worked for nothing on Anima—but still, it seemed like a real swindle.

Ophelia lifted her gloved hands up to her face and contemplated them thoughtfully. This evening more than ever, she was missing the Museum of Primitive History. How long ago was it now since she'd read an antiquity? These ten clumsy fingers, whose only skill was evaluating, would they now just serve to satisfy Berenilde's whims?

She laid her hands back on the mattress. She was feeling homesick. Since her arrival in the Pole, she hadn't received a single letter, either from her parents or her sister or her great-uncle. Had she already been forgotten?

I mustn't linger here, she told herself, flat on her back. Berenilde's going to need me. And yet she let the sounds of the sleeping quarters gently wash over her. The hurried footsteps. The ringing of bells. The flushing of toilets, next door.

The ceiling started to move. Tall fir trees shot up across it, and the cobwebs turned into a wild forest, stretching as far as the eye could see. Ophelia knew that beyond this forest was the land, and then the sea, and then towns, with no abyss, no break, because that was the land of the old world. The landscape became hazy and a figure, long and thin, emerged in the distance. Swept along against her will, Ophelia was hurled towards this man, who kept snapping his fob watch in her face. "Your fate is of real concern to me."

Ophelia woke up with a start and stared at the ceiling of her room in shock. Had Thorn really uttered such words? She sat up to a creaking of springs, took her glasses off her nose, and rubbed her eyes. Yes, he really had said them. At the time she'd been far too anxious to dwell on it, but now it was rising to surface like an air bubble. That's how it went with Ophelia, she always had a delayed reaction.

She fiddled nervously with her glasses. Thorn worried about her? He had a peculiar way of showing it; she didn't know what to make of it at all.

Suddenly, Ophelia was worried about the time. She put her glasses back in place, and Mime's fake face absorbed them into his white skin. Poking her head out of her half-open door, she consulted the corridor clock. She had to do so several times. If she could believe those hands, it was already five in the morning! How could she have slept so long without even realizing it? To her, it felt as though her sleep had lasted but the blink of an eye.

No sooner had Ophelia set off in a hurry, than she turned back. She'd almost forgotten her key on the door. The steward had been quite clear: without the key, her presence at Clairdelune had no legitimacy.

She got lost for a while in the maze of the sleeping quarters, jostled by servants in a hurry, coming to one dead end, and then another. Could Archibald's guests really still be up at this hour? If Ophelia had failed in her duties, Berenilde would set her claws on her as never before.

She ended up finding a spiral staircase. Barely had she set foot on the first step than she was already at the top. She didn't question this phenomenon—she was becoming accustomed to such spatial anomalies. The staircase led to a narrow service corridor, long and windowless. One side was punctuated with countless closed doors: music room; spice boudoir; gentlemen's smoking room; ladies' smoking room . . . As she continued along it, she realized that the service corridor went right round the castle. She finally plumped for the door labeled "rear gallery." Next, she had to find her way around these passages, but they all looked alike, with their glossy parquet flooring, velvet benches, and grand wall mirrors. Ophelia raised her eyebrows when she saw couples passionately embracing each other at the back of the alcoves, and frowned when women in just their petticoats crossed an antechamber in fits of laughter. She wasn't sure she approved of the turn Archibald's little party was taking.

Ophelia popped her head around every half-opened door and pressed her nose against every window. Peacocks were freely strutting around on the large table in the lounge. In a theater auditorium, to rapturous applause, two men were simulating a duel while declaiming poetry. In the garden, young aristocrats were enjoying a motor race between the flowerbeds. Beneath the thick fug of the smoking rooms, many nobles had lost their wigs, while some, on the other hand, were wearing little but their wigs. In the library, elderly ladies were reading licentious tales aloud to each other. Ophelia was flabbergasted when she noticed Thorn's grandmother cooing with laughter among them. Nowhere had she seen Berenilde or Aunt Rosaline, and she wasn't sure whether she should find that reassuring or not.

Posted in all the rooms were policemen in cocked hats and blue-and-red uniforms. They remained standing to attention, with a fixed stare, just like lead soldiers. Ophelia wondered what purpose they could be serving.

She went into a games room and breathed a sigh of relief when she saw Aunt Rosaline, easily recognizable in her black dress, asleep on a divan. She gently shook her shoulder, but couldn't wake her. The air here was heavy with narcotic fumes. Her eyes watering, Ophelia peered around at the billiard and card players nodding off at every table. Valets as discreet as shadows continued to offer cognacs and boxes of cigars to the most resilient among them.

She found Archibald sitting upside down in an armchair,

his back on the seat and his legs crossed on the back, the tip of a hookah in his mouth. His eyes stared vacantly, with a look of pensive melancholy that contrasted with his usual smiling. Ophelia thought that if there was one man she'd never trust, it was definitely him. One really doesn't organize an orgy in honor of an expectant mother.

At the back of the room, half-reclining on a sofa, Berenilde was playing chess lethargically. Ophelia made a beeline for her. Although not allowed to speak, she'd surely find a way to convince her to return to her room with Aunt Rosaline, before everything really started to degenerate. She bowed and snapped her heels, as the servants did to announce their presence, but Berenilde barely glanced at her, continuing her game as though nothing had changed.

Ophelia knew how furniture must feel.

"Watch out, Knight," murmured Berenilde, moving her castle forward. "I'm going to put your queen in difficulty."

Knight? A valet wasn't allowed to stare at a noble, but Ophelia couldn't resist having a quick look at the neighboring armchair. Her surprise was enormous. With his golden curls, chubby cheeks, and round spectacles, Berenilde's adversary was biting his nails and looking devastated. He couldn't be more than ten years old—his slippers barely touched the ground. What was this child doing here at this hour?

"Check," Berenilde alerted him. The Knight yawned at length and knocked his piece over with the back of his hand. "If Mr. Thorn were my private tutor," he said in a thick voice, "I'd make a better chess player."

"Come now, Knight, I made sure to find you the best private tutor around. Your progress is undeniable, I assure you. And to be honest, I wouldn't wish my nephew as teacher on any child in the world."

The Knight dunked a biscuit into a glass of milk and took a bite, scattering crumbs over his fine velvet trousers. "Forgive me, madam, you're absolutely right. I'm already grateful for all you do for me."

"Are you happy at your uncle's?"

"Yes, madam. He's a little hard of hearing, but I get on splendidly with his dogs."

Ophelia found this scene eerie. A few corridors away, men and women were indulging in every excess. The narcotic fumes shrouding the room were starting to get to her, and she had no desire to end up on the divan with Aunt Rosaline. She would have readily coughed to remind Berenilde of her presence, but she was afraid of revealing her true self. She jumped when it was the Knight who raised his bottle-bottom glasses towards her. From eyelid to brow, he bore the Mirage tattoo. "Are you in madam's service? Do you work at the manor? Do you find my room pretty?"

Ophelia just blinked foolishly. So the child's room, it was his? The Knight's curiosity at least had the merit of getting a reaction from Berenilde, who gave a semblance of stifling a yawn. "Please excuse me, Knight, but it's getting late. I've had my fill of dancing and playing!"

"Madam," said the child, politely bowing his head, "we'll continue our conversation another time, if you like."

Ophelia swiftly offered her arm to Berenilde when she noticed her swaying. Her eyes, normally so limpid, had a glassy appearance. She'd drunk and smoked more than she should, which Ophelia deemed entirely unreasonable in her condition.

"What are you doing like that?" Berenilde asked Archibald. Sitting upside down in his chair, he removed the hookah from his lips and blew out a ribbon of blue smoke. His old top hat had fallen off and his light hair cascaded down to the carpet.

"I'm contemplating my existence from a different angle," he declared, seriously.

"Are you now! And what do you deduce?"

"That, right way up or wrong way up, it's totally devoid of meaning. And that this position makes the blood rush to the head," he added, grinning sardonically. "You're leaving us already? Would you like me to accompany you?"

"No, no, carry on with your meditation."

Ophelia understood that it was up to her to take control of the situation. With Berenilde putting all of her weight on her shoulder, she supported her firmly across the games room and along the corridors. Fortunately, they soon arrived in front of the lovely golden gate of the lift. "Good evening, madam!" the liftboy called out cheerily while bowing.

"My room," ordered Berenilde.

"Certainly, madam."

The liftboy took them up to the top floor of Clairdelune. Ophelia gritted her teeth as they made their way to Archibald's quarters. Berenilde was leaning heavily on her and her nails were digging into the skin of her shoulder like blades. Her wedding-cake wig alone must weigh several kilos.

They went into the antechamber, where the gramophone was singing to itself, and on to the apartments assigned to Berenilde. The maids had already unpacked the trunks and put everything away. As soon as Ophelia had helped Berenilde to sit down, she started rummaging in the cupboards. Any lady's boudoir worthy of the name should have smelling salts in it. She ended up coming across a closet in which mineral waters, cod-liver oil, and a collection of little bottles were lined up. She opened one and reclosed it as soon as the pungent smell reached her nose. She'd found it.

Ophelia nearly spilt the salts on the carpet when Berenilde grabbed her by the wrist. "That child you saw me with," she said in a hoarse voice, "never go near him, is that clear?"

The only thing that was clear right now in Ophelia's eyes was that Aunt Rosaline was alone down below. She pulled back her wrist and Berenilde finally let go.

Out in the corridor, the lift had already gone down. Ophelia pressed on the call lever; as soon as the gate opened, the lift-boy dropped his friendly smile. "Did you call the lift?" Ophelia nodded and went in, but the boy threw her out so roughly, she was winded. "Who do you think you are? A marquis? Bother me once more, half-wit, and I'll smash your teeth in."

Stupefied, Ophelia watched him shut the gate and take his luxurious lift back down. She had to go through the long corridor of bedrooms to return to the maids' room. Even the service stairway proved contrary: it obliged Ophelia to go down all the steps of each floor, like any ordinary stairway.

Fortunately, Aunt Rosaline hadn't moved from her divan, intoxicated by the ambient fumes. The salts that Ophelia slipped under her nose had the effect of a slap. "Stink bomb and dirty socks!" she babbled, pushing the phial away. Ophelia blinked several times to prompt her aunt to be more guarded. If she started swearing like an Animist, their imposture would go up in flames. Rosaline got a grip on herself when she saw Mime's pale face peering over her, and she cast a disorientated look around the players of tarot and billiards. "Where's Be . . . madam?"

Ophelia's only response was to hold out her hand. They left the place discreetly and, several floors later, arrived at Berenilde's. She had thrown off her wig and unwound the cable of the telephone handset right up to her bed. "My staff have returned," she told the person on the line, "are you happy now? This first evening went by without the slightest hitch."

Aunt Rosaline, who had just found herself a fan, was waving it with an offended dignity. Apparently, she had a different opinion on the evening she'd just had.

"I'll use my key, don't you worry at all," continued Berenilde. "No, I'll call you. Good bye." She handed the ivory telephone to Ophelia. "That boy is becoming remarkably thoughtful," she said to her, not without a touch of sarcasm.

Ophelia replaced the phone more impatiently than she should have. *Your fate is of real concern to me*, hey? Great help that was to her! Berenilde and Archibald were as irresponsible as spoilt children, and Thorn knew it. A man who agrees to abandon his own fiancée in such a den of decadents can't decently claim to care about her.

"Close the door," Berenilde requested from her bed. She had undone her chain to give Ophelia the pretty key studded with precious stones that Archibald had given her. At the first click of the lock, a leaden silence fell upon them. In the antechamber, on the other side of the door, the croaking music from the gramophone had abruptly stopped. "Now we can speak freely," declared Berenilde with an exhausted sigh. "We'll be safe from the indiscreet as long as that door remains locked."

As Ophelia and Aunt Rosaline looked dubiously at each

other, Berenilde clicked her tongue with annoyance. As she removed each pin from her hair, the golden curls bounced gracefully onto her shoulder. "The bedrooms at Clairdelune are the most secure in the Pole, ladies. Each turn of the key places us at one remove from the world. It's a little as though we were no longer really there, do you understand? You could shout yourself hoarse, and you wouldn't be heard in the adjoining room, even if an ear were stuck to the door."

"I'm not sure I find that so reassuring," hissed Aunt Rosaline.

"We'll only lock ourselves in while we're resting," Berenilde assured her, wearily. "And for pity's sake, lower that light!"

On those words, she buried her head in her pillow and massaged her temples with a pained expression. The wig had mussed her lovely hair, and her skin, usually so silky, was as wan as a candle. And yet Ophelia had to admit that fatigue made her beauty even more affecting.

Aunt Rosaline lowered the room's lighting and shuddered when her eyes crossed Mime's unfamiliar ones. "I can't get used to that grotesque disguise! Can't you take it off, just while we're together?"

"Better not," said Berenilde. "Ophelia won't be sleeping with us—only lady's companions and nannies are allowed to share their mistress's privacy."

Aunt Rosaline's naturally jaundiced complexion turned waxen. "And so where will she go? It's my goddaughter that I'm supposed to be watching over, not you!"

"I already have a bedroom linked to yours," Ophelia hastened to reassure her, showing her the key. "I won't be far away." Deep down, she hoped her aunt would never set foot in Baths Road.

"Where's Mother?" asked Berenilde with concern, having suddenly noticed her absence.

"In the library," said Ophelia. "She didn't seem to be having too boring a time." She said nothing of the licentious stories she'd seen her enjoying with the other ladies of her age.

"You must go and fetch her soon, dear girl. In the meantime, make us some tea."

Berenilde's apartments included a small kitchen. While Aunt Rosaline put a cast-iron kettle on the gas ring, Ophelia prepared the cups. She broke only one. "Why mustn't I go near the Knight?" she asked, while looking for the sugar bowl in the pantry. Prostrate on her bed, Berenilde mopped her brow with her lace handkerchief. She would have been lucky not to feel ill after all she'd drunk and inhaled that night.

"Neither you nor Madam Rosaline must," she sighed. "He's a redoubtable illusionist. You would be the loser in his game, my dear."

"And yet together you made a charming picture," said Ophelia with surprise, as she now gathered up the sugar cubes she'd scattered on the floor.

"A different battle was going on behind our innocent game of chess. That child tries to catch me in the trap of his imagination and I exhaust myself eluding him! He'd be quite capable of toying with you simply because you're part of my retinue."

"Toying with us?" queried the aunt, frowning.

Berenilde turned her head on the pillow to give her a mocking smile. "Are you familiar with hypnosis, Madam Rosaline? It's like dreaming while remaining awake," she said, rolling each "r." "Except that dream is forcibly imposed upon you."

"What a little horror! Back home, kids aren't always angels,

I'll admit, but their most reprehensible pastime consists of ringing a doorbell and then bolting like rabbits."

As she listened, Berenilde let out a laugh so devoid of joy, it sent shivers down Ophelia's spine. "But what's he got against you?" she insisted. "To me, you seemed pretty kind to him."

Berenilde slipped her shoes off with her toe and contemplated the canvas sky above her bed. "I'm indebted to him. It's an old story, I'll tell you about it some other time."

The whistling of the kettle filled the silence that ensued. Aunt Rosaline served the tea, her lips tight as a clothes peg, but Berenilde pushed her cup away with a grimace of disgust. "My dear Ophelia, could you bring me my cigarette case, my lighter, and a little brandy, please?"

"No."

Berenilde sat up on her pillow and Aunt Rosaline spilt her tea. As incredulous as each other, they stared at the little man planted in the middle of the carpet, sugar bowl in hand.

"I don't think I quite understood you," Berenilde said, in a falsely sweet tone.

"No," Ophelia repeated, calmly. "Forgive my candor, but I can smell your breath from where I stand. Can't you see what you're putting yourself through, you and your baby? If you're incapable of being reasonable, I will be, in your place."

Aunt Rosaline's horsey teeth revealed themselves, just long enough for a fleeting smile. "She's right, a woman of your age should be particularly careful."

Aghast, Berenilde arched her brows and crossed her hands over her stomach. "Of my age?" she stammered in a flat voice. "How dare you?" Too weary to show her anger, she instantly let her head fall back on the pillow in a cascade of blond curls. "It's true that I feel a bit weird. I fear I've been unwise."

"I'm going to get you some nightclothes," Aunt Rosaline declared, drily.

Lying on her bed, lost in her beautiful crumpled dress, Berenilde suddenly seemed so vulnerable that Ophelia softened, despite herself. I should hate this woman, she thought. She's capricious, narcissistic, and calculating. So why can't I stop myself from worrying about her?

Ophelia pulled a chair over to the bed and sat down. She'd just understood that that would doubtless be her true role here: protecting Berenilde from her enemies, from her family . . . and from herself, too.

The Library

The weeks that followed were the strangest that Ophelia had ever lived through. Not a day went by—or rather, "a night," since there was no daylight at Clairdelune—without Archibald having the urge to organize a costumed ball, a grand banquet, an improvised play, or some other eccentric pastime of his own invention. Berenilde made it a point of honor to attend every event. She made conversation, smiled, embroidered, played, danced, and, back in the privacy of her room, passed out with exhaustion. These episodes of weakness didn't last long; Berenilde was keen to show herself once again in public, more radiant than ever.

"At the court, it's survival of the fittest," she would repeat to Ophelia at the rare moments they were alone. "Reveal a sign of weakness in front of others, and tomorrow, all the newspapers will talk only of your decline."

This was all fine, but Ophelia now had to live at the same rhythm as her. Every room in Clairdelune had its own "service clock," that little device on which one only had to move the hands to the right room, in the sleeping quarters, to call one's valet from anywhere at all in the castle. The 6, Baths Road bell board rang out at all hours, allowing Ophelia no rest, to such an extent that once, she found herself falling asleep while serving the tea.

Satisfying Berenilde was exhausting. She demanded blocks of ice, ginger biscuits, menthol tobacco, a footrest at the right height, cushions not filled with feathers, and then it was up to Ophelia to track down what was required. She suspected Berenilde of taking advantage of the situation, but her aunt's fate, forced into the passivity of a lady's companion, didn't appeal, either.

Indeed, sometimes, Archibald ordered long sessions of idleness. His guests then had to remain seated doing nothing other than smoking. Those who read or chatted quietly to keep boredom at bay during these sessions were very badly thought of. Ophelia would have been eternally grateful for them if she hadn't been obliged to remain beside Berenilde, standing around in the opium fumes.

However, the hardest problem for Ophelia to resolve was that of the lavatories. As a valet, she didn't have access to the conveniences for women. As for those for men, they were cruelly lacking in privacy. Ophelia had to look out for occasions when no one was around, and they were rare.

The upkeep of her personal effects wasn't an easy task, either. Ophelia could take her shirts, handkerchiefs, trousers, and stockings to the laundry, but she didn't have a spare livery. And without a livery, she was no longer Mime. So she had to wash it all herself, in the basin in her room, and put it on before it was dry. She so frequently had a cold that Fox himself ended up sympathizing with her. "What a pity they palmed such a damp corner off on you, kid!" he sighed when he saw Ophelia blowing her nose mid-service. "Give me an extra sandglass and I'll arrange for Gail to link you up to the main stove."

Easy to say. Since Ophelia had been working for Berenilde, she hadn't obtained a single break. One had to recognize that by continually breaking Archibald's earthenware dishes, she couldn't really hope for any favorable treatment. Fortunately, in Thorn's grandmother, she had found a precious ally; it was she who had given her her very first green sandglass, to thank her for bringing her a shawl. When Ophelia was looking for a snuffbox she bumped into Fox, who was himself off to serve a herbal tea to Lady Clothilde. She took the opportunity to pass him her gratuity.

"Congratulations, sonny!" he crowed, instantly pocketing it. "Promises are made to be kept, so I'm going to teach you your first lesson." With his eyes he discreetly indicated the policemen posted in the corridor. "Those gentlemen aren't there just to look good," he whispered very quietly. "They assure the safety of the family and the guests. Each one possesses a white sandglass—a one-way ticket to the dungeons! Lose your key just once, do the slightest untoward action, my lad, and they'll pitch into you."

That same day, Ophelia got herself a chain so she'd always have her key around her neck. She was checked every morning; she no longer wanted to take any risk.

All things considered, these measures were understandable. Archibald offered sanctuary to nobles who feared for their lives, prominent ministers, envied favorites. Indeed, Ophelia realized that no one here really liked anyone else. The Mirages disliked Berenilde's presence among them, but they also distrusted Archibald and his sisters, in whose hands they had placed their lives. There was plenty of smiling, but looks were equivocal, utterances ambiguous, and the atmosphere was toxic. No one trusted anyone, and if all these people drowned their sorrows with parties, it was to forget how scared they all were of each other.

The one among them who disturbed Ophelia the most was the little Knight. He was so young, so polite, so gauche behind his thick glasses that he gave the impression of being innocence itself. And yet he made everyone feel uncomfortable, in particular Berenilde, whose company he fervently sought. She conversed with him without ever looking him in the eye.

Ophelia soon discovered some new faces at Clairdelune. Many courtiers and officials came and went as though they were just passing through. Ophelia would see them hurrying into lifts that were under close surveillance, in the central gallery of the castle. They would only come back down a few days later; some never returned.

Berenilde turned away whenever she came across someone going into one of these lifts. That's when Ophelia understood that they were going to Farouk's tower. Puzzled, she studied the embassy carefully from the gardens. The castle had every appearance of being a totally enclosed space, with regular roofs and pepperpot towers beneath the starry night sky. And yet, some of these lifts rose beyond the sky, towards an invisible world.

"Lesson No. 2," said Fox when Ophelia was able to pass him another sandglass. "You'll have noticed that the architecture here is highly changeable. Never linger in the provisional rooms if you can't see anyone else there. Mother Hildegarde has been known to erase rooms when mates were still in them."

Ophelia shuddered with horror.

She'd still never met Mother Hildegarde, but, having heard her spoken about, she was starting to know her better. This Hildegarde was a foreign architect. She came from a distant and little known ark, the LandmArk, where people played with space as though with an elastic band. Ophelia had finally understood that it wasn't the Mirages' illusions that distorted the laws of physics on the Citaceleste, it was the prodigious power of Mother Hildegarde. If the bedrooms at Clairdelune were more secure than safes, it was because each turn of the key locked them into an enclosed space, that's to say, cut off from the rest of the world, totally impregnable.

Ophelia got hold of some paper and a pencil, and, during their breakfast in the servants' hall, made Fox draw her a plan of the premises. She was tired of getting lost due to the absurdities of this space. How many staircases led to impossible destinations? How many rooms had windows that defied logic?

"Whoa! You're asking too much of me!" Fox protested, scratching his red mane. "Just you try to make rooms containing more space than they should fit on to a page. What, what's up?"

With her pencil, Ophelia was hammering on a small corridor that she just couldn't get her head around. "That?" said Fox. "It's what's called a Compass Rose. Never seen one? There are loads round here." He took the pencil and drew large arrows going off in all directions. "With this Compass Rose, you've got a shortcut to the gardens on the cascades side; a shortcut to the large dining room; a shortcut to the men's smoking room; and a normal door that leads to the service corridor. The trick," he concluded, "is to memorize the colors of the doors. You get the idea?"

As she was staring at her sketch, what Ophelia grasped was that she was going to have to put her memory to work, rather than her sense of direction. She'd have liked to ask Fox where this famous Mother Hildegarde, whom he was always going on about, lived, but, alas, a mute doesn't ask questions.

That didn't stop her from learning a good deal from her contact with him—much more than with Thorn and Berenilde, in any case. As they ate meals together, Fox became increasingly talkative with Mime, sometimes giving advice without having received a sandglass in exchange: "Kid, you really mustn't bow the same way to a duke and a baron, even if they're from the same family! With the first, you bow until you can see your kneecaps; with the second, a simple bow of the head will do."

Ophelia was starting to know her way around all these aristocrats; she even went so far as to learn the order of precedence and its numerous exceptions. Titles corresponded to the nobles' fiefdoms, on the Citaceleste or in the Pole's provinces; or to honorary offices; or to privileges bestowed by Farouk. Sometimes, to all three at once.

"All notorious incompetents!" bewailed Gail. "Who can pin fake suns on to fake skies, but are incapable of fixing a boiler."

Ophelia nearly choked on her lentil stew and Fox raised his bushy eyebrows. Normally, the mechanic didn't mix with them, but on that occasion she had invited herself to their supper. She pushed Fox along the bench, planted her elbows on the table, and trained her electric-blue eye on Ophelia. Her pitch-dark, cropped hair and black monocle obscured half of her face.

"You, I've been observing you for a while now and, I must say, you intrigue me. Behind your standoffishness, you're finding out about everything and everyone. You wouldn't be a bit of a *spy*, in your own way?"

Gail had placed an ironic emphasis on that *spy* that made Ophelia uncomfortable. This woman, with her brusque manners, did she intend to denounce her to Archibald's policemen?

"You always see evil everywhere, my lovely," Fox broke in, half-smiling. "This poor chap has never seen anything other than his mistress's little manor, so it's normal he feels disorientated. And anyhow, keep out of our conversations, they're our business."

Gail paid him no attention. She remained focused on Ophelia, who was trying to chew her lentils as innocently as possible. "I'm not convinced," she muttered, finally. "The fact is, you intrigue me." She slapped her hand on the table to reinforce her words, and got up as abruptly as she'd sat down.

"Not happy about that," admitted Fox, looking peeved, when Gail had gone. "Seems like you *seriously* took her fancy. Years I've been after that woman, me."

Ophelia finished what was on her plate, feeling a little anxious. When playing the part of Mime, she wasn't supposed to attract too much attention. Then she thought about Gail's opinion of the nobles. In this world, servants had very little value. They weren't descendants of Farouk, issuing instead from the people with no powers, so had to compensate with their hands for what they couldn't contribute with their talents. It certainly gave one food for thought. A Mirage who conjures up illusions is thus considered better than those who clean his linen and prepare his meals?

The closer Ophelia got to Pole society, the more disenchanted she became. She'd come here hoping to find trustworthy people, but all she saw around her were big, capricious children . . . starting with the host. Ophelia just couldn't understand how the role of ambassador could have fallen to such an offhand and provocative man. Archibald never combed his hair, barely shaved, displayed holes in every glove, every frock coat, every hat he wore, without any of it diminishing his seraphic beauty. And this beauty he used and abused in his dealings with women. Ophelia better understood why Thorn and Berenilde were protecting her from him: Archibald's way of life consisted of leading women to commit adultery. He got all of his female guests into his bed, and then spoke to their husbands with staggering candor:

"You're as fat as a pig!" he guffawed to the provost of the merchants. "Beware, your wife is the most unsatisfied of all those whom I've had the pleasure of *visiting*."

"You seem to be showing a lot of interest in my sister Relish," he said softly to the Keeper of the Seals. "Touch her but once, and I'll make you the biggest cuckold of all the arks put together."

"Do you occasionally find yourself doing your job?" he asked the police lieutenant. "As I was saying to your wife only yesterday, anyone can just walk right into the Citaceleste! Not that it displeases me, but I've found myself bumping into the least expected people in places where they really shouldn't be . . . "

On hearing these last words, Ophelia almost tipped her tray of pastries over Berenilde's dress. She was touching wood, but Archibald still hadn't mentioned their meeting. If the Web had witnessed the scene through him, as Thorn seemed to believe they could, Archibald's sisters were likewise remaining discreet.

Did they all not care a fig about it? Or were they waiting for the right moment to slip a note to Berenilde? Ophelia felt as though she were permanently walking a tightrope.

One morning, however, it was her turn to uncover one of Archibald's little secrets. It was during one of those rare lulls when the guests were sleeping off the drunkenness of the last party and Clairdelune's metronome hadn't yet been restarted. Apart from a glassy-eyed noble wandering the corridors like a sleepwalker, only a few servants were tidying up on the ground floor.

Ophelia had gone down to find a poetry anthology that Berenilde, subject to one of those strange cravings of pregnant women, had urgently requested. When she opened the door of the library, Ophelia at first wondered whether her glasses weren't playing tricks on her. There were no more pink armchairs or crystal chandeliers. There was a musty smell, the furniture was arranged differently, and, when she scanned the shelves, she couldn't see the usual books. Gone were the licentious works; gone the doctrines of pleasure; gone the romantic poetry! All that was there were specialist dictionaries, strange encyclopedias, and, especially, an impressive collection of linguistic studies. Semiotics, phonemics, cryptanalysis, linguistic typology . . . What were such serious tomes doing in the home of the frivolous Archibald?

Her curiosity piqued, Ophelia began to leaf through a randomly plucked book—*In the Days When Our Ancestors Spoke Several Languages*—but it nearly fell from her hands when she heard Archibald's voice behind her:

"Inspiring reading?"

Ophelia turned around and breathed a sigh of relief. It wasn't her being spoken to. She hadn't noticed them when she came in, but Archibald and another man were at the back of the room, leaning over a wooden lectern. Apparently, they hadn't noticed her either.

"Certainly, it's a remarkable reproduction," commented the man with Archibald. "If I weren't an expert, I would have sworn we were dealing with an original."

He spoke with an accent Ophelia had never heard before. Concealed behind some shelving, she wasn't entirely sure she was allowed to be here, but she couldn't resist a quick, surreptitious look. The stranger was so small, he must have been standing on a stool to reach the height of the lectern.

"If you hadn't been an expert," Archibald replied, nonchalantly, "I wouldn't have treated myself to your services."

"Where's the original, *signore*?"

"Only Farouk knows. Let's make do with this copy for now. What I need to be sure of first is that you're up to this translation. Our Lord officially charged me with distributing it to all my relations, but he's losing patience, and I'm harboring under my roof a female competitor who wants to beat me to it. So I'm in rather a hurry."

"Come, come," the stranger said in his reedy little voice, laughing nervously. "I may be the best, but don't expect miracles from me! To this day, no one has ever deciphered the Book of a family spirit. What I can propose to you is a statistical study of all the distinctive features of this document: the number of signs, the frequency of each one, the size of the spacing. Then I could proceed to a comparative study of the other reproductions, of which I am the proud owner."

"And that's it? You've traveled across the world at my expense to inform me of what I already know?" Archibald's tone didn't betray any annoyance, but there was something about his honeyed diction that seemed to make the stranger uneasy.

"Forgive me, *signore*, but no one can be expected to do the impossible. What I can assure you is that the more we compare, the more the overall statistics gain in precision. Perhaps one day we'll succeed in getting some logic to emerge from the chaos of this alphabet?"

"And you're described as the best in your discipline!" sighed Archibald with disappointment. We are wasting each other's time, sir. Allow me to see you out."

Ophelia hid behind a marble bust while the two men left the library. As soon as the door was closed, she tiptoed over to the lectern. A huge book was resting on it. It was so like the one in Artemis's archives that it would be hard to tell them apart. With her reader's gloved fingertips, she carefully turned the pages. There were the same enigmatic arabesques, the same silent story, the same skin-like texture. The expert was right, this reproduction was a small masterpiece.

So, there were other Books across the arks? If that little stranger were to be believed, each family spirit possessed a copy, and if Archibald were to be believed, Lord Farouk had a burning desire to decipher his own.

Perturbed, Ophelia had a sudden premonition. The pieces of an astounding jigsaw puzzle were falling into place in her mind. That "female competitor" mentioned by Archibald, she was convinced that he meant Berenilde. This was neither the place nor the time to think, however. Her instinct told her that she shouldn't have heard what she'd heard, so best not to linger in the vicinity.

Ophelia made for the door. When she couldn't turn the handle, she realized that she'd got locked in. She looked around for a window, or a service door, but this library didn't resemble the one she knew in any way. There wasn't even a fireplace. The only source of light came from the ceiling, where an illusion, quite a successful one at that, imitated a sunrise on the sea.

Ophelia could hear her own heart beating, and suddenly realized that the silence here was abnormal. The sounds of the servants' activities no longer reached her through the walls. Anxious, she ended up banging on the door to make her presence known. Her blows produced not the slightest sound, as though she were hitting a pillow.

A double room.

Fox had already spoken to her of these rooms that superimposed two places in a single space. Only Archibald possessed the key that allowed access to each one. Ophelia was trapped in the double of the library. She sat on a chair and clarified her thoughts. Force open the door? It led nowhere. One part was there, the other no longer was, and one can't do anything to something that doesn't exist. Await Archibald's return? If he didn't come back for weeks, it promised to be a long wait.

"I must find a mirror," Ophelia then decided, getting up.

Unfortunately for her, this library wasn't as vain as the other rooms in Clairdelune. It sought neither to be visually pleasing nor to create lighting effects. Unearthing a mirror among these scholarly tomes would be a challenge. There were certainly pocket mirrors on the shelves, for deciphering texts written backwards, but Ophelia couldn't have got her hand through those.

302

She finally spotted a silver tray on which bottles of ink were kept. She cleared it and polished it with a handkerchief until she could see her reflection in it. It was narrow, but would do. Ophelia leant it against some library steps. Archibald would surely wonder what the tray was doing in such an unlikely place, but she had no choice.

Kneeling on the carpet, Ophelia conjured the image of her sleeping quarters in her mind and dived headlong into the tray. Her nose bent, her glasses crunched and her forehead rang out like a gong. Dazed, she stared at the expressionless face of Mime in front of her. The passage hadn't worked?

"Traveling through mirrors, that requires facing up to one-self," her great-uncle had said. "Those who close their eyes, those who lie to themselves, those who see themselves as better than they are, they could never do it."

Ophelia understood why the mirror had rejected her. She was wearing Mime's face and playing the part of someone other than herself. She unbuttoned her livery, and confronted her dear old reflection head-on. She had a red nose and bent glasses from the impact. It felt strange to see once again her vague expression, messy bun, shy mouth, and those shadows under her eyes. This face might be a little rough around the edges, but at least it was hers.

With Mime's livery under her arm, Ophelia was now able to pass through the tray. She landed awkwardly on the floor of her room at 6, Baths Road, and hastened to put her uniform back on. Her hands were shaking like leaves. She'd really had a narrow escape this time.

When she finally made it to Berenilde's room on the top floor of the castle, the widow looked at her with impatience from her bath. "For goodness' sake! I had to send Rosaline in search of you and I'm left with no staff to get me ready. Don't tell me you've forgotten my poetry anthology, on top of all that?" she moaned, seeing Mime return empty-handed.

Ophelia had a quick look to check no one else was in the apartments, and turned the key in the door. The nauseating gramophone in the adjoining antechamber could no longer be heard: Ophelia and Berenilde had been transported to a separate world.

"What am I to you?" Ophelia then asked, in a muted voice. Berenilde's anger instantly abated. She stretched her lovely tattooed arms along the rim of the bath.

"Pardon?"

"I'm not rich, I'm not powerful, I'm not beautiful, and I'm not loved by your nephew," Ophelia intoned. "Why force him to marry me, when just my presence causes you so many problems?"

Once over her initial astonishment, Berenilde erupted into musical laughter. The foamy water lapped against the porcelain bath while her hilarity lasted. "What kind of tragedy is playing out inside your head? I chose you by chance, my dear; it could just as easily have been the girl next door. So stop being childish and help me up. This water's getting cold!"

Ophelia then knew for certain that she was lying to her; "chance" was a word that didn't feature in the court's vocabulary. Lord Farouk was trying to find an expert to unlock the secret of his Book. What if Berenilde thought she'd finally found that expert?

The Visit

"Young man, you're a disgrace to your profession," muttered Gustave.

Ophelia looked at the brown imprint her iron had left on the paper. Of all her daily tasks, if there was one that she found particularly thankless, it was ironing the newspaper. Every morning, a bundle of papers was delivered to the servants' lobby. The valets had to redo the folds themselves, to make them more manageable for the masters. Ophelia always scorched three or four papers before ironing one properly. Fox had got into the habit of doing it for her, but not today: there had been a green sandglass, so he was enjoying a well-deserved break. And just Ophelia's bad luck, that morning the head butler was inspecting in the servants' hall.

"You will understand that I can't tolerate such wastage," he told her with a wide smile. "From now on, you're not allowed to touch the newspapers. For this once, go and give the fruits of your clumsiness to Madam Berenilde. You haven't a tongue, so at least try to have some guts, hmm?"

Gustave chuckled and left, with his hurried little steps. It wasn't the first time the head butler had amused himself by playing that little game with Mime. Behind his oily manner, he took a sly pleasure in humiliating and bad-mouthing those of a lower rank. He was no example to anyone, with his wonky wig, badly attached dicky, and alcoholic breath, and yet, according to Fox, he'd already pushed some to suicide.

Ophelia felt much too tired to protest. As she set off for the white boudoir, her scorched newspaper on a salver, she had the impression of wading through cotton wool. Between the dampness of her room, the deceptive mildness of the corridors, and the lack of sleep, she'd ended up catching tonsillitis. Her head ached, throat ached, nose ached, ears ached, eyes ached, and she was missing her old scarf. If she hadn't given Fox all her sandglasses, she would have readily reported sick.

Ophelia took advantage of the service corridor to scan the headlines on the scorched newspaper:

COUNCIL OF MINISTERS AGAIN DELIVERS SQUIB
POETRY COMPETITION—TO YOUR QUILLS, KIDS!
CARRIAGE 'DECAPITATED' AT CLAIRDELUNE
GREAT SPRING HUNT: DRAGONS SHARPEN CLAWS

Spring, already? Time had flown by so fast . . . Ophelia turned the paper over to see the weather forecast. Minus twenty-five degrees. This ark's thermometer seemed stuck at the same temperature, month after month. Would the weather be milder when the sun returned in the summer? She wasn't that keen to find out, in fact: each day that went by brought her closer to the wedding, at the end of summer.

With Berenilde's frantic pace of life, Ophelia had rarely had time to think of Thorn. And if she was sure of one thing, it was that the same would be true of him. "Your fate is of real concern to me," he'd said. Well, if he really was concerned about his fiancée's fate, it was only from a distance. He'd never shown up again since the evening of their arrival at Clairdelune; Ophelia wouldn't have been surprised if he'd totally forgotten her existence.

A fit of coughing shook her chest. She waited for it to subside before pushing open the service door that led to the white boudoir. This feminine little lounge was the most comfortable and refined in the castle; it was all lace, cushions, softness, velvet. A poetic illusion made snowflakes fall from the ceiling, without ever reaching the carpet.

Today, Berenilde and Archibald's seven sisters had gathered in the white boudoir to admire Baron Melchior's latest collection of hats. "This one shouldn't fail to please you, young lady," he said to Dulcie, passing her a leafy confection. "The roses open and bloom as the ball progresses, right up to the grand finale. I've named it 'Evening Flowering.'"

All the ladies applauded. Mirage right up to his majestic portliness, Baron Melchior had launched his own couture house. The illusory fabrics with which he embellished his creations outdid each other in originality. The more daring he was, the more successful he was. He was said to have "golden fingers." Trousers whose pattern changed throughout the day, that was Melchior. Musical ties for big occasions, Melchior. Lingerie that became invisible upon the twelfth strike of midday, Melchior.

"I really like that interior bonnet of silk tulle," Berenilde complimented him. Even though her dresses were designed to camouflage her rounded stomach, her pregnancy was becoming increasingly obvious. Standing in a corner of the boudoir, Ophelia was observing her. She couldn't understand how the widow managed to remain so beautiful and so radiant despite all her excesses.

"You're a connoisseur," responded the baron, smoothing his waxed moustache. "I've always considered you to be an exception within your family. You have the good taste of the Mirages!"

"Come, come, baron, don't be insulting," said Berenilde with her tinkling little laugh.

"Ah, the news of the day!" exclaimed Joy, helping herself from Ophelia's salver. The young girl sat elegantly on a wing chair, and then frowned. "It looks as if this paper has got a bit too close to the iron."

"Mime, you'll be deprived of your break today," declared Berenilde.

Being under no illusions, Ophelia wouldn't have expected any less of her. Aunt Rosaline, who was serving tea to all these ladies, stiffened with anger. She couldn't forgive Berenilde for any of the punishments inflicted on her goddaughter.

"Listen up, they've written about it!" said Joy, laughing, her pretty nose deep in the paper. "'The carriage procession in the Clairdelune gardens has always succeeded in standing out from the rest. Yesterday evening, the hapless Countess Ingrid demonstrated that to her own cost. Did she request too imposing a carriage? Did she select stallions too vigorous for the occasion? Cracking the whip, tightening the reins, nothing worked: the countess sped along the large avenue like a cannonball, clamoring for help.' Hold on, don't laugh yet, the best is still to come! 'Whether the carriage was too high, or the porch too low, the fact is that the vehicle saw its roof lopped off in less time than it takes to write it down. Happily, the wild ride ended well, and the countess got away with a big fright and a few bruises.'"

"What a lamentable spectacle!" exclaimed Melody.

"If being ridiculous could kill . . . " sighed Grace, leaving her sentence hanging.

"She'll pick a more modest carriage in future," reasoned Clarimond.

"Or less impetuous stallions," countered Relish.

Archibald's sisters laughed so hard they had to reach for their handkerchiefs. Ophelia's head was buzzing like a hive; she found all this babbling terribly boring. Berenilde, who looked kindly upon such youthfulness, fluttered a fan in front of her neck. "Now, now, dear girls, don't mock the mishaps of poor Ingrid too much."

"Well said," Patience concurred, stiffly. "Control yourselves a little, now, silly girls. The countess is our guest."

Archibald's sisters lived up to their names. Patience always showed levelheadedness; Joy made light of everything; Melody saw everything as a pretext for a work of art; Grace attached the utmost importance to appearances; Clarimond enlightened her audience with her sensible opinions; and Relish saw life as being all about sensuality. As for little Dulcie, she was so smooth that even the rudest words fell from her mouth as pearls.

The Web. The clan's name made total sense when one saw them all together. Despite their differences in age and temperament, the sisters seemed to form one and the same person. If one held out her hand, another immediately passed her powder compact, sugar tongs, gloves, without them even needing to consult each other. When one began a sentence, another finished it as naturally as anything. On some occasions, they all started to laugh at the same time for no apparent reason. On others, quite the opposite: they blushed with embarrassment and none of them could follow the conversation anymore. This generally happened when Archibald "visited" one of his guests in a castle bedroom.

Archibald . . . Since the episode in the library, Ophelia could no longer stifle a feeling of some uneasiness. She felt as though she had put her finger on something essential, but she could speak about it to no one, especially not to Berenilde. The more she thought about it, the more she was convinced that the favorite had orchestrated Thorn's marriage to bolster her position with regards to Farouk.

"Baron, may I have a quick look at your ribbons?" asked Dulcie in her beguiling voice. Baron Melchior put down his cup of tea and broke into a smile that lifted both sides of his moustache upright, like sticks. "I was waiting for you to ask me that, young lady. I thought especially of you for my new collection."

"Of me?" When the baron opened up his case, Dulcie squealed with delight. Against a black velvet backing, each colored ribbon had a butterfly on it, fluttering its wings. The young girl was determined to try every one of them. "Bring me the large mirror."

Dazed with tiredness, it took Ophelia a while to realize that the order was addressed to her.

"It's impolite to appropriate someone else's servant like that," lectured Patience.

"Use my staff as you please, my darling," said Berenilde, affectionately stroking the little girl's hair. "I don't need them at the moment."

310

The large mirror weighed a ton, but Dulcie proved to be as ruthless as Berenilde. "Don't put it down," she ordered Ophelia. "Hold it like this so it's at my height. No, don't lean it over, bend your legs instead. Right, stay in that position."

Dulcie gave her orders in a caressing voice, as though doing a great favor. With long hair of incomparable fineness, a pearly complexion, and eyes like pure, deep pools, she already enjoyed exploiting her charms. Ophelia wasn't very sensitive to them. Having already seen her throwing spectacular tantrums, she knew that these refined manners were but a varnish that cracked at the first aggravation. She sincerely pitied the man who would marry her.

While Ophelia, gripping the mirror, battled an uncontrollable urge to sneeze, the ladies chatted, laughed, drank tea, tried on hats.

"Madam Berenilde, you should dismiss your valet," Melchior suddenly declared, putting a handkerchief to his nose. "He keeps coughing and sniffing, it's utterly unpleasant."

If Ophelia had been able to speak, she'd have readily agreed with the baron, but a discreet knock at the door saved Berenilde from having to respond. "Go and open," she told her.

Stiff with cramps, Ophelia wasn't sorry to put the mirror down for a moment. When she opened the door she was far too startled to bow. Two heads above her, rigid in his black uniform with epaulettes, thinner and gloomier than ever, Thorn was winding his watch.

He entered without a glance at Ophelia. "Ladies," he half-heartedly greeted them. A stunned silence had fallen on the little boudoir. Berenilde stopped fluttering her fan, Aunt Rosaline hiccupped with surprise, the sisters held their teacups in midair, and Dulcie ran to hide in the petticoats of the eldest. This huge, taciturn man shattered, merely by his presence, the feminine charm of the room. He was so tall that the fake snow fluttered down before his eyes like a swarm of white flies. Berenilde was the first to pull herself together.

"You've got no manners!" she teased him in her lovely husky accent. "You should have announced your arrival, you've caught us off guard."

Thorn chose an armchair that wasn't overflowing with either cushions or lace, and, bending his great wader's legs, sat in it. "I had to drop off some files at the ambassador's office. I'm taking advantage of my visit to check on how you're feeling, aunt. I won't stay long."

At this last sentence, all of Archibald's sisters breathed a sigh of relief. For her part, Ophelia found it the hardest thing in the world to maintain her role, motionless in her corner, without being able to look Thorn in the face. She knew that he wasn't very popular, but it was something else to observe it for herself. Did he know what Mime actually looked like? Did he have any idea that his fiancée was present in the room, a mute spectator of his unpopularity?

Thorn seemed unconcerned about the chill his arrival had cast. He rested his briefcase on his knees and lit himself a pipe, despite the disapproving coughs all around him. With a frown he turned down the tea Aunt Rosaline offered him; out of the two of them, it was hard to decide whose lips were most pursed.

"Mr. Treasurer!" exclaimed Baron Melchior with a smile. "I'm very pleased to see you; I've been requesting an audience for months!" Thorn gave him a steely look that would have put more than a few off, but the fat baron didn't let it bother him. He rubbed his heavily ringed hands together, gleefully. "Your marriage is eagerly awaited, you know? Such a ceremony can't just be thrown together at the last moment, as I'm sure a man as organized as you well knows. I undertake to concoct the most adorable wedding dress ever for your beloved!"

Ophelia almost gave herself away with a sudden urge to cough.

"I'll see when the time comes," declared Thorn, lugubriously.

The baron plucked a notebook from his hat as a magician would a white rabbit. "It won't take a minute. Could you give me the lady's measurements?"

It was without doubt the most embarrassing situation Ophelia had ever been in. She wished she could disappear under the carpet.

"I'm not interested," insisted Thorn, his voice thundery. Melchior's heavily brilliantined moustache collapsed in tandem with his smile. His tattooed eyelids blinked several times, and he put his notebook away. "As you please, Mr. Treasurer," he said with a fearsome sweetness. He closed his case of ribbons and piled all of his hats in a box. Ophelia was sure that Thorn had seriously offended him. "I bid you good day," Melchior muttered to the ladies, and then left.

An awkward silence returned to the boudoir. From the depths of the eldest's petticoats, little Dulcie eyed Thorn's scars with a pout of disgust.

"You've lost weight again," Berenilde chided. "With all those ministerial banquets, don't you ever take the time to eat, then?"

Relish winked at her sisters and approached Thorn's chair, a mischievous smile on her lips. "We're longing to meet your little Animist, Mr. Thorn," she cooed. "You're so secretive!"

Ophelia was starting to worry about being the subject of all these conversations. She hoped her meeting with Archibald wasn't about to be laid on the table. Since Thorn merely consulted his fob watch, Relish got bolder and leant towards him. Her little blonde curls wriggled with every movement of her head. "Could you at least tell us what she looks like?"

Thorn fixed his ferrous eyes so abruptly on hers that Relish lost her smile. "I could tell you what she doesn't look like."

Behind Mime's impassive mask, Ophelia raised her eyebrows. What did he mean by that?

"My Treasury needs me," concluded Thorn, closing the cover of his watch. He rose and, in two long strides, was gone. Disconcerted, Ophelia closed the door behind him. It wasn't really worth him coming by for so little . . .

Conversations immediately resumed in the boudoir as though never interrupted: "Oh, Madam Berenilde! Would you accept to perform with us in the Spring Opera?"

"You'd be perfect in the part of the beautiful Isolde!"

"And Lord Farouk is to attend the performance. It will be a chance for you to give him your kind regards!"

"Perhaps," Berenilde replied, flapping her fan and paying barely any attention.

As she blew her nose, Ophelia wondered whether Berenilde was angry. She only understood the cause much later, when Berenilde pointed to the floor with her fan: "What do I see there, on the carpet?" Ophelia crouched at the foot of the chair Thorn had sat in and picked up a lovely silver stamp.

"It's the seal of the Treasury," observed Clarimond. "Your nephew must be very put out to have mislaid it."

Since Ophelia just stood there, arms dangling, Berenilde struck her with her fan. "Well," she said, annoyed, "what are you waiting for to return it to him?"

The Treasury

Ophelia stared at the pale, flat figure of Mime in the mirror on the wall. Only she and an aristocrat remained in the waiting room, and he kept fiddling with his top hat and, every now and then, glancing impatiently at the office's frosted-glass door. Ophelia watched him without appearing to, through the mirror. Like many Mirages, he was a healthy-looking man, almost bursting out of his jacket, and with both eyelids stamped with tattoos. Since his arrival, he had been continually checking the mantel clock. Nine twenty. Ten forty. Eleven fifty-five. Quarter past midnight.

Ophelia stifled a sigh. At least he hadn't been waiting since morning. Having got lost in countless lifts, she'd been standing here all day. She felt so tired that her vision was starting to blur, despite her glasses. Visitors were received in order of precedence, and valets were at the bottom of the list. Ophelia avoided looking at the many empty chairs, and the sideboard on which coffee and petits fours had been served. She wasn't allowed any of that.

She would have been perfectly happy to drop the seal off at the office, but she knew she couldn't. If Berenilde had been that annoyed, it was because Thorn had forgotten it deliberately, and if he'd forgotten it deliberately, it was because he'd wanted to instigate a meeting.

The glass door finally opened. A man came out, politely tipping his hat at the colleague who remained in the waiting room. "Goodbye, Mr. Vice President," said the secretary. "Mr. Councillor? If you'd care to follow me."

The Mirage went into the office with an irate grunt and Ophelia found herself alone. No longer able to resist, she grabbed a cup of coffee, dunked a petit four in it, and sat on the nearest chair. The coffee was cold and swallowing was painful, but she was famished. Ophelia gobbled up all the petits fours on the sideboard, blew her nose twice, and then instantly fell asleep.

She had to stand up smartly when the door opened, an hour later. The Mirage councillor left, even more disgruntled than when he'd gone in. The secretary closed the glass door without a glance at Ophelia.

Unsure, she waited a little, then knocked a few times to remind him of her presence. "What do you want?" he asked through the half-open door. Ophelia indicated that she was unable to speak, and pointed inside the office. She wanted to come in like the others, wasn't that obvious?

"The Treasurer needs some rest. I'm not disturbing him for a valet. If you have a message, give it to me."

Ophelia couldn't believe it. She'd been stuck here for hours and she wasn't even afforded the favor of an audience? She shook Mime's head and pointed obstinately at the door the secretary was blocking with his foot.

"Are you deaf as well as mute? Too bad." He slammed the door in Ophelia's face. She could have left the seal in the waiting room and gone back empty-handed, but she did nothing

318

of the sort. Her mood was souring. Thorn had wanted to lure her over here? He would have to accept the consequences. She hammered at the door until the bewigged silhouette of the secretary reappeared behind the frosted glass. "Clear off or I'll call the police!"

"So, what's going on here?"

Ophelia recognized Thorn's hard accent.

"Oh, sir has come down?" stammered the secretary. "Sir mustn't worry, it's just a little ruffian I'm about to kick on his way."

Behind the glass, the silhouette of the secretary was replaced by the tall, thin one of Thorn. When he opened the door and lowered his sharp nose down to Ophelia, for a moment she feared he didn't recognize her. She raised her chin to look directly back at him.

"Insolent!" exclaimed the secretary. "That's too much, I'm calling the police."

"It's my aunt's messenger," Thorn rasped through gritted teeth. The secretary's face fell and then adopted a mortified expression. "As sir can see, I'm utterly embarrassed. A regrettable misunderstanding."

Ophelia shivered. Thorn had placed a large, freezing-cold hand on the nape of her neck to push her into a lift, at the back of the office. "Switch off the unnecessary lights, I will be receiving no one else for today."

"Yes, sir."

"My appointments for tomorrow?"

The secretary donned thick spectacles and flicked through a notebook. "I had to cancel them, sir. As he left, Mr. Vice President handed me notification for you to attend the Council of Ministers, at five o'clock this morning."

"Have you received the chef's inventory of cellars and store-rooms?"

"No, sir."

"I need that report for the Council. Get hold of it."

"The storerooms, sir?" They couldn't have been next door, since the secretary didn't seem keen on the prospect of going there. He bowed, nevertheless. "Certainly, sir. Goodbye, sir."

With an endless sequence of bows and "sir"s, the obsequious secretary departed.

Thorn pulled back the gate of the lift. Ophelia was finally alone with him. And yet they exchanged not a word or a look as the lift slowly gained altitude. The Treasury had been established in one of the Citaceleste's many turrets. The distance between stops from the office to Thorn's study seemed interminable to Ophelia, so oppressive was the silence in the lift. As much as she blew her nose, sneezed, coughed, stared at her shoes, Thorn said nothing to put her at ease.

The lift stopped in front of a vast corridor with as many doors as a piano has keys. Probably a Compass Rose. Thorn pushed open a double door at the end of the corridor. As the saying goes, it's the job that makes the man, not the man that makes the job. When Ophelia saw the Treasury, she wondered whether that wasn't particularly true in Thorn's case. The study was an austere, cold room that allowed for not the slightest eccentricity. The office furnishings were reduced to a large desk, a few seats, and filing cabinets in the four corners of the room. No carpet on the floor, no pictures on the paneling, no knickknacks on the shelves. Of all the gas lamps, only the one on the desk was lit. The somber atmosphere of the wood wasn't brightened up by any colors, apart from the book

320

bindings all along the shelving. Abacuses, maps, and graphs served as decoration. In fact, the single frivolous touch was a threadbare old sofa, placed under a bull's-eye window.

"You can express yourself here without fear," said Thorn, after locking the doors behind him.

He took off the uniform with the epaulettes. Now he was just in a simple jacket, buttoned over an impeccably white shirt. How come he wasn't cold? Despite the cast-iron radiator, it was freezing cold in the study.

Ophelia pointed at the bull's-eye window. "What does that window look onto?" She put her hand to her neck. Her voice was rusty as an old gate. Between the sore throat and Mime's mutism, her vocal cords had suffered. Hearing it, Thorn had arched his scarred brow. That was the only movement animating his long, rigid face. Maybe she was imagining it, but Ophelia found him even stiffer than usual.

"The outdoors," he finally replied.

"The real outdoors?"

"Indeed."

Ophelia couldn't resist the temptation. She perched on the sofa, like a little girl, to press her nose against the porthole. Despite its double thickness, the glass was as cold as ice. Ophelia looked down below and saw the shadows of the ramparts, arches, and towers. It was breathtaking. There was even an airship landing strip! With her glove she wiped the condensation from the glass. As she glimpsed a patch of night sky through a lace of frost and icicles, she held her breath. Strange whirlwinds were leaving colored trails in the midst of the stars. Could they be the aurora borealis? Mesmerized, Ophelia wondered how long it was since she'd last seen the sky.

Suddenly, her throat tightened, and it wasn't just due to her illness. She was thinking of all those starry nights back in her little Valley that she'd never taken time to contemplate.

Ophelia would have forgotten all about Thorn, behind her, if the shrill ring of a telephone hadn't snatched her from her thoughts. He gave her a quick look to urge discretion, and answered the call. "Yes? Brought forward? Four o'clock, I'll be there."

He put the ear trumpet back on the phone's hook and returned to Ophelia. She expected an explanation, but Thorn just leant on his desk, arms crossed, as though he were the one expecting something. So she rummaged in her uniform's pockets, placed the seal on the desk, and cleared her throat to help her voice. "Your ruse didn't please your aunt. And, to be perfectly frank, I didn't particularly appreciate it, either," she added, thinking back to the waiting room. "Wouldn't it have been simpler just to phone Clairdelune?"

Thorn's large nose emitted an annoyed snort. "The lines in Citaceleste aren't secure. And it wasn't my aunt I wanted to speak to."

"In that case, I'm listening." Ophelia had spoken more curtly than intended. No doubt Thorn had a good reason for prompting this meeting, but she wasn't feeling herself. If he beat around the bush for too long, he'd pay the price.

"That disguise makes me feel uncomfortable," Thorn declared, checking his watch. "Remove it, please."

Ophelia fiddled nervously with the button on her collar. "I'm only wearing a shift under my livery." She instantly felt ashamed for having revealed her prudery. This was exactly the kind of conversation she didn't want to be having with Thorn.

In any case, he wasn't a man to be stirred by such things. Indeed, he impatiently snapped shut the cover of his watch and, with his eyes, indicated a wardrobe behind the desk. "Take a coat."

Do this, do that . . . In some respects, Thorn took after his aunt. Ophelia went around the solid-wood desk to open the door of the wardrobe. Inside there were only clothes belonging to Thorn, all excessively austere and inordinately large. Having no choice, she took a long coat off its hanger. With a quick look, she reassured herself that Thorn wasn't watching her; he conspicuously had his back to her. Courtesy? Irony? Indifference?

Ophelia unbuttoned her livery and pulled on the coat. She frowned on seeing her reflection in the mirror inside the door. She was so small and the coat so big, she looked like a child in adult clothing. With her chapped lips and inflamed nose, she really looked a mess. Her dark curls, badly tied in a bun, fell around her cheeks, emphasizing the paleness of her skin. Her gray-tinted glasses didn't even conceal the dark rings shadowing her eyes. Ophelia looked so pitiful, she felt her attack of prudery was even more ridiculous.

Too tired to remain standing, she sat in the desk chair. It had been made to measure for Thorn; her feet no longer touched the ground. "I'm listening," she then repeated.

Leaning on the other side of the large desk, Thorn pulled a small piece of paper from his jacket pocket and slid it across the writing folder to Ophelia. "Read."

Taken aback, Ophelia rolled up the coat's flapping sleeves and seized the rectangle of paper. A telegram?

ery

MR. THORN TREASURY CITACELESTE, POLE
NO NEWS FROM YOU SINCE YOUR DEPARTURE
YOU COULD REPLY TO MOTHER'S LETTERS
ANGERED BY YOUR SILENCE AND INGRATITUDE
COUNTING ON ROSALINE TO WRITE TO US—AGATHA

Staggered, Ophelia read the message several times.

"It's rather annoying," said Thorn, flatly. "Your Doyennes have committed a blunder in revealing this address to your family. I must absolutely not be contacted at the Treasury, particularly by telegram."

Ophelia raised her chin to look him straight in the eye, from the other side of the desk. This time she was well and truly furious with him. Thorn was responsible for her letters. Because of him, she had felt forgotten by her parents, while they had been worried. "What are these letters my sister is talking about?" she asked, accusingly. "You've never delivered a thing to me. Did you even send those that we entrusted to you?"

She must have looked really angry because Thorn lost his composure. "It's not me who inadvertently mislaid all those letters," he protested.

"So, who is playing at intercepting our correspondence?"

Thorn lifted and then closed the cover of his watch. Ophelia was starting to find it annoying, his forever checking the time like this.

"I don't know, but that person is skillful. Control of the postal system is part of the remit of my position. Without this telegram, I would never have been alerted to these disappearances."

Ophelia tucked a curl of hair, which was bobbing against her nose, behind her ear. "Do I have your permission to read it?" The phrase could have been confusing, but Thorn understood immediately what she was getting at. "I'm not the owner. You don't need to seek my permission."

In the shade of her glasses, Ophelia raised her eyebrows. How did he know that? Ah, yes, Aunt Rosaline and she had talked about it in the airship, at the second-in-command's table. Behind his haughty demeanor, Thorn was quite attentive after all. "You were the last person to touch it," she explained. "I can't avoid reading you in the process."

The idea didn't seem to appeal to Thorn. His thumb opened, closed, reopened, reclosed the cover of his fob watch. "The stamp on the telegram is authentic," he said. "I doubt it's a fake, if that's what concerns you." Thorn's eyes, like two slivers of metal, shone strangely in the light of the desk lamp. Each time they were turned on Ophelia, as they were now, she felt as though they were trying to penetrate her very soul. "Unless, of course, it's my word that you're questioning," he concluded in his hard accent. "Would you not rather be seeking to read me?"

Ophelia shook her head. "You overestimate me. A reader doesn't penetrate the depths of people's minds. What I can capture is a fleeting state of mind, what you've seen, heard, felt at the very moment of handling the object, but I assure you it remains superficial."

Arguing had never been Ophelia's strong point. The cover of Thorn's watch was now relentlessly going click click, click click, click click. "Someone is messing with my correspondence," she sighed, "I no longer want to run the risk of being manipulated."

To her great relief, Thorn finally put his watch back into his jacket pocket. "You have my permission."

As Ophelia was unbuttoning her protective glove, he was observing her with the distant curiosity peculiar to him. "Can you read absolutely everything?"

"Not everything, no. I can read neither organic matter nor raw materials. People, animals, plants, minerals in their crude state are all beyond my scope." Ophelia looked at Thorn over the top of her glasses, but he asked no further questions. When she took the telegram with her bare hand, she was instantly traversed by a mental turmoil that took her breath away. As she had expected, Thorn wasn't truly calm. On the outside, he was a slab of marble; on the inside, one thought immediately led to another, at such a pace that Ophelia was incapable of intercepting a single one. Thorn thought a lot, and he thought very fast. She'd never read anything like it in anyone else.

Going back in time, she soon detected the astonishment that had hit him when he had discovered the telegram. He hadn't lied, he knew nothing about the stolen letters.

Ophelia delved further into the past. The telegram went from Thorn to an unknown person, and from an unknown person to another unknown person. They were all employees of the postal service, all preoccupied with the petty concerns of daily life. They were cold, they had sore feet, they wanted a better wage, but not one of them showed the slightest curiosity about the message destined for the Treasury. Ophelia couldn't go back further than the hands of the telegraphic operator who transcribed into letters the sound signals from a receiver.

"Where's the telegraphic station?" she asked.

"In Citaceleste, near the airship hangars."

Thorn had taken advantage of this reading to tidy his papers, sitting at the other end of the desk, which he normally kept for visitors. He was classifying, stamping, filing bills.

"And where does she receive the signals from?"

"When it's a telegram from another ark, like this one, she receives it directly from North Wind," he said, not looking up from his sorting. "It's a minor interfamilial ark, dedicated to airmail and the postal service."

As ever when Ophelia asked him questions, Thorn replied reluctantly, as though forcing himself to remain patient.

Ophelia was seriously wondering whether he thought her mind too slow. The fact is that she couldn't rival the frantic workings of his brain. "Like you, I believe this telegram is authentic," Ophelia declared while re-buttoning her glove. "And I also believe you're being honest. Forgive me for having doubted you."

At that, Thorn did look up from his bills. He clearly wasn't used to such politeness as he found nothing to say and remained stiff as a scarecrow. It could have been because it was the end of the day, but his light hair, which he always combed back, now fell over his forehead, casting a shadow over the scar on his eyebrow.

"That doesn't resolve the mystery of the letters' disappearance," added Ophelia, embarrassed by the silence. "My presence in the Pole is no longer much of a secret. What do you suggest?"

"We know nothing of the interceptor or the motive," Thorn finally said. "So we won't change our strategy. You will play the mute valet at Clairdelune, while a servant pretends to be you at my aunt's manor." At which he unscrewed the globe from the lamp, exposing the bluish flame, and burnt the telegram without further ado.

Ophelia took off her glasses to massage her eyelids. Her reading had intensified her headache. Even if she'd only skimmed the surface, Thorn's accelerated thoughts had made her feel dizzy. Did he live with that all the time?

"This masquerade is becoming absurd," she whispered. "In any case, what does it matter to us if I'm discovered after our marriage rather than before it? Being married won't make me less vulnerable to the family's outrageous behavior, to petty acts of vengeance and other conspiracies." Ophelia coughed to clear her voice. She was becoming increasingly hoarse. At this rate, she'd end up truly voiceless. "I think we should stop being so cautious and I should stop hiding," she concluded. "Come what may."

She put her glasses back on with a resolute flourish. Doing so, her elbow knocked an ink pot, spilling its contents over the fine, glossy wood of the desk. Thorn got up and swiftly saved his bills from the black tide, while Ophelia rummaged in the pockets of her livery, folded on the chair, to pull out all her handkerchiefs. "I'm so sorry," she said, wiping the mess. Then she noticed that she'd smeared ink on Thorn's coat. "I'll take it to the dry cleaner's," she promised, even more embarrassed.

Gripping his bills, Thorn looked at her without saying a word. When Ophelia's eyes met his, right at the top of the tall, thin body, she was surprised not to detect a trace of anger in them. Thorn mainly seemed disconcerted. He ended up looking away, as if he were more at fault than Ophelia. "You're mistaken," he muttered, putting his papers away in a drawer.

"When I've married you, if everything works out as I'm hoping, our situation will be very different."

"Why?"

Thorn passed her a sheaf of blotting paper. "You've been living at Archibald's for a while, perhaps you're more familiar now with the particularities of his family?"

"Some of them, yes." Ophelia laid the blotting paper wherever ink was still spreading on the desk. "Is there something else I need to know about them?"

"Have you heard talk of the ceremony of the Gift?"

"No."

Thorn looked exasperated. He would have preferred a "yes." This time he started going through the registers stored in a cabinet, as though he wanted at all costs to keep his eyes focused on something. "A member of the Web is present at every marriage," he explained in his voice of eternal gloom. "By a placing of hands, they forge a link between the couple that enables them to be 'twinned.'"

"What are you trying to tell me?" stammered Ophelia, who had stopped wiping the desk.

Thorn again seemed irritated. "That soon, you will have taken part of me and I part of you."

Ophelia's entire body shuddered under the big, black coat. "I'm not sure I quite understand," she whispered. "I'll make you a gift of my Animism, and you of . . . of your claws trick?"

Hunched over his cabinet, nose deep in an accounts register, Thorn grunted a reply that was more a clearing of the throat. "This marriage will at least have the advantage of making you stronger, no? You should feel pleased."

For Ophelia, this was one sarcasm too many. She threw all

the blotting paper onto the desk, went over to the cabinet, and placed her ink-stained glove on the page Thorn was busy reading. When he lowered his razor blade eyes onto her, she defied him with her glasses. "When were you intending to tell me about this?"

"In due course," he grunted.

Thorn was uncomfortable, which only put Ophelia into an even worse mood. He wasn't behaving as usual and it made her nervous. "Do you have so little confidence in me, to do all this hiding from me?" she persisted. "And yet I think I've shown plenty of goodwill up to now."

With her croaky voice, Ophelia felt pathetic, but her reproaches caught Thorn off guard. His stern features had all loosened due to the surprise. "I am conscious of the efforts that you make."

"But it's not enough," she muttered, "and you're right. You can keep your no-go world. I'm far too clumsy to be entrusted with Dragon's claws." Shaken by a coughing fit, Ophelia removed her hand from the register.

Thorn contemplated the inky imprint left by the little glove for a long time, as though hesitating to say something. "I will teach you," he suddenly declared. He seemed as embarrassed at saying these four words as Ophelia was at hearing them. No, she thought. Not that. He has no right.

"It would certainly be the first time you went to such trouble," she said, reproachfully and looking away. Increasingly disturbed, Thorn opened his mouth, but the ringing of the telephone stopped him short.

"What?" he muttered, on answering it. "Three o'clock? Fine. Yes, good night."

As he was replacing the receiver, Ophelia gave a final, totally pointless, wipe with her handkerchief to the vast ink stain imprinted on the desk. "I'd better go back. Could I borrow your wardrobe, please?" With Mime's livery over her arm, she was indicating the mirror on the still-open door. She needed to leave before it was too late.

Deep down, she knew it was already too late.

As she leant towards the mirror, Ophelia saw Thorn's lofty figure approaching stiffly. His face had turned dark and thunderous. He hadn't appreciated the turn their conversation had taken. "Are you coming back?" he said, gruffly.

"Why?" She couldn't stop herself from being on the defensive. In the mirror, she saw Thorn's reflection frowning hard enough to distort his scar.

"Thanks to your ability to travel through mirrors, you could keep me informed of the situation at Clairdelune. And," he added more quietly, taking a sudden interest in his shoes, "I think I'm starting to get used to you." He had said this last sentence in the neutral tone of an accountant, but Ophelia started to shake. Her head was spinning. Her vision was blurred.

He didn't have the right.

"I'll lock the wardrobe when I'm receiving visitors," Thorn continued. "If the door is open, it means you can enter here in total safety, at any time of the day, or of the night."

Ophelia stuck her finger into the mirror as though it were dense water and, suddenly, she caught sight of the two of them. A small Animist swallowed by her too-big coat, looking sickly and dazed. A Dragon, huge, edgy, brow furrowed by constant mental tension. Two irreconcilable worlds.

"Thorn, I must be honest with you. I think we're making

331

a mistake. This marriage . . . " Ophelia stopped just in time, realizing what she'd almost said: this marriage is but a plot of Berenilde's; she's using us for her own ends, we mustn't enter into her game.

She couldn't reasonably announce that to Thorn without having proof of what she was suggesting. "I know we can no longer turn back," she sighed. "The future you're offering me simply doesn't appeal to me."

In the mirror, Thorn's jaws had tightened. He, who never attached any importance to the opinion of others, seemed humiliated. "I had predicted that you wouldn't last the winter, and you've proved me wrong. You deem me incapable of one day offering you a decent life; would you permit me, in turn, to prove myself?"

He was speaking in small bursts, his teeth clenched, as if this matter demanded an enormous effort from him. As for Ophelia, she didn't feel at all well. She had no desire to reply to him.

He didn't have the right.

"Could you send a telegram to my family to reassure them?" she stammered pathetically.

Ophelia noticed a spark of anger in the reflection of Thorn's eyes. For a second, she thought he was going to send her packing, but, instead, he agreed. She immersed herself entirely in the wardrobe mirror and stepped out into her sleeping quarters, at the other end of the Citaceleste. She stood still in the cold darkness, lost inside her coat, her stomach so knotted she felt nauseous. From Thorn she'd been ready for anything. Brutality. Disdain. Indifference.

He didn't have the right to fall in love with her.

The Orange

Ophelia contemplated her buttered bread without appetite. All around her, the servants' hall was buzzing with gossiping and giggling. She felt as if the merest clink of a cup was reverberating on the surface of her skull.

Since she'd returned from the Treasury, several days ago now, she couldn't get to sleep anymore. And yet it wasn't for lack of exhausting herself at work. On top of his usual duties, Mime now served as a page turner. Berenilde had ended up accepting the part of Isolde for the Spring Opera, and she didn't miss a single rehearsal in the music room. "I'm going to be more demanding of you than ever," she had declared to Ophelia after learning of the disappearance of the letters. "No one here must doubt that you could be anything other than a valet to me."

In truth, Ophelia didn't care. She had just one desire: to get Thorn out of her head. He had had the poor taste to turn a conventional marriage arrangement into a soppy little story, and she hadn't forgiven him for that. In her eyes, he'd just broken a tacit agreement. Cordial and dispassionate relations, that's all she aspired to. Because of him, an unease hovered between them that hadn't been there before.

As Ophelia was trying to swallow down her coffee, a slap on the back made her spill half of it over the table. Fox straddled the bench and shoved his watch under her nose, knocking into a colleague as he did so. "Get a move on, sonny. The funeral ceremony's about to begin!"

Madam Frida, an elderly cousin of Archibald, had been struck down by a heart attack at the last Clairdelune ball, after an excessively boisterous dance. This morning she was being buried in the family vault.

As Ophelia indicated to Fox to go on ahead, he squinted at her while frowning with his enormous red eyebrows. "So what's up with you? You never say a thing anymore! Well, yes, you've never been chatty, but before, you'd speak to me with your eyes, or hands, or scribbles, and we understood each other. Now, I feel like I'm alone, waffling to a wall! It's starting to really worry me."

Ophelia looked at Fox in astonishment. He was worried about her? She jumped when a basket of oranges landed right in the middle of her buttered bread. "Can you deliver that for me?"

It was Gail, the black-monocled mechanic. As usual, she was swimming in her soot-covered overalls and hiding her face behind a cloud of dark hair.

"Bloody hell!" swore Fox. "Where d'you get those oranges?" Like all exotic fruit, oranges were only ever seen on the nobles' tables. Archibald owned a private orchard on the distant ark of LandmArk. Ophelia knew that a Compass Rose provided access to it, spanning thousands of kilometers with no regard for the basic laws of geography, but only the steward possessed the key.

"To my knowlege, the LandmArk orange grove also belongs to Mother Hildegarde," said Gail in a grating voice. "It's her home, after all."

"Exactly as I thought," sighed Fox, scratching his side-whiskers, "you helped yourself in the master's larder. Out of the question that I touch stolen fruit. Ask me whatever you like apart from that."

"I'm not asking you anything. I'm talking to the new guy." Gail rolled her single eye over to Ophelia. An eye so blue, so bright, so sparkling that the black curls that cascaded over it didn't manage to obscure it. "Deliver that to my boss, will you? She'll be at the funeral of the old lady and I know you have to go, too. Promise it won't cause you any problems."

"Why him?" grumbled Fox, scowling. "Why not you, for example?"

Ophelia was wondering the same thing, but the thought of finally meeting Mother Hildegarde didn't displease her. She was a foreigner, like her, and yet she'd succeeded in making herself indispensable to all the important people in this world. The elevation of the Citaceleste into the sky, the air currents for the dog sleighs, the distortions of space, the strong rooms, the concept of the sandglasses: there wasn't a thing here that didn't bear her trademark. Her stroke of genius had been to combine her power over space with the Mirages' illusions. Ophelia had a lot to learn from her.

She stiffened when Gail leaned over the table until nose to nose with Mime's face. She spoke in such a low voice that Ophelia could barely hear her in the midst of the general hubbub. "Why you, hey? Because I've not stopped watching you since you got here. You feel as if you don't fit in, and you're absolutely right. Know why my boss is called 'Mother,' and not 'Duchess' or 'Countess'? Because she's not one of them. She's the mother of folk like you and me. Bring her these oranges, she'll understand."

Under Ophelia's flabbergasted gaze, Gail sauntered off with her tomboy swagger, hands in pockets. "Don't fit in?" What did she mean by that?

"Well, didn't understand a word of that, me," declared Fox, combing his fiery mop. "Known her since she was a young thing, that woman, but don't think I'll ever understand her." He let out a dreamy, almost admiring, sigh, then shook his watch in front of Ophelia. "We're less and less early. Lift your bum off this bench!"

The funeral ceremony of the late Madam Frida was held at the Clairdelune chapel, right at the back of the estate, beyond the fir-tree forest, beyond the Plate-of-Silver pond. As soon as she set foot inside, following a procession of nobles clad in black, Ophelia sensed a change of atmosphere. Seen from outside, the chapel looked like the ruin of a small, unpretentious fortified castle, which added a romantic touch to the gardens. Once past the large door, one entered a dark and disturbing world. The marble tiling made every step, every whisper echo right up to the vaulted roof. Imposing stained-glass windows were lashed by fake rain and lit up by fake lightning. Each flash allowed a glimpse of the glass images between the lead borders: a chained wolf; a water serpent; a hammer struck by a thunderbolt; an eight-legged horse; a half-dark, half-light face.

With basket of oranges under arm, Ophelia cast an anxious look around the chapel, which was packed with the high society. How was she going to recognize Mother Hildegarde?

"Key, if you please," a policeman posted at the entrance said to her. Ophelia tugged on her chain and presented him with her key. To her great astonishment, he then gave her a black umbrella. It was so heavy, it took her breath away. The policeman was distributing them to all the valets he was in charge of. They then held them aloft over the heads of their masters, as if to protect them from invisible rain. Was this whole performance part of the funeral ceremony? Ophelia felt sorry for the family. It couldn't be easy to mourn in such a ludicrous scenario.

Ophelia spotted Berenilde and her mother. Aunt Rosaline wasn't with them—only valets were authorized to attend the funeral. "Why these oranges?" asked Berenilde, unashamedly beautiful in her mourning dress. "Did I ask for any such thing?" Ophelia tried to explain to her, with the help of much gesticulating, that she had to deliver them to someone in the crowd. "We don't have time," decreed Berenilde, "the ceremony is about to begin. What are you waiting for to open your umbrella?"

Ophelia hastened to obey, but there were crystal pendants dangling from every rib of the umbrella. That explained its weight. Burdened with Gail's basket, Ophelia would have ended up dropping everything on the floor if Thorn's grandmother hadn't, yet again, come to her aid. She relieved her of the oranges, much to Berenilde's annoyance.

"You're too good to this boy, Mother."

The grandmother must have only half-grasped this warning as her wrinkled face broke into a contrite smile. "It's really that I'm too greedy, my dear. I adore oranges!"

"Don't touch those, we don't know where they've been lying around. Let's get going," continued Berenilde, taking her mother's arm, "I'd like to sit close to Odin's altar."

Lifting her umberella as high as possible to make up for her shortness, Ophelia followed close behind them. Too bad, Mother Hildegarde would have to wait. She threaded her way as best she could through the other umbrellas, a strange forest of black mushrooms, until they reached the benches reserved for those close to the deceased.

Recognizable by his tattered top hat, Archibald was slumped in the front row. Ophelia had never seen him looking so serious. So he had been affected by the death of Madam Frida? Just for that, he went up in Ophelia's esteem.

The ambassador was surrounded by his sisters and an impressive cohort of aunts and cousins. It was the first time Ophelia saw the Web in its entirety, because the members of the clan didn't all live at Clairdelune. The predominance of women in this family was notable. She spotted Fox, who was standing behind the third row of benches, holding his umbrella above Lady Clothilde. Archibald's grandmother was a little hard of hearing, so she was holding her ear trumpet in the direction of the harmonium, frowning like a music critic despite the fact that no one yet sat at the keyboard.

Ophelia positioned herself with her umbrella behind Berenilde and her mother, a row further back. Clearly visible to all, at the far end of the chapel, the coffin had been placed at the foot of a statue of a giant seated on a throne. Ophelia looked at it with curiosity: was that "Odin's altar?" Gripping her umbrella with both hands to stop the pendants swinging, she glanced, intrigued, at the walls of the nave. Between the stained-glass windows, other stone statues, wide-eyed and stern-featured, supported the vaulted ceiling with their arms.

The forgotten gods.

This chapel was a reproduction of the churches of the old world, from the time when humans believed they were ruled by all-powerful forces. Ophelia had never seen one anywhere else, apart from in old illustrations. On Anima, baptisms, marriages and funerals were all celebrated very simply, at the Familistery. The people over here certainly had a sense of decorum.

The hum of murmuring from the benches ceased. The policemen, lining the walls in a guard of honor, stood to attention. The solemn music from the harmonium rose to fill the entire chapel. The master of ceremonies had just appeared at Odin's altar. He was an elderly, bewigged man, clearly deeply upset, with the mark of the Web on his forehead. Ophelia recognized the widower of Madam Frida.

"A thread has snapped!" he declared in a quavering voice. He fell silent and closed his eyes. Moved, Ophelia thought for a moment that he couldn't find his words, but then realized that all the members of the Web were collecting their thoughts. The silence continued, disturbed only by a cough here, a yawn there from guests on the benches. Ophelia was finding it increasingly hard to hold her umbrella straight. She hoped her basket of oranges wasn't too heavy for Thorn's grandmother; she'd rested it on her knees and was clinging to the handle to stop it spilling onto the flagstones.

When Ophelia saw all of Archibald's sisters blowing their noses, overcome by the same emotion, she understood that the family weren't collecting their thoughts. The ceremony was actually continuing, but without words. The Web didn't need them, they were all linked to each other. What one felt, everyone felt. Ophelia looked again at Archibald, in the front row, whose profile was all she could make out. A provocative smile no longer lit up his face. He'd even combed his hair and shaved his cheeks for the occasion.

This family were united by a bond of which neither Ophelia nor any clan in the Pole had the slightest conception. A death wasn't just the loss of a loved one. It was a whole part of one-self disappearing into oblivion.

Ophelia felt ashamed for having entered this chapel without a single thought for the woman lying inside the coffin. Forgetting the dead was like killing them a second time. She focused on her only memory of Madam Frida—that of an old lady dancing rather too fast—and concentrated on it with all her might. It was all she could do for them.

The umbrella seemed less heavy to Ophelia, the time less long. She was almost startled when the widower thanked those assembled and they all stood up. Each valet closed his umbrella and hung it by its curved handle on the back of a bench. The shaking of all those pendants sounded like a shower of crystal rain.

Ophelia copied them and, with a bow of the head, thanked Thorn's grandmother as she returned her basket to her. While Berenilde was busy conveying her condolences to Archibald's family, she took her chance to go in search of Hildegarde. She had to find her before the chapel had emptied.

"Benches at the back," Fox whispered in her ear. "Don't hang around in her company, son, she hasn't got the best reputation."

As soon as Ophelia spotted an old woman sitting in the back row of benches, she knew, without any hesitation, that this was Mother Hildegarde. She was a perfectly hideous relic. With her thick, salt-and-pepper hair, swarthy complexion, tacky spotted dress, and cigar planted in a smirk, she stuck out among the pale nobles surrounding her. She swiveled her small black eyes, sunk like marbles in her big face, to scrutinize all these toffs with a kind of impertinent irony. Mother Hildegarde seemed to derive great pleasure from seeing people turn away as soon as their eyes met hers, and then calling out to them by name in her guttural voice.

"Are you satisfied with your new shortcut, Mr. Ulric?"

The person in question mustered a polite smile and hurried off.

"I'm not forgetting your pavilion, Madam Astrid!" she promised a lady hiding, in vain, behind a fan. Ophelia watched the scene with unavoidable sympathy. All of these people requested the services of the architect but were ashamed to be seen with her. And the more unwelcome they made her feel, the more she behaved like she owned the place. As she kept shouting out to the nobles, the policemen considered intervening, but Archibald signaled to them not to get involved. He calmly crossed the chapel and leant over the back bench, his old opera hat pressed to his chest. "Madam, you are disrupting our mourning. Could you behave yourself?"

Mother Hildegarde's face cracked into a witch's smile. "How could I refuse a favor to you, Augustine?"

"Archibald, madam. Archibald."

Mother Hildegarde sniggered as she watched the ambassador moving off, but she kept her word and stopped making the guests scarper. Ophelia decided this was the ideal moment to deliver her oranges.

"What's he after, that midget?" Hildegarde asked, while drawing deeply on her cigar.

Ophelia placed the basket beside her on the bench and

thought it best to salute her. Mother Hildegarde might not be a noble, and her manners were certainly lacking in refinement, but she still deserved a minimum of respect. "She's the mother of folk like you and me," Gail had said. It was silly, but Ophelia suddenly felt full of expectation. She didn't understand why she'd been chosen to make this strange delivery, but she realized that she was hoping for a small miracle out of it. A word, a look, some encouragement, anything that would enable her finally to feel at home here. Gail's words had affected her more than she'd thought.

Mother Hildegarde slowly picked up an orange. Her small black eyes darted from the fruit to Ophelia and from Ophelia to the fruit with a vivacity that was surprising for her age. "Did my little brunette send you?"

She spoke croakily, but Ophelia couldn't tell whether that was due to her foreign accent or too many cigars. "Lost your tongue, midget? What's your name? Whom do you serve?"

Ophelia placed a helpless hand on her mouth, truly sorry not to be able to reply to her. Mother Hildegarde was enjoying rolling the orange in her plump, wrinkled hand. She studied Mime from head to toe with a sneering curiosity, then beckoned him over to whisper something in his ear: "You look so insignificant, it almost makes you special. Do you, too, have a few little things to hide, sonny? Deal done."

To Ophelia's amazement, the Mother slipped three blue sandglasses into her livery pocket and dismissed her with a slap on the bottom. Ophelia had understood absolutely nothing of what had just taken place. She hadn't got over her astonishment when Fox caught her by the arm and spun her round like a weather vane. "I saw everything!" he hissed between his teeth. "Three blues for a basket of oranges! You knew it, hey? Wanted to keep your paradise all to yourself, false brother!"

He was unrecognizable. Greed and bitterness had erased all trace of friendliness from his big green eyes. Ophelia felt ineffably sad. She shook her head to say to him, no, she didn't know, she didn't understand, she didn't even want those sandglasses, but then a yell distracted their attention: "Murder!"

All around them there was chaos. The noble ladies left the vicinity with panicked cries, while the men, shocked, formed a circle around the chapel's back bench. Mother Hildegarde had gone totally stiff in her spotted dress, eyes frozen in their sockets, pale as a corpse. The orange she'd been holding a moment ago had rolled onto the flagstones. Her hand was all black and swollen.

"It's him!" shouted someone, pointing at Ophelia. "He poisoned the architect!"

There followed an eruption of echoes throughout the chapel: "Poisoner! Poisoner! Poisoner!" Ophelia felt as if she'd plunged into a nightmare. As she was spinning around, accused by dozens of fingers, she glimpsed, fleetingly, Fox's contorted face, Berenilde's shattered face, Archibald's intrigued face. She jostled the policemen trying to get hold of her, quickly pulled off her glove, ran to the basket of oranges, and touched the handle with her fingertips. A risky move, but perhaps her only chance of knowing. Then, in two blinks of an eye, she read the devastating truth.

The next moment, all Ophelia could see was an avalanche of truncheons.

The Dungeons

Lying on a carpet that stank of mold, Ophelia was thinking. At least, she was trying to think. She had a distorted vision of the room in which she found herself. Her glasses had got bent on her nose and she couldn't put them back on properly as her wrists had been handcuffed behind her back. The only source of light was the fanlight of a door, and it caused strange silhouettes to spring out from the shadows: broken chairs, torn paintings, stuffed animals, stopped clocks. There was even a bicycle wheel, alone in its corner.

So, is that all they were, the Clairdelune dungeons? An old junk room?

Ophelia made an attempt to get up, instantly abandoned. Her handcuffs were hurting her. Moving hurt her. Breathing hurt her. She probably had a cracked rib; those policemen hadn't pulled their punches. They'd even been scrupulous enough to confiscate the three blue sandglasses Mother Hildegarde had given her.

All her thoughts were for Aunt Rosaline, who must be worried sick. And Thorn? Had he been informed of what was going on? Ophelia hadn't received a single visit since she'd been thrown onto that carpet a few hours earlier. In all her life, she'd rarely known time to drag this much.

What would she be expected to do when they came for her? Keep playing her part to the end, so as not to reveal Mime's imposture? Disobey Thorn and speak out loud to plead her case? Her only defense rested on her reading of the poisoned basket; why would anyone take her word for it? She found it hard enough to believe herself.

And Ophelia did feel partly guilty of what she was being accused of: if Mother Hildegarde was dead, it was due to her naivety.

She blew on a strand of hair that was sticking to her glasses. She couldn't see it, due to the effective camouflage of her livery, but the sensation bothered her. She seized up when she noticed a movement in the shadows, close to her, on the ground, and then she realized that it was just Mime's reflection. There was a mirror right there, leaning against a pile of furniture. The thought of escaping crossed her mind, but then, disappointment: on closer inspection, the mirror was broken.

Ophelia raised her head to look at the door, her heart pounding. Someone was turning a key in the lock. A bewigged silhouette, round as a barrel, stood out against the light of the corridor. It was Gustave, head butler at Clairdelune. Closing the door behind him, candleholder in hand, he moved forward through the junk until Ophelia could see him more clearly. The light from the flame emphasized his chalky skin and red lips, turning his fat, grinning face into a grotesque comedy mask. "I thought I'd find you more battered and bruised," he cooed in his reedy voice. "Although our little policemen aren't known for their soft touch."

Ophelia had blood sticking to her hair and an eyelid so swollen that she could barely open it, but the butler couldn't see that: the illusion of the livery concealed it all behind Mime's immutable face. Gustave leant over her with a condescending little tut-tut. "It would certainly seem that you were manipulated, hmm? Murdering in such a crude way, in full diplomatic territory, right in the middle of a funeral ceremony! No one, not even you, is that stupid. Alas, barring a miracle, I can't see what could save your insignificant little self. Madam Hildegarde wasn't popular, I'll grant you, but we don't kill at Clairdelune. That's the rule."

Bothered by her handcuffs, Ophelia stared wide-eyed with her one working eye. Since when did this fat butler care about her fate? He leant closer and his smile widened. "As I speak to you, Madam Berenilde is pleading your case to the master, as if her own honor were at stake. She's doing it with such fervor that no one's fooled. I don't know what you do to her in private, but she's seriously infatuated with you, hmm? And I must admit that that makes you particularly precious in my eyes."

Ophelia was listening to him as though in a dream. This scene was unreal.

"I think Madam Berenilde could even end up convincing the master to give you a fair verdict," Gustave continued with an amused chuckle. "Unfortunately, time is against you, hmm? Our dear policemen are overzealous, and I heard that they're shortly to put the rope round your neck, with no inquest, no trial, no witnesses. It'll be over before your mistress is even informed."

Ophelia felt her whole body go into a cold sweat. She was really starting to be afraid. If she revealed her true identity, would they show more clemency towards her or would she worsen the situation? Wouldn't she risk dragging Berenilde down with her?

Breathless from leaning over too long, fat Gustave stood up straight. He looked for a chair that still had its four legs, put it beside Ophelia's carpet, and sat on it. The wood creaked ominously under his weight. "Would you like to do a deal with me, young man?"

In too much pain to sit up, all Ophelia could see of Gustave was a pair of patent shoes and white stockings. She indicated that she was listening to him by blinking.

"It is in my power to save you from the policemen," Gustave's shrill little voice continued. "I give you my word that no one will come to bother you until the master has made his decision. That's your only chance of salvation, hmm?" He guffawed, as though the situation truly was hilarious. "If the master decides to give you a chance and if, by a miracle, you come through, then you'll owe me a small favor."

Ophelia waited for what was coming, but Gustave said nothing more. She realized that he was writing when she heard a light scratching sound. He leant over close enough to stick his message on her nose, with backup from the candle: *Berenilde must have lost her baby before the evening of the opera.*

For the first time in her life, Ophelia knew what it meant to hate. This man disgusted her. He burnt the message on the flame of the candle.

"Since you're so intimate with madam, you should be up to it, hmm? And no trickery," he warned her, in a sugary voice. "The person commissioning me is powerful. If you so much as think of betraying me, or fail in this task, your miserable existence will immediately be over, hmm?"

Gustave left with his hurried little steps without even waiting for a sign of consent. After all, it wasn't as if Mime was in a position to refuse his offer. He closed the door with the click of a key, and Ophelia found herself alone again on her dusty carpet, curled up in the dark.

A reprieve. That's all she'd just obtained.

Ophelia struggled for a long time with anxiety and pain before sinking into a dreamless sleep. The click of the door roused her from her torpor a few hours later. Three policemen in black cocked hats entered the junk room. When they grabbed her under the armpits to get her on her feet, Ophelia almost groaned out loud in pain.

"Buck up! You've been summoned to the ambassador's office."

Supported by a firm grip, Ophelia stumbled out of the junk room. She blinked, dazzled by the light of the corridor, which seemed to go on forever, punctuated by countless doors leading to other junk rooms. Ophelia knew that beyond this corridor there was nothing. Fox had told her about the dungeons: they were a vast enclosed space, with no stairs, no lift, no windows, no possibility of leaving. Only the policemen could come and go as they pleased.

One of them collected a white sandglass from a little recess close to Ophelia's cell. The sand it contained trickled slowly, one grain at a time. Each servant thrown into the dungeons was linked to such a sandglass; their detention ended once it was empty. When one knew that some sandglasses were designed to turn around automatically, in perpetual motion, it sent shivers down the spine.

The policeman smashed Ophelia's sandglass on the floor.

Before she'd even had time to blink, she found herself back in the Clairdelune chapel, at the precise spot she'd been arrested. "An emptied sandglass always takes you back to your starting point," Fox had explained to her. It was the first time she was experiencing it. Other policemen were already there to seize her by the shoulders and request she follow them. Their orders echoed against the checkered flagging, the large stained-glass windows, and the stone statues. They alone remained in the chapel. Ophelia couldn't believe that a funeral ceremony had taken place here that very morning. Or was it yesterday?

She was led from shortcut to shortcut, and from Compass Rose to Compass Rose, in order to cross the Clairdelune estate. She could only just put one foot in front of the other. Every breath tore at her ribs. Her mind a blank, she hadn't the faintest idea what she should do to get them out of this mess, Berenilde, Rosaline and herself. Speak or say nothing? Ophelia felt so alone with her uncertainty that she surprised herself by wishing that Thorn was there to help them out. She could barely stand anymore when the policemen pushed her into the private office of the ambassador.

Ophelia wasn't prepared for what awaited her there.

Archibald and Berenilde were calmly drinking tea. Sitting in comfortable armchairs, they were chatting amiably while a chubby little girl was playing them a little piano. They didn't even seem to have noticed Mime's presence.

Only Aunt Rosaline, who was serving the tea, started to shake nervously. Her jaundiced complexion had become very pale—pale with rage against the entire world, pale with anxiety for her niece. Ophelia would have liked to rush into her arms.

350

She alone seemed to her to have a human face in the midst of all this indifference.

"My sisters are not exhausting you too much?" inquired Archibald with polite interest. "I'm not sure all these rehearsals are necessary."

"They're just keen to make a good impression on our Lord," replied Berenilde. "This opera will be their first official appearance up there, at the court."

"More importantly, it will be your great return, my dear. If Farouk sees you again, he'll undoubtedly want to tear you away from Clairdelune immediately. You have never been so beautiful."

Berenilde accepted the compliment with an affected flutter of her eyelashes, but her smile was rather stiff. "I'm not as sure as you on that, Archie. You know how much 'small feminine issues' annoy him," she explained, laying a hand on her stomach. "As long as I'm in this state, he'll refuse to receive me. That was the price to pay, as I knew from the start."

Ophelia's head was spinning. All this was so far removed from what she was going through right now . . . A woman was dead, another was going to be judged for a crime she hadn't committed, and they were sipping their tea and talking affairs of the heart!

A man lurking in a corner of the office coughed on his hand to attract their attention. It was Papier-Mâché, the steward. He was so narrow, so gray, so stiff that he became invisible when he remained silent. "Madam, sir, the accused has arrived."

Ophelia didn't know whether she was supposed to bow or not. Her ribs were so painful that just standing was torture. She stared desperately at Berenilde, asking her with her eyes what she should do, but her protector barely looked at her. She was happy merely to place her cup back on its saucer and wait. As for Aunt Rosaline, she looked as if she were fighting the urge to smash the porcelain teapot over someone's head.

Archibald, on the other hand, was fanning himself with his top hat and looking bored. "Let's get it over with! We're listening, Philibert."

Papier-Mâché put on a pair of spectacles, opened an envelope, and read the letter it contained in a monotonous voice: "I the undersigned, Madam Meredith Hildegarde, certify, on my honor, that I take total responsibility for the events that took place during the funeral ceremony of the late Madam Frida. I ordered a basket of oranges for the occasion, but neither its contents nor the delivery boy are at fault. My indisposition was caused by an extreme allergic reaction to a spider bite. In the hope of having cleared up any misunderstanding, please accept, Mr. Ambassador—"

"Et cetera, et cetera," Archibald interrupted him, flapping his hand. "Thank you, Philibert."

Pursing his lips, the steward refolded the letter and put his glasses away. Ophelia couldn't believe her ears. It was a cock-and-bull story.

"The matter is thus closed," declared Archibald, without looking at Ophelia. "Please accept my humblest apologies, dear friend."

He had spoken directly to Berenilde, as though the only injured party were the mistress, and not the valet. Ophelia felt as though she didn't exist.

"It was just a regrettable misunderstanding," murmured Berenilde, while giving a sign to Aunt Rosaline to serve them some more tea. "Poor Madam Hildegarde, those spiders are a veritable scourge! We can't see them, due to the illusions, but they're crawling all over the place! Anyhow, a few days in bed and it clears up. You can leave us," she added with a careless glance at Ophelia. "I'm giving you the day off."

Ophelia started moving again as though in a dream. One policeman removed her handcuffs, another opened the door for her. She went out into the corridor, took a few erratic steps, repeating to herself, again and again, that it was over, that she was alive, and then her legs gave way beneath her. She would have been sent sprawling if a helping hand hadn't caught her in time. "Costly, those sandglasses, eh?" It was Fox. He'd waited outside the office to be there when she came out. Ophelia felt so grateful that the emotion made her eyes smart. "I didn't cover myself in glory," he added with an embarrassed smile. "No hard feelings, lad?"

Ophelia accepted with all her heart. No hard feelings.

The Nihilist

In the basement sleeping quarters, bedroom doors were for-ever opening and closing, regardless of how late it was. The gaslights had been dimmed for the night. Some servants were going off to work, others were coming back to sleep, all were barging into each other without a word of apology. If a few, clutching their coffee, took the time to chat with a neighbor, most totally ignored each other.

Right at the end of the sleeping quarters, Baths Road was engulfed in clouds of steam. The valets were queuing, towels over shoulders, to enter the communal showers. Reeking of sweat was among the job's taboos. The cacoph-ony of water jets, singing exercises, and insults rang out along the corridor.

On the other side of door No. 6, which had been double-locked, Aunt Rosaline couldn't control her outrage. "Cornets alive, how can you sleep with such a racket?"

"You get used to it," murmured Ophelia.

"Does it never stop?"

"Never."

"This is no place for a young lady. And this room is appall-ing. Just look at those walls rotting with damp—not surprising

355

you're always sick! Oh, you're wincing . . . Is this where it hurts?"

Rosaline pressed lightly on the rib and Ophelia nodded, gritting her teeth. She had lain down on the bed, not wearing her livery, shirt pushed up, while her aunt's long, nervy hands were prodding her sides. "Definitely a cracked rib. You're going to have to rest, avoid sudden movements, and, most importantly, carry nothing heavy for at least three weeks."

"But Berenilde . . . "

"She's proved her powerlessness to protect you. You were saved thanks only to that Hildegarde's honesty."

Ophelia opened her mouth, then changed her mind. It wasn't to Hildegarde's honesty but rather to her lie that she owed her life. She wasn't so naïve as to think that nothing would be asked of her in return.

"Enough playing at being flunkies!" ranted Rosaline. "This whole malarkey has gone much too far. At this rate, you'll be dead before marrying your maniac of a fiancé."

"Not so loud," whispered Ophelia, with a knowing look towards the door.

Her aunt pursed her big, horsey mouth. She plunged a cloth into a bowl of cold water, and cleaned up the dried blood on Ophelia's split lip, gashed forehead, and matted hair. For a long while, neither of them said anything else, and the racket of Baths Road took over.

Lying on her back, having taken off her glasses, Ophelia couldn't breathe comfortably. The relief of being alive had slowly given way to a bitter aftertaste. She felt betrayed and disgusted; after what had just occurred, it seemed to her that she couldn't really trust anyone. She watched the narrow, rather blurred figure nursing her with small, careful gestures. If Aunt Rosaline had had the slightest notion of what had actually happened, first at the chapel, then in the dungeons, she'd have made herself sick with worry. Ophelia couldn't speak about it to her, as she'd have been capable of doing something stupid and putting herself in danger.

"Aunt?"

"Yes?"

Ophelia wanted to tell her that she was pleased she was there, and that she feared for her, too, but all her words stuck in her throat like stones. Why did she never manage to speak of such things? "Don't show your feelings to others," she mumbled instead. "Keep your anger secret, melt into the background, count only on yourself."

Aunt Rosaline raised her eyebrows, and her whole forehead, on display thanks to her tight bun, seemed to shrink all at once. With slow movements, she wrung out the cloth and laid it flat over the bowl. "Seeing enemies everywhere," she said, solemnly, "do you think that's a tolerable existence?"

"I'm so sorry, aunt. Try to keep going until the wedding."

"I wasn't talking about myself, silly! I believe it's you who's going to live here for the rest of your days."

Ophelia felt a knot in her stomach. She'd promised herself never to give up. She turned her head away, and that simple movement hurt her entire body. "I think I need to think," she murmured. "To be honest, I can't see things very clearly anymore."

"In that case, you can start by putting these on." Aunt Rosaline placed her glasses on her nose, not without a touch of mischief. The insalubrious little room regained its clean lines, its precise contours, its familiar untidiness. Old filched newspapers, dirty coffee cups, a box of cakes, a basket of clean, ironed shirts—Fox came to see Mime on his every break, and never empty-handed. Ophelia promptly felt ashamed for feeling sorry for herself. Fox had welcomed her the day she'd arrived, initiated her in all the workings of Clairdelune, advised her as best he could, and he'd been there when she'd got out of the dungeons. He wasn't entirely disinterested, but he'd never tried to harm her, and Ophelia was starting to realize that that was a rare quality.

"You're right," she whispered. "I can already see a bit clearer."

Aunt Rosaline passed a caring, rather rough, hand through her heavy brown curls. "Combs alive! Your hair's in a right muddle! Sit up and I'll try to untangle it all." A few tugs later, the "music room" bell rang out from the board above the bed. "Your wicked stepmother and her accursed opera!" sighed Aunt Rosaline. "She can say what she likes, she's completely obsessed with it. I'll look after the scores; you, rest yourself."

When her aunt had gone, Ophelia decided to get dressed. Better not to hang around for too long with her true face above her neck. Putting her livery back on took much careful maneuvering, but just as well she had: she'd just finished buttoning herself up when there was a knock on the door.

The first thing she saw on opening it was the giant horn of a gramophone. Her surprise increased when she saw that it was Gail bringing it to her. "Apparently you're convalescing," she grunted. "I've brought a little music. Hey, can I come in?"

Ophelia had thought she'd have to deal with her sooner or later, but hadn't expected it to be that quick. Gail was grinding her teeth and, with the eyebrow holding her black monocle in place, she frowned in annoyance. She was wearing a simple shirt and dungarees; all the valets emerging from the showers and lavatories were whistling as they passed behind her. It didn't show when she wore her usual baggy overalls, but the mechanic was pretty curvaceous.

Ophelia indicated to her to come in and locked the door behind her. Without wasting a second, Gail put the gramophone on the small table, carefully took a record out of the bag slung around her, placed it on the turntable, and cranked up the mechanism. Deafening brass-band music filled the whole room.

"The walls have ears," she explained, in a low voice. "This way, we'll be able to speak at ease." Gail dived onto the bed as though it were her own, and lit a cigarette. "Woman to woman," she added, with a mocking smile. Ophelia let out a resigned sigh and sat down on a stool, slowly so as to spare her ribs. She suspected that the mechanic had seen through her.

"Don't put on your timid act," insisted Gail, her smile widening even more. "I bet you're no more mute than you are male."

"Since when have you known?" Ophelia then asked.

"From the first moment. You can fool everyone else, my sweet, but not the Gail."

The mechanic blew her cigarette smoke out through her nose, her electric-blue eye fixed on Ophelia, who was much more disturbed than she wanted to show.

"Listen," she spat out through clenched teeth, "I know what you must think and that's why I'm here. I'm not responsible for the trap you fell into. Incredible as it may seem, I didn't know those oranges were poisoned. I don't know what went on, but me, I never wanted to cause you any trouble. Quite the opposite, in fact."

The brass-band music from the gramophone covered her tense voice so well that Ophelia was struggling to hear her.

"I know who you are. Or at any rate, I'm assuming I do. A little new girl who has to dress as a man to serve the haughty Berenilde? You can only be the fiancée of her nephew, whose arrival here everyone's waiting for. You hadn't even arrived, and already everyone hated you, you know that?"

Ophelia blinked in agreement. Oh yes, she knew it. Thorn's enemies had become hers, and he had a daunting number of them.

"I find that disgusting," continued Gail, after taking a fresh drag from her cigarette. "I know what it does to one to be hated for being born into the wrong family. I've been watching you from the start, and I thought you were going to be eaten alive. That's why I wanted to recommend you to my boss. The oranges, they're a kind of code between us. I swear to you that I was sincere when I told you she was different, that she'd accept you as you are, without judging you."

"I never doubted your sincerity," Ophelia assured her. "How is Mother Hildegarde doing?"

Gail's monocle almost popped out. "You've never doubted me? Well, I don't know what more you'd need!" She stubbed her cigarette out on the iron bar of the bed and immediately lit herself a second one. "The Mother will soon be up and about," she said, shaking her match out. "She has a constitution of steel—the poison that will kill her hasn't yet been invented.

Her allergy story wasn't very believable, but then, the important thing is that she exonerated you."

"Why did she do that?" asked Ophelia, cautiously. "Does she know who I am, too?"

"No, and she'll only know if you decide to tell her. I won't interfere anymore, you have my word of honor."

To Ophelia's great regret, Gail felt obliged to underline the pledge with a giant gob of spit on the already far from spotless floor of her small bedroom. "I still don't understand why your Madam Hildegarde helped me out. After all, nothing proves that I didn't try to poison her. All the appearances are against me."

Gail sniggered between her teeth. She crossed her legs, shamelessly displaying her heavy, dirty footwear, and the bedsprings creaked in unison. Her dungarees were stained with coal dust and oil; Ophelia would definitely have to change the sheets after her visit. "Because, as you say, all the appearances are against you. By poisoning the oranges, you'd have been sentencing yourself to death. And also, the Mother has the weakness of trusting me, and me, I have the weakness of trusting you. Without wishing to offend you, you've got the lovely face of an ingénue."

Ophelia stiffened on her stool, checked with a quick glance at the mirror that she still had Mime's neutral appearance, and looked back at Gail, astounded. "You see me as I actually am?"

Gail puckered her lips, hesitating, and then raised her eyebrow and took out her monocle. It was the first time Ophelia was seeing her left eye. It was as black as the one on the right was blue. Heterochromia. Gail had a tattoo on her eyelid, a bit like the Mirages did.

"I work in the service of Mother Hildegarde, but I was born here. I'm the last survivor of my clan. Have you ever heard mention of the Nihilists?"

Ophelia, gripped by these revelations, shook her head.

"Hardly surprising," Gail continued, wryly, "as they all died about twenty years ago."

"They all died?" asked an ashen Ophelia.

"A strange epidemic," said Gail in a mocking tone. "That's the way of the court . . . "

Ophelia gulped. It certainly sounded like a sordid business. "You escaped it."

"By passing myself off as a little, insignificant servant, exactly like you today. I was a kid at the time, but I'd already understood many things." Gail took off her cap and shook her short, dark hair, which fell over her face in an unspeakable mess. "All the minor nobles are little blondies, me included. We get that from Farouk, our very badly named family spirit. I manage to go unnoticed by dyeing my hair black. If my presence here became known, I'd be dead before I could tighten my final nut and bolt," she added with an amused grin. "I uncovered your secret, I reveal my own to you, seems fair to me."

"Why?" whispered Ophelia. "Why would anyone seek to kill you?"

"Look at yourself in the mirror."

Ophelia frowned, and turned again to her reflection. To her great astonishment, this time she saw her real face, covered in bumps and bruises, with big eyes staring out from behind a pair of glasses. "How do you do that?"

Gail tapped her tattooed eyelid. "I only have to look at you with my 'evil eye.' I'm a Nihilist. I cancel the power of others and your livery is a pure Mirage concoction. You can understand why I prefer not to scream it from the rooftops." She put her monocle back in place and Ophelia became Mime once again on the mirror's surface. "This special lens prevents me from cancelling all the illusions I lay my eyes on. It acts as a filter."

"A bit like the gloves of a reader," murmured Ophelia, looking at her hands. "But you unmasked me despite your monocle. Does it then allow you to see what's hiding behind illusions?"

"My family used to sell plenty of them," grumbled Gail in a cloud of cigarette smoke. "The Mirages didn't appreciate everyone being able to see all that their little tricks conceal. Our monocles mysteriously disappeared along with my entire family . . . I managed to save only this one."

With these words, she brought as much hair as possible over her eye and rammed her cap down as far as possible. Ophelia observed her as she finished her cigarette in silence. She understood that if this woman's features were so hard, it was due to all the ordeals she'd gone through. She sees herself again through me, thought Ophelia. She wants to protect me as she would have liked someone to protect her.

Suddenly, Ophelia felt her heart racing, right up to her throat. The sisters, cousins, aunts she knew; Gail was the closest she had to a very first friend. Ophelia would have liked to find a fitting phrase, words strong enough to express the immense gratitude overwhelming her, but she decidedly wasn't good at that kind of thing.

"It's very nice of you to trust me," she stammered, ashamed not to have found anything better to say.

"Your secret against my secret," grunted the mechanic, stubbing out her cigarette. "I'm no angel, my darling. If you betray me, I'll betray you, too."

Ophelia pushed her glasses up her nose, a gesture she could finally allow herself in front of someone. "Fair enough."

Gail got up with a creaking of bedsprings, and cracked her knuckles like a man. "So what's your real name?"

"Ophelia."

"Well, Ophelia, you're not as insignificant as you seem. But I'd still advise you to make a courtesy visit to my boss. She lied for you, and she can't stand ingratitude."

"I'll try to remember."

Indicating her gramophone with her chin, Gail smiled with a grimace. The brass-band music hurt the ears after a while. "I'll bring you some other records. Get well soon." She tweaked the brim of her cap in farewell and slammed the door behind her.

The Trust

Ophelia lifted the arm of the gramophone to stop the deafening music. She double-locked her door, took off her livery, and stretched out on her bed, which now reeked of motor oil and cigarettes. Facing the ceiling, she let out a deep sigh. She'd been duped like an idiot, beaten with truncheons, threatened by a corrupt butler, and astounded by a fallen noble. That was a lot of trauma for one little person.

Ophelia realized that she was going to have to speak to Thorn that very evening. Her heart started pounding painfully against her ribs. She dreaded seeing him again. She still wasn't entirely sure what had really occurred the last time, and still hoped she'd got the wrong idea, but Thorn's attitude had definitely been ambiguous.

Ophelia was scared, viscerally scared, that he might have grown fond of her. She felt incapable of loving him in return. She certainly didn't know much on the subject of feelings, but for that alchemy to work, didn't a man and a woman need to enjoy a minimum amount of affinity? Thorn and she had absolutely nothing in common, and their two temperaments were incompatible. The exchange of their family powers, on the day of the wedding, would change nothing.

Ophelia chewed away at the seams of her glove. She'd been discouraging to Thorn. If he felt rejected once again, would he continue to offer her his support? She was still going to need it, today more than ever.

She got up carefully and passed a hand through the mirror in her room. While Ophelia's body remained at 6, Baths Road, her arm was penetrating inside the wardrobe at the Treasury, on the other side of Citaceleste. She could feel the thickness of the coats. Thorn had said he would close the door of the wardrobe if he was consulting. Ophelia knew he could receive visitors until midnight, it was doubtless still too early.

She pulled back her arm. All she could do now was wait. She lowered the flame of the gas lamp, curled up under her sheets, and soon drifted off into a restless half-sleep. She dreamt she was imprisoned in a huge, white sandglass, and every grain that trickled down resounded like a veritable thunderbolt. When she awoke with a start, her shirt soaked in sweat, she realized that what she'd been hearing was just the tap dripping in her basin. She drank a little water, wiped her neck with a damp sponge, and plunged her hand back into the mirror. This time, she could push her arm through up to the elbow. The wardrobe at the Treasury was open.

Ophelia had second thoughts as soon as she saw her reflection in the mirror. She had on a simple shirt and short hose, no shoes on her feet, and her long, brown hair flowed freely down her back. Entering Thorn's room looking like this wasn't a great idea. She had to rummage about in her mess to find the big coat he'd lent her. She buttoned it up from top to bottom, and rolled up the flapping sleeves. It wouldn't hide the bruises on her face, but would at least look more decent.

Ophelia darkened the lenses of her glasses to conceal her black eye, and then tipped herself, all in one go, into her reflection. The cold instantly took her breath away. She could see no further than the end of her nose. Thorn had turned off the heating and switched off the lights. Had he gone, leaving his wardrobe open?

Ophelia waited until she'd got used to the surrounding darkness, her heart pounding. The bull's-eye window, at the back of the room, allowed a little moonlight to filter through the feathery frost. She was starting to distinguish the outline of the large desk, the lines of the shelves, the curves of the seats. Beneath the bull's-eye window, there was a silhouette, all hollows and angles, seated on the sofa, totally still. Thorn was there.

Ophelia moved forward, tripping on bumps in the floorboards, banging into the corners of furniture. When she reached the sofa, she saw that Thorn's pale eyes, bladelike flashes against a dark background, were following her every move. He was hunched over, forearms resting on thighs, but he still seemed just as big. Of his Treasurer's uniform, only the golden epaulettes shone in the dark.

"Did I wake you?" whispered Ophelia.

"No. What do you want?"

As frosty receptions go, it was definitely a frosty reception. Thorn's voice was even more gloomy than usual. He didn't seem particularly pleased to see Ophelia, and, in a certain way, that reassured her. He'd clearly reconsidered his opinion of her since the previous time.

"There are one or two things I have to speak to you about. It's rather important."

"Do sit down," said Thorn. He had a talent for turning what

367

could pass as a polite formula into a despotic command. Ophelia felt around for a chair, but once she'd found one, had to give up on moving it. Made of velvet and fine wood, it was too heavy for her cracked rib. So she sat at a distance, her back to the sofa, obliging Thorn to move. He relinquished his hunched position with an annoyed snort, and sat on his official chair, on the other side of the desk. Dazzled when he turned on his reading lamp, Ophelia blinked. "I'm listening to you," he said, in a hurry to get it over with. She didn't have time to say a word before he cut in: "What's happened to you?"

Thorn's long face had hardened even more, if that were possible. Ophelia had concealed all she could behind her glasses and her hair, hoping he wouldn't notice the bruises, but it hadn't worked. "A funeral ceremony ended badly. That's what I must talk to you about."

Thorn linked his long, gnarled fingers on the desk and waited for her explanation. So stern was his demeanor, Ophelia felt as though in the dock, facing an implacable judge. "Do you know Madam Hildegarde?"

"The architect? Everyone knows her."

"I delivered some oranges to her. She'd barely touched one when she fell to the ground. My guilt wasn't even questioned and the policemen immediately threw me into the dungeons."

Thorn's entwined fingers tightened on the desk. "Why didn't my aunt phone me?"

"Maybe she didn't have the time or a chance to," Ophelia replied, cautiously. "In any case, Madam Hildegarde didn't die. According to her, she had a violent allergic reaction."

"An allergic reaction," Thorn repeated, sounding skeptical.

Ophelia swallowed and clenched her fists on her knees. The moment of truth had arrived. "She lied. Someone definitely did poison those oranges . . . with the aim of harming me, not Madam Hildegarde."

"You seem to have a very precise idea on the matter," observed Thorn.

"It was your grandmother."

At this announcement, Thorn moved not an inch. He remained hands linked, back hunched, brow furrowed, nose pinched. Ophelia had rarely felt so uncomfortable. Now she'd launched into it, she felt fearful. After all, why should Thorn trust her?

"I read it by touching the basket of oranges," she continued. "Your grandmother relieved me of it, but that was just to allow her to pour her concoction on to the oranges. Her hatred of me, as gauged through the tips of my fingers, is spine-chilling." Ophelia watched for a flicker of emotion in Thorn's metallic eyes—surprise, denial, incomprehension— but he seemed to have turned into marble. "She detests everything I represent," she insisted, hoping to convince him. "A parvenu, a cause of shame, tainted blood. She doesn't want me dead, she wants to discredit me publicly." Ophelia jumped when the bell of the telephone rang out on the desk. Thorn let it ring, his eyes searching deeply into her dark glasses. "I said nothing about it to your aunt," she stammered. "I've no idea whether or not she suspects the two-faced behavior of her mother. First I wanted to know what you felt about it," she concluded, her voice fading.

Thorn finally moved again. He unlinked his fingers, sat up straight in his chair, thereby gaining height, and consulted his fob watch. Ophelia was flabbergasted. Did he not take her seriously? Did he think he was wasting his time with her?

"You want to know what I feel?" he said at last, not taking his eyes from his watch.

"Please." Ophelia was almost imploring him. Thorn wound his watch, put it back in his uniform pocket, and, totally unpredictably, violently swept everything off his desk with his arm. Quill-holders, ink pots, blotters, letters, even the telephone, were all sent spinning to the floor with a deafening clatter. Ophelia gripped the armrests of her chair with both hands to stop herself from running away. It was the first time she'd seen Thorn succumbing to an outburst of violence, and she feared it would be directed at her next.

And yet, with his elbows on the desk, hands pressed together, finger to finger, Thorn didn't seem at all like someone who had recently been angered. Now uncluttered, the desk displayed a nasty dark stain: the contents of the ink pot Ophelia had knocked over the previous time. "I'm pretty annoyed," said Thorn. "Somewhat more than that, even."

"Sorry," whispered Ophelia.

Thorn clicked his tongue with irritation. "I said I was annoyed, not that *you* had annoyed me."

"So you've decided to believe me?" murmured Ophelia, with relief.

Thorn raised his eyebrows in surprise, his long scar following suit. "And why wouldn't I believe you?"

Caught off guard, Ophelia stared at the writing materials piled up on the floor. Such chaos looked wrong in the middle of the perfectly ordered world of the office. "Well . . . it would be understandable that you'd give more credit to your grandmother than to a person you hardly know." She cleared her throat and added, "I think you've snapped the cable of your phone."

Thorn looked at her closely. "Take off your glasses, please."

Surprised by this unexpected request, Ophelia did as she was asked. Thorn's thin figure at the other end of the desk got lost in the blur. If he wanted to assess the damage for himself, she wasn't going to stop him. "It's the policemen," she sighed. "They don't hold back."

"Did they discover your true identity?"

"No."

"Did they make you suffer other things that I can't see now?"

Ophelia put her glasses back on clumsily, terribly embarrassed. She hated it when Thorn put her under interrogation like this, as though incapable of dropping his role of Treasurer. "Nothing serious."

"On second thought, I correct what I said," continued Thorn in a monotone voice. "You are partly responsible for my annoyance."

"Oh?"

"I asked you to trust no one other than my aunt. No one. Does one really have to dot every 'i' for you?"

Thorn's tone was so exasperated that Ophelia was flabbergasted. "How could I have suspected your grandmother for a second? She was kinder to me than any of you."

All of a sudden, Thorn went so deathly pale that his skin was the color of his scars. Ophelia realized too late what she'd just said. Some truths are better left unsaid. "And she lives under your own roof," she stammered.

"You will often have enemies under your own roof. Try to get used to the idea."

"So you didn't trust her from the start?" said Ophelia, shocked. "Your own grandmother?"

A sound of mechanical bellows invaded the office, followed by a resounding click. "The dumbwaiter," explained Thorn. His long legs extended like springs. He went over to a wall, lifted a wooden shutter and retrieved an aluminum coffeepot.

"May I have some?" Ophelia asked, impulsively. She could no longer survive without coffee since living in the Pole. She noticed too late that there was only one cup, but Thorn let her have it with no objection. Coming from him, she found the gesture very gracious.

"I, too, have been made to pay by that old vixen," he said, pouring her some coffee.

Ophelia looked right up at him. With her seated and him standing, it was enough to give you vertigo. "She had it in for you, too?"

"She tried to suffocate me under a pillow," said Thorn, languidly. "Luckily, I'm tougher than I look."

"And . . . you were young?"

"I'd only just been born."

Ophelia's eyes fell into her cup, brown and steaming. "That's monstrous."

"It's the fate generally reserved for bastards."

"And no one said anything, did anything against her? How can Berenilde still even tolerate that woman in her home?"

Thorn reopened the shutter of the dumbwaiter, this time to collect some tobacco. He sat back down in his chair, looked for his pipe in a drawer, and started filling it. "You've seen for yourself how talented that old lady is at deceiving those around her."

"So no one knows what she made you suffer?" asked Ophelia, astonished.

Thorn struck a match to light up the bowl of his pipe. The flame highlighted his angular, tense features, evidence of a strained mind. As soon as he stopped interrogating, his eyes became evasive. "No one," he growled. "Just as is happening to you today."

"Without wishing to offend you," Ophelia gently insisted, "how can you actually know what happened? You've just told me you were a newborn."

Thorn shook his match and silvery smoke rings rolled out of his pipe. "I have a very good memory."

Behind her glasses, Ophelia's swollen eyelid half-opened in surprise. Remembering events that occurred during the first months of one's life—she didn't think it was even possible. On the other hand, such a memory would explain Thorn's brilliance at accounting. Ophelia took a sip of coffee. The bitter liquid warmed her inside. She would have liked a little sugar and milk, but she couldn't be too demanding, either. "And your grandmother, does she know that you remember it?"

"Perhaps, perhaps not," grunted Thorn between two puffs on his pipe. "We've never spoken of it."

Ophelia saw him once more, rebuffing his grandmother when she'd welcomed them on the perron. She had to admit that she'd misjudged the one as much as the other, that day.

"I thought that, with age, she'd got out of her murderous little habits," continued Thorn, stressing each consonant. "The trick she's just played on you proves the opposite."

"What should I do, then?" asked Ophelia.

"You? Nothing."

"I don't think I can look her in the face as though nothing happened."

Beneath Thorn's furrowed brow, in the shadow of his eyelids, the metallic flashes hardened. There was lightning in his eyes. Ophelia found it almost worrying.

"You will no longer have to look her in the face. I'm going to send that woman away, very far from Citaceleste. Didn't I tell you that I would take my revenge on all those who went for you?"

Ophelia quickly took refuge behind her cup of coffee. Suddenly, she had a big lump in her throat. She'd just grasped that she really was important to Thorn. It was neither an act nor just empty words. He expressed his feelings rather crudely, certainly, but he was terribly sincere.

He takes this marriage much more seriously than I do, Ophelia thought, and that thought wrenched her stomach. Much as he wasn't the easiest man to deal with, she had no desire to make him suffer or to humiliate him by refusing to give herself to him. Well . . . maybe that had crossed her mind in the early days, but she'd reconsidered her position since then.

She was lost in the contemplation of the bottom of her empty cup for so long that Thorn ended up unhooking his pipe from his mouth and pointing at the coffeepot. "Have some more."

Ophelia needed no persuading. She poured herself a full cup of coffee, and sat further back in her seat, trying to find a bearable position. Remaining seated crushed her ribs and made breathing uncomfortable. "I have another urgent problem to put to you," she said, her voice hoarse. "Your grandmother aside, I've made a second enemy."

Thorn's pale eyebrows collided. "Who?"

Ophelia took a deep breath and, without stopping, told him about Gustave's blackmail. The more she spoke, the more Thorn's body was lengthening. He stared at her, utterly perplexed, as if she were the most unlikely creature nature had produced.

"If Berenilde hasn't lost her child before the Spring Opera, I'm done for," she concluded, fiddling with her gloves.

Thorn sat back in his chair and passed his hand over his silver-blond hair, flattening it even more. "You're severely testing my nerves. You certainly have a talent for getting yourself into a fix." Pensive, he blew out all the smoke through his large, hawkish nose. "So be it. I'll take care of that, too."

"How?" breathed Ophelia.

"Don't worry about the details. You simply have my word that that butler will do you no harm, not to you, not to my aunt."

Ophelia downed the rest of her coffee in one gulp. The lump in her throat wouldn't go away. Thorn was going to help her beyond all expectations. She felt perfectly ungrateful to have treated him with such disdain up until now.

The Treasury's clock chimed six in the morning. "I must return to my room," said Ophelia, putting her cup down. "I didn't realize it was so late."

Thorn got up and held open the mirrored door of the wardrobe for her as though it were an ordinary door. Ophelia didn't have the heart to leave like this, without a friendly word for him. "I . . . I thank you," she stammered.

Thorn raised his eyebrows. He suddenly looked all stiff and starchy in his uniform with its epaulettes, too confined by his big, thin body. "It's a good thing that you opened up to me," he said, gruffly. There was a brief, awkward silence, and then he added, between his teeth: "I may have seemed a bit cold, earlier—"

"It's my fault," Ophelia cut in. "Last time I behaved unpleasantly." Thorn's lips convulsed. She couldn't tell whether it was an attempted smile or an embarrassed grimace.

"Put your trust in only my aunt," he reminded her.

Ophelia was sad to see how much credit he gave Berenilde. She was manipulating them like puppets and he was playing her game without even realizing it. "In her, I don't know. But in you, no longer any doubt about that."

Ophelia thought she was doing the right thing by saying that to him. Unable to play the loving couple, she at least wanted to be honest with Thorn. He had her trust, he should know it. But she did wonder whether it wasn't a mistake when the gray eyes abruptly turned from hers in the sternest way.

"You must go, now," he muttered. "I must tidy my office and mend the telephone before my first appointments of the day. As for what you spoke to me about, I'll see to it."

Ophelia merged into the mirror and resurfaced in her room. She was so absorbed in her thoughts that she didn't at first notice that the gramophone had started playing again in her absence. She stared, baffled, at the record blaring out its brass-band music.

"Here you are at last!" sighed a voice behind her. "I was starting to get a bit worried."

Ophelia turned around. A little boy was sitting on her bed.

The Threat

The Knight was wearing striped pajamas. Licking what remained of a lollipop, he raisied his round glasses towards Ophelia. "You shouldn't leave your key on the door. You don't know the trick of pushing it with a pin from the other side, then? First you slip a piece of paper under the door, then, once the key has fallen, all that remains is to pull it towards you. If the space under the door is wide enough, it works every time."

With arms dangling in her big black coat, Ophelia wasn't listening to a word the Knight was saying to her. The presence here of this little Mirage was a disaster. Totally calm and expressionless, he tapped the bed to invite her to sit beside him. "You don't look very well, miss. Make yourself comfortable. The music doesn't bother you too much?"

Ophelia remained standing. She was so traumatized that she'd forgotten her pain. She hadn't the remotest idea of what she was supposed to say or do. She was even more thrown when the boy awkwardly pulled out a bundle of envelopes from under his pajamas.

"I had a quick look at your personal mail. I hope that doesn't bother you—I'm often told off for being too curious."

The letters that had disappeared. How on earth had they ended up in the hands of this child?

"Your mother's very worried about you," commented the Knight, randomly picking out a letter. "You're lucky; my first mom is dead. Thank goodness I have Madam Berenilde. She's extremely important to me." He looked at Ophelia with his placid eyes, enlarged by his thick glasses. "Have you thought about Gustave's proposal? You have until this evening to honor your part of the contract."

"Are you behind this?" asked Ophelia, in a weak voice.

Unruffled, the Knight pointed at the gramophone, which was blaring out its brass-band music. "You'll have to speak up a bit for me to hear you, miss. If you don't kill the baby," he continued, calmly, "Gustave will set the policemen on to you. Personally, I don't have much influence on them. He does."

The little boy noisily crunched the rest of his lollipop. "You absolutely mustn't kill Berenilde, just the baby. A nasty fall should suffice, I think. It's essential that it dies. It could take my place in Madam Berenilde's heart, you understand?"

No, Ophelia didn't understand. That a little ten-year-old body could contain such a sick mind, it was beyond her comprehension. It was the fault of the place, of the nobles, of all those clan wars; in this world, children had no chance of developing a sense of right and wrong.

The Knight threw his lollipop stick on the floor and started carefully going through Ophelia's letters. "I keep a very close watch over everything that concerns Madam Berenilde. Intercepting her family's mail is a real little obsession. It's when I came across yours that I learnt that you were at the manor.

Don't worry," he added, pushing his glasses back up his nose, "I've said nothing to no one, not even Gustave."

He swung his legs at the end of the bed, gripped by a sudden interest in his little furry slippers. "To be honest, I'm a trifle offended. First an unknown girl is put up in my house without my permission being asked. And when I decide to pay you a visit myself, I discover that a servant is pretending to be you. A decoy for the curious, is that it? I'm afraid I don't share that particular sense of humor, miss. As that poor girl discovered to her cost."

Ophelia shook with nervous shivers. Who had replaced her at the manor? Pistache? She'd never worried about it. She hadn't spared a single thought for the girl risking her life in her place. "Did you harm her?"

The Knight shrugged his shoulders. "I just delved inside her head. That's how I knew that the little valet was, in reality, you. I wanted to see for myself what you looked like and I'm totally reassured now that I have. You're much too ordinary for Madam Berenilde to feel affection for you." He dived back into the letters, wrinkling his nose in concentration.

"That other lady, she's a relation of yours, isn't she?"

"Don't you go near her." Ophelia had been quicker to speak than to think. Provoking this child was a reckless, dangerous thing to do—she sensed it with every fiber of her being. He raised his round glasses back up at her and, for the first time, she saw him smile. An awkward, almost timid smile.

"If Madam Berenilde loses her baby before this evening, I'll have no reason to attack your relation." The Knight tucked Ophelia's letters back inside his pajama top and almost tripped as he got up from the bed. For such a clumsy child, he certainly wasn't lacking in cheek. Cracked rib or not, Ophelia would have given him the spanking of the century if she'd been capable of moving, but she felt as if she were drowning, body and soul, in those bottle-bottom glasses. Young as he was, the Knight, once standing, wasn't that much smaller than her. She could no longer tear herself away from his placid eyes, which tattooed eyelids closed.

No, thought Ophelia, with all her might. I must not allow him to manipulate my mind.

"I'm really sorry, miss," the Knight sighed, "but you will retain no memory of this conversation. I am, however, convinced that it will leave an impression on you. A very bad and very tenacious impression." With these words, he took his leave with a bow of the head, and closed the door behind him.

Ophelia remained stock-still in Thorn's big coat. She had the most splitting headache. She stopped the gramophone to shut it up; why had she restarted it, anyway? She frowned on seeing the key not properly inserted in the lock. She hadn't locked the door, what a scatterbrain! As she crossed the room, something stuck to her stocking. Ophelia rubbed her foot on the ground to get rid of it, and looked closely to see what it was. A small stick. This room was turning into a dump.

Carefully, she sat on the bed, and looked anxiously around her. Her livery was folded over the back of a chair. The basin had been emptied of its dirty water. The door was at last locked. Why, then, did she have that feeling of having forgotten something very important?

"He hanged himself? Lot of good that'll do him."

Ophelia had only just sat at the table in the servants' hall when Fox had hurled that statement at her, between two gulps of coffee. Who hanged himself, she would have liked to have asked him. She stared at him for a long time until he decided to say more. With his chin, he indicated the feverish commotion of the servants around the tables. "You really must get your head out of the clouds, sonny. It's all everyone's talking about! Gustave, the head butler. Found attached to a beam in his room."

If Ophelia hadn't been sitting on a bench already, her legs would have given way beneath her. Gustave was dead. She'd spoken to Thorn about him and he was dead. She urged Fox with her eyes, eager to know what had happened.

"You seem really shaken," said a surprised Fox, raising his eyebrows. "You're definitely the only one to shed a tear over his fate, believe me. He was a real pervert, that guy. And he didn't have a totally clear conscience, you know. Apparently, they found a summons from the Chamber of Justice: illegal possession of yellow sandglasses, abuse of trust, and more!" Fox ran his thumb under his imposing jaw in a meaningful gesture. "He was finished in any case. Play too much with fire, and you get your butt burnt."

Ophelia barely touched the coffee that Fox had served her with a theatrical flourish. The Chamber of Justice was closely linked to the Treasury; it was Thorn all right who was behind all this. He'd kept his word. Ophelia should have felt relieved, for herself and for the baby, but her stomach remained in knots. And now? Thorn surely wasn't going to invite his grandmother to throw herself from a window, was he?

As Fox was insistently scratching his throat, she put aside her thoughts to return to him. He was contemplating the bottom of his empty cup with an uneasy expression. "You're returning to service today, eh? For that singsong?"

Ophelia nodded. She had no choice. This evening it was the Spring Opera, presented in Farouk's honor. Berenilde was absolutely counting on her presence; she'd even managed to secure her a minor role, as a gondolier. With a cracked rib, it promised to be a long evening.

"Me, I won't be there," grumbled Fox. "My mistress is deaf as a post, so operas bore her to death." He hadn't looked up from his cup, and a furrow had appeared between his eyebrows. "Isn't it a bit soon, for you?" he suddenly asked. "I mean, after all you've been through . . . A single day of rest, it's really not that much, eh?"

Ophelia waited patiently for him to say what he had to say. Fox scratched his throat, combed his side-whiskers, and glanced warily around him. Suddenly, he thrust a hand in his pocket. "Here. But don't get used to it, eh? It's just for this once, to give you a chance to breathe, eh?"

Dazed by all those "eh?"s, Ophelia looked at the green sandglass placed near her cup of coffee. She was grateful for her enforced silence: had she been able to speak, she wouldn't have known what to say. Until now, it was she who handed over all of her tips.

Fox crossed his arms on the table with a sulky expression, as if playing it charitable was bad for his reputation. "The three blue sandglasses," he grumbled between his teeth, "the ones Mother Hildegarde gave you. The policemen didn't return them to you, eh? I just don't think that's right, that's all."

Ophelia studied Fox closely—his strong face, his expressive

eyes under the burning bush of his eyebrows, his flaming hair. She felt she was suddenly seeing him with more clarity than before. Thorn had ordered her not to put her trust in anyone; at that moment, she felt incapable of obeying him.

"Don't look at me like that," said Fox, turning away. "It gives you, like, a woman's eyes . . . It's really unnerving, you know?"

Ophelia gave him back his sandglass. Whatever he thought, he would need it more than she would. Once he'd got over his surprise, Fox broke into a mocking smile. "Ah, I think I understand! You want to see *him* and be seen by *him*, is that it?" He lay flat on the table like a big ginger cat, elbows forward, to be able to speak to her, nose to nose. "The Immortal Lord," he whispered. "He whom only the toffs are allowed to look at directly. Me, my boy, I've already met him. Cross my heart and hope to die! It was only an instant, when I was escorting Madam Clothilde, but I could see him just as I'm seeing you, yourself. And, believe me or not, lad, he glanced at me. Being seen by an Immortal, can you imagine?"

Fox seemed so proud that Ophelia wasn't quite sure whether to smile or grimace. While rubbing shoulders with the servants, she'd soon noticed that they were incredibly superstitious when it came to Farouk. They seemed convinced that the slightest attention from him, even involuntary, left such an imprint on the soul that it became immortal. Those who were fortunate enough to be looked at by the family spirit, a privilege normally reserved for nobles, would survive the death of the body. The others were condemned to oblivion.

Animists didn't entertain this kind of belief with regards to Artemis. They were pleased to think that they would continue to exist through the memory of their possessions, and that was as far as it went.

Fox patted Ophelia's shoulder as if to console her. "I know you have a minor role in the show, but don't hope to be noticed for that. You and me, we're invisible to the eyes of those in high places."

Ophelia pondered these words as she elbowed her way along the ground-floor service corridor. There was so much traffic this morning that valets, maids, and messengers were treading on each other's toes amid indescribable confusion. All of them now spoke only of the opera; Gustave's death was already ancient history.

Ophelia's ribs rattled with every breath she took. She looked for less busy routes, but the gardens and sitting rooms were swarming with people. In addition to the embassy's usual guests, there were now ministers, councilors, fashionable ladies, diplomats, artists, and dandies. They had all come here for Archibald's lifts, the only ones to serve Farouk's tower. The spring celebration must be a much-awaited event in the Pole. The number of policemen had doubled for the occasion.

In the music room, the atmosphere was, alas, not much calmer. Archibald's sisters were panicking over problems with costumes. The dresses hindered their movement, the headdresses were too heavy, they were running out of pins . . .

Ophelia found Berenilde behind a screen, standing on a footrest, her gloved arms gracefully raised. Majestic in her ruff-collared dress, she disapproved of the tailor making her try on satin belts. "I asked you to conceal my stomach, not to emphasize its roundness."

"Don't you worry about that, madam. I'm planning on

adding some veils that will reveal only what's required of your figure."

Ophelia thought it best to stay in the background for the moment, but she could see Berenilde perfectly in the large, swiveling cheval mirror. Her cheeks were all flushed with emotion. She really was smitten with Farouk; that much she wasn't pretending.

Ophelia could almost read her thoughts in her big, limpid eyes: I'm finally seeing him again. I must be the most beautiful. I can reconquer him.

"I'm sorry about your mother, madam," sighed the tailor, with a fitting expression on his face. "Falling ill on the day of your performance, that's really bad luck."

Ophelia held her breath. Thorn's grandmother was unwell? That couldn't be a coincidence. Berenilde didn't appear particularly concerned, however. She was far too obsessed with her image reflected in the mirror. "Mother always had weak lungs," she said, distractedly. "Each summer she goes to the Opal Sands sanatorium. She'll be going earlier this year, that's all."

Ophelia would have liked to know how Thorn had managed to get his grandmother to report sick. Maybe he'd openly threatened her? The air had suddenly become much more breathable, and for that, Ophelia was indebted to him. And yet, she still didn't feel at ease. She felt as if a threat were still hovering in the atmosphere, but without her being able to name it.

Mime's black-and-white reflection in the mirror caught Berenilde's eye. "There you are! You'll find your props on the bench. Don't lose them, we haven't any spares."

Ophelia got the message. She'd also be appearing at the

court this evening. Even hidden behind the face of a servant, she'd better not make a bad impression. She looked over at the bench, in the midst of harpsichords and dresses. On it she saw a flat hat with a long blue ribbon, the oar of a gondola, and Aunt Rosaline. A nervous wreck, she was so pale that her skin had lost its usual sallowness. "In front of the entire court . . . " she moaned between her long teeth. "Handing over the phial in front of the entire court."

Aunt Rosaline was playing Isolde's lady-in-waiting, who, unable to bring herself to provide the poison requested by her mistress, swaps it for a love potion. It was a small, wordless part, of the sort saved for servants, but the thought of appearing onstage in front of such a large audience made her feel sick with nerves.

As Ophelia put on the flat hat, she was wondering whether Thorn would also attend the performance. She didn't particularly fancy pretending to row right under his nose. In fact, thinking about it, she didn't fancy doing it under anyone's nose.

The hours that followed trickled by. Berenilde, Archibald's sisters, and the ladies of the chorus were all busy getting ready, only allowing themselves a break to drink herbal teas with honey. Ophelia and her aunt had to wait patiently on their bench.

Towards the end of the morning, Archibald dropped by at the music room. He'd put on clothes that were tattier than ever, and his hair was such a mess, it looked like a pile of straw. He made it a real point of honor to appear scruffy when the circumstances were least appropriate. It was, along with his implacable frankness, one of the few traits that Ophelia liked in him.

Archibald was making last-minute recommendations to his sisters' dressmakers. "These dresses are far too revealing for their age. Add leg-of-mutton sleeves to replace those gloves, and add wide ribbons to hide those low necklines."

"But, sir . . . " stammered one dressmaker, with an alarmed glance at the clock.

"Of their skin, allow only that of their faces to be visible." Archibald ignored the horrified cries of his sisters. His smile wasn't as airy as usual, as though he found the thought of serving them up to the court repugnant. He was a very protective brother, Ophelia had to give him that.

"It's nonnegotiable," he declared, as his sisters wouldn't stop protesting. "And now, I'm returning to my guests. I've just lost my head butler, so I've been saddled with some admin problems."

Once Archibald had left, Ophelia's eyes kept going back and forth between the clock, Berenilde, and Aunt Rosaline. She felt stressed under her livery, as if a countdown were proceeding in silence. Only seven hours before the performance. Only five hours. Only three hours. Gustave was dead, but, despite that, absurdly, she still felt bound by his blackmail. She should have warned Berenilde of what had taken place in the dungeons. Seeing her so carefree in front of her mirror wasn't reassuring. Ophelia feared for her, for the baby, for her aunt, too, without any real reason.

Tiredness finally got the better of her anxiety, and she dozed off on the bench.

It was the silence that woke her. A silence so sudden, it hurt the ears. Archibald's sisters were no longer chattering; the dressmakers had stopped working; Berenilde's cheeks had lost their bloom.

Some men and women had just burst into the music room. These people looked nothing like the other Clairdelune nobles. They wore neither wigs nor frills and flounces, but all stood so tall that one might have thought them the owners of the place. Their fine fur garments, more suited to the forest than the salon, left the tattoos on their arms uncovered. They all had a hard look in common, cutting as steel. The same look as Thorn.

Dragons.

Encumbered with her oar, Ophelia got up from the bench to bow, as any valet who remotely valued his life would. Thorn had warned her: his family was extremely touchy.

When she straightened up, Ophelia recognized Freya from her pursed lips and thornlike nose. She was surveying the costumes and musical instruments with her icy eyes, and then fixed them on Archibald's pale and silent sisters. "You don't greet us, young ladies?" she said, slowly. "Are we thus unworthy to be your guests for one day? We're allowed to come up to Clairdelune only once a year, but maybe that's already too often for your liking?"

At a loss, the sisters all turned as one, like weather vanes, to the eldest. Patience raised her chin with dignity and clutched her hands to stop them trembling. She may have been the least pretty, due to her stern features, but she didn't lack bravado. "Forgive us, Madame Freya, we weren't expecting this surprise visit. Just looking around you will, I think, suffice to understand our embarrassment. We're all in the middle of dressing for the opera."

Patience threw a meaningful look at the Dragons with shaggy beards and scarred arms. In their white fur coats, they looked like polar bears who had strayed into the world of humans.

There were indignant cries from among the ladies of the chorus. Freya's triplets were laughing uncontrollably as they poked their shaved heads under the dresses. Their mother said not a word to make them behave. On the contrary, she sat on the stool of a harpsichord, elbows on the lid, with every intention of staying there. On her lips was a smile that Ophelia knew well: it was the very one she'd displayed in the carriage before vigorously slapping her.

"Carry on as you were, young ladies, we'll not disturb you. This is just a simple family reunion."

Some suspicious policemen entered the room to check everything was all right, but Patience indicated that they should go, and then asked the dressmakers to finish their work.

Freya then turned her forced smile towards Berenilde. "It's been a long time, aunt. You appear to have aged."

"A very long time indeed, dear niece."

Behind Mime's unassuming posture, Ophelia noted everything that transpired. From having played the valet, she'd learnt how to capture every detail in a few attentive glances. She couldn't blatantly stare at Berenilde, but she could compute what she noticed. The controlled tone of her voice. Her perfect stillness in Isolde's beautiful dress. Her gloved arms, kept along her body to stop them instinctively crossing over her stomach. Under her veneer of calm, Berenilde was tense.

"You're unfair, little sister. Our aunt has never been as radiant!"

A man unknown to Ophelia had boldly gone up to Berenilde to kiss her hand. He had a prominent jaw, athletic shoulders, and a glowing complexion. If he was Freya's brother, then he was Thorn's half-brother. He didn't resemble him at all. His intervention had the merit of relaxing Berenilde, who slid an affectionate finger down his cheek. "Godfrey! It's getting so hard to prise you away from your province! Every year, I wonder whether you'll survive the terrible winter, out there, in the depths of your forest."

The man burst into resounding laughter, a laughter that bore no resemblance to the usual tittering of the courtiers. "Come, come, dear aunt, I would never allow myself to die without taking tea with you one last time."

"Berenilde, where's Catherine? She's not with you?" This time it was an old man who had spoken. At least, Ophelia supposed he was old—despite his wrinkles and white beard, he was built like an ox. He cast a disdainful look at the elegant furniture surrounding him. As soon as he had started speaking, all the members of the family had turned towards him to listen. A real patriarch.

"No, Father Vladimir," said Berenilde, gently. "Mother has left Citaceleste. She's unwell, and won't be at tomorrow's hunt."

"A Dragon who doesn't hunt is no longer a Dragon," the old man muttered into his beard. "From spending too much time in salons, your mother and you have become delicate little flowers. Perhaps you're going to tell us now that you won't be there, either?"

"Father Vladimir, I believe Aunt Berenilde has attenuating circumstances."

"If you weren't our best hunter, Godfrey, I'd chop off your hands for uttering such shameful words. Do I have to remind you what it represents for us, this great spring hunt? A noble skill practiced by us alone that reminds those at the top who we are. The meat the courtiers find on their plates, it's the Dragons that bring it to them!"

Father Vladimir had magnified his voice so that every person present in the room could hear him. Ophelia had heard him, certainly, but she'd barely understood him. The man had an atrocious accent.

"It's a highly respected tradition," agreed Godfrey, "but one not without danger. In her condition, Aunt Berenilde could be excused—"

"Fiddlesticks!" exclaimed a woman, who had remained silent until then. "When I was about to give birth to you, my boy, I was still hunting in the tundra."

Thorn's stepmother, Ophelia noted to herself. She was the spitting image of Freya, but with more pronounced features. She'd probably never become a friend, either. As for Godfrey, Ophelia wasn't really sure what to think of him. She felt an instinctive liking for him, but she'd been wary of those oozing goodness ever since the grandmother had played that odious trick on her.

Father Vladimir raised his great tattooed hand to point at the triplets, who were busy demolishing a harp. "Look at them, all of you! Behold the Dragons! Not yet ten years old, and tomorrow they'll be hunting their first Beasts with nothing but their claws."

Sitting at her harpsichord, Freya was exultant. She exchanged a complicit look with Haldor, her husband with the huge blond beard.

"Which woman among you can boast of perpetuating our

line in this way?" continued Father Vladimir, casting a hard look at all around him. "You, Anastasia, too ugly to unearth a husband? You, Irina, who've never carried a single one of your pregnancies to term?"

Everyone looked down under the implacable beam of his gaze, like that of a lighthouse, scanning the horizon. An embarrassed silence fell on the whole room. Archibald's sisters pretended to be busy getting ready, but missed not a jot of what was being said.

As for Ophelia, she couldn't believe her ears. Making women feel guilty in that way, it was appalling. Beside her, Aunt Rosaline was so choked, she could hear her every breath.

"Don't get enraged, Father Vladimir," said Berenilde, in a calm voice. "I'll be one of you tomorrow, just as I've always been."

The old man looked scathingly at her. "No, Berenilde, you haven't always been one of us. By taking the bastard under your wing and by turning him into what he is today, you betrayed us all."

"Thorn belongs to our family, Father Vladimir. The same blood flows in our veins."

At these words, Freya let out a scornful laugh that made all the harpsichord's strings jangle. "He's power-hungry, a shameless schemer! He'll disinherit my children to benefit his own, once he's married his ridiculous little woman."

"Calm down," whispered Berenilde. "You're attributing to Thorn a power he doesn't have."

"He's the Treasurer, aunt. Of course he has that power."

Ophelia clung to her gondolier's oar with both hands. She was starting to understand why her future in-laws hated her so much.

"That bastard is not a Dragon," Father Vladimir insisted, in a fearsome voice. "If he so much as shows his ugly nose tomorrow at *our* hunt, I'll take great pleasure in adding a new scar to his body. As for you," he said, pointing his finger at Berenilde, "if I don't see you there, you will be dishonored. And don't rely too much on the attentions of Lord Farouk, my lovely, as they now hang but by a thread."

Berenilde responded to his threat with a sweet smile. "Please excuse me, Father Vladimir, but I must finish getting ready. We'll meet again after the performance."

The old man let out a contemptuous snort, and all the Dragons followed him closely out of the room. Ophelia counted them with her eyes as they went though the doorway. There were twelve of them, including the triplets. Was that it, the entire clan?

As soon as the Dragons had gone, the chattering resumed in the music room, like birdsong after a storm.

"Madam?" stammered the tailor, returning to Berenilde. "Can we finish your dress?"

Berenilde didn't hear him. She was stroking her stomach with a melancholy tenderness. "Charming family, isn't it?" she murmured to her baby.

The Opera

When the clock in the main gallery struck seven, Clairdelune was already empty of its denizens. Everyone, from the embassy's permanent guests to the little courtiers just passing through, had taken the lifts that went up to the tower.

Archibald had waited until the last minute to gather the opera performers around him. They comprised his seven sisters, Berenilde and her retinue, the ladies of the chorus, and the dukes Hans and Otto, who were singing the only two male roles in the piece. "Please give me all your attention," he said, taking his watch out of a pocket full of holes. "In a few moments, we're going to take the lift and leave diplomatic sanctuary. I therefore urge you to take care. The tower is situated out of my jurisdiction. Up there, it will no longer be within my power to protect you from your enemies."

He plunged his sky-blue eyes into those of Berenilde, as though addressing her in particular. She smiled at him, mischievously. In truth, she seemed so sure of herself right now that she emanated an aura of invulnerability.

Hiding under her gondolier's hat, Ophelia wished she shared her confidence. Her encounter with her future in-laws had had the effect of an avalanche on her.

"As for you," continued Archibald, this time turning to his sisters, "I'll bring you back to Clairdelune as soon as the performance is over." He turned a deaf ear when they made a big fuss, protesting that they weren't children anymore, and that he was heartless. Ophelia wondered whether these young girls had ever known anything other than their brother's estate.

When Archibald offered his arm to Berenilde, the whole group rushed up to the lift's golden gate, jealously guarded by four policemen. Ophelia couldn't stop her heart from beating harder. How many nobles had she seen going up in one of these lifts? And what did it look like, then, this world on high towards which everything converged?

A porter opened the gate and pulled a request cord. A few minutes later, the lift descended from the tower. Seen from the corridor, it only looked big enough to carry three or four people. And yet, all twenty-two members of the group entered it without needing to jostle. Ophelia wasn't surprised to discover a vast room with velvet-covered banquettes and tables laden with pastries. Such spatial absurdities were now part and parcel of her daily life. Trompe l'oeils of sunny gardens and galleries of statues seemed to extend the already considerable space. They were so convincing that Ophelia banged into a wall, believing she was entering an alcove.

The air around her was heavy with heady perfumes. The two bewigged dukes were leaning on the knobs of their canes. The ladies of the chorus elegantly re-powdered their noses. Milling around all these people without hitting anyone with her oar was a real challenge. Aunt Rosaline, beside her, didn't have the same problem as her only prop was the phial she had to give

Berenilde on stage. She was fingering it nervously, increasingly agitated, as though holding a burning coal.

A liftboy in honey-yellow livery shook a little bell. "Ladies, young ladies and gentlemen, we're about to depart. We will be stopping at the Council chamber, the hanging gardens, the courtesans' thermal baths, and, our last stop, the Family Opera House. The Lifts Company wishes you an excellent ascent!"

The golden gate closed and the lift rose with lumbering slowness.

Clutching her oar as if her life depended on it, Ophelia didn't take her eyes off Berenilde. With the evening in prospect, it seemed crucial to her that at least one of them remained vigilant. Never had the atmosphere felt so oppressively stormy to her. Lightning would strike, that was certain; all that remained now was to know where and when.

When she saw Archibald leaning towards Berenilde's ear, Ophelia moved a step closer, the better to hear: "I was present, much against my will, at your little family reunion."

Ophelia frowned, and then recalled that Archibald could see and hear everything his sisters saw and heard.

"You shouldn't take any notice of all that provocation, dear friend," he continued.

"Do you think I'm made of glass?" Berenilde teased him, with a shake of her little blonde curls. Ophelia saw a smile spreading across Archibald's angelic face.

"I know full well what you are capable of, but I'm obliged to watch over you and the child you're carrying. Every year, your great family hunt brings its tally of deaths. Just don't forget that."

Ophelia's whole body shuddered. She saw once again the

immense carcasses of mammoths and bears that her forebear, Augustus, had sketched in his travel journal. Was Berenilde seriously contemplating taking them to the hunt, tomorrow? With all the goodwill in the world, Ophelia couldn't imagine herself participating in a hunt in the snow and the dark, in minus twenty-five degrees. She was suffocating from having to remain forever silent.

"The Family Opera House!" announced the liftboy.

Lost in thought, Ophelia followed the movement of the group. What was bound to happen did happen: she hit some-one with her gondolier's oar. She kept bowing to apologize, before realizing that she was doing so to a little boy.

"It's nothing," said the Knight, rubbing the back of his head. "It didn't hurt me." Behind his thick, round glasses, his face was expressionless. What was this child doing with them in the lift? He was so discreet that Ophelia hadn't noticed him. This incident left her with an inexplicable feeling of uneasiness.

In the large foyer, a few gentlemen still lingered to smoke their cigars. As the group went by, they turned their heads and joshed. Ophelia was too dazzled to see them clearly. The twelve crystal chandeliers up in the gallery were reflected perfectly in the highly polished parquet floor; she felt as if she were walk-ing on candles.

The foyer led to the foot of a monumentally grand double staircase. All marble and copper, mosaics and gilt, it led to the Opera House's auditorium. At each landing, bronze statues brandished gas lamps in the form of lyres. The two symmet-rical flights led to the circular corridors, where the curtains of the boxes and dress circle were already nearly all drawn. The air there hummed with murmurs and stifled laughter.

Ophelia felt dizzy at the thought of having to the scale those endless steps. Every movement plunged an invisible blade into her ribs. Fortunately, however, the group skirted the grand staircase, went down a few steps, and through the stage door, situated just under the auditorium.

"This is where I leave you," whispered Archibald. "I must return to my seat in the box of honor before the arrival of our Lord."

"You will tell us what you think after the show?" Berenilde asked him. "Others will flatter me without an ounce of sincerity. At least I know I can count on your unfailing frankness."

"At your own risk. I'm no great lover of opera." Archibald raised his hat to her and closed the door behind him.

The stage door opened onto a complex maze of corridors that led to the scenery storage rooms, the workshops, and the singers' dressing rooms. Ophelia had never set foot in an opera house in her life; penetrating this world behind the scenes was a fascinating experience. She looked with curiosity at the costumed performers and the capstans for drawing curtains or changing scenery.

It was only once she'd arrived at the singers' dressing room that she noticed that Aunt Rosaline was no longer following them. "Go quickly to find her," ordered Berenilde, sitting at a dressing table. "She only appears at the end of Act I, but she absolutely must stay close to us."

Ophelia completely agreed. She put her oar down, not to be pointlessly burdened, and set off along the gangways. The orchestra pit must be directly above—she could hear the musicians tuning their instruments. To her great relief, she found Aunt Rosaline without difficulty. Planted in the middle of a corridor, rigid in her austere black dress, she was blocking the way for the stagehands. Ophelia gestured for her to follow, but her aunt seemed not to see her. She was spinning around, completely disorientated, clutching her phial. "Close all these doors," she grumbled between her teeth. "I detest drafts."

Ophelia quickly took her by the arm to guide her to the dressing room. It was doubtless due to stage fright, but Aunt Rosaline was being careless. She really mustn't let herself go by talking like that in public. Her Animist accent could be heard as soon as she diverged from "yes, madam" and "very well, madam." Aunt Rosaline pulled herself together once Ophelia found her a seat in the singers' dressing room. She sat up, straight and silent, hugging her phial, while Berenilde did her singing exercises.

Archibald's sisters had already gone up to the wings; they were onstage from the overture. Berenilde only made her entrance in scene three of Act I.

"Take these." Berenilde had just turned to Ophelia to hand her some opera glasses. Aggrandized by her costume and extravagantly styled hair, she looked regal. "Go up and discreetly take a look at Farouk's box. When those charming children make their appearance, watch him closely. You have ten minutes, not a minute longer."

Ophelia realized that it was *her* whom Berenilde was addressing, not Mime. She left the dressing room, crossed a corridor, and went up some stairs. She looked up at the gangway, but the large pelmet was in the way; from up there she wouldn't see the auditorium. She reached the wings, plunged in darkness, where rustling dresses jostled like restless swans. Archibald's sisters were waiting impatiently to make their entrance onstage.

Some applause could be heard; the curtain had risen. The orchestra launched into the first bars of the overture and the ladies of the chorus all sang out in unison: "My lords, does it please you to hear a noble tale of love and of death?" Ophelia went around the stage and spotted some floating drapes hung in the background to conceal the wings. She took a furtive look between the curtains. First she saw the back of the set of a two-dimensional town, then the backs of the ladies of the chorus, and, finally, the great auditorium of the opera house.

Ophelia took off her long-ribboned hat, and positioned the opera glasses over her own glasses. This time she could see very clearly the rows of seats, gold and crimson, covering the stalls. Few seats were empty. Even though the show had officially started, the nobles continued to chat among themselves, behind their gloves and fans. Ophelia thought them outrageously rude; the ladies of the chorus had rehearsed for days for this performance. Annoyed, she raised the opera glasses to the upper circles, which ascended the auditorium on five levels. All the boxes were taken. Inside them there was chatting, laughing, card-playing, but no one listening to the chorus.

When the grand box of honor appeared in the double circles of the glasses, Ophelia held her breath. Thorn was there. Stiff in his black uniform with frogging, he was consulting what she presumed was his trusty fob watch. So, his position of Treasurer must be important for him to have a seat here . . . Ophelia recognized Archibald by his old top hat, sitting right beside him. He was casually looking at his nails. The two men were ignoring each other so pointedly, without even pretending to be interested in the show, that Ophelia couldn't stifle an exasperated sigh. They really weren't setting a good example.

With a swerve of the glasses, she took in a whole row of diamond-smothered women—probably favorites—before discovering a giant clad in an elegant fur coat. Ophelia stared wide-eyed: so was that him, the family spirit around whom all those nobles, all those clans, all those women revolved? For whom Berenilde felt such boundless passion? For whom people killed each other left, right, and center? As the weeks had passed, Ophelia's fertile imagination had conjured up contradictory portraits, from icy to fiery, gentle to cruel, splendid to terrifying.

Apathetic. That was the first word that came to her mind on discovering this hulking form slumped on his throne. Farouk was sitting the way bored children do, right on the edge of the seat, elbows on armrests, back stooped into a hump. He'd propped his chin on his fist to stop it from falling forward, and the tubing of a hookah was wound around his other hand. Ophelia would have thought him sound asleep if she hadn't glimpsed, between his half-closed eyelids, the flicker of a gloomy look.

Despite the opera glasses, she couldn't make out the details of his face. Maybe it would have been possible if Farouk had been endowed with powerful, strongly contrasting features, but he possessed the purity of marble. Seeing him now, Ophelia understood why his descendants were all so pale, of both complexion and hair. His beardless face, on which one could barely distinguish the arch of the eyebrows, the bridge of the nose, the crease of the mouth, seemed to be made of mother-of-pearl. Farouk was perfectly smooth, without shadows, without bumps. His long, white plait was coiled around his body like some strange river of ice. He seemed at once as old as the world and as young as a god. No doubt he was handsome, but Ophelia found him too devoid of human warmth to have any effect on her.

She finally spotted a glimmer of interest amid all that torpor when Archibald's sisters appeared onstage. Farouk chewed on the tip of his hookah, and, with the slinky slowness of a snake, turned his head towards his favorites. The rest of his body hadn't moved, so his neck ended up at an unlikely angle. Ophelia saw the lips of his profile moving, and all the favorites, green with envy, passed the message from one to the other until it reached Archibald. The compliment couldn't have been to his liking, as Ophelia saw him get up from his seat and leave the box.

As for Thorn, he hadn't taken his eyes off his watch; he was keen to get back to his Treasury, and made no bones about it.

Farouk's show of interest in the ambassador's sisters spread from boxes to stalls. All the nobles, who had ignored the show up until now, started to applaud enthusiastically. What the family spirit approved of, his entire court approved of.

Ophelia rearranged the drapes and put the gondolier's hat back on her head. She could return these opera glasses to Berenilde; she'd certainly learnt her lesson.

In the wings, admirers were already rushing to declare their undying love to Archibald's sisters. None of them even looked at Berenilde, erect in her gondola on rails, like a solitary queen. When Ophelia climbed into the back to assume the rower's position, she heard her mutter through her smile: "Make the most of these crumbs of glory, sweethearts, because they won't last."

Ophelia pulled the wide brim of her hat over her face. Berenilde sometimes sent shivers down her spine.

In the distance, the violins and harps in the orchestra were heralding Isolde's entrance. The mechanism gently propelled the gondola along the rails. Ophelia took a deep breath to give herself courage. She would have to keep up the part of rower for the whole of the first act.

As the boat arrived onstage, Ophelia looked at her empty hands in disbelief. She'd forgotten her oar in the dressing room. She threw a panicked look at Berenilde, hoping for a miracle from her to save them from ridicule, but the diva, stunning under the footlights, was already preparing to sing. Ophelia had to resort to improvisation, finding no better solution than to mime the action of a rower, without her precious prop.

She probably wouldn't have attracted any attention had she not been standing, perched high on the edge of the gondola. Mortified, she bit her lip when bursts of laughter rose up from the auditorium, interrupting Berenilde in full flow as she was singing: "Night of love, in the city of heaven, unlike any other . . . " Disconcerted, and blinded by the stage lighting, Berenilde choked back several breaths before realizing that it wasn't she who was being mocked, but her rower. Behind her, Ophelia tried to maintain her composure, silently swaying her hips to the rhythm of an invisible oar. It was either that, or standing like an idiot with arms dangling. Berenilde summoned up the most beautiful smile, which put a stop to the derision, and picked up her song as though never interrupted.

Ophelia sincerely admired her. As for herself, it took a good many imaginary oar strokes before she stopped staring at her shoes. While around her love, hatred, and revenge were being sung about, Ophelia's ribs were increasingly painful. She tried concentrating on the illusory water that flowed endlessly between cardboard houses and makeshift bridges, but the sight didn't distract her for very long.

Under the cover of her hat, she then risked a curious glance over at the box of honor. Sitting on his throne, Farouk had been transformed. His eyes were blazing like flames. His waxen face was visibly melting. It was neither the plot of the opera nor the beauty of the singing that had this effect on him, but Berenilde, and Berenilde alone. Ophelia understood now why she had been so determined to reappear in front of him. She knew exactly the hold she had over him. She had mastered to perfection the science of sensuality, which knows how to fan the embers of desire with just the language of the body.

Seeing that marble giant turning to jelly at the sight of this woman was a disturbing spectacle for Ophelia. She'd never felt so alien to their world as right now. The passion that linked them was no doubt the most true and most sincere thing she'd witnessed since her arrival in the Pole. But that truth was something Ophelia would never experience herself. The more she watched them both, the more convinced she became. She could make an effort to be more tolerant of Thorn, but it would never be love. Was he aware of that, too?

If she hadn't forgotten her oar, Ophelia would probably have dropped it in surprise. She'd only just noticed the sharp look Thorn was giving her from the box of honor. Seen from another part of the set, no one would have noticed the slight difference in the angle of his look, or doubted, therefore, that it was directed entirely at his aunt. However, from where Ophelia was standing, at the end of her gondola, she could clearly see that it was Mime he was staring at like that, without the slightest embarrassment.

No, Ophelia thought then, with a wrench to her stomach. He has no idea. He's expecting something from me that I'm incapable of giving him.

As the act was drawing to a close, a new incident brought her back to the immediate reality. Aunt Rosaline, who was supposed to bring the love potion to Isolde, never appeared onstage. An awkward silence fell among the singers, and Berenilde herself remained dumbstruck for a long while. It was another performer who helped her out by handing her a goblet instead of the phial.

From then on, Ophelia thought no more of Thorn, or of Farouk, or of the opera, or of the hunt, or of her rib. She wanted to know if her aunt was all right—nothing else was more important in her eyes. When the curtains fell for the interval, in the midst of all the applause and the bravos, she got down from the gondola without even glancing at Berenilde. In any case, she wasn't needed for Act II.

Ophelia was relieved to find Aunt Rosaline in the dressing room, exactly where she'd left her. Sitting on her chair, very straight, phial in hands, she seemed quite simply unaware that time had passed. Ophelia gently shook her by the shoulder. "We won't succeed if we keep moving," Aunt Rosaline declared, stiffly, her eyes staring into space. "For a good photograph, you have to hold the pose."

Was she delirious? Ophelia pressed a hand to her forehead, but it seemed a normal temperature. That just worried her even more. Already, earlier on, Aunt Rosaline was behaving strangely. Quite clearly, something wasn't right. First checking that they were alone in the dressing room, Ophelia warily spoke out loud: "You don't feel well?"

Aunt Rosaline flapped her hand as if a fly were buzzing around her, but didn't reply. She seemed totally lost in her thoughts.

"Aunt?" Ophelia called out to her, increasingly anxious.

"You know full well what I think of your aunt, my poor George," mumbled Rosaline. "She's an illiterate who uses books as kindling. I refuse to have anything to do with someone with so little respect for paper."

Ophelia stared at her with wide-open, baffled eyes. Uncle George had died about twenty years ago. Aunt Rosaline wasn't lost in her thoughts; she was lost in her memories. "Godmother," Ophelia implored her in a whisper. "Do you at least recognize me?"

Her aunt didn't even look at her, as though Ophelia were made of glass. She was overwhelmed by an uncontrollable feeling of guilt. She didn't know why or how, but she had the vague impression that what was happening to Aunt Rosaline was her fault. She was afraid. Perhaps it was nothing, just a temporary aberration, but a little voice within her was whispering that it was much more serious than that. They were going to need Berenilde.

Very carefully, Ophelia removed the phial from her aunt's clenched hands, and then remained sitting beside her for the entire duration of Acts II and III. It was an extremely long wait, which Aunt Rosaline punctuated with nonsensical sentences, never wanting to resurface. It was unbearable seeing her sitting on this chair, with that faraway look, at once close and unreachable.

"I'm coming back," whispered Ophelia when the applause made the dressing room's ceiling vibrate. "I'm going to get Berenilde; she'll know what to do."

"You just need to open your umbrella," replied Aunt Rosaline.

Ophelia went back up the stairs that led to the wings as quickly as her rib allowed her to. As she kept moving, the pain almost stopped her from breathing. She slipped between the performers crowded onstage to take their bows. The thundering applause made the ground shake beneath her feet. Bouquets of roses were thrown by the dozen onto the boards.

Ophelia understood the cause of all this adulation better when she saw Berenilde receiving a kiss on the hand from Farouk. The family spirit had come onstage in person to express his admiration publicly. Berenilde was in a state of grace: radiant, exhausted, splendid, and victorious. This evening, thanks to her performance, she had just recovered her title of favorite among favorites.

Heart thumping, Ophelia couldn't take her eyes off Farouk. Close up, this magnificent white giant was much more impressive. It wasn't surprising that he was considered a living god. The look he was giving Berenilde, who was aquiver with emotion, shone with a possessive glint. Ophelia could read his lips for the single word he uttered: "Come."

He wrapped his huge fingers around the delicate curve of her shoulder, and slowly, slowly, they descended the steps of the stage. The crowd of nobles surged around them as they passed, like a breaking wave.

Ophelia knew that she couldn't count on Berenilde that evening. She had to find Thorn.

The Station

Ophelia let herself be swept along by the surge of spectators heading for the auditorium's exits. As she followed them
down the grand staircase, her feet were trodden on at least
five times. All spectators had been invited to a large reception
in the Sun Salon. There were buffets laid on, and servants in
yellow livery carried their trays from one noble to another,
serving sweet drinks.

An idle valet would attract attention. Ophelia took a glass
of champagne and went through the crowd with small,
hurried steps, like a servant eager to quench his master's
thirst. All around her, Berenilde's performance was being
commented on: her too-broad mezzo, her too-tight sharps,
her breathlessness as the show ended. Now that Farouk
was gone, the criticism was more scathing. The diamond-
covered favorites, now neglected, had gathered around the
pastries. When Ophelia passed by them, musical critique had
already given way to talk of bad makeup, weight gain, and
ageing beauty. That was the price to be paid for being loved
by Farouk.

Ophelia feared for a moment that Thorn had already taken
refuge in his Treasury, but she finally spotted him. Which

wasn't hard: his sullen, scarred face, stuck on his great bean-pole body, loomed over the whole crowd. Being taciturn, he clearly wanted to be left alone, but he was all anyone saw: men in frock coats were endlessly flocking over to him.

"That tax on doors and windows is a piece of nonsense!"

"Fourteen letters I've sent you, Mr. Treasurer, and not a reply to this day!"

"Larders are starting to empty. Ministers tightening their belts, what is the world coming to?"

"It's your duty to keep us from famine. That big hunt had better be good, or you'll be hearing about it at the next Council meeting!"

Ophelia made her way through all these portly civil servants to get to Thorn. He couldn't help raising his eyebrows in surprise when she hoisted her glass of champagne up to him. She tried to fix an insistent expression onto Mime's face. Would he understand that she was seeking his help?

"Make an appointment with my secretary," Thorn declared, dismissively, to all the gentlemen. Glass of champagne in hand, he turned his back on them. He gave not a sign, not a look to Ophelia, but she followed close on his heels with total confidence. He would lead her to a safe place, she would tell him about Aunt Rosaline, they would find a solution.

Her relief was short-lived. A strapping fellow gave Thorn a resounding slap on the back, making him spill his champagne on the tiled floor. "Dear little brother!"

It was Godfrey, Berenilde's other nephew. To Ophelia's great dismay, he wasn't alone: Freya was on his arm. Beneath her pretty fur hat, her eyes were dissecting Thorn as if he were some freak of nature. He, however, merely pulled out his handkerchief to wipe the champagne from his uniform. He didn't seem particularly overjoyed to see his family.

There was an oppressive silence, underlined by the buzz of conversation and the chamber music. Godfrey shattered it with a masterful laugh. "For goodness' sake, you're not *still* sulking! It's been five years now since we three last saw each other!"

"Fifteen," said Freya, icily.

"Sixteen," corrected Thorn with his usual stiffness.

"Well, time's most definitely passing!" sighed Godfrey, without dropping his smile.

Standing back a little, Ophelia struggled to resist staring at the handsome hunter. With his strong jaw and long, golden locks, Godfrey was very arresting. When he spoke, the Northern accent took on a cheery ring. He seemed as comfortable in his supple, muscular skin as Thorn was cramped in his big, bony body.

"Wasn't Aunt Berenilde extraordinary this evening? She was a credit to our family!"

"We'll see about that, Godfrey," jeered Freya. "Our aunt should preserve her energy rather than exhausting herself with warbling. An accident can easily happen when hunting."

Thorn darted his hawk's eyes at his sister. He said not a word, but Ophelia wouldn't have fancied facing him right then. Freya smiled fiercely at him, seeming to defy him with her thornlike nose.

"None of that concerns you. You don't have the right to join us, despite being Treasurer. Isn't that wonderfully ironic?" She left her brother's arm and lifted her fur dress to avoid the puddle of champagne. "I vow never to see you again," she said, by way of farewell.

Thorn clenched his jaw, but made no comment. Ophelia was so struck by the harshness of these words that she didn't immediately realize that she was in Freya's way. She stepped aside, but wasn't forgiven for this little contretemps. A valet had made Freya wait, and Freya didn't do waiting. She looked down at Mime with the disgust one would normally save for creepy-crawlies.

Ophelia brought her hand swiftly to her cheek. A searing pain had just shot through her skin, as if an invisible cat had scratched her right in the face. If Thorn had noticed the incident, he didn't show it.

Freya disappeared into the crowd, leaving a chill behind her that even Godfrey himself couldn't dispel. "She wasn't as unpleasant when we were little," he said, shaking his head. "Being a mother doesn't really suit her. Since our arrival on Citaceleste, she hasn't stopped jeering at us, my wife and me. No doubt you already know, but Irina suffered another miscarriage."

"I really couldn't care less." Thorn's tone wasn't particularly hostile, but he didn't mince his words. Godfrey didn't seem in the least offended.

"Of course, you must be thinking about your own marriage now!" he exclaimed, landing another slap on his back. "I pity the woman who'll see your sinister face every morning."

"A sinister face that you decorated in your own way," Thorn reminded him, in a flat voice.

Beaming, Godfrey slid a finger across his own eyebrow, as though redrawing Thorn's scar on his own face. "I gave it some character, you should be thanking me. After all, you did keep your eye."

Massaging her burning cheek, Ophelia had just lost her remaining illusions. The jovial, warm Godfrey was just a cynical brute. As she watched him move away, laughing his head off, she hoped never to encounter another Dragon for the rest of her life. These in-laws were horrible, she'd seen quite enough of them.

"The Opera foyer," said Thorn, simply, turning on his heel and walking off.

In the grand hall, the atmosphere was more bearable, but there were still too many people around for Ophelia to be able to speak out loud. She was thinking of Aunt Rosaline, all alone in the dressing room. She followed Thorn, who was striding ahead of her, hoping that he wouldn't lead her too far away. He passed behind the ticket office and went into the cloakrooms. There, not a soul. Ophelia thought the place ideal, so was disconcerted to see Thorn not stopping, for all that. He advanced between the rows of cupboards, heading straight for the one marked "Treasurer." Did he want to collect his coat? He pulled out a bunch of keys from his uniform and inserted one of them, all golden, into the lock of the cupboard.

When he opened the door, Ophelia saw neither hangers nor coats, but a small room. With a movement of his chin, Thorn invited her to go in, and then locked the door behind them. The room was circular, barely heated, devoid of furniture. It did, however, have doors painted in many colors. A Compass Rose. No doubt they could have spoken there, but it was cramped and Thorn had already put his key into a new lock.

"I mustn't go too far away," Ophelia muttered.

"It's just a matter of a few doors," responded Thorn in a formal tone.

413

They crossed a series of Compass Roses, finally ending up in freezing darkness. Winded by the cold, Ophelia coughed clouds of mist. When she finally breathed in, her lungs seemed to solidify inside her chest. Her valet's livery wasn't designed for such temperatures. All she could now see of Thorn was a scrawny shadow groping its way forward. In some places, his black uniform merged so well into the darkness that Ophelia guessed his movements just from the creaking of a floorboard.

"Don't move, I'm putting the light on."

She waited, shivering. A flame crackled. Ophelia first saw Thorn's profile, with its low forehead, its large, steep nose, and its combed-back fair hair. He turned on a wall gas lamp, extending the flame, and the light pushed back the shadows. Ophelia looked around her, flabbergasted. They were inside a waiting room where the benches were covered in frost. There were also ticket counters hung with icicles, rusted luggage trolleys, and a clock face that hadn't told the time for ages. "A disused station?"

"Only in winter," grumbled Thorn in a cloud of mist. "The snow covers the rails and stops the trains moving for half the year."

Ophelia went over to a window, but the panes were streaked with frost. If there were a platform and tracks out in the dark, she couldn't see them. "Have we left Citaceleste?" Articulating each word was a challenge. Ophelia had never been so cold in her life. As for Thorn, he didn't seem at all bothered. The man had ice in his veins.

"I thought we wouldn't be disturbed here."

Ophelia glanced at the door they'd come through. It, too, was marked "Treasurer." Thorn had closed it, but it was reassuring to know that it was nearby. "Can you travel every-where with your bunch of keys?" she asked, her teeth chatter-ing. In a recess in the waiting room, Thorn was busy in front of the cast-iron stove. He stuffed it with newspaper, struck a first match, waited to see if the chimney was drawing proper-ly, added more newspaper, threw in a second match, fanned the flames. He hadn't looked once at Ophelia since she'd given him his glass of champagne. Was it her masculine appearance that made him uncomfortable?

"Only to public facilities and administrative premises," he finally replied.

Ophelia went over to the stove and offered her gloved hands to the warmth. The smell of old paper burning was so good. Thorn remained squatting, his eyes lost in the flames, his face all shadow and light. For once, Ophelia was the taller of the two, and she wasn't about to complain.

"You wanted to speak to me," he muttered. "I'm listening."

"I had to leave my aunt alone at the Opera. She's behav-ing strangely, this evening. She's going over old memories and doesn't seem to hear me when I speak to her."

At that, Thorn threw her a steely look over his shoulder. His blond eyebrow, sliced in two by his scar, was arched in surprise. "That's what you wanted to tell me?" he asked, incredulous.

Ophelia wrinkled her nose. "Her condition is really worry-ing. I assure you, she's not herself."

"Wine, opium, homesickness," Thorn cited between his teeth. "She'll get over it."

Ophelia would have liked to retort that Aunt Rosaline was too strong a woman for such weaknesses, but the stove blew back some smoke and a violent sneeze tore at her ribs.

"I, too, needed to speak to you," Thorn announced. Still squatting, he was staring again into the red glow of the stove's panes. Ophelia was terribly disappointed. He hadn't taken her fears seriously, dismissing them as if casually closing a file on his desk. She didn't feel that inclined to listen to him in turn. She looked around at the frosty benches, stopped clock, shuttered ticket counter, snow-whitened windows. She felt as if she'd taken a step beyond time, as if she were all alone with this man in a pocket of eternity. And she wasn't very sure she liked it.

"Stop my aunt from going on the hunt tomorrow."

Ophelia had to admit, she hadn't expected him to say that. "She seemed pretty determined to be there," she countered.

"That's madness," Thorn spat out. "The whole tradition is madness. The starving Beasts are only just emerging from their hibernation. Every year, we lose hunters." His profile, set in anger, was even sharper than usual. "And I didn't appreciate Freya's insinuation," he continued. "The Dragons don't look very favorably upon my aunt's pregnancy. She's becoming too independent for their liking."

Ophelia's whole body was shivering, and it was no longer just from the cold. "Believe me, I myself have no desire to go to this hunt," she said, massaging her ribs. "Unfortunately, I don't see how I could go against the will of a Berenilde."

"It's up to you to find the right arguments."

Ophelia took some time to consider the matter. She could have been angry with Thorn for worrying more about *his* aunt than about *her* aunt, but what use would that have been? And also, she shared his foreboding. If they did nothing, this whole business would end badly.

She looked down at Thorn. He was squatting just a step away from her, totally engrossed in the station stove. She couldn't resist tracing the long gash cutting across half of his face. A family that inflicts that on you is not a true family. "You've never spoken to me of your mother," she murmured.

"Because I have no desire to speak of her," Thorn immediately snapped.

Ophelia suspected that it was probably a taboo subject. Thorn's father had committed adultery with a girl from another clan. If Berenilde had taken their child into her clutches, it was probably because the mother didn't want it. "And yet it does concern me a little," she said, gently. "I know nothing about this woman, I don't even know if she's still alive. Your aunt just told me that her family had fallen into disgrace. Don't you miss her?" she added, in a small voice.

Thorn's big forehead furrowed. "Neither you nor I will ever know her. There's nothing else you need to know."

Ophelia didn't push it. Thorn must have taken her silence for offense, as he threw a nervous glance over his shoulder. "I'm not expressing myself well," he muttered, gruffly. "It's because of this hunt . . . The truth is, I'm less concerned for my aunt than I am for you."

He had caught Ophelia unawares. Her mind blank, she didn't know what to say to him, so foolishly just held her hands out to the stove. Thorn was watching her now with the intensity of a bird of prey. With his big body drawn in, he seemed to hesitate, but then awkwardly unfolded an arm towards Ophelia. He seized her wrist before she had time to react. "You have blood on your hand," he said.

Stupefied, Ophelia looked at her reader's glove. She had

to blink several times before realizing what that blood was doing there. She took the glove off and felt her cheek. With her fingers she felt the outline of an open wound. Thorn hadn't noticed it due to Mime's livery; that illusion concealed everything—freckles, glasses, beauty spots—behind a perfectly blank skin. "It was your sister," said Ophelia, putting her glove back on. "She didn't hold back."

Thorn unfolded his long wader's legs and returned to being unreasonably tall. His features had all tightened into razor blades. "She attacked you?"

"Earlier on, at the reception. I didn't get out of her way fast enough."

Thorn had turned as pale as his scars. "I didn't know. I didn't realize . . . " He had whispered these words in a barely audible, almost humiliated voice, as if he'd failed in his duty.

"It's nothing," Ophelia assured him.

"Show me."

Ophelia felt all her limbs stiffen under her valet's livery. Undressing in this freezing-cold waiting room, right under Thorn's big nose, was the last thing she felt like doing. "I tell you it's nothing."

"Let me be the judge."

"It's not for you to judge!"

Thorn considered Ophelia with astonishment, but she was the more surprised of the two. It was the first time in her life she'd raised her voice like that. "So who, then, if not me?" Thorn asked in a tense voice.

Ophelia knew she'd offended him. His question was justified: one day, this man would be her husband. She took a deep breath to stop her hands from shaking. She was cold, she was in pain, and, most of all, she was afraid. Afraid of what she was about to say. "Listen," she muttered. "I'm grateful to you for wanting to watch over me, and I thank you for the support you've given me. But there is one thing that you need to know about me." Ophelia forced herself not to look away from Thorn's piercing eyes, two heads above her. "I don't love you."

Thorn just stood there, arms dangling, for several long seconds. His face was totally expressionless. When he did finally move, it was to tug on the chain of his watch, as if the time was suddenly of utmost importance. Ophelia derived no pleasure from seeing him like this, staring at the dial, lips pulled into an indefinable furrow. "Is it due to something I've said to you . . . or haven't said to you?" Thorn had asked this stiffly, without taking his eyes off his watch.

Ophelia had rarely felt so profoundly uncomfortable. "It's not your fault," she whispered in a tiny voice. "I'm marrying you because I wasn't given any other choice, but I feel nothing for you. I won't share your bed, I won't give you children. I'm very sorry," she whispered even more quietly, "but your aunt hasn't chosen the right person for you."

She jumped when Thorn's fingers closed the cover of his watch. He hunched his big body onto a bench, which the heat from the stove had started to defrost. His face, pale and gaunt, had never looked so devoid of emotion. "I now have the right to repudiate you. Are you aware of that?"

Slowly, Ophelia confirmed that she was. With her admission, she had called into question the official clauses of the conjugal contract. Thorn could denounce her and choose another wife for himself, totally legitimately. As for Ophelia, she would be dishonored for life.

"I wanted to speak to you in all honesty," she stammered. "I wouldn't be worthy of your trust if I lied to you on this issue."

Thorn stared at his hands, pressed against each other, finger to finger. "In that case, I'll carry on as if I'd heard nothing."

"Thorn," sighed Ophelia, "you're not obliged . . . "

"Of course I am," he cut in, brusquely. "Do you have any idea of the fate reserved for betrayers here? Do you think you just have to present your excuses to me and my aunt, and then go back home? You're not on Anima here."

Frozen to the bone, Ophelia no longer dared to move, or to breathe. Thorn maintained a lengthy silence, back hunched, then straightened his endless spine to look at her straight on. Ophelia had never felt as daunted by these two hawk's eyes as she did right now.

"What you've just said to me, repeat it to no one, if you value your life. We'll marry, as agreed, and after that, well, it will be only our business."

As Thorn got up, his joints all cracked in unison. "You don't want me? Let's not mention it again. You don't want brats? Perfect, I detest them. There'll be plenty of tongues wagging behind our backs, and so what."

Ophelia was dumbfounded. Thorn had just accepted her conditions, as humiliating as they were, to save her life. She felt so guilty about not returning his feelings that she had a lump in her throat. "I'm so sorry . . . " she repeated, pathetically.

Thorn then lowered a metallic look at her that made her feel as if nails were being hammered into her face. "Don't apologize too quickly," he said, his accent even harsher than usual. "You'll be regretting having me for a husband soon enough."

The Illusions

After returning Ophelia to the Opera cloakroom, Thorn left without a backward glance. They hadn't exchanged another word.

Ophelia felt as though walking in a dream as, alone, she moved across the foyer's shimmering parquet floor. The chandeliers, still burning bright, hurt her eyes. She found the grand staircase, now deserted, and the stage door, a flight of stairs further down. Apart from a few security lamps, all the lights were off. No one was around, neither stagehands nor performers. Ophelia stood quite still in the corridor, surrounded by bits of scenery, abandoned in the shadows—a pasteboard boat here, some fake marble columns there. She was listening to the painful wheeze of her own breath.

"I don't love you."

She'd said it. Never would she have thought that such simple words could trigger such a stomachache. Her rib seemed to be crushing her very insides.

Ophelia got a little lost in the badly lit corridors, ending up first at the workshops, then at the lavatories, before finding the singers' dressing room. Aunt Rosaline had stayed there in the dark, sitting on her chair, staring into space, like a marionette whose strings have been cut.

Ophelia turned the light on and went over to her. "Aunt?" she whispered in her ear. Aunt Rosaline didn't reply. Only her hands were moving, tearing a musical score, and then restoring it with a slide of the fingers; tearing it again, restoring it again. Maybe she believed she was back in her old restoration studio? No one must witness this.

Ophelia pushed her glasses back up her nose. She would have to do her best on her own to get Aunt Rosaline to a safe place. Gently, not wishing to distress her, she took away the score, and then took her by the arm. She was relieved when she got up willingly.

"I hope we're not going to the public gardens," muttered Aunt Rosaline between her long, horsey teeth. "I hate the public gardens."

"We're going to the Archives," Ophelia lied. "Great-uncle is in need of your services." Aunt Rosaline nodded her head, looking professional. Whenever a book needed saving from the ravages of time, she'd answer the call.

Still holding her arm, Ophelia got her out of the dressing room; it really felt like guiding a sleepwalker. They went along one corridor, turned into a second, turned back down a third. The basement of the Opera House was a veritable labyrinth, and the poor lighting didn't help with finding one's way.

Ophelia froze when she heard stifled laughter not far off. She let go of her aunt's arm and had a quick look through any nearby doors left ajar. In the performers' wardrobe room, where the costumes were lined up like strange sentinels, a man and a woman were languorously kissing. They were half-lying on a daybed, their position verging on indecent.

Ophelia would have continued on her way had she not recognized, by the light of the safety lamps, Archibald's tattered top hat. She thought he'd returned to Clairdelune with his sisters. The way he was kissing his partner was so lacking in tenderness, so fast and furious, that she ended up pushing him away, and wiping her lips. She was an elegant woman, dripping in jewelry, who must have been at least twenty years older than him.

"You beast! You bit me!"

Her anger wasn't very convincing—she was smiling, longingly. "I suspect you're taking your nerves out on me, you rotter. Even my husband wouldn't dare do that."

Archibald looked at the woman with his relentlessly bright eyes, but with no passion. It never ceased to amaze Ophelia that he got so many ladies into his bed by showing them so little affection. Even though he did have the face of an angel, they were pretty weak to give in to him . . .

"You're spot on," he readily admitted. "I am indeed taking my nerves out on you."

The woman burst into the shrillest laughter, and slid her ringed fingers along Archibald's beardless chin. "You're still angry from earlier on, my boy. Yet you should feel honored that Lord Farouk has designs on your sisters!"

"I hate him." Archibald had said it just as he would have said, "Oh, it's raining," or, "This tea's cold."

"You're blaspheming!" said the woman, laughing nervously. "Try, at least, not to say such things out loud. If it's disgrace that tempts you, don't drag me down with you." She lay down again on the velvet daybed, head thrown back, in a theatrical pose. "Our Lord has two obsessions, my dearest! His pleasure and his Book. If you don't pander to the first, you'll have to think about deciphering the second."

"I fear that Berenilde may have already checkmated me on both counts," Archibald sighed. Had he but glanced at the half-open door, he would have discovered Mime's colorless face staring, wide-eyed, back at him.

So, Ophelia thought, clenching her gloved fists, I got it right. That rival he fears, it's none other than me . . . me, and my little reader's hands. Berenilde had certainly maneuvered skillfully.

"I'll just accept it!" added Archibald, with a shrug of his shoulders. "As long as Farouk is interested in her, he's not interested in my sisters."

"For a man who enjoys the company of women so much, I find you adorably old-fashioned."

"Women are one thing, Madam Cassandra. My sisters are quite another."

"If only you could be as jealous about me as you are about them!"

Looking baffled, Archibald pushed his top hat back from his forehead. "You're asking for the impossible. You mean nothing to me."

Madam Cassandra, visibly chastened, leant her elbows on the padded edge of the daybed. "That's your main failing, ambassador. You never lie. If you didn't use and abuse your charm, it would be so easy to resist you!"

A smile broke across Archibald's pure, smooth profile. "Would you care to experience it again?" he asked in a honeyed voice. Madam Cassandra immediately stopped simpering. Looking very pale in the subdued lighting of the safety lamps,

and gripped by sudden emotion, she looked at him with ado-
ration. "To my great regret, I would care to," she wheedled.
"Make me not feel alone in the world anymore. . ."

As Archibald, with eyes half-closed like a cat, leant over
Madam Cassandra, Ophelia turned away. She had no desire to
watch what would come next in that wardrobe room.

She found Aunt Rosaline exactly where she'd left her. She
took her hand to lead her far away from this place.

Ophelia soon realized that leaving the great Family Opera
House wasn't going to be easy. Much as she kept showing her
room key to the liftboy, proving that she lived at Clairdelune,
he just didn't want to know. "I only take respectable people on
board, little mute. And that one," he said, pointing a disdainful finger at Aunt Rosaline, "looks to me like she's overdone it
on the champagne."

Bun held high with dignity, she was clasping and unclasp-
ing her hands while mumbling disjointed sentences. Ophelia
was starting to think that they'd be spending the night in the
foyer when a guttural voice, with a strong foreign accent, came
to her aid: "Let them on board, my boy. These two are with
me."

Mother Hildegarde was approaching with small steps,
making a solid-gold walking stick ring out on the parquet floor.
She had lost weight since her poisoning, but that didn't stop
her flowery dress from being too narrow for her extreme stout-
ness. She had a cigar in her mouth, and had dyed her thick,
salt-and-pepper hair black, which certainly didn't make her
look any younger.

"You are requested not to smoke in the lift, madam," the
liftboy said, stiffly. Mother Hildegarde stubbed out her cigar,

not in the ashtray he held out to her, but on his honey-yellow livery. The liftboy stared at the burnt hole with a look of devastation.

"That'll teach you to address me respectfully," she sniggered. "These lifts, it's me that manufactured them. Try to remember that in future."

She settled down inside the lift, leaning with all her weight on her stick and smiling proprietorially. A little boudoir with padded walls, this lift was more modest than the one the opera group had gone up in. Carefully, Ophelia pushed Aunt Rosaline inside, hoping to goodness that she wouldn't break their cover, and then bowed as low as her cracked rib would allow. It was the second time Mother Hildegarde had come to her aid. She was disconcerted when the old architect responded to her bow with a booming burst of laughter. "We're even, kid! A rower with no oar—just what I needed not to die of boredom at that opera. I was splitting my sides right up to the intermission!"

The liftboy lowered the lever roughly, clearly mortified to have such an unrespectable woman on board. Ophelia, on the other hand, felt a certain admiration for Mother Hildegarde. She might have the manners of an innkeeper, but at least she shook up the conventions of this ossified world.

When they arrived at Clairdelune's central gallery, the Mother tapped her on the head with familiarity. "I've helped you out twice, my boy. I ask for just one thing in return: that you don't forget it. People here have short memories," she added, turning her little black eyes on the liftboy, "but me, I remember on their behalf."

Ophelia was really sorry to see the old architect walk off

with little taps of her stick. She felt so vulnerable this evening, she was ready to accept anyone's help. Gently, she led her aunt through the gallery, avoiding meeting the eyes of the policemen who stood to attention along the walls. It would probably take years before she'd be able to walk in front of them without feeling nervous.

Clairdelune was unusually quiet. Its countless clocks were showing quarter past midnight; the nobles wouldn't come back down from the tower before the small hours of the morning. In the service corridors, however, there was a party atmosphere. Maids, lifting their aprons so they could run, were tapping each other and shouting, "You're it!", and then running off in fits of laughter. They didn't even glance at little Mime as he helped Madam Berenilde's companion up the stairs.

Having reached the top floor of the castle and, right at the end of the big corridor, Berenilde's fine apartments, Ophelia finally felt safe. She got her aunt to stretch out on a divan, wedged a round cushion under her head, unbuttoned her collar to help her breathe more easily, and managed, with perseverance, to get her to swallow a little mineral water. The smelling salts Ophelia wafted under her nose had no effect. Aunt Rosaline let out some loud sighs, her eyes rolling between her fluttering eyelashes, and then finally dozed off. That, at least, is what Ophelia supposed. Sleep, she willed her aunt, sleep and then wake up for good.

As soon as she was slumped in a squat armchair, close to the radiator, Ophelia realized that she was totally exhausted. Gustave's suicide, the Dragons' visit, that interminable opera, Aunt Rosaline's delirium, Freya's clawing, the unused station, Archibald's smile, and that rib, that blasted rib that never let up . . . Ophelia felt as if she now weighed double whatever she had the day before.

She would have liked to melt into the armchair's velvet. She couldn't get Thorn out of her head. He must have felt terribly humiliated because of her. Mustn't he already be starting to regret getting involved with such an ungrateful woman? The more she pondered on all this, the more angry Ophelia was with Berenilde for organizing this marriage. That woman thought only about possessing Farouk. Couldn't she see that she was making them suffer, Thorn and her, for her personal gain?

I mustn't let myself go, reasoned Ophelia. I'll make some coffee, watch over Aunt Rosaline, take care of my cheek . . .

She was asleep before she'd even finished going through all she still had to do.

It was the click of the doorknob that roused her from sleep. From her armchair, she saw Berenilde come into the room. In the pink light of the lamps, she seemed at once radiant and drained. Her curls, free of all their pins, cascaded around her delicate face like a golden cloud. She was still wearing her stage costume, but the lace collar, colored ribbons, and long, silky gloves had got lost along the way.

Berenilde looked at Aunt Rosaline, slouched on the divan, then at Mime, sitting beside the radiator. Then she locked the door to cut them off from the outside world.

Ophelia had to make two attempts at standing up. She was rustier than an old automaton. "My aunt . . . " she said in a hoarse voice. "She's not at all well."

Berenilde responded with her loveliest smile. She came towards her with the silent grace of a swan gliding on a lake.

Ophelia then noticed that her eyes, normally so limpid, were clouded. Berenilde smelt of brandy. "Your aunt?" she repeated, gently. "Your aunt?"

Berenilde didn't lift a finger, but Ophelia felt an almighty slap twisting her head from her shoulders. Freya's scratch throbbed painfully on her cheek. "That's for the shame that *your* aunt brought on me." Ophelia hadn't even had time to recover when a fresh slap propelled her face in the opposite direction. "And that's for the ridicule that *you*, forgetful little rower, didn't spare me."

Ophelia's cheeks were burning as if actually on fire. She saw red. Grabbing a crystal carafe, she threw the water in it at Berenilde's face. She stood there, utterly stupefied, while her makeup ran from her eyes in long, gray tears. "And that should freshen up your ideas," said Ophelia in a subdued voice. "Now you will examine my aunt."

Having sobered up, Berenilde wiped her face, gathered her skirts, and knelt beside the divan. "Madam Rosaline," she called, shaking her shoulder. Aunt Rosaline stirred, sighed, mumbled, but nothing she said was intelligible. Berenilde lifted her eyelids but didn't manage to catch her eye. "Madam Rosaline, can you hear me?"

"You should go to the barber, my dear friend," replied the aunt.

Leaning over Berenilde's shoulder, Ophelia was holding her breath. "Do you think someone might have drugged her?"

"How long has she been like this?"

"I think it came over her just before the performance. She was totally herself all day long. She had a little stage fright, but not to that degree . . . She seems not to differentiate anymore between the present moment and her memories."

Berenilde got up with difficulty, exhausted. She opened a little glass-fronted cupboard, poured herself a glass of brandy, and settled in the squat armchair. Her wet hair was dripping down her neck. "It would seem that your aunt's mind has been imprisoned in an illusion."

Ophelia thought she'd been hit by a thunderbolt. "If Madam Berenilde loses her baby before this evening, I'll have no reason to attack your relation." Where had she heard those words? Who had said them? It wasn't Gustave, was it? It felt as if her memory were thrashing about inside her head to make her remember something essential. "The Knight," she muttered, vaguely. "He was in the lift with us."

Berenilde raised her eyebrows, and then studied the play of light through her glass of brandy. "I know that child's trademark. When he locks a consciousness within those strata, one can only escape from the inside. It grabs you from behind, it seeps into you, it overlaps with reality, and then all at once, without warning, you're trapped. Without wishing to be a killjoy, my dear, I doubt whether your aunt has a strong enough mind to get herself out of there."

Ophelia's vision became blurred. The lamps, the divan, and Aunt Rosaline all started swirling around as if the world would never know stability ever again. "Release her," she said, in the ghost of a voice.

Berenilde stamped her feet, annoyed. "Are you listening to me, you fool? Your aunt is lost in her own meandering thoughts, and there's nothing I can do to stop that."

"Then ask the Knight," Ophelia stammered. "He can't have done this without an ulterior motive, can he? He must be expecting something from us—"

"You can't bargain with that child!" Berenilde interrupted her. "What he does, he never undoes. Come on, console yourself, my dear. Madam Rosaline isn't suffering and we have other things to worry about."

Ophelia stared at her in horror as she sipped her drink in small gulps.

"I've just learnt that the servant who was pretending to be you at the manor has thrown herself out of a window. An episode of 'temporary insanity,'" explained Berenilde, with obvious irony. "The Knight has uncovered our secret, and wants us to know it. And then this hunt is starting in a few hours!" sighed Berenilde, exasperated. "All this is truly regrettable."

"Regrettable," Ophelia repeated slowly, incredulous. An innocent girl had been murdered due to them, Aunt Rosaline had just been sent on a journey of no return, and Berenilde found that *regrettable*? Ophelia's glasses darkened as if night had suddenly fallen on them. A night haunted with nightmares. No . . . all of this was just a misunderstanding. That little servant wasn't really dead. Aunt Rosaline was going to stretch, yawn, and resurface.

"I confess that I'm starting to lose patience," sighed Berenilde, while contemplating her streaked makeup in her hand mirror. "I wanted to respect tradition, but this betrothal is really dragging. I can't wait for Thorn finally to marry you!"

As she was putting her glass to her lips, Ophelia snatched it out of her hands and smashed it onto the carpet. She unbuttoned her livery to throw it far away. She wanted rid, once and for all, of Mime's face, which masked her own expressions, determined that her anger be out in the open.

When Berenilde saw her as she was, thinner under her shirt,

skin covered in bruises and blood, glasses bent, she couldn't stop herself from raising her eyebrows. "I didn't realize that the policemen had beaten you up that much."

"How much longer are you going to play with us?" cried Ophelia, losing her temper. "We're not your dolls!"

Sitting comfortably in her chair, hair and makeup awry, Berenilde didn't lose her cool. "So this is how you behave when driven into a corner," she murmured, looking at the broken glass on the carpet. "What makes you think that I'm manipulating you?"

"I've overheard some conversations, madam. They enlightened me on certain things you made very sure not to inform me of." Exasperated, Ophelia held out her arms, hands lifted, fingers fanned. "These are what you've wanted from the beginning. You've got your nephew betrothed to a reader because up there, somewhere in that tower, a family spirit wants someone to decipher his Book." Ophelia was at last offloading her thoughts, like a cotton reel unwinding as it falls. "What worries everyone at the court is not our marriage, but that you should be the one who gives Farouk what he desires the most: someone able to satisfy his curiosity. Then you would be forever impossible to topple, wouldn't you? Free to make all the heads you don't like roll."

Since Berenilde, her smile frozen on her lips, didn't deign to reply, Ophelia brought her arms back down. "I have bad news, madam. If Farouk's Book is made of the same material as Artemis's Book, then it isn't readable."

"It is readable." Her hands crossed on her stomach, Berenilde had finally decided to lay her cards on the table. "It is readable even to the extent that other readers have already done so," she continued, calmly. "Your own ancestors, my dear. It was a very, very long time ago."

Behind her glasses, Ophelia was staring wide-eyed. The last entry in her forebear Adelaide's journal came back to her like a slap in the face: *Rudolf has finally signed his contract with one of Lord Farouk's solicitors. I am not allowed to write anything more—it is a professional secret—but we will meet their family spirit tomorrow. If my brother puts on a good show, we will become rich.*

"To whom am I contracted? To you, madam, or to you family spirit?"

"You understand at last!" Berenilde sighed, stifling a yawn. "The truth, my dear, is that you belong as much to Farouk as you do to Thorn."

Shocked, Ophelia thought back of the mysterious casket handed to Artemis to seal the alliance between the two families. What had this box contained? Jewelry? Precious stones? No doubt something less valuable. It couldn't cost that much, a girl like Ophelia.

"No one asked my opinion. I refuse."

"Refuse, and you will anger both of our families," Berenilde warned her in her velvety voice. "If, on the other hand, you do what is hoped of you, you will be Farouk's protégée, sheltered from all the nastiness of the court."

Ophelia didn't believe a single word. "Some of my ancestors have already read his Book, you say? I suppose if I'm needed today, then their attempts weren't conclusive."

"The fact is that they never succeeded in going far enough back into the past," said Berenilde with a joyless smile. Aunt Rosaline moved on the divan. Heart thumping, Ophelia leant over her, but was immediately disappointed: her aunt was

433

still wittering between her long teeth. Ophelia considered her waxen face for a moment, then returned to Berenilde, frowning. "I don't see why I would offer a better service, or why you're marrying me off to meet your ends."

Annoyed, Berenilde clicked her tongue with impatience. "Because your ancestors had neither your talent nor that of Thorn."

"Thorn's talent?" questioned Ophelia, taken aback. "His claws?"

"His memory." Berenilde settled into her chair, stretching her tattooed arms on its armrests. "A formidable and implacable memory that he inherited from his mother's clan, the Chroniclers."

Ophelia raised her eyebrows. Thorn's memory was a family power? "If you say so," she stammered, "but I don't understand what his memory and our marriage have got to do with this reading."

Berenilde burst into laughter. "They've got absolutely everything to do with it! Have you been told about the ceremony of the Gift? It enables family powers to be combined. This ceremony takes place at marriages, and only at marriages. It's Thorn who will be Farouk's reader, not you."

It took a considerable time for Ophelia to take in what Berenilde was telling her. "You want to transplant my skills as a reader onto his memory?"

"The alchemy promises to be effective. I'm convinced that the dear child will work wonders!"

Ophelia looked at Berenilde from the depths of her glasses. Now that she'd got her anger out of her system, she felt horribly sad. "You are contemptible."

Berenilde's harmonious features collapsed and her beautiful eyes widened. She clasped her hands around her stomach as if a blade had just stabbed her. "What have I done for you to judge me so harshly?"

"You're asking me that question?" asked Ophelia, amazed. "I saw you at the Opera, madam. You have secured Farouk's love. You're carrying his child, you're his favorite, and will be for a long time to come. So why, why involve Thorn in your schemes?"

"Because he's the one who decided it should be like this!" Berenilde defended herself, shaking her wet hair. "I only organized your marriage because he expressed the desire for it."

Ophelia was sickened by this display of dishonesty. "You're lying again. When we were on the airship, Thorn tried to persuade me not to marry him."

Berenilde's lovely face looked distraught, as if the thought that Ophelia might hate her was unbearable to her. "Do you really think he's a man who would allow himself to be manipulated in that way? The boy is much more ambitious than you seem to think. He wanted the hands of a reader, I found him the hands of a reader. Maybe he thought, on seeing you for the first time, that my choice wasn't the most inspired one. I'll admit having my own doubts about you, too."

Against her will, Ophelia was starting to feel shocked. In fact, it was much worse than that. She felt as if a pernicious chill were now entering her blood, slowly rising in her veins, and, finally, reaching her heart. When she had declared to Thorn that she would never fulfill the role of his wife, he had proved to be so accommodating . . . Far too accommodating. He hadn't lost his cool, he hadn't sought to argue about it, he hadn't behaved as a rejected husband would behave. "How naïve I've been!" Ophelia whispered. For all these past weeks, it wasn't her that Thorn had strived to protect. It was her reader's hands.

She collapsed heavily onto a stool and stared at Mime's patent shoes, on her feet. She'd said to Thorn, looking him straight in the eye, that she trusted him, and, like a coward, he had looked away. She'd felt so guilty for rejecting him and so grateful that he hadn't repudiated her!

She felt nauseous.

Slumped on her stool, Ophelia didn't immediately notice that Berenilde was kneeling down beside her. She stroked the knots in her dark hair and then the gashes on her face with a sorrowful expression. "Ophelia, my little Ophelia. I thought that you were lacking in heart and common sense, and now I realize my error. For pity's sake, don't be too hard on Thorn and on me. We're simply trying to survive; we're not exploiting you for the pleasure of it."

Ophelia would have preferred her to say nothing. The more Berenilde spoke, the more her stomach ached.

Overcome with tiredness and the worse for drink, Berenilde laid her cheek on Ophelia's knee, like a child craving affection. Ophelia didn't have the heart to push her away when she noticed that she was crying. "You've drunk too much," she chided her.

"My . . . children," hiccupped Berenilde, burying her face in Ophelia's stomach. "They were taken from me, one by one. One morning, it was hemlock poured into Thomas's hot chocolate. One summer's day, my little Marian was pushed into a pond. She would have been your age . . . she would have been your age."

"Madam," Ophelia murmured.

Berenilde could no longer hold back her tears. She was sniffing, groaning, hiding her face in Ophelia's shirt, ashamed of this weakness she was giving in to.

"And Peter who was found hanging from that branch! One by one. I thought I would die. I wanted to die. And he, he . . . You can tell me that he has every failing, but he was there when Nicholas . . . my husband . . . died while hunting. He made me his favorite. He saved me from despair, showered me with presents, promised the only thing in the world that could give meaning to my life!" Berenilde's sobbing made her choke, and then, with difficulty, she said: "A baby."

Ophelia let out a deep sigh. She gently cleared Berenilde's face, shrouded as it was in tears and hair. "You have finally been honest with me, madam. I forgive you."

The Maid

Ophelia helped Berenilde back to her bed. She fell instant-ly asleep. With her creased skin, smudged eyelashes, and hol-lowed eyes, her face seemed older against the white pillowcase. Ophelia contemplated her sadly, and then switched off the bedside lamp. How could one hate someone devastated by the loss of her children?

Stirring on the divan, stuck in her past, Aunt Rosaline was cursing some paper of second-rate quality. Ophelia stole an eiderdown from the grandmother's empty bed and spread it over her godmother. Once she realized there was nothing else she could do, she slid slowly down onto the carpet and drew her legs up. Her chest was hurting. More than her gashed cheek. More than her ribs. A deep, searing, incurable pain.

She felt ashamed. Ashamed of not being able to bring Aunt Rosaline back to reality. Ashamed of thinking herself capable of regaining control of her life. Ashamed, so ashamed, of having been so naïve.

Ophelia drew her chin to her knees and looked at her hands with bitterness: some women are married for their fortunes; me, I'm married for my fingers.

Deep in her chest, suffering gave way to an anger as hard

and cold as ice. Yes, she forgave Berenilde for her scheming and her meanness, but she forgave Thorn nothing. Had he been sincere with her, had he not led her to believe certain things, she might have excused him. There'd been no shortage of opportunities to tell her the truth; not only had he let them pass, but he'd also had the cheek to pepper their encounters with, "I'm starting to get used to you," and, "Your fate is of real concern to me." Because of him, Ophelia had seen feelings where there had only ever been ambition.

That man, he was the worst of them all.

The clock struck five. Ophelia got herself up, wiped her eyes, and, with a look of determination, put her glasses back on her nose. She no longer felt at all downhearted. Her heart was beating furiously within her ribs, producing a surge of willpower with every beat. However long it took, she would get her revenge on Thorn and this life he was imposing on her.

Ophelia opened the medicine cupboard, and took out some sticking plaster and surgical spirit. When she took a look at herself in Berenilde's hand mirror, she discovered a face covered in bruises, a split lip, scary shadows under her eyes, and a somber expression that wasn't really her. Her bedraggled plait was spilling brown curls onto her forehead. Ophelia clenched her jaw as she wiped the surgical spirit over Freya's claw mark. It was a clean cut, as if done by a splinter of glass. She'd probably be left with a small scar.

She folded a clean handkerchief, stuck on a cross of plaster, and, after three attempts, got the dressing to hold on her cheek. That done, she planted a kiss on her aunt's forehead. "I'm going to get you out of there," she promised, speaking into her ear.

Ophelia picked up Mime's livery, which she'd thrown to the floor, and buttoned it back on. This disguise would certainly no longer protect her from the Knight, so she'd have to avoid crossing his path.

She went over to Berenilde's bed and, not without difficulty, removed her chain with the little key studded with precious stones. She unlocked the door. From now on, she'd have to act fast. For security reasons, the apartments in the embassy could only be locked from the inside. Aunt Rosaline and Berenilde were both fast asleep, as vulnerable as children; they would be exposed to external dangers until her return.

Ophelia trotted along the corridor. She took the service stairs to get down to the basement. When she went past the servants' dining hall, she was surprised to see policemen there, distinguishable by their cocked hats and blue-and-red uniforms. They were surrounding a table full of valets having their morning coffee, and seemed to be putting them through a thorough interrogation. A surprise inspection? Best not to linger in the vicinity.

Ophelia went from the warehouses to the coal-fired boiler to the plumbing room. She found Gail in none of them. However, she did come across a printed notice plastered all over the walls:

WANTED

Last night a deplorable incident was reported to us. Yesterday evening, a valet serving at Clairdelune hit a defenseless child. The embassy's reputation is at stake! Distinguishing features: black hair, small stature, youngish. He was armed with an oar (?) at the time in question. If you know a valet fitting this description, contact the steward's office without delay. Reward guaranteed.

Philibert, steward of Clairdelune

Ophelia frowned. That little Knight was real poison; he'd
definitely got it in for her. If she encountered the policemen,
she'd end up in the dungeons. She'd have to change her face,
and fast.

She continued along more corridors, hugging the walls, and
sneaked into the laundry like a thief. There, she slipped into
the steam of the boiling vats, between two rows of shirts on
sliding racks. She borrowed a white apron and bonnet. She
made another detour to the washhouse, where she stole a black
dress that was drying on a line. The less Ophelia wanted to
attract attention, the more she kept banging into linen baskets
and washerwomen.

Since she couldn't decently change in the corridors, she
hurried off to Baths Road. She had to change direction several times to avoid the police knocking on doors. Having
made it to her room, she double-locked herself in, caught her
breath back, undressed as quickly as her rib would allow, hid
Mime's livery under her pillow, and put on the dress from
the washhouse. In her haste, she'd started with it on back
to front.

As she was tying the apron around her waist and pinning
the bonnet onto her mass of brown hair, Ophelia was trying
to reason with herself as methodically as possible. What if I'm
inspected? No, the police are prioritizing interrogating valets.
And what if I'm asked questions? I stick to "yes" and "no,"
because my accent mustn't betray me. And if I betray myself
anyhow? I'm in the service of Mother Hildegarde. She's a foreigner, she hires foreigners, full stop.

Ophelia froze when she caught sight of her reflection, her
real reflection, in the wall mirror. She'd completely forgotten

about the state of her face! With her dressing and her bruises, she looked like some poor abused girl. She looked around for some solution amid all her mess. Thorn's coat. Ophelia unhooked it from its peg and examined it from top to bottom. It was the clothing of an official, one could tell at a glance. It was the final ingredient missing from her character: what could be more plausible, for a little servant, than taking "sir's" clothing to the dry cleaner? Ophelia slipped the coat onto a wooden hanger, folded it over one arm, and held it up high with the other. With the coat hoisted before her like a mainsail, no one would notice her face too much.

All of this should afford her enough time to find Gail.

Barely had Ophelia stuck her nose outside her room than a fist almost came down on her. It was Fox who was about to bang on the door. His big, green eyes popped out and his mouth hung half-open in surprise; behind her coat, Ophelia couldn't have looked much less surprised.

"Well I never!" muttered Fox, scratching his red mane. "If I'd thought for a second the mute had company. Sorry, lovey, need to talk to him." He placed his strong hands on Ophelia's shoulders and pushed her gently into Baths Road, as one would dismiss a little girl who hasn't been good. She'd not taken three steps before Fox called her back: "Hey, lovey! Wait!" In a few strides, he'd planted his body, solid as a dresser, fists on hips, in front of her. He lent forward, eyes squinting, trying to get a better look at what was hiding like that behind the big, black coat Ophelia was holding up between them. "His room's empty. What were you getting up to in there, like that, all alone?"

Ophelia would have preferred a question she could have

answered with a yes or a no. Making an enemy of Fox was the last thing she needed to do. Hindered by her coat, she awkwardly pulled her key chain out of an apron pocket. "Lent," she muttered.

Fox raised his thick red eyebrows and checked the label saying 6, Baths Road with the suspicious curled lip of a policeman. "He'd be crazy to go around without his key! You wouldn't have been trying to nick some sandglasses off my buddy, by any chance?" In an authoritarian manner, he pushed Thorn's coat aside like a curtain. His mistrust turned to embarrassment as soon as he saw Ophelia up close, under her glasses and bonnet. "Well, my poor kid!" he sighed, mellowing. "Don't know who your masters are, but they don't hold back. You new? Didn't want to scare you, eh, it's just that I'm looking for my friend. Know where I might find him? There's been, like, a 'Wanted' notice circulating for the past hour. With his guilty old look, he'll be in for it again."

Ophelia was disarmed to realize that this big valet was more deserving of her trust than her own fiancé was. She raised her chin, no longer trying to hide from him, and looked him straight in the eye. "Help me, please. I must see Gail, it's very important."

For the duration of a few blinks, Fox was speechless. "Gail? But what's she . . . What've you . . . Sandglasses alive, who are you?"

"Where is she?" implored Ophelia. "Please."

At the other end of Baths Road, the police made a noisy appearance. They broke into the showers and lavatories by force, dragged out half-naked men, rained truncheon blows on anyone who protested. The cries and insults were bouncing off the walls as gruesome echoes.

Ophelia was terrified. "Come," muttered Fox, taking her by the hand. "If they notice you've got someone else's key on you, they'll lay into you."

Ophelia followed Fox, crushed by his manly grip, tangled up in Thorn's long coat. The sleeping quarters' roads followed one after the other, all alike with their checkered tiles and little lamps. Panicked by the police searches, the servants were standing on their doorsteps and pointing the finger at anyone unfortunate enough to match the description. There were more and more policemen around, but Fox managed to avoid them by taking side routes. He was continually checking his pocket watch. "My mistress is going to wake up soon," he sighed. "Normally, at this time, I've already prepared her tea and ironed her newspaper."

He showed Ophelia into a Compass Rose and opened the door that led directly to the back of the castle. They crossed the exotic menagerie, the aviary, the sheepfold, and the dairy. The geese in the farmyard honked furiously as they passed.

Fox led Ophelia as far as the automobile garage. "The master's organizing a race tomorrow," he explained. "As the chauffeur-mechanic is ill, Gail's been picked to check over the motors. She's in a stinker, I'd better warn you."

Ophelia laid a hand on his arm just as he was about to open the garage doors. "Thank you for helping me, but it would be better if you stay out here," she whispered. "I'll go in alone."

Fox frowned. The lantern hanging over the garage entrance, directly above them, set all his red hair alight. With a cautious look around, he checked that they were definitely alone in this part of the estate. "I've no idea what's going on, I don't know what you're after or who you really are, but one thing is clear to me, right now." He looked down at the silver-buckled patent shoes pointing out from under Ophelia's black dress. "Those are valet's pumps, and of valets with such small feet, I know only one."

"The less you know about me, the better it will be for you," Ophelia tried to persuade him. "People have suffered from knowing me too well. I couldn't forgive myself if anything happened to you through my fault."

Perplexed, Fox scratched the side-whiskers that sprouted on his cheeks like burning bushes. "So, I'm not wrong. It's . . . it's really you? Gadzooks," he muttered, tapping his forehead with his palm, "as embarrassing situations go, this is definitely one. And yet I've witnessed plenty of weird things around here." His great red-haired hands grabbed the ring handles on both doors. "Another reason for going in here with you," he concluded, with a determined pout. "Heck, I've got the right to understand."

It was the first time Ophelia was setting foot in the garage. The place, where the heady smell of petrol hung in the air, seemed deserted. Lit by three ceiling lamps, the elegant cabins of sedan chairs were lined up in the foreground. Apple-green wood, sky-blue curtains, old-rose shafts, floral motifs—no two were the same. The Clairdelune cars were parked at the back of the garage, as they were more rarely brought out. They were objects of luxury displayed mainly to please the eye. The uneven and winding roads of the Citaceleste weren't suited to motorized transport. All of the cars were covered in sheets, except one. From a distance, it resembled a perambulator, with its large, narrow, spoked wheels and flowery hood. Probably a lady's car.

Gail was swearing like a trooper as she bent over the internal combustion engine. Ophelia had only ever seen one in her museum, and only in separate parts. On Anima, the vehicles propelled themselves, like well-trained animals; they didn't need a motor.

"Hey, my lovely!" called out Fox. "A visitor for you!"

Gail let out her final expletive, hit the motor with her monkey wrench, angrily pulled off her gloves, and lifted her protective goggles onto her forehead. Her bright-blue eye and black monocle stared at the little maid Fox had brought to her. Ophelia submitted silently to this scrutiny; she knew that Gail would recognize her, since she'd always seen her as she really was.

"I hope, for your sake, that it's important," she finally spat out, impatiently. And that was it. She asked no question, said not a word that could have compromised Ophelia in front of Fox. "Your secret against my secret." Ophelia awkwardly refolded Thorn's coat, as it was weighing her hands down. It was her turn not to betray Gail.

"I'm in difficulty, and you're the only person I can turn to. I'm going to need your talents."

Cautious, Gail tapped the monocle that cast an impressive shadow under her eyebrow. "*My* talents?"

Ophelia nodded while tucking the curls which were flowing out of her bonnet behind her ear.

"It's not to help out a toff, at least?"

"You have my word that it isn't."

"But what on earth are you muttering about?" asked Fox, exasperated. "So you know each other, you two? What's it mean, all this secrecy?"

Gail tore off her goggles, shook her black curls, and pulled her straps back onto her shoulders. "Don't get involved, Foster. The less you know, the better it'll be for you."

Fox looked so flummoxed that Ophelia felt sorry for him. He was the last person she wanted to hide from, but she had no choice. She'd shown him her real face, and that was already too much.

Gail placed a finger on her mouth to make them be silent. Outside, the geese were honking. "Someone's coming."

"The police," cursed Fox, checking his watch. "They're searching every corner of Clairdelune. Speedy, those guys!" He indicated a low door, barely visible behind the rows of shrouded cars. "We must scram. They absolutely mustn't get their hands on the girl."

Gail tightened the clench of her eyebrow around the monocle. "All the lights are on," she spluttered, "this car's innards are out in the open! They'll realize that we've run away from the place, and sound the alert."

"Not if they find someone right here." Fox hastily took off his livery, rolled up his shirtsleeves, and sprayed himself with motor oil. "Ladies, I present an overworked mechanic!" he sniggered, raising his hands. "I'll take care of the police. Go quickly around the back, both of you."

Ophelia looked at him with both sadness and amazement. She realized what a significant place in her life this big redhead had taken. Inexplicably, she was afraid she'd never see him again once they'd gone through the low door. "Thank you, Foster," she muttered. "Thank you for everything."

He responded with a cheeky wink. "Tell the mute to watch his backside."

"Put these on," muttered Gail, handing him her goggles. "You'll look more credible."

Fox pulled them onto his forehead, took a deep breath to give himself courage, cupped Gail's fierce face in his hands, and kissed her with conviction. She was so shocked that her blue eye widened without her even thinking of pushing him away. When he released her, a huge smile stretched from side-whisker to side-whisker. "Been after her for years, that woman," he whispered.

In the distance, the doors opened onto the silhouettes of the policemen. Gail pushed Ophelia behind a tarpaulin-covered car, led her along the wall in the shadows, and went out with her through the back door.

"Imbecile," she hissed between her teeth.

Ophelia couldn't see much, out in the fake starry night. But she could have sworn that Gail's mouth, usually so hard, had softened.

The Dice

Along corridors and up stairs, Ophelia and Gail made it to the top floor of Clairdelune without crossing the policemen's path. It was a relief to close the door and turn the key in the lock. Ophelia threw Thorn's big coat onto a chair, lifted the drape of the bed's canopy to check Berenilde was still sleeping, and then indicated the divan to Gail. On it, Aunt Rosaline was tossing and turning as though having a bad dream.

"A Mirage has imprisoned her mind in an illusion," Ophelia quietly whispered. "Can you help her to resurface?"

Gail crouched beside the divan and scrutinized Aunt Rosaline. With arms crossed and lips pursed, she peered at her through her black curls for a long time. "Strong stuff," she grumbled. "My compliments to the chef, sterling work. May I wash my hands? I'm covered in grease."

Ophelia filled Berenilde's basin and looked for some soap. She was so nervous she spilt water on the carpet. "Can you help her?" she asked again in a tiny voice, as Gail was having a wash.

"The issue isn't whether I can help her, but why would I help her. Who is this woman, first of all? A friend of the Dragoness?" she spat, with a disdainful glance at the four-poster. "If so, she means little to me."

451

From the depth of her glasses, Ophelia focused on the black monocle to reach the person hiding on the other side of it. "Believe me, this woman's only fault is having me for a niece." Within the darkness of the monocle, Ophelia detected what she'd hoped for: a spark of anger. Gail hated injustice with all her being. "Bring me a stool."

Gail sat opposite the divan and took off her monocle. Her left eye, darker and more unfathomable than a bottomless well, scathingly surveyed Berenilde's apartments. She wanted Ophelia to learn from the spectacle, to show her what this world looked like once the curtain of illusions had been lifted. Wherever her eye fell, that place's appearance changed. The majestic carpet was nothing but a cheap rug. The elegant wallpaper turned into a mold-stained wall. The porcelain vases became plain terra-cotta pots. The canopy was now moth-eaten, the screen ripped, the armchairs faded, the tea service chipped. If the web of illusions unraveled under Gail's implacable gaze, it respun itself as soon as that gaze turned elsewhere.

"Varnish over filth," Archibald had said. Ophelia was gauging how true that was. She would never see Clairdelune in the same way ever again.

Gail leant forward on her stool and gently lifted the aunt's sleeping face between her hands. "What's her name?"

"Rosaline."

"Rosaline," repeated Gail, focusing on her with the closest attention. Her eyes, one blue, the other black, were wide open. Leaning on her elbows on the back of the divan, Ophelia was twisting her fingers with anxiety. Aunt Rosaline's closed eyelids began to quiver, and that quivering spread through the rest of her body. She started to shake violently, but Gail tightened her grip around her face, turning the devastating beam of her Nihilism on her. "Rosaline," she murmured. "Come back, Rosaline. Follow my voice, Rosaline."

The shaking ceased and Gail placed the waxen head back on its cushion. She leapt off the stool, put her monocle back in place, and swiped some cigarettes out of Berenilde's personal box. "Right, I'm off. Fox knows nothing about mechanics and the cars won't service themselves."

Ophelia was dumbfounded. Aunt Rosaline was still lying on the divan with her eyes closed. "It's just that she doesn't seem that awake."

As she was lighting herself a cigarette, Gail attempted a smile that was probably supposed to be reassuring. "There'll be sleeping for a little while longer. Most importantly, don't rush her, she needs to resurface, and believe you me, she's returning from far away. A few hours later, and I wouldn't have caught her."

Ophelia hugged herself to control the shaking of her entire body. Suddenly, she realized that she was burning hot. Her rib seemed to be throbbing to the same rhythm as her heart. It was at once painful and soothing.

"Everything alright?" murmured Gail, concerned.

"It certainly is," Ophelia assured her with a weak smile. "It's . . . it's nerves. I've never been so relieved in my life."

"One mustn't get into such a state." Cigarette in hand, Gail seemed totally perplexed.

Ophelia pushed her glasses up her nose to look her straight in the face. "I owe you a great deal. I don't know what the future holds, but you'll always have an ally in me."

"Spare the fine words," Gail cut in. "Not wishing to upset

you, my darling, but either the court will break all your bones, or it will rot them to the marrow. And I'm not someone to be associated with. I did you a favor, I paid myself in cigarettes, we're quits."

Gail looked thoughtfully, almost sadly, at Aunt Rosaline, and then, with a fierce smile, tweaked Ophelia's nose. "If you really want to do me a favor, don't become one of them. Make the right choices, don't compromise yourself, and find your own path. We'll talk about it again in a few years' time, okay?" She opened the door and tipped the peak of her cap. "Be seeing you!"

When Gail had gone, Ophelia locked the door behind her. The embassy's bedrooms were the safest in the whole of Citaceleste; nothing harmful could happen anymore to anyone here while that door remained locked.

Ophelia leant over Aunt Rosaline and stroked her pinned-back hair. She wanted to wake her up, to be reassured that she really had returned from her past, but Gail had advised not to rush her.

The best she could do now was sleep. Ophelia yawned so hard her eyes watered. She felt as if she had a whole lifetime of sleep to catch up with. She pulled off her maid's bonnet, untied her apron, pushed off her shoes with her toes, and sank into an armchair. When she started flying over forests, towns, and oceans, Ophelia knew that she was dreaming. She spanned the surface of the old world, the one that was but a single entity, as round as an orange. She saw it in a wealth of detail. The sun bouncing off the water, the leaves on the trees, the avenues in the towns, everything leapt out at her with perfect clarity.

Suddenly, the horizon was blocked by a gigantic top hat.

The hat grew bigger and bigger and bigger, and beneath it was Archibald's bittersweet smile. He soon filled the entire landscape, holding Farouk's Book open in his hands. "And yet I did warn you," he said to Ophelia. "Everyone hates the Treasurer, and the Treasurer hates everyone. Did you really think you were so special as to be an exception to the rule?"

Ophelia decided she didn't like this dream and opened her eyes. Despite the warmth from the radiator, she was shivering. She blew on her palm and hot breath returned. A touch of fever? She got up to find a blanket but, between them, Berenilde and Aunt Rosaline already had them all. Ironically, all that was left to Ophelia was Thorn's big coat. She wasn't so proud as to cold-shoulder it. She returned to her chair and curled up in a ball inside the coat. The clock chimed, but she couldn't bear to count the chimes.

The chair wasn't very comfortable—it was too crowded. Space had to be made for the ministers with their haughty moustaches. Would they ever shut up? Ophelia could never sleep with all this waffle. And what were they discussing? Food and drink, of course; it's all that came out of their mouths. "Provisions are running short!" "Let's levy a tax!" "We must punish the poachers!" "Let's discuss it round a table!" Ophelia felt only revulsion for their bulging bellies, but none sickened her more than Farouk. His very existence was a mistake. His courtiers tried to impress him, they intoxicated him with pleasures, and they held the reins of power in his place. No, Ophelia could definitely never rest here. She would have liked to leave this place, to go outdoors, the real outdoors, to gulp enough wind to vitrify her lungs, but she lacked time. She always lacked time. She sat on tribunals, in councils, at parliaments. She kept herself to herself; listened to the opinions of one side and then the other; sometimes deliberated, when those idiots were rushing headlong down a dead end. In any case, it was the numbers that decided. Numbers never get it wrong, do they? The potential of the resources, the number of inhabitants, that's all concrete. So that little fatso, there, who's claiming more than he's due, he'll go off empty-handed, quietly cursing Ophelia, complaining about her, and that's it. As far as complaints, Ophelia would receive a daily dose. She no longer counted her enemies, but her implacable logic always carried the day over their biased interpretation of sharing. They'd already tried to saddle her with a legal clerk, just to check, you know, that her integrity was unimpeachable. And they'd fallen flat on their faces because she relied only on numbers. Not on her conscience, or on ethics, only on numbers. So much for a legal clerk!

But that was actually a strange thought, because Ophelia suddenly realized that she was herself a legal clerk. A legal clerk with an astronomical memory, keen to prove herself, inexperienced. A young clerk who never made mistakes, which infuriated the old treasurer. He saw her as a pernicious insect, an opportunist prepared to push him down the stairs to usurp him. What an imbecile! He'd never know that, behind her stubborn silences, all she sought was his approval, and that at least one person would grieve on the day he died. But that would be much later.

For now, Ophelia was writhing in pain. Poison. It was so predictable; she couldn't trust anyone, anyone but her aunt. Was she going to die here, on this carpet? No, Ophelia was far from death. She was just a little girl who spent her days playing with dice, alone and silent, keeping herself to herself. Berenilde tried everything under the sun to entertain her—she'd even given her a lovely gold watch—but Ophelia preferred the dice. The dice were random, full of surprises; they weren't inevitably disappointing like human beings.

Ophelia felt less bitter as she continued to become younger. She ran around Berenilde's estate until she was breathless. She tried to catch an already well-built adolescent who taunted her from the top of stairs by sticking his tongue out at her. It was her brother, Godfrey. That is, her half-brother—she wasn't allowed to say "brother." It was a stupid expression; it wasn't, after all, half a boy who was charging just ahead of her. And it wasn't half a girl who, around the corner of a corridor, threw herself at her legs in fits of laughter. Ophelia liked it when Berenilde invited Godfrey and Freya over, even if they did sometimes hurt her with their claws. She didn't like it, on the other hand, when their mother came, too, and gave her that disgusted look. Ophelia hated that look. It was a look that tore into one's head, tortured one from the inside without anyone seeing a thing. Ophelia spat into her tea as revenge. But that was after, long after the disgrace of her mother, long after the death of her father, long after her aunt had taken her under her wing. Right now, Ophelia is playing her favorite game with Freya, up on the ramparts, at that rare time of year when it was mild enough to make the most of the sunshine. The dice game, with dice carved by Godfrey himself. Freya throws them, decides on the combination of numbers—"you add them," "you divide them," "you multiply them," "you subtract them"—and then she checks on her abacus. The game in itself bores Ophelia. She would have preferred it tougher, with fractions, equations, powers, but catching her sister's look of admiration every time, it warmed the cockles. When Freya throws the dice, she feels at last that she exists.

An alarm sounded. Ophelia blinked, dazed, all twisted in her chair. As she was untangling the strands of hair caught up in her glasses, she looked frantically around her. Where was that noise coming from? The sleeping shadow of Berenilde was quite still behind the drape of the canopy. The flames of the gas lamps were gently sputtering. Aunt Rosaline was snoring on her divan. It took Ophelia a long while to realize that it was the ringing of the telephone that she was hearing.

Finally, it shut up, leaving a deafening silence in the apartments.

Ophelia dragged herself out of her chair, feeling stiff all over, her head humming. The fever must have gone down, but her legs were all numb. She leant over her aunt, hoping to see her open her eyes at last, but she had to resign herself to waiting a bit longer. Gail had said she would resurface on her own; she must trust her. She padded over to the bathroom, rolled up the flapping sleeves of Thorn's coat, pulled off her gloves, folded her glasses, turned the tap on, and splashed plenty of water on her face. She needed to cleanse herself of all those strange dreams.

Her shortsighted eyes met in the mirror above the sink. Her dressing had come unstuck and the gash on her cheek had been bleeding again. It was when she put her gloves back on that she noticed the hole through which her little finger was poking. "Well," she muttered to herself, taking a closer look, "that's what you get for chewing on the seams."

Ophelia sat on the edge of the bath and stared at the huge

coat she was wrapped up in. Had she read Thorn's memories due to the hole in her glove? It was an adult's coat, and she'd gone back to his childhood—it must be something else. She rummaged in the pockets and finally found what she was looking for under a seam in the lining. Two little dice, clumsily carved by hand. It was them that, totally unintentionally, she'd read.

Ophelia looked at them with nostalgia, even a little sadness, and then got a grip by closing her fist. She mustn't confuse Thorn's feelings with her own. That thought stopped her in her tracks. Thorn's feelings? If that schemer had once had any, he'd lost them along the way. Doubtless, life hadn't been kind to him, but Ophelia wasn't in the mood for showing compassion.

She got rid of the coat as she would have shed a skin that didn't belong to her. She changed her dressing, shuffled around the little sitting room, and consulted the clock. Eleven o'clock—well into the morning. The Dragons must have set off for the hunt a long time ago; Ophelia was delighted to have escaped that family duty.

The phone started ringing again, and finally succeeded in waking up Berenilde. "The devil take that invention!" she grumbled, pushing back the drape of her bed. But she still didn't answer it. Her tattooed hands fluttered like butterflies to fluff up her waves of blonde hair. Sleep had given her back the freshness of a young girl, but it had crumpled her lovely costume. "Do make us some coffee, dear girl. We're really going to need it."

Ophelia was of the same opinion. She put a saucepan of water on the gas cooker, almost set fire to her glove striking a match, and worked the coffee grinder. She found Berenilde leaning her elbows on the little table in the sitting room, her chin resting on her linked fingers, her eyes searching her cigarette box. "Did I really smoke that much, yesterday?"

Ophelia put a cup of coffee in front of her, deeming it not essential to inform her that a female mechanic had helped herself to her supply. As soon as she sat at the table, Berenilde turned her crystal-clear eyes on her. "I don't have a very detailed memory of our conversation yesterday, but I remember enough to declare this a grave time." Ophelia passed her the sugar bowl, expecting the verdict. "Speaking of time, what is it?" asked Berenilde, glancing at the clock.

"Past eleven, madam."

Gripping her coffee spoon, Ophelia braced herself for the thunderbolt that was about to hit the table: "What! And the thought of getting me up never entered your little bird brain? Are you not aware of how important this hunting party was to me? Because of you, I'm going to be called feeble, good-for-nothing, past it!"

But not a bit of it. Berenilde dropped a sugar cube into her coffee and sighed. "Never mind. To be frank, I stopped thinking about that hunt the very moment Farouk laid eyes on me. And honestly," she added with a dreamy smile, "he's exhausted me!"

Ophelia brought her cup to her lips. That was the sort of detail she'd have gladly done without.

"Your coffee's terrible," Berenilde declared, puckering her pretty lips. "You really haven't any talent for life in society."

Ophelia had to admit that she wasn't wrong. Even after adding sugar and milk, she was struggling to drink her own cup.

"I think the Knight leaves us no choice," continued Berenilde. "Even if I gave you another face and another identity, that child would strip you bare in the blink of an eye. The secret of your presence here is unravelling. There are two options: either we find you a better hiding place until the day of the wedding . . . (Berenilde's long, smooth nails tapped the handle of her porcelain cup) . . . or you make your official entrance at court."

With a flick of her napkin, Ophelia wiped the coffee she'd just spilt on the tablecloth. She'd envisaged this possibility, but it pained her to hear it spoken. As things stood now, she'd actually prefer to play at being Berenilde's valet than at being Thorn's fiancée.

Berenilde leant back in her armchair and crossed her hands over her rounded stomach. "Obviously, if you want to survive until your marriage, that can only be done on one condition, and one condition alone. You'll have to be Farouk's official ward."

"His ward?" repeated Ophelia, stressing both words. "What qualities are required to deserve such an honor?"

"In your situation, I think that you yourself are all that's required!" Berenilde teased her. "Farouk's dying to know you, you represent a great deal in his eyes. Too much, in fact. That's why Thorn has always categorically refused for you to go near him."

Ophelia pushed her glasses up her nose. "What do you mean by that?"

"If I had the slightest idea, you wouldn't see me hesitating like this," said Berenilde, annoyed. "Who knows with Farouk, he's so unpredictable! What I dread is his impatience. Until now, I've concealed your presence in his own Citaceleste—do you know why?"

Ophelia was already preparing for the worst.

"Because I dread that he'll get you started on his Book. The outcome of such a reading terrifies me. If you fail, which I don't doubt given the difficulties of your predecessors, I fear that he'll succumb to a fit of bad temper."

Ophelia gave up on her coffee, and put the cup back on the saucer. "You're telling me that he might punish me if I don't give him immediate satisfaction?"

"He certainly wouldn't want to make you suffer," sighed Berenilde, "but I fear that the outcome will be the same in the end. So many others have left their spirit there before you! And he, child that he is, will be sorry when it's too late, as usual. Farouk can't get used to the vulnerability of mortals, in particular those who haven't inherited his powers. In his hands, you're but a wisp of straw."

"Might he be a bit stupid, your family spirit?"

Berenilde looked with astonishment at Ophelia, but she didn't bat an eyelid. She'd lived through too much recently to keep her thoughts to herself any longer. "That's the kind of suggestion that will shorten your stay with us if you make it in public," Berenilde warned her.

"What makes Farouk's Book so different from Artemis's?" asked Ophelia, adopting a professional tone. "Why should one be readable, and the other not?"

Berenilde shrugged a shoulder, which escaped seductively from her dress. "To be honest with you, my girl, I'm barely interested in this business. I've only seen this Book once, and that was enough for me. It's a totally hideous and unwholesome object. It looks like—"

"Human skin," murmured Ophelia, "or something resembling

it. I was wondering whether a particular element featured in its composition."

Berenilde gave her a look sparkling with malice. "Well, that's not your business, it's Thorn's. Be content with marrying him, giving him your family power, and a few heirs along the way. We ask nothing more of you."

Cut to the quick, Ophelia's lips tightened. She felt negated, both as a person and as a professional. "In that case, what do you suggest we do?"

Berenilde stood up, looking resolute. "I'm going to reason with Farouk. He will understand that, in his own interest, he must guarantee your safety until the marriage, and, in particular, not expect anything of you. He'll listen to me, I carry influence with him. Thorn will be furious with me, but I can't see a better solution."

Ophelia contemplated the light playing on the surface of her coffee, disturbed by the movement of her spoon. What would really make Thorn furious? That wrong be done to his fiancée, or that she become unusable before even being of any use? And what then, she asked herself, bitterly. Once she'd transmitted her power to him, and he'd used it, what would become of her? Wouldn't her life in the Pole just be reduced to drinking tea and making polite conversation? No, she decided, observing her face upside down in the bowl of her spoon, I'll be sure to create a different future for myself, whether they like it or not.

Berenilde's astonished gasp jolted Ophelia from her ruminations. Aunt Rosaline had just sat up on the divan to give a sharp look at the clock. "Second-hands alive!" she cursed. "Soon midday and I'm still lounging in bed."

Ophelia's dark thoughts were instantly dispelled. She leapt up so suddenly from her chair that she knocked it over on to the carpet. Berenilde, in contrast, sat down, hands on stomach, flabbergasted. "Madam Rosaline? Are you really here, among us?"

Aunt Rosaline stuck pins into her loosened bun. "Do I look as if I'm somewhere else?"

"It's quite simply impossible."

"The more time I spend with you, the less I understand you," muttered Aunt Rosaline, frowning. "And you, what have you got to smile about like that?" she asked, turning to Ophelia. "You're wearing a dress now? And what's that dressing on your cheek? Gadzooks, what did you go and tear that on?" Aunt Rosaline seized her hand and squinted at her little finger, playing peekaboo through the hole. "You're going to be reading here, there, and everywhere! Where are your spare pairs? Pass me that glove so I can mend it for you. And put that grin away, it sends shivers down my spine."

Try as she might, Ophelia couldn't put it away; it was either that or crying. As for Berenilde, she still hadn't got over her surprise, as Aunt Rosaline was fetching the sewing box from a cupboard. "Was I mistaken?"

Ophelia felt sorry for her, but she certainly wasn't about to tell her that she'd sought the services of a Nihilist.

The wall telephone started ringing again. "The phone's ringing," remarked Aunt Rosaline with her unshakeable sense of reality. "It may be important."

Berenilde, sitting pensively, concurred, and looked up at Ophelia. "Answer it, my dear."

Aunt Rosaline, who was pushing thread through the eye of her needle, panicked. "Her? But her voice? Her accent?"

"The time for secrets is over," declared Berenilde. "Answer it, dear girl."

Ophelia breathed in. If it was Archibald, it would make a great prologue to her entrance on the scene. Awkwardly, she unhooked the ivory telephone with her remaining gloved hand. She'd seen her parents using a telephone occasionally, but had never used one herself. Barely had she pressed the receiver to her ear when a crash of thunder burst her eardrum: "Hello!" Ophelia almost dropped the phone. "Thorn?"

There was a sudden silence, broken by Thorn's choked breathing. Ophelia resisted the urge to hang up on him. She would have preferred to settle her scores with him face-to-face. If he ever had the gall to get angry with her, she was ready for him.

"You?" Thorn uttered, reluctantly. "Very good. That's . . . that's very good. And my aunt, she is . . . is she near you?" Ophelia stared, wide-eyed. Such confused stuttering, coming from Thorn's mouth, was certainly unusual. "Yes, in the end we stayed here, all three of us."

In the receiver, she heard Thorn catching his breath. It was impressive, being able to hear him like this, as if he were close by, without having to face him. "No doubt you would like to speak to her?" suggested Ophelia, coldly. "I think you have plenty to talk about."

It was when she was no longer expecting it that the explosion occurred. "Stayed here?" roared Thorn. "I've been trying to join you for hours now, banging on your door. Do you have the slightest idea what I . . . No, clearly, it didn't even occur to you!"

Ophelia held the receiver a few centimeters away. She was

starting to think that Thorn must have been drinking. "You're bursting my eardrum. You don't need to shout, I'm receiving you loud and clear. For your information, it's not yet midday, and we've just woken up."

"Midday?" repeated Thorn, bewildered. "How in god's name can one confuse midday and midnight?"

"Midnight?" asked Ophelia, astonished.

"Midnight?" echoed Berenilde and Aunt Rosaline in unison behind her.

"So you're aware of nothing? You've been sleeping all this time?" Thorn's voice was bristling with static electricity. Ophelia clung to the receiver. He hadn't been drinking, it was much more serious than that. "What's happened?" she whispered.

Another silence filled the telephone, so lengthy that Ophelia thought they'd been cut off. When Thorn spoke once more, his voice had regained its distant tone and hard accent. "I'm calling you from Archibald's office. Allow three minutes for me to come up and join you. Don't open your door before then."

"Why? Thorn, what's going on?"

"Freya, Godfrey, Father Vladimir, and the others," he said slowly. "It would seem that they are all dead."

The Angel

Berenilde had turned so white that Ophelia and Aunt Rosaline each held her by an arm to help her up. But she displayed Olympian calm as she gave them her advice. "Awaiting us, on the other side of that door, are nothing but vultures. Answer none of their questions, avoid revealing anything about yourself."

She grabbed her little key studded with precious stones and pushed it into the lock. With a simple click, she plunged all three of them into Clairdelune's mayhem. The antechamber next door had been besieged by policemen and nobles. All was confusion, the sounds of coming and going, stifled exclamations. As soon as they saw the door half-opening, silence fell. Everyone stared at Berenilde with unseemly curiosity, and then the questions shot out like fireworks.

"Madam Berenilde, we've been told your whole family has perished due to a poorly organized hunt. Have the Dragons belied their reputation as peerless hunters?"

"Why weren't you with your family? It's said you had words with them, only yesterday. Did you, then, have a premonition of what was going to happen?"

"Your clan has gone; do you think your position at court is still legitimate?"

Ophelia, unsurprised at such maliciousness, heard it all without seeing those who were spouting it. Standing bravely in the doorway, Berenilde blocked her view of the antechamber. She faced the onslaught in silence, her hands crossed on her dress, searching for Thorn. Ophelia stiffened when she heard a woman start to speak. "The rumor's going around that you're hiding a reader from Anima. Is she in these apartments? Why aren't you introducing her to us?"

The woman cried out and several voices protested. Ophelia didn't have to witness the scene to know that Thorn had just arrived, and was pushing aside all these charming people.

"Mr. Treasurer, will the death of the hunters affect our larder?"

"What measures do you intend to take?"

Thorn's only response was to push his aunt inside, usher Archibald and another man in, and then lock the apartments. The din from the antechamber ceased immediately; they had now moved beyond space. Berenilde then threw herself at Thorn with a fervor that knocked them both against the door. She gripped his big, thin body, a head taller than hers, with all her might. "My dear boy, I'm so relieved to see you!"

Stiff as a post, Thorn didn't seem to know what to do with his too-long arms. His hawk's eyes bored into Ophelia's glasses. She mustn't have looked great, with her bruised face, streaming hair, maid's dress, bare arms, and only one hand gloved out of two, but none of that bothered her. What bothered her was to be bursting with an anger that she couldn't express. She was furious with Thorn, but given the circumstances, couldn't have a go at him.

Ophelia went from this predicament straight into another one. Archibald bowed low before her, top hat held to chest.

"My humble respects, Thorn's fiancée! How the devil have you landed at my place?"

His angelic face, pale and delicate, tipped her a knowing wink. As was to be expected, Ophelia's little improvisation in the poppy garden hadn't deceived him. All she could hope was that he wouldn't choose this very evening to give her away.

"Might I finally know your name?" he persisted, with a candid smile.

"Ophelia," replied Berenilde, on her behalf. "If you don't mind, we'll do the introductions some other time. We have much more urgent business to discuss."

Archibald barely listened to her. His luminous eyes were studying Ophelia more closely. "Have you suffered ill-treatment, little Ophelia?"

She struggled to answer him. She was hardly going to accuse his own policemen, was she? Since she lowered her eyes, Archibald passed a finger over the dressing on her cheek with such familiarity that Aunt Rosaline coughed against her fist. As for Thorn, he frowned hard enough to split his forehead. "We've gathered this evening to talk," declared Archibald. "So, let's talk!"

He threw himself into an armchair and perched his gaping shoes on a footrest. Aunt Rosaline prepared tea. Thorn folded each limb down on to the divan, awkward among such feminine furnishings. When Berenilde sat beside him and collapsed against the epaulettes of his uniform, he didn't look at her once; his ferrous eyes followed Ophelia's slightest move and gesture. Feeling uncomfortable, she didn't know where to put herself, or what to do with her hands. She backed into a corner of the room, even banging her head on a shelf.

The man who had entered with Thorn and Archibald remained standing in the middle of the carpet. Clad in a thick, gray fur, he was no young thing. His prominent nose, reddened with rosacea, dominated his ill-shaven face. He was rubbing his dirty shoes against his trousers to make them more presentable.

"Jan," said Archibald, "deliver your report to Madam Berenilde."

"A nasty business," muttered the man. "A nasty business."

Ophelia had no memory for faces, so it took her a while to recall where she'd seen him before. He was the gamekeeper who had escorted them to Citaceleste, on the day they'd arrived in the Pole.

"We're listening to you, Jan," Berenilde said, gently. "Express yourself freely, you'll be rewarded for your sincerity."

"A massacre, my dear lady," growled the man. "If I escaped meself, it's a miracle. A true miracle, lady." He clumsily grabbed the cup of tea Aunt Rosaline was serving him, emptied it noisily, put it down on a pedestal table, and started shaking his hands about as if they were puppets. "I'm going to repeat to you what I told yer nephew and the ambassador. Yer family, they were all there, down yonder. Even three kids whose mugs I'd never seen before. 'Scuse me if I seem coarse, but I mustn't keep nothing from you, eh? So, I'd better warn you, lady, yer absence was fiercely criticized. They was saying that you was disowning yer own, and about to start yer own line, and that they'd got the message, loud and clear. And that the 'bastard's fiancée,' to use their words—I'd be ashamed, I would, to come out with the like—they'd never recognize her, not her, and not the brats she'd pull out the oven. At that, they launched the hunt, just like they do every year. Me, knowing the forest like

470

the back of me hand, I played me part and I picked 'em some Beasts. Not the knocked-up females, eh, them we never touch. But I'd got three big males there, enough to give you meat all year. All that was left was to comb, surround, isolate, and kill—just the old routine!"

Ophelia was listening to him with increasing apprehension. This man had the strongest of accents, but she found him easier to understand today.

"Never witnessed the like, I haven't. The Beasts, they started charging from all directions, randomly, all foaming at the mouth. As if possessed. Well, the Dragons, they went for it with their claws, slashing away straight into the flesh, again, and again, and again. But the Beasts, there were always more of 'em, it were never-ending! They trampled over those they didn't devour. I thought . . . Dammit, I thought I was a goner, and yet I know my job."

Hidden in her corner, Ophelia closed her eyes. Yesterday, she'd wanted never to see her in-laws ever again. But never, ever would she have wanted things to end up like this. She thought of Thorn's memories, she thought of Godfrey and Freya as children, she thought of the triplets, whom Father Vladimir was so proud to take hunting . . . All night, Ophelia had felt stifled by a stormy atmosphere. The lightning had well and truly struck.

The gamekeeper rubbed his chin, on which a bushy beard grew. His eyes glazed over. "You'll think I've lost the plot, and even I, when I hear meself, I think I'm nuts. An angel, lady, an angel saved me from the carnage. He appeared in the middle of the snow and the Beasts, they all left, gentle as lambs. It's thanks to that angel I were spared. One hell of a miracle . . . with all due respect, madam." The man opened a flask of spirits and downed several swigs. "Why me?" he asked, wiping his moustache on his sleeve. "Why that cherub saved me, and not them others. That I'll never understand."

Stunned, Ophelia couldn't resist a sidelong glance at Thorn to see his reaction, but she couldn't gauge his state of mind. He'd been staring at his fob watch for some time, as if its hands had frozen.

"So, you are confirming to me that all the members of my family died during this hunt?" Berenilde asked, patiently. "Every single one of them?"

The gamekeeper couldn't bring himself to look anyone in the eye. "We found not one survivor. Some bodies, they're unrecognizable. I swear to you on me life, we'll comb that forest as long as it takes to collect them bodies. Give 'em a decent burial, you know? And who knows, eh? The angel might have saved some others?"

Berenilde managed a voluptuous smile. "You're naïve! What did he look like, then, this cherub who fell from the sky? Like a well-dressed child, with golden-blond hair and cute chubby cheeks?"

Ophelia puffed on the lenses of her glasses and wiped them on her dress. The Knight. Again, and always, the Knight.

"You know 'im?" asked the man, alarmed.

Berenilde let out a resounding laugh. Thorn, roused from his lethargy, looked sharply down at her to make her control herself. She was very flushed and her curls were tumbling over her cheeks with an abandon that wasn't like her. "Possessed Beasts, is that it? Your angel blew illusions into their brains that only a depraved imagination could conceive of. Illusions that

472

enraged them, starved them, and that he then dismissed with a click of his fingers." Berenilde matched the action to the words with such a flourish that it took the gamekeeper's breath away. Overcome, he stared with eyes like plates. "Do you know why that little angel saved you?" continued Berenilde. "So that you could then describe, in the minutest detail, exactly how my family was massacred."

"That's a very serious accusation, dear friend," Archibald intervened, pointing at his tattooed forehead. "An accusation in front of a multitude of witnesses." His lips curled into a smile, but it was at Ophelia that he directed it. Through him, the whole Web was witnessing the scene and she was part of the show.

In the blink of an eye, Berenilde found her serene face again. Her chest, which was heaving in fits and starts, calmed down, along with her breathing. Her skin returned to being as white as porcelain. "An accusation? Have I even suggested a name?"

Archibald peered deep into his punctured top hat, as if he found that hole more fascinating than all the people present. "I believed, listening to you, that this 'angel' was no stranger to you."

Berenilde looked up at Thorn for guidance. Rigid on the divan, he responded with a scathing look. From the depths of his silence, he seemed to be exhorting her: "Play the game." This silent exchange had lasted but an instant, but it allowed Ophelia to realize how mistaken she'd been about Thorn. She'd long seen him as Berenilde's puppet when, in fact, he'd always been pulling the strings.

"I'm distraught by the death of my family," Berenilde murmured with a weak smile. "I'm distracted with pain. What really happened today, no one knows and no one ever will know."

With her eyes of honey and face of marble, she was back onstage playing a part. Poor Jan, totally flummoxed, couldn't make head or tail of it all.

As for Ophelia, she really didn't know what to think of all she'd just heard. By setting the policemen on Mime, and imprisoning Aunt Rosaline's mind, and compelling that poor servant to jump out of the window, had the Knight been maneuvering to keep Berenilde here to stop her from going to that hunt? It was only a hypothesis. It was forever only hypotheses. That child was formidable. His shadow hung over every disaster, but one could never accuse him of anything.

"So, we'll consider the matter closed?" chirped Archibald. "A deplorable hunting accident?"

At least one person was relishing the situation this evening. Ophelia would have found him hateful had she not got the feeling that each of his interventions was aimed at protecting Berenilde from her own state of mind.

"Provisionally, at least." All eyes turned to Thorn. These were the first words he had uttered since the start of their little meeting.

"That stands to reason," said Archibald, with a touch of irony. "If the inquest brings to light aspects that would suggest criminal goings-on, I don't doubt that you will reopen the file, Mr. Treasurer. It's right up your alley, it seems to me."

"As it will be up yours to compile your report for Farouk, Mr. Ambassador," Thorn retorted, shooting him a razor-sharp look. "My aunt's position at court has become precarious; can I count on you to defend her interests?"

Ophelia sensed from his tone that it was more of a threat than a request. Archibald's smile broadened. One by one, he lifted his shoes off the footrest and put his old top hat back on. "Would Mr. Treasurer be casting doubt over the zeal with which I will defend his aunt?"

"Haven't you already let her down in the past?" Thorn hissed between his teeth.

Still inhabited by her alter ego, Ophelia wore a faraway, barely concerned look on her face. Yet she didn't miss a scrap of what was being said and not being said. So Archibald had betrayed Berenilde in the past? Was that why Thorn hated him even more than the others?

"You're speaking of bygone days," Archibald whispered, without dropping his smile. "What a tenacious memory! But I understand your concern. You owe your social advancement to the support of your aunt. If she falls, you could well fall with her."

"Ambassador!" protested Berenilde. "Your role is not to add fuel to the flames."

Ophelia watched Thorn, motionless on the divan, closely. Archibald's comment didn't seem to have affected him, but his long, gnarled hands had tightened around his knees.

"My role, madam, is to tell the truth, the whole truth, and nothing but the truth," responded Archibald, suavely. "Your nephew only lost half of his family today. The other half is still very much alive, somewhere in the provinces. And that half, Mr. Treasurer," he concluded, calmly looking at Thorn, "was brought down by your mother's misdemeanor."

Thorn's eyes narrowed into two gray slits, but Berenilde laid her hand over his to calm him down. "For goodness' sake, gentlemen, let's stop stirring up all those old stories! We have to think of the future. Archibald, can I count on your support?"

With a flick, he straightened up his top hat, uncovering his big, clear eyes. "I have something better to propose to you than support, dear friend. I propose an alliance. Make me the godfather of your child, and henceforth you can consider my whole family as your own."

Ophelia dived into a handkerchief so she could cough at will. Godfather to Farouk's direct descendant? Here was a man who didn't miss a trick. Taken aback, Berenilde had instinctively laid her hands on her stomach. Thorn, on the other hand, went white with rage and seemed to be battling a desire to make Archibald swallow his hat.

"I'm not in a position to refuse your help," Berenilde finally responded, sounding resigned. "So that is how it will be."

"Is that an official announcement?" insisted Archibald, again tapping his forehead tattoo.

"Archibald, I make you the godfather of my child," she declared, as patiently as she could. "Will your protection extend to my nephew?"

Archibald tempered his smile. "You're asking a great deal of me, madam. People of my own gender inspire me with the most profound indifference and I have no desire to introduce such a lugubrious individual into my family."

"And I have no desire to be your relation," spat Thorn.

"Supposing I bend my principles," Archibald continued, regardless. "I would only accept to offer my protection to your little fiancée if she herself made the request."

Ophelia's eyebrows shot up as she felt the force of Archibald's twinkling wink. From having been continuously treated like part of the furniture, she no longer expected to be asked her opinion.

"Decline his offer," Thorn commanded her.

"For once, I totally agree with him," Aunt Rosaline suddenly broke in, angrily putting down her tea tray. "I will not permit you to mix with such an unseemly crowd."

Archibald looked at her with obvious curiosity. "So the lady's companion was an Animist? I was deceived under my own roof!" Far from being offended, he seemed quite the opposite: agreeably surprised. He turned to Ophelia, clicking his heels, and opened his eyes wide, so wide that the sky seemed to take over his face. From their divan, Thorn and Berenilde were glaring at her to convey that they expected more than just idiotic silence from her.

In Ophelia's head, an alien thought now dominated all other thoughts: "Make your own choices, little miss. If you don't seize your freedom today, it will be too late tomorrow."

Archibald continued innocently staring at her, as though that thought really hadn't come from him. Ophelia decided that he was right, she must make her own choices from now on. "You are a man without morals," she declared, as loudly as possible. "But I know you never lie, and it's truth that I need. I consent to listen to all the advice that you care to give me."

Ophelia had looked Thorn straight in the eye as she'd said these words, because she was addressing him, too. She saw his angular body crumple. Archibald, on the other hand, couldn't stop smiling.

"I think we're going to get on famously, Thorn's fiancée. We're friends from this moment onwards!" He tipped his hat

477

at her, deposited a kiss on Berenilde's hand, and left, taking the poor, disorientated gamekeeper with him. The cries and questions of the nobles burst through when the ambassador went through the antechamber door; calm returned as soon as Aunt Rosaline turned the key.

There was a long, tense silence during which Ophelia felt the general disapproval bearing down on her. "I'm staggered by your arrogance," said an indignant Berenilde as she stood up.

"I was asked for my opinion and I gave it," responded Ophelia, as placidly as she could.

"Your opinion? You're in no position to have an opinion. Your only opinions will be those dictated to you by my nephew."

Stiff as a corpse, Thorn's eyes didn't leave the carpet. His chiselled profile was expressionless.

"By what right do you publicly oppose the wishes of your future husband?" Berenilde continued, her voice icy. Ophelia didn't need to think about the question for very long. Her face was in a dreadful state, one more clawing wasn't going to stop her. "By the right that I granted to myself," she said, with confidence. "From the moment I discovered that you were manipulating me."

In the clear water of Berenilde's eyes there was a kind of eddy. "How dare you speak to us in that tone?" she whispered, choked. "You're nothing without us, my poor girl, absolutely nothing—"

"Be quiet."

Berenilde spun around. Thorn had issued this order in a voice full of thunder. He unfolded his big body from the divan and gave his aunt a look so piercing it made her blanch.

478

"It so happens that her opinion does have importance. What exactly did you say to her?"

Berenilde was so shocked he was attacking her that she was struck dumb. Ophelia decided to reply in her stead. She raised her chin to meet Thorn's scarred eye, right up there. The dark shadows around it were scary and his pale hair had never been so badly combed. He had been too tested today for her to unleash her full fury on him, but she couldn't postpone this conversation. "I know about the Book. I know your true ambitions. You're using the marriage to take away part of my power and fortify yourself with it. What I regret is not having heard about it from your mouth."

"And what I regret, personally," grumbled Aunt Rosaline, giving her back her mended glove, "is not understanding what you're wittering on about."

Thorn had taken refuge behind his watch, as he always did when a situation was out of his control. He wound it up, closed the cover, reopened the cover, but it changed nothing: the timeline had been broken. From today, nothing would ever be as it was. "What's done is done," was all he said, in a neutral tone. "We have other fish to fry right now."

Ophelia wouldn't have thought it possible, but she felt even more disappointed in Thorn. He'd expressed no regret, come up with no excuse. She suddenly realized that a small part of her had continued secretly to hope that Berenilde had lied to her and that he had nothing to do with this scheming.

Exasperated, Ophelia pulled on her glove and helped her aunt clear away the tea things. She was in such a nervous state that she broke two cups and a saucer.

"We no longer have any choice, Thorn," Berenilde sighed.

479

"We must present your fiancée to Farouk, and the sooner the better. Everyone's soon going to know she's here. It would be dangerous to hide her from him for any longer."

"Isn't it even more dangerous to just spring her on him?" he muttered.

"I'll ensure that he takes her under his wing. I promise you it will all go well."

"But of course," hissed Thorn, scathingly. "It was just so simple, why didn't we think of it sooner?"

In the little kitchen, Aunt Rosaline exchanged an astonished glance with Ophelia. It was the first time Thorn was being so insolent to Berenilde in their presence.

"Will you no longer trust me, then?" she asked, reproachfully.

Heavy steps approached the kitchen. Thorn bowed his head to avoid banging it on the lintel, too low for his height, and leant against the door frame. Busy drying up, Ophelia ignored his eyes boring into her. What was he expecting? A kind word? She didn't want to look him in the face anymore.

"It's Farouk that I don't trust at all," said Thorn in a hard voice. "He's so forgetful and so impatient."

"Not if I stay by his side to bring him to reason," declared Berenilde, standing behind him.

"You'll be sacrificing what independence you have left."

"I'm prepared for that."

Thorn didn't take his eyes off Ophelia. Concentrate as she might on drying a teapot, she could still sense him out of the corner of her glasses.

"You keep drawing her closer to the epicenter that I, personally, wanted to keep her away from," he complained.

"I can't see any alternatives."

"Please, do just carry on as if I weren't here," said Ophelia, riled. "It's not as if it concerns me, after all." She looked up and, this time, couldn't avoid Thorn's eyes bearing down on her. She discovered what she'd feared seeing in them. A profound weariness. She didn't want to feel sorry for him, to think about those two little dice.

Thorn came right into the kitchen. "Leave us for a moment," he asked Aunt Rosaline, who was putting the tea service away in a cupboard. She gritted her long horse's teeth. "On the condition that this door remains open."

Aunt Rosaline joined Berenilde in the sitting room, and Thorn pulled the door to as much as possible. There was only a gas lamp in the kitchen; it projected Thorn's skeletal shadow onto the wallpaper as he stood, at full height, before Ophelia.

"You knew him." He'd whispered these words very stiffly. "It's not the first time that you're meeting him," he continued. "As your real self, I mean."

It took Ophelia a while to understand that he was talking about Archibald. She pushed back the wave of hair falling over her glasses like a curtain. "No, indeed. I'd already met him by accident."

"The night of your getaway."

"Yes."

"And he knew who you were for all this time."

"I lied to him. Not very well, I'll admit, but he never made the connection between Mime and me."

"You might have informed me."

"No doubt."

"Maybe you had reasons for not telling me about this meeting?"

Ophelia's neck was aching from looking up at Thorn. She noticed, in the lamplight, that the muscles along his jaw had tightened. "I hope you're not alluding to what I think you are," she said in a subdued voice.

"Should I deduce that he didn't dishonor you?"

Ophelia was exploding inside. Well, that really took the cake! "No. You, on the other hand, have humiliated me more than anyone has."

Thorn raised his eyebrows and breathed in deeply through his big nose. "You're annoyed with me because I concealed things from you? You, too, lied to me by omission. It would seem that we both got on the wrong track from the start." He'd come out with that in a totally dispassionate tone. Ophelia felt increasingly baffled. Did he really think he could sort out their differences as easily as he filed away his Treasury cases? "And I'm not accusing you of anything," he added, unperturbed. "I just recommend that you don't trust Archibald. Protect yourself from him, never remain alone in his company. And I can't recommend strongly enough the same caution with Farouk. Be constantly escorted by someone when you're obliged to frequent him."

Ophelia didn't know whether to laugh or get really annoyed. Thorn seemed serious. She sneezed three times, blew her nose, and continued in a snuffly voice: "Your concern is misplaced. No one really notices me."

Thorn went quiet, pensive, and then leant forward, one vertebra at a time, until he could grasp Ophelia's hand. She would have pulled away had he not straightened up almost instantly of his own accord. "You believe that?" he asked, sardonically.

And as Thorn left the kitchen, Ophelia realized that he had slipped a piece of paper into her hand. A telegram?

MR. THORN TREASURY CITACELESTE, POLE CONCERNED BY YOUR SILENCE ARRIVING AS SOON AS POSSIBLE—FATHER MOTHER AGATHA CHARLES HECTOR DOMITILLA BERTRAND ALPHONSE BEATRICE ROGER MATHILDA MARK LEONORA, ETC.

The Mirror Visitor

"Always lower your eyes in the presence of Lord Farouk."

"But don't let that stop you from standing up straight."

"Speak only if you are specifically invited to do so."

"Show yourself to be as frank as a whistle."

"You have to deserve the protection afforded you, Ophelia, so show humility and gratitude."

"You're representing the Animists, dear girl, so allow no one to lack respect for you."

Bombarded with the contradictory recommendations of Berenilde and Aunt Rosaline, Ophelia wasn't really listening to either. She was trying to soothe the scarf, which, half mad with joy and half with anger, was coiling itself round her neck, her arms, and her waist for fear of again being separated from its mistress.

"I should have burnt that thing when your back was turned," sighed Berenilde, shaking her fan. "One doesn't make one's entrance at the Pole's court with a badly behaved scarf."

Ophelia picked up the parasol she'd just dropped. Berenilde had decked her out in a veiled hat and a vanilla-colored dress, as light as whipped cream, which reminded her of childhood outfits worn when her whole family went on summer picnics.

This getup seemed infinitely more incongruous than her scarf on an ark where it never reached more than minus fifteen degrees in spring.

Their lift gently came to a halt. "The Family Opera House, ladies!" the liftboy announced. "The Lifts Company would like to inform you that a connecting service awaits you on the other side of the foyer."

The last time Ophelia had crossed the Opera foyer's glimmering parquet floor, she'd been wearing a valet's livery rather than a lady's dress, and carrying an oar instead of a parasol. She felt as if she had swapped one disguise for another, but one thing hadn't changed: her rib was just as painful.

A new liftboy, tugging at his elastic-strapped hat, came to meet them. "Your connection awaits you, ladies! Lord Farouk has made known his ardent desire to receive you."

In other words, he was already getting impatient. Berenilde entered the lift as if she were floating on clouds. Ophelia, in contrast, was more walking on eggshells as she went past the throng of policemen guarding the entrance gate. She didn't find it that reassuring, being afforded such protection to go up just one floor.

"We're no longer in the embassy," Berenilde warned as the porter was closing the golden gate. "From today onwards, eat nothing, drink nothing, accept no gift without my authorization. If you value your health or your virtue, you will also avoid any alcoves and little-used corridors."

Aunt Rosaline, who had helped herself to a cream bun from the lift's enticing buffet, put it back without batting an eyelid.

"What measures are you thinking of taking concerning our family?" asked Ophelia. "It's out of the question to make them come here." Just imagining her brother and sisters being in this nest of vipers, it sent her into a cold sweat.

Berenilde sat voluptuously on one of the lift's banquettes. "You can trust Thorn to resolve that problem with his usual efficiency. For now, your greatest concern should be not making too bad an impression on our family spirit. Our future at the court will partly depend on the opinion Farouk forms of you." Berenilde and Aunt Rosaline immediately returned to their recommendations, with one wanting to correct Ophelia's accent, the other to keep it as it was; one requesting that any Animism be kept private, the other that it be publicly promoted. It was as if they'd each been learning their lines all day long.

Ophelia picked at the fluff on her scarf, as much to calm it down as herself. Behind the veil of her hat, she was pursing her lips to contain her thoughts. "Trust" and "Thorn": she'd no longer make the mistake of putting those two words side by side. The little conversation they'd had the previous day would make no difference, whatever Mr. Treasurer might think.

As the lift creaked from its every nook and cranny, as a luxurious liner does when setting sail, Ophelia felt as if these sounds were emanating from her own body. She felt more fragile than she had the day she'd watched Anima disappear into the night; than the day her in-laws had clawed her; than the day the policemen had beaten her and thrown her into Clairdelune's dungeons. So fragile, in fact, that she felt that, at the next crack, she could shatter.

It's my fault, she thought, bitterly. I promised myself not to expect anything of that man. If I'd kept my promise, I wouldn't be in such a state.

Agreeing automatically with the advice she was being given, Ophelia stared apprehensively at the lift's golden gate. In a few moments, it would open onto a world more hostile than everything she'd experienced until now. She had no desire to smile at people who despised her without knowing her, who saw her merely as a pair of hands.

Ophelia dropped her parasol again, but this time didn't pick it up. Instead, she looked at her reader's gloves. These ten fingers were exactly like her: they no longer belonged to her. She'd been sold to strangers by her own family. She was now the property of Thorn, of Berenilde, and, soon, of Farouk, three people in whom she had absolutely no trust, but to whom she would have to submit for the rest of her days.

The lift carriage came to such a sudden stop that the buffet china tinkled; the champagne spilt over the tablecloth; Berenilde put both hands on her stomach; and Aunt Rosaline swore, in the name of all the stairs in the world, that no one would catch her taking a lift ever again.

"Ladies, please accept all the Company's apologies," said the distraught liftboy. "It's just a small mechanical issue, our ascent will resume shortly."

Ophelia didn't understand why this boy was apologizing when, in fact, he deserved her utmost gratitude. The jolt had caused such pain to her rib that she was still winded; it was more effective than any slap. How could she have allowed herself to keep turning over such defeatist thoughts? It wasn't just other people, it was also she, Ophelia, who had constructed her whole identity around her hands. It was she who had decided that she'd never be anything other than a reader, a museum curator, a creature more at home in the company of objects than of human beings. Reading had always been a passion, but since when were passions the only foundations of a life?

Ophelia looked up from her gloves and caught her own reflection. Between two illusory frescoes in which fauns were playing hide-and-seek with nymphs, a wall mirror returned a version of reality: a slip of a woman in a summer dress, her three-colored scarf lovingly wrapped around her.

While Berenilde was threatening to have the poor liftboy hanged if the lift's jolting had the slightest effect on her pregnancy, Ophelia slowly approached the mirror. She lifted the veil of her hat and looked closely at herself, glasses to glasses. Soon, when the bruises had faded, when Freya's clawing had turned into a scar on her cheek, Ophelia would see a familiar face once more. But the look in her eyes, that would never return to how it once was. From having seen so many illusions, it had lost its own, and that was just fine. When illusions disappear, only the truth remains. Those eyes would look less within, and more out to the world. They still had much to see, much to learn.

Ophelia plunged the tips of her fingers into the liquid surface of the mirror. She suddenly recalled that day when her sister had given her some advice, in the hair salon, a few hours before Thorn's arrival. What was it she'd said, again? "Charm is the strongest weapon given to women, you must use it without scruples."

As the lift began to ascend again, the mechanical issue having been resolved, Ophelia promised herself never to follow her sister's advice. Scruples were very important. They were even more important than her hands. "Traveling through mirrors," her great-uncle had said before their separation, "that requires facing up to oneself." As long as Ophelia had scruples, as long as she acted according to her conscience, as long as she could face up to her reflection every morning, she would belong to no one else but herself.

"That's what I am before being a pair of hands," Ophelia concluded, pulling her fingers out of the mirror. "I'm the Mirror Visitor."

"The court, ladies!" the liftboy announced, lowering the brake lever. "The Lifts Company hopes your ascent was enjoyable and offers all its apologies for the delay."

Ophelia picked up her parasol, fired with renewed determination. This time, she was ready to brave this world of pretense, this labyrinth of illusions, and resolved never to lose her way in it again.

The golden gate opened on to a blinding light.

Fragment, postscript

It's coming back to me—God was punished. On that day, I understood that God wasn't all-powerful. Since then, I've never seen him again.